D0612566

SEALed with a Promise

MARY MARGRET DAUGHTRIDGE

Sourcebooks Casablanca™
An Imprint of Sourcebooks, Inc.®
Naperville, Illinois

Copyright © 2009 by Mary Margret Daughtridge
Cover and internal design © 2009 by Sourcebooks, Inc.
Cover photo © Maxfx/dreamstime.com, Fintastiqu/dreamstime.com

Sourcebooks and the colophon are registered trademarks of Sourcebooks, Inc.

All rights reserved. No part of this book may be reproduced in any form or by any electronic or mechanical means including information storage and retrieval systems—except in the case of brief quotations embodied in critical articles or reviews—without permission in writing from its publisher, Sourcebooks, Inc.

The characters and events portrayed in this book are fictitious or are used fictitiously. Any similarity to real persons, living or dead, is purely coincidental and not intended by the author.

Published by Sourcebooks Casablanca, an imprint of Sourcebooks, Inc.
P.O. Box 4410, Naperville, Illinois 60567–4410
(630) 961–3900
FAX: (630) 961–2168
www.sourcebooks.com

Library of Congress Cataloging-in-Publication Data

Daughtridge, Mary Margret.
SEALed with a promise / Mary Margret Daughtridge.
p. cm.
1. United States. Navy. SEALs—Fiction. 2. Women college teachers—Fiction. 3. Illegitimacy—Fiction. 4. Revenge—Fiction. I. Title.
PS3604.A92S435 2009
813'.6—dc22

2008041433

Printed and bound in the United States of America
QW 10 9 8 7 6 5 4 3 2 1

For Pat,
Whose name should be beside friendship *in every dictionary, because she defines it.*

Prologue

Chief Petty Officer Caleb "Do-Lord" Dulaude always said if he ever saw Teague Calhoun again, he'd kill him. Do-Lord huffed a mirthless chuckle and shook his head. Wouldn't you know fate would test his resolve when he had an M-14 rifle in his hand?

In less than five minutes, Calhoun, a United States Senator with his escort of security contractors, would come through the brass doors of the best hotel in Kandahar.

All SEALs respected Murphy's Law the way they did the law of gravity. According to Murphy anything that can go wrong, will go wrong, and at the worst possible moment. Murphy must have worked overtime to arrange this. The third floor room of a bombed out school, where Do-Lord and his spotter waited, offered the perfect vantage point for a sniper targeting anyone exiting the hotel—one reason Do-Lord's commanding officer, Jax Graham, had made sure *his* team commanded it. Jax was positioned in a window across the plaza. Other SEALs were scattered among the pedestrians who thronged the barricaded street.

The only problem was that Do-Lord's role was to protect Calhoun from assassination—not do the job himself. The black plastic barrel grip of his sniper rifle was slick with sweat again. Do-Lord wiped it, then rubbed his Kevlar-gloved hands, trigger finger removed, on the pants of his desert camouflage BDUs.

"Hot up here," whispered Warren, his spotter, though no one in the plaza three stories below could have heard a normal voice. They were making no effort to hide, but still Warren clung to the shadows as he checked distances with his range finder. He gave Do-Lord a measuring glance. "You okay?"

Guilt, as unusual as it was unwelcome, stabbed Do-Lord. He should be thinking of nothing but the task and how to meld his actions into seamless teamwork with the others.

From the day he was eighteen he had wanted nothing more than to be one of these men, these SEALs, the warrior elite of the world. These extraordinary men had all the strength, cunning, and mastery of weapons a boyhood spent on the dirty fringes of society had taught him to respect. He had come to them tough. He had already known how to push himself past being wet, cold, hungry, and exhausted. And he had come streetsmart. From the time he was ten, he had simply done what he had to, neither cringing from necessity, nor looking back with regret. To be one of them, he had ruthlessly eliminated his past, and his essential pragmatism had stood him in good stead.

The past he had locked away had stayed away. He had become a SEAL and a good one. In the process, almost against his will, he had acquired concepts like honor, accountability, trust, and pride. As the years had gone by, he had felt that the man he was had less and less in common with the boy he had been.

Now it was as if the single-minded closing of the doors to his past had never happened. He pulsed with old anger. Anger he thought gone, forgotten, meaningless.

And guilt that he could contemplate abandoning his training tore at his gut like ground glass.

If he told Warren a tenth of what was going on, he would be removed from duty instantly. Without taking his eyes from the dusty, rubble-strewn plaza, Do-Lord lifted his thumb in assent.

No matter what he did when Calhoun appeared, he was going to have a hard time living with himself.

Well, at least he wasn't bored anymore.

Lately, it was harder and harder to keep his mind on track.

He was just tired, he told himself. Jax had called him a super-computer this morning, and he felt like one: a laptop that had been running off batteries far too long, and was close to shutting down. He was ready for deployment in this sere, harsh, beautiful country to be over. He didn't get lonely and homesick as some of his buddies did. The Teams were his home, his fellow SEALs his family. So it stood to reason that when he was sick of a deployment, what he would feel would be boredom. Sometimes when they were on patrol in the mountains, he imagined the grey and tan and ochre landscape of sharp crags and black shadows was the moon. But when he tried to imagine what aliens hid in the shadows, he cut off his mind's attempts to escape. Anybody who didn't stay in the here and now focused on what was real could find themselves dead in a heartbeat.

At oh-dark-thirty this morning Do-Lord had stumbled into the briefing room, where Jax already sat clicking through pages on his laptop. He should have felt a little kick of anticipation, a rising of the blood. Jax wouldn't have sent a yeoman to waken him for any routine matter. But whatever was going down, he had little enthusiasm for.

"What's up?" He rubbed his freshly shaven cheeks, trying to wake up. After months of letting his beard grow, the better to blend in where most men were bearded, the smooth skin felt strange. "Something tells me you're not trying to get a leg up on your post-deployment paperwork."

Jax looked as if he'd never gone to bed. He shook his head in disgust. "Since we ship home tomorrow, the powers that be have decided we don't have anything to do."

"Meaning we've drawn a job nobody else wants."

"You've got it. We're tasked to provide perimeter security for a visiting congressman," Jax paused, and sifted through a pile of faxes. "Here." He passed Do-Lord a bio with photograph. "Senator Calhoun of North Carolina. Intel has credible reports a terrorist cell plans an assassination attempt."

Cold sweat broke out on the small of Do-Lord's back. He took the bio and sank into one of the rolling chairs that surrounded the table without waiting for permission. Jax and he had never stood on ceremony when alone, and Do-Lord wasn't sure his legs would hold him.

"Do you know him?" Jax's gray eyes narrowed. "You've got a funny look on your face."

Jax was his best friend as well as his CO. Antiauthoritarian to the bone, Do-Lord wouldn't have made it through BUD/S, the basic SEAL training, without Jax's help. For one crazy moment Do-Lord contemplated telling Jax everything.

But a childhood of confiding in no one, of making his life look *normal* so Social Services wouldn't be called, had built a wall that couldn't be scaled—not in the few moments before the others arrived. Do-Lord forced his face into his trademark easygoing smile. "Know who he is, of course."

Everybody knew who the senator was. He was on several of the most influential senate committees, including the defense budget. He was known for his ability to grab headlines. Political pundits speculated that he was already running for president even though the election was a couple of years away. And now Do-Lord had to plan how his team would protect the bastard.

"I know that super-computer brain of yours has already figured out why I wanted you to get here first. Here are satellite photos of the square," Jax went on. "Work out placements for Warren, Barry, and the rest. We have to trust your ability to visualize. There's no time to run a rehearsal. As soon as the guys get up, we'll brief, and then there's just enough time to get into position. I want you on sniper," he added.

All SEALs were expert marksmen, but even among them, Do-Lord was an acknowledged top gun. Do-Lord had known Jax would want him for sniper from the first words out of his mouth. And yet when Jax confirmed his hypothesis, for the second time Do-Lord almost spoke up to tell his friend why he couldn't see Teague Calhoun with a gun in his hand.

But he didn't.

Jax looked exhausted. Not just from one night of missed sleep. He was tired, as they all were with their deployment almost at an end, but in addition, he'd flown home ten days ago when the death of his ex-wife left his four-year-old son Tyler motherless. He'd attended the funeral, made arrangements for Tyler to live with his grandmother temporarily, and come back—all in four days. He didn't have to. Deployment could have been over for him. But as long as they were in harm's way, Jax couldn't abandon his platoon. Looking after his men meant everything to Jax. They could always depend on him.

How could Do-Lord tell Jax not to depend on *him* this time? Keeping the unit ready to operate at all times was a chief's job. There wasn't anybody else Jax could call on. Jason Hew was almost as good a shot, but he had an eye infection. By noon the plaza would throng with people. No random or missed shots could be allowed to put innocent people in danger.

How could he tell the man he trusted with his life, "Don't trust *me*"? Jax needed him to pull his weight, not turn himself into an emotional liability.

Do-Lord knew where his duty as a SEAL lay. To forge a bunch of alpha males into a unit that would act as a team at all times. BUD/S instructors drove home the lesson again and again. Where one failed, all would pay. But for the first time in years, the anger threatened to find its way to the surface. He wanted to do something not in the team's best interests.

The dilemma made him feel ripped in two, but as Samuel Johnson said about hanging, it wonderfully concentrated the mind. He wasn't bored anymore.

He waited in the hot wind that whistled through the blank windows of what had once been a school. He waited like the sniper he was, ready for the moment when the target would appear. No sirree. He was not bored.

"Showtime," Jax's voice, dead level calm, spoke softly in Do-Lord's earpiece. "They'll be at the door in two minutes. If Intel's sources are good, there's a tango in this crowd planning assassination. He won't care who else he kills. Nobody go to sleep on me. We'll have twenty seconds to get it right."

Do-Lord swept the plaza with his gaze. There was Gonzo on the east side of the square, and Davy, their hospital corpsman behind the twisted, burned-out car that looked like a sculptor's nightmare. Jax had made sure his men held all the best sniper positions, but the terrorist, if there was one, was probably hiding in plain sight.

Yelling erupted from the sector Barry controlled, and was followed by silence as Barry moved in. Do-Lord didn't see what had caused the yelling. He had zoned out for an instant. A hollow feeling opened at the base of Do-Lord's spine. Trying to suppress anger and frustration about seeing the only man he'd ever wanted to kill, he was doing his job mechanically, confident the others had it under control. Not acceptable. Another wave of guilt slid greasily into his stomach.

The tall brass doors of the hotel opened and black-suited men appeared—that would be the security contractors ready to stop a bullet with their own bodies. Did they know the manner of man they were willing to give their lives for? Stupid question. Most of them, like most SEALs, took satisfaction from their patriotism and their sense of honor fulfilled, and left political ramifications to others.

Behind them another head appeared. He spotted Calhoun's Colonel Sanders white, wavy hair. From the ground he would be completely covered by his escort, but from Do-Lord's vantage three stories above the street, he was completely open.

Do-Lord brought the scope to his eye. The thing about the high-powered scope was that it brought objects into intimate closeness while it eliminated the rest of the world from consciousness. Waiting for a shot through a high-powered scope was strangely akin to meditation. There was the same detached peacefulness, the same merging of consciousness.

Calhoun was two hundred yards away, but his face was all Do-Lord could see. It was closer than a handshake's distance. So easy. A nice clear shot, and the man's polished, smooth face, the kind of face it takes generations of money, power, and prestige to produce, would be replaced by a pink haze. You never see the bullet hit. Only the target centered in the scope, and then the pink haze. Sight, inhale…

"Do-Lord, we have a bad guy in Alpha-2—east side of the newsstand—he's getting to his feet."

Damn! He'd lost focus again. Jax's ability to spot one terrorist in a mass of innocent people, was so acute it looked like ESP, but Do-Lord should have been scanning the crowd too, from his even higher vantage point.

"I've got him." Warren checked his distance finder. "Tan pakol hat, right? I make it 225 yards. Light wind. Easy shot."

Do-Lord found the target. A beggar, drowsing in the scant shade cast by the ramshackle stand, stirred as if awakened and rose slowly. His pakol hat, worn only by those who fought the Taliban in the early days of the war, was an ironic touch. And beggars were a common sight in this city. Even as Do-Lord spared a thought to wonder how on earth Jax *knew,* the man raised a Russian-made semiautomatic rifle to his shoulder.

"Take him down, Do-Lord," Jax ordered quietly.

The rifle the bad guy hoisted wasn't terribly accurate, and it was prone to jamming, Do-Lord assessed with absentminded professionalism. The man held the shoulder on which he rested the stock too high. Not a professional then. Maybe not trained. Vic and Littletree were converging on him, but the assassin could probably get a few rounds off before they tackled him.

It was Do-Lord's answer. The terrorist was a weapon already aimed at the man Do-Lord wanted dead. One slight hesitation. The terrorist could be the instrument of Do-Lord's revenge.

Jax wouldn't order anyone else to fire into a crowd this dense, but the terrorist mentality had no such scruples. He wouldn't care how many of his own people would be cut down by the spray of bullets. He didn't care that his was a suicide mission. He probably didn't care whether he killed the senator or not. His object was to cause fear, disrupt normal life, and force the U.S. to tie up resources.

"Do-Lord, take him down," Jax repeated. His voice sounded almost bored, but flexible and deadly as a rapier, it cut anyway.

Do-Lord could see runnels of sweat making lighter streaks through the dirt on the man's cheeks. From the moment he had the tango in his scope Do-Lord had been unconsciously tracking his own slow heartbeats. He inhaled, found the space between one heartbeat and the next, and squeezed the trigger.

❖❖❖

"What the hell took you so long?" Jax asked. Shoulder-to-shoulder they were jammed into the Humvee to be transported back to the base on the outskirts of the city near the airport.

"Couldn't get a clear shot."

SEALs lie. They succeed in their dangerous and deadly work by not appearing where they are expected and by not being what they appear to be. A cynical SEAL saying was: "Never tell the truth, when a lie will do as well."

Lying didn't bother Do-Lord. He hadn't told the truth much since he was ten years old. But until now, he'd never lied to Jax. Do-Lord passed a hand over his face, pressing his thumbs against his eyes, fighting the urge to weep.

"God, I'm tired," he said.

"Yeah," said Jax, slumping beside him. "And we've lost almost twelve of the twenty-four hours we had to get squared away before we leave."

"Grab some rack time when we hit the base. I'll write your after-action report for you."

Jax grumbled and shook his head.

"Shut up." Do-Lord cuffed him lightly on the arm. "You know I write better than you do. I can do it in half the time. It'll be waiting for your signature before chow."

Jax didn't answer, but packed together as they were, Do-Lord felt him relax and his breathing become more regular. To let Jax nap for a few minutes, Do-Lord angled his shoulder to brace his friend against the jolts of a road that was more pothole than pavement.

In his bones he still felt the deep tremors where past and present, like tectonic plates, ground together. When he'd made his vow, he'd been thinking like a kid, boiling with a violent compound of grief and teenage testosterone, pressurized by his sheer powerlessness.

But he wasn't a kid anymore.

He had a promise to keep. It was time he stopped reacting and started thinking like a SEAL.

Chapter 1

Little Creek, Virginia

Funerals, yes. He'd pulled honor guard duty at too many of them. But in all his thirty-two years, Caleb "Do-Lord" Dulaude had never attended a wedding. In a surprise development, barely four months since the platoon's return from the 'Stan, Jax was getting married, and Do-Lord had to be the best man at one.

Mellow November sunshine trickled into his cubicle from the window in the hallway, and his stomach growled. He pushed back the cuff of his gray and tan desert camo BDU's to check his watch then rifled the pages of the etiquette book open on his desk to see if he had a chance of finishing it in time to get some lunch.

His battered *2002 Bluejacket's Guide,* a chief petty officer's bible, specified in detail how to render military honors at a funeral, but it hadn't helped much with a wedding. It said very little about his duties during the ceremony, only that he would be in charge of the arch of swords, which would take place outside the church. He figured there was a lot more to a wedding than that, especially among the upper-crust of North Carolina.

This book on etiquette was the third he'd read. In his palm pilot he had a twenty-six item list of his duties as best man. He wouldn't necessarily need to know all, but it was always the little things that got you killed. Since he had no idea which details would prove to be crucial, he ignored the rumbling of his stomach.

Harder to ignore were his boredom with what he read and the tiny niggle of fear that the two staves on which he had depended, feeding his mind's thirst for information and the engrossment of SEAL life, were failing him.

The tall white cake typically served at wedding receptions today was once the bride's cake, whereas the wedding cake was a fruitcake, filled with nuts...

"I looked for you in the NCO mess." Burly Master Chief Lon Swales, also dressed in camo, interrupted him. From the first, although he didn't take well to regulations, Do-Lord had loved the Navy's prescribed dress code for every occasion. He always knew exactly what to wear in order not to draw attention to himself. "What are you missing lunch to read?"

Do-Lord slid the yellow highlighter through his fingers while he considered lying. His fellow SEALs accepted his reading mania. He had a paperback stashed in a pocket anytime he wasn't in combat gear—and a lot of times when he was. In desperation, after he'd exhausted all other printed matter, he'd even read paperback romances while in Afghanistan. Since pictures of scantily clad women were offensive to Muslims, the covers of many had been torn off, adding a new layer of meaning to the term "bodice ripper."

Everyone would really razz him, if they found out he'd moved on to etiquette books. On the other hand, the razzing would be worse if the guys learned he'd *lied* about reading up on etiquette.

"Emily Post. Research. Boning up for Jax's wedding."

The weathered skin around the Master Chief's eyes folded into deep crow's feet, and his lips quirked, but the expected teasing didn't come. Instead, with perfect seriousness, he asked, "Have you read *Service Etiquette?*"

"Swartz, Fourth Edition? Read it first. When I'm invited to the White House, I'll sho'nuff do you proud."

Lon chuckled at Do-Lord's tongue-in-cheek reference to the fact that *Service Etiquette* covered protocol for every social occasion a person in the military could encounter, no matter how unlikely. "Stranger things have happened." He took a seat in the straight metal chair in front of Do-Lord's desk, and in an almost gentle voice he asked, "How's it going?"

"Tell you what…" Caleb let the sentence hang while he tossed the highlighter on the desk and rolled his desk chair back to stretch out his legs. "It's boring as hell, but it's not as bad as that outboard motor service manual you made us read during Hell Week."

Do-Lord saw with satisfaction he'd struck the right note with the Master Chief. Twelve years ago, Lon had been a BUD/S instructor to the class that included Jax, an ensign, and Do-Lord, except he hadn't earned his nickname yet.

"Hey, I was just trying to help you stay awake." Lon settled into his chair and hooked his thumbs over his belt, his innocent tone belied by a devilish grin.

"Yeah, right." During Hell Week the trainees were allowed a total of four hours sleep. During so-called rest periods, harsh consequences would descend on anyone who fell asleep *and* on all those near who allowed him to nod off. Listening while someone read aloud was bad enough, since few people did it well. Trying to stay alert while boring material was read aloud would turn their few minutes of respite into torture.

Lon's expression grew thoughtful, his eyes on a distant past. "Until that night I didn't think you were going to graduate. Some guys never get it that being a SEAL isn't about taking punishment, or endurance, or even being the best or the baddest."

Though fewer than twenty percent graduated from the toughest training in the world, it wasn't because instructors tried to wash a trainee out. They did, however, use any means to make a trainee aware of his weak areas and the need to overcome them. "You were doing your part, but that's all you were doing. For all the physical stuff we do, ultimately, making a SEAL is mental. A man must decide he's personally responsible for the success of the team and the welfare of every member. He has to find within himself whatever makes him able to do that. You were holding back, side-stepping opportunities for leadership, letting your boat crew not do as well as they might have, because you didn't like being noticed." Lon's eyes twinkled. "So we noticed you—a lot."

"That's why you handed *me* the manual to read aloud!" Until this moment, Dulaude had never suspected the instructors had intended to make him *uncomfortable* by singling him out. He shouted with laughter at the double irony. For Dulaude, being *made* to read was a "get out of jail free" card. Thinking only of himself, he had known exactly how Br'er Rabbit felt in the briar patch. He could easily pretend to mumble through it.

"Yup. We figured you'd be miserable trying to read aloud, and you'd make everybody else miserable." Lon chuckled in reminiscence.

But Dulaude had looked out at the faces of the men gathered in the mess hall at 3:00 a.m. Of a starting class of one hundred twenty-nine, around fifty red-eyed, battered men remained. More would quit before the night was over, because the pain, cold, and exhaustion would only get worse. White with fatigue, shoulders slumped, neither hopeful nor interested, longing only for sleep, they had watched him with faces set to endure.

Except for Jax. His eyes had been so bloodshot he looked like a creature from a horror movie, but still they lit with expectation. He seemed to think Dulaude intended to do something to keep them awake.

Dulaude had glanced down at the manual Chief Swales had stuffed in his hands. Gray print on flimsy gray paper, it was designed to blind any reader it didn't render comatose. However, Dulaude could read a page at a glance and had something close to eidetic memory. Up to now, he had concealed his reading ability as he had his real IQ. He had learned early that both made him stand out, and drawing the attention of authorities was never a good thing.

A crazy idea came to him, one that would blow his "average" cover forever, but would get everyone else through the next fifteen minutes.

"My brothers-s! *Listen-n* to the *word-d* of the *naval command-d,*" he began with the over-articulated cadences of a tent preacher. "Verily I say unto you, *this*"—he waved the manual—"is what you must know about the 175 horsepower four-stroke outboard, and *if* you have faith, it is *all* you need to know."

A murmur went through the assembled men, a rustle, as awareness that something novel was happening penetrated their tired brains.

"The *outboard* is secured with four three-inch bolts—four, did you hear me brothers, *four!*"

"Preach it, brother!" yelled Jax, a huge grin breaking across his face.

"Hallelujah!" someone in the back exulted.

"Which should always be tightened—"

As they caught on to the joke, more joined into the irreverent fun. Their instructors *did* pursue safety and equipment maintenance with something close to religious fervor.

"Before and after each use—"

"Thank you, Jesus!"

"Or after four hours elapsed running time."

"I believe! I believe!"

"Praise the Lord!"

"Yeah. Praise Duluade!" Jax added.

Lon rose laughing. Instructors made training as tough as they could, but they gloried to see trainees demonstrate the out-of-the-box thinking that was the SEALs' hallmark. "Metcalf, lead us in a closing hymn."

"I've got a home in glory-land that outshines the sun." Metcalf's rich baritone began the old church-camp song, so easy anyone could sing along. When he got to the chorus of "Do, Lord, oh do, Lord, oh do, remember me," the mess hall rang with clapping and stomping.

"That's when the guys nicknamed you Do-Lord, isn't it?" Lon broke in on Do-Lord's train of thought, returning him to the present. "And you and Jax have been friends since BUD/S."

"Yeah, the Philadelphian with a silver spoon in his mouth and the Alabama cracker, raised in trailer located on the hind end of nowhere."

The older man's eyes sharpened. "Alabama?"

"Sure. You knew that," Do-Lord deepened his drawl. "That's why I talk this way."

Lon snorted and crossed his arms over his chest. "How much you drawl depends on how much bullshit you're spreading."

Do-Lord nodded gravely. "That too. Why did you come looking for me?"

"I just got the report on Delvecchio's condition."

"Carmine? How is he?" Carmine was a trainee who had finished BUD/S but who still had a six-month apprenticeship to serve before he would be a full-fledged SEAL, ready to operate.

Lon took a deep breath, eyes squinted with pain. "He's been moved to Bethesda. He's got leukemia."

"*What?*" Do-Lord's eyes narrowed in disbelief. "I told him to report for sick call—three, four days ago, but I didn't think anything was wrong with him. I was tired of him saying he was tired." Do-Lord slammed the stupid book on etiquette shut, disgusted that he had been studying the social customs of the upper class while a man he was responsible for had been seriously ill, and he hadn't realized it. "I thought he was goldbricking. Showing up late looking like hell. Phoning in his PT." Do-Lord pushed his hair back from his forehead, a gesture left over from Afghanistan. Dark red hair like his wasn't uncommon among Afghanis, so while there he'd let it grow, and with his more rangy than stocky build he'd blended in better than some of the darker guys. SEALs, who might have to leave the country undercover at any time, were allowed relaxed grooming standards, but Do-Lord had cut his hair as soon as he returned to the U.S. "The poor SOB."

"Cut yourself some slack. You took the appropriate action when you had cause to do so. You know how these gung-ho kids try to cover up."

"That's right. I *do* know." Do-Lord wasn't going to let himself off the hook. "I've seen men trying to run on broken legs and showing up for roll call with one-hundred-four-degree temperatures. I should have suspected something else was going on." Do-Lord felt like breaking something, but SEALs don't make violent gestures. When they're violent, it's for real.

"I should have been paying better attention to his motivation." Maintaining smooth function of the team on a day-to-day basis was done by chiefs. The blend of skills and personalities that would meld a pack of all-alpha dogs into a cooperating team was as difficult to analyze as an alchemical formula. A man whose performance was lackluster might be outstanding if assigned to a different group. "And don't bother reminding me the platoon Jax led in Afghanistan was tight," Do-Lord went on. "Unusually so, even for SEALs. It's breaking up now, scattering to different posts. It's normal for us to resent the new guy, although he isn't the cause of the changes. It wouldn't be rational to expect him to fit in."

"Are you going to have both sides of this conversation, or am I allowed to speak now?" The older man's amused drawl was a gentle, but unmistakable, rebuke.

Do-Lord pressed his lips together and nodded.

"I'm not holding you responsible for Delvecchio, and neither is anyone else. But I am worried about you. You haven't been yourself since Afghanistan. You fake being laid-back better than anybody I know, but you're too tight. I know you've got a degree in clinical psychology, but you can't treat yourself. Find somebody to talk to, get it off your chest, and get your head back where it needs to be."

Lon was thinking post-traumatic stress. The thought had occurred to Do-Lord too. It explained the difficulty paying attention, the sense that some nameless something was wrong, the oppressive boredom. He was sure it explained the crazy moment in Afghanistan when he'd almost fired on a man he was tasked to protect. He still woke up in a cold sweat from nightmares in which he saw Calhoun in his rifle scope and *did* squeeze the trigger.

He'd put the whole event down to combat stress, some aberration induced by the fatigue of unrelenting vigilance in a land where the enemy could be anyone, anywhere. The popular press often attributed Post-Traumatic Stress Disorder (once called "battle fatigue" until it was recognized that many people who hadn't been in wars had the same symptoms) to one horrific, traumatic event.

In fact, people were amazingly resilient, and one terrible event in an otherwise stable, supportive environment didn't usually induce PTSD. Instead it was an accumulation of stresses: being in constant danger from which there was no escape, assaults on the emotions which one dare not feel, morally ambiguous situations which many were far too young to comprehend, much less grapple with, that eventually overwhelmed the mind's defenses.

The men he was responsible for, he carefully monitored for signs of combat stress, but apparently it had snuck up on him. He still couldn't believe that, even for a second, he had risked the careers of every man in the unit, especially Jax's, his best friend. His own career he wouldn't have needed to worry about. Someone would have seen to it that he left Afghanistan in a body bag. And he would have thought the punishment just. He was grateful that the deeply indoctrinated ideals of loyalty, responsibility, and awareness of consequences had pulled him back from the brink, but the shame of that moment crawled up his face in a hot slither. He couldn't possibly, ever, tell anyone.

Anyway, he already knew what a therapist would tell him. In Afghanistan, though he had done what he *should,* he hadn't done what he wanted to. Therefore, what was troubling him now was lack of closure.

He was determined to stop thinking like a hotheaded teenager and start thinking like a SEAL. Whether caused by PTSD or not, if he had lived up to his promise, instead of burying his past when he buried his mother, the moment in Afghanistan would never have happened.

When he made the vow with a teenager's intensity, he'd wanted justice and seen it in black and white, a life for a life. With planning, nothing would be easier than to kill Calhoun. But now that he'd had time to think rationally, a clean head shot was too good for the senator. If he thought about justice for his mother in a balanced way, Calhoun hadn't murdered Do-Lord's mother. He had destroyed her life. It was a subtle, but important distinction.

So, thinking like a SEAL, he needed to do the most damage to Calhoun's life with the least expenditure of resources. That was exactly what Calhoun had coming.

The first step was to gather intelligence, and he had begun. He had bought a cheap laptop to be destroyed later, which he used only for surfing the Net for every detail he could glean about Calhoun. Eventually, he would learn where Calhoun was vulnerable.

Most men returning from deployment had the occasional image or idea they couldn't dismiss. He had it under control. His symptoms weren't anything to worry about unless they didn't go away. He slid his trademark lazy smile onto his face hoping it was good enough to get past Lon's radar. "You're right. I guess I just feel sorry for Carmine—it's a tough break. It sucks, and I wouldn't want it to happen to anybody."

Lon appeared satisfied. "Right. In case a bone marrow transplant will help, Davy will take blood samples from anyone who wants to donate. In the meantime, see if there's anything Carmine or his family need." Lon shoved out of his chair. "But while you're at it, plan to get away. You know I'll approve leave anytime you ask. We call the world of operations the 'real' world, but if we really believe that's reality, we're in trouble."

Chapter 2

Sessoms Corner, North Carolina

THE TRAILER HE GREW UP IN COULD HAVE FITTED, with room left over, into the double parlor of the late Victorian house where a wedding breakfast for Jax and his bride Pickett was taking place. A corner of Do-Lord's mouth kicked up in amusement. The *most* room would have been left at the ceiling. Decorated with intricate crown molding, these ceilings were easily fifteen feet.

Painted a cheerful lime green and filled with comfortable upholstered sofas and chairs as well as what even he recognized as priceless antiques, these were clearly rooms to be lived in, not just displayed to company. The house had been in the family for over a hundred years, and oil portraits of ancestors, not all terribly good, were scattered among hunting scenes and landscapes.

By the time he'd helped himself to the sausage casserole, fruit compote, fried green tomatoes, venison loin in gravy, and grits on the table in the dining room, the autumn leaf design on the porcelain plate was completely obliterated. He carried it very carefully across priceless Oriental carpets, grateful he wasn't expected to balance it on his knee. The warm sunny day, unusually balmy for November in North Carolina, had allowed the hostesses to set tables outside on the wide porches where thick white paint gleamed on columns and rails.

A light breeze carried the scent of autumn leaves and the earthy tang of newly-dug peanuts. It fluttered the peach tablecloths and played with pretty girls' hair. A couple of the girls smiled invitingly. He smiled in return, but he set his plate down at an empty place at the table where Jax's bride, Pickett, sat with two of her cousins. Pickett looked bright as an autumn leaf herself with her gold tumble of curls and orange silk dress.

Last night at the wedding rehearsal, Jax had caught him watching Pickett and leaned over to say, "Pickett's mine. Get one of your own." Jax's words kept reverberating in his mind. They popped up at the oddest, and sometimes most inconvenient, times. Jax had said them in jest—well, partly in jest. Jax laughed when he said it, but there wasn't a doubt in Do-Lord's mind he'd also been warned away.

Jax had it wrong. Do-Lord liked Pickett. He thought she was perfect—for Jax. During the rehearsal he hadn't been eyeing Pickett so much as trying to understand how she came to be best friends with Emmie Caddington, who was the maid of honor. Pickett and her sisters, who were her other attendants, were all remarkably pretty, remarkably poised women, while the friend had to be one of the blandest people he'd ever seen. It was like she intended to be a nonentity, but in a reverse way she stood out precisely because there was nothing about her to draw the eye. Still, birds of a feather flock together. Puzzling how she could be Pickett's friend was a way to keep himself entertained through the interminably silly proceedings.

SEALs believed in rehearsal. A practice run for the ceremony was the first item on the three-day wedding agenda that had made total sense to Do-Lord—until he found out it was bad luck for the bride to rehearse her own part, so she sat on a pew, while the maid of honor pretended to be the bride. SEALs rehearsed one another's roles all the time. But unless they thought Emmie would marry Jax if Pickett was out of commission, making her rehearse Pickett's role in addition to her own didn't make a lick of sense.

He also hadn't seen why Emmie, whose arm was in a cobalt blue sling (the only colorful thing about her) had to mime bending down to straighten Pickett's train, which as maid of honor was one of her duties. She shouldn't have been doing it at all. Being able to use only one arm made her clumsy, and it had to hurt like hell. He was standing right there, he could move the damn train. He'd give her credit. She hadn't complained once, but he'd been so irritated after a while, he'd had to find a way to take his mind off it.

Pickett smiled and indicated the empty chair when she saw him approach the table. Do-Lord carefully laid his fork to the left of his plate and put his knife on the right. Chiefs were taken in hand by older chiefs as soon as they were promoted and taught table manners that could get them through a formal seven-course banquet. The wedge of quiche on Pickett's plate looked untouched. Offering to serve others before seating oneself was good manners, but it was genuine concern that made him ask, "Can I get you anything from the buffet?"

Pickett shook her head. "Thank you, but I have to leave in a minute. Jax and Tyler will be here soon, and I can't let Jax see me. Bad luck, you know."

Oh yes, the notion that it was bad luck for the groom to see the bride before the wedding. There seemed to be no end to traditions and superstitions surrounding a wedding. No limit to how seriously intelligent, educated people took them. “Why is it bad luck?”

“Because, if he *sees* her, he might change his mind,” one of the cousins joked with a horsey laugh. Between guys a jab like that might be a sign of affection, but Do-Lord didn’t miss the way she flicked her eyes to see if the punch connected.

Pickett laughed too, but the corners of her mouth looked tight.

He pretended to think it over. “Naw. That cain’t be it. A smart man like Jax? He knows he’s getting the prettiest girl here—don’t you think?” Do-Lord kept his country-boy smile until she dropped her eyes.

“Everybody has always said Pickett’s sister Grace is the beauty of the family. Pickett’s the smartest.” The other cousin covered Pickett’s hand. “But I have to say, Pickett you look the prettiest today I’ve ever seen you.” Meaning what? What was the matter with these people? “I’m so happy for you,” she added with a genuine smile.

Pickett squeezed her cousin’s hand in return, then folded her napkin. “Well, I don’t know what my bad luck would be, and I don’t want to find out. I’m going to take my leave now.”

In a few minutes the other two women excused themselves.

Alone at his table at last, Do-Lord checked the master schedule of events he’d loaded into his smart phone, cross-referenced with directions to every breakfast, lunch, dinner, and dance, and the names of the hosts with degree of kinship to Pickett's family. Etiquette demanded he thank his hostess before departing. As soon as he found at least one (there were twelve), he could return to the hotel and nap awhile.

Do-Lord returned his phone to his belt and hefted his empty plate. It didn't seem right to leave it on the table.

"Here, I'll take that." Pickett's grey-haired great-aunt spoke from his elbow. Her complexion was artfully preserved. Except for the obviously young, all the women appeared at least twenty years younger than they probably were. "Isn't it nice the weather has cooperated? On the Saturday after Thanksgiving, you never know what the weather will do. But with Pickett's sister Grace directing the wedding, why am I surprised? Everything she does is perfect." The old lady rattled on in seemingly inexhaustible chatter. This was the woman he was looking for. He called up the correct leave-taking phrases and waited for an opening. "Nobody else could have pulled off a wedding with only a month's preparation," she continued. "It won't be what it could have been, of course, but Grace *swears* Pickett wanted a small wedding. You should have seen the weddings we did for Pickett's older sisters," she sighed. "Still, family has to rally at times like this, don't you think?"

Do-Lord wouldn't know. His family had consisted of himself and his mother. When Social Services had returned him to his mother, he'd made sure any shortcomings about his home life were never noticed again. Theoretically, he must have had grandparents, cousins, maybe aunts and uncles, but not a one that he knew of had ever *rallied.*

"Yes ma'am." He used the smile older ladies in almost any culture reacted well to. "Having family you can count on makes all the difference."

Emmie Caddington was looking for a man. In a very short-term-goal, *temporary* sort of way, that is. Right now, before the wedding breakfast could break up, she needed to find Caleb Dulaude, the one everybody called Do-Lord.

Eastern North Carolina men carry nicknames like Potlikker and Choo-choo to their graves without loss of dignity. Among them, a name like Do-Lord was unexceptional, but somehow, she couldn't make herself use it. Despite his down-home persona, his rust-red hair, and the tan-over-freckles skin of an outdoorsman, there was an austere integrity to his features, not as obvious as handsomeness, that made the name all wrong for him.

Whenever she saw him she longed for her pencil, or better yet, pen and ink to trace the relationships of broad, rather prominent brow ridges and longish nose, uncompromising cheekbones, and mobile mouth. When he was a boy, he'd probably been on the homely side. Bony features like his would take some growing in to.

Even the unconscious flexing of her fingers as she mentally drew him started up the throb in her shoulder. Having her right arm immobilized in a sling while a dislocated shoulder healed was the reason, the only reason, she needed him. If she hadn't been in denial about how long it would be before her arm was usable, she wouldn't have waited so long before seeking him out.

Of course, she might not have been in denial, if the thought of being anything but carefully polite to him wasn't anathema to her. He and those like him represented everything she thought the world would be better without.

Pickett's sister Grace, her knit dress of lapis silk jersey nailing the "dressy casual" the invitation had called for, halted Emmie's attempt to thread her way through the crowd around the buffet table.

Every few millennia nature reaches the apex of an evolutionary line and produces a creature so perfect, so exquisitely adapted to its ecological niche, that it seems the environment was made only to be a setting for it.

Such a creature was the exceedingly well-named Grace. She was absolutely everything a young matron of her class should be. She was beautiful, smart, alarmingly competent, and tireless in her devotion to her family and her life's work, which was (as the oldest of the sisters and her mother's right hand) to present them to the world as polished and perfected as she could make them. Aiding her mission, she had the sublime confidence of one who has never questioned, or needed to question, her place in the great scheme of things.

"Where are you going," Grace asked, "and with *that* look on your face?"

Emmie wasn't sure what expression might be on *her* face, but she didn't miss the look of exasperated affection with which Grace swept Emmie's beige Land's End blazer and matching beige skirt. Emmie wasn't by nature rebellious. With her logical mind, the thousand slippery rules governing style were simply incomprehensible. By the time she'd entered college she was already a true eccentric—a nerd who couldn't even conform to the rules of nerd-dom. She had accepted her singular state and come to prefer it. Accepting it was easier than trying to fit in.

She always bought generic clothes, efficiency and comfort being her wardrobe goals. Catalog shopping saved time since everything already matched, and the clothes, never in—or out of—style, lasted for years.

This morning she hadn't been able to move her arm enough to hook her bra, so she'd left it off. She'd added the blazer over her white blouse, hoping to disguise the deficiency.

Her outfit wouldn't have incited envy, but it would have passed muster as dressy casual on the campus of UNC-Wilmington where she was a junior faculty member. It was wrong for the breakfast.

Emmie didn't know what to say. She couldn't tell Grace, of all people, the truth: she was looking for Caleb. Grace would want to know why, and she wasn't a good liar. To lie well one had to understand a society's unwritten expectations.

Grace waived her hesitation aside. "Forget I asked. Do you have a ride back to Mother's house?"

"Yes." She would if she could find Caleb, at any rate. Emmie had an otherworldly innocence, plain and fresh as warm milk, that made men twice her age, balding deacons and loan officers with grown children, hit on her. The good thing about it was that people rarely questioned her intentions.

"Fine, just remember it's going to take a long time to dress." Fortunately, before she could add more admonishments, someone interrupted to ask Grace for an opinion about some wedding detail. Emmie made her escape with a little wave.

She could have screamed with impatience when Pickett's sixtyish cousin Annalynn planted herself in her path, determined to pump Emmie for news.

"Pickett's finally getting married! Can you believe it? And to a real hottie!" Annalynn gushed. Annalynn gushed about everything, but she needn't sound as if a miracle had transpired. In Emmie's opinion, Pickett was far too frequently relegated to "poor thing" status. Her relatives still saw Pickett as the baby of the family, the chubby, frequently-ill teenager with unruly hair and her nose stuck in a book.

Emmie nodded but refused to reply.

As college freshmen Emmie and Pickett were nerds together and soon best friends. Pickett's health and figure had improved once she learned to control her diet. She discovered a haircut that made the most of her exuberant gold curls and overcame her nerdishness with her warmth and compassion. It was no surprise to Emmie an attractive man could fall in love with Pickett.

She *was* surprised at Pickett's choice in a groom: a SEAL. Take everything bad about the military, multiply it by ten, and you had a SEAL. Pickett had always sworn up and down she'd never marry a military man—it was something they'd always been in perfect agreement about—and yet, Pickett had changed her mind. It deeply, deeply scared Emmie. Nothing could ever change the fact that she loved Pickett with all her heart, but she wasn't sure how they would maintain their friendship. Once Pickett was absorbed into the military-industrial complex, she would become part of a culture antithetical to Emmie's most basic beliefs.

Pickett would tell her she was worrying about events that hadn't happened yet, and that she would never allow anything to threaten their friendship. None of this was anything Emmie was going to discuss with Annalynn.

Patience wasn't Emmie's strong suit. Once she had a goal in mind, she tended to fix on it to the exclusion of all else. She didn't have *time* to trade party chatter with Pickett's cousins, aunts, uncles, and assorted others whose degree of kinship was distant enough to confound the most determined genealogist, but who, nevertheless, qualified as family. It seemed like every one of them had stopped her. Emmie was utterly sick of explaining why her arm was in a cobalt blue canvas sling. Once the wedding breakfast broke up, the high-ceilinged rooms of the late Victorian house would empty quickly. If Caleb left before she talked to him, all her plans were ruined. There was a very small window before she had to get rigged out in the bridesmaid getup Grace had chosen.

The sling was rubbing the collar of the beige blazer against her neck again. Her wardrobe goal was efficiency and comfort, but she'd sacrificed comfort today for clothes she could get into unaided. She regretted the decision to add the blazer, but since she couldn't hook a bra she didn't see what else she could have done.

The worst part about the blazer was that it encouraged her hair to work its way under the sling. Painful tugs accompanied any incautious movement of her head. Emmie adjusted the sling impatiently and scanned the thinning crowd, while trying at least to *appea*r to listen to Annalynn. Impatient as she felt, Emmie didn't want to be rude. From the first time Pickett had brought her home for a college holiday, these people had hugged her and teased her and admonished her as if she belonged.

"I guess you're next." Failing to get Emmie to talk about Pickett, Annalynn tried another subject. "When are you going to find yourself a man?"

"Actually, I'm looking for a man right now. Have you seen Jax's best man?"

Emmie caught the avid interest that widened Annalynn's rather watery eyes and gave herself a mental slap. She'd done it again! Sometimes she got so focused on her goals she forgot to consider how others would interpret her words and actions. The story that she and the best man were an item would make the rounds before the opening ta-dums of the wedding march.

"I didn't mean it like *that,*" she protested with a pained laugh. "But I really am looking for him. I need to speak to him before he leaves."

"I saw him on the front porch talking to Lilly Hale," Annalynn panted, thrilled to be fostering a romance. "Run quick. I think he was taking his leave."

"Aunt Lilly Hale, can I borrow Caleb for a minute?"

Do-Lord felt the odd little internal shiver, like the supercharged air of a thunderstorm, a half-second before the woman appeared at his elbow. Without turning, he knew Emelina Caddington, Pickett's best friend and maid of honor, stood beside him.

Something about her irritated him, something besides the way she called him Caleb in her cool, precise voice, oddly devoid of southern accent. Nobody had called him Caleb since he left Alabama. He'd joined the Navy the day he turned eighteen, and since then he'd been Dulaude. Do-Lord to his friends.

She wasn't attention-worthy in any way except for her wide blue eyes that gave her the look of a serious, intelligent kitten. Appealing image, but it was canceled by her shapeless clothes and sensible shoes.

Spinsterish. The old-fashioned word fit her and matched her name, Emelina. Beside Pickett's tall, elegant sisters, almost awe-inspiring in their cool, blonde beauty, or Pickett herself, the sweetest, most feminine thing he'd ever seen, Emmie didn't rate a second glance.

SEALs might love one another like brothers and be willing to die for one another, but that didn't mean they liked every SEAL. Any man who earned the Trident, the symbol of brotherhood with other elite warriors, had learned to control his reaction to people. Above all, he did not let things get to him. Which made it even more irritating that anytime she was in the room, he watched her.

"Emmie, darling! It's so good to see you." The older woman leaned forward to carefully lay her cheek against Emmie's, avoiding the bright blue harness that held Emmie's arm close to her chest. "But your poor arm! Are you still going to be Pickett's maid of honor? How are you going to manage two bouquets and Pickett's train and everything?"

Emmie favored Pickett's great aunt with a stiff smile. "That's what I need to talk to the best man about. Excuse us please?" Without waiting for a reply Emmie looped her good arm through his and tugged him back into the house.

It went against his grain to let a stranger inside his personal space where a knife could be used; or to let anyone hamper his right arm preventing him from going for his weapon; or to let himself be taken anywhere he hadn't decided for himself to go. A tiny bit amused by her presumption in believing she *could,* he allowed her to lead him.

The very novelty sent a tingle of anticipation through his boredom. She seemed unaware she'd crossed lines men twice her size wouldn't have dared, and she pressed his arm so close he could feel the soft give of the side of her breast.

Her full, soft breast that wasn't confined by a bra.

He wouldn't be a man if he didn't notice.

The irritation he always felt around her morphed into a more primal awareness. He suddenly noticed her smell. She wore no perfume that he could detect. She just smelled basic. Sweet. Like a woman.

She intended to pull him past the parlors into the wide hall that would take them deeper into the house. He didn't *think* she was coming on to him—not after the stiff way she always acted around him—but she was up to something. "Where are we going?"

"To Aunt Lilly Hale's office. Someplace we can talk."

"Talk?" Do-Lord halted so he could look into her face. He squashed an absurd blossom of hope. She was the last woman in the world who would pull him aside for a quickie. And close to the last woman in the world he would want to pull him aside. Yeah, suddenly she interested him, but not *that* way. Even though she reminded him more than ever of a serious, and right this minute, very determined kitten. A Siamese kitten with big, blue eyes and silvery beige fur.

Emmie intercepted the rather calculating look of masculine assessment he gave her, and suddenly became aware of the heat and steely strength of the arm under the fine tweed of his coat, and of the fact that she had left off her bra this morning. Could he tell? Surely not.

She wanted to grind her teeth with frustration. It was that goal-directed thing again making her unaware of how she was coming across. Grabbing his arm had been a stupid move, but for a man who stood out as he did, he could be amazingly elusive. For thirty minutes she'd searched the crowd for his russet head and broad shoulders, dodging jocular inanities about when she was going to find herself a man. The irony hadn't escaped her.

Or improved her disposition, she was afraid. Her shoulder hurt with a deep, grinding ache. All she really wanted to do was take her pain medication and lie very still until it was time for the wedding.

By the time she'd spotted him framed by the double doors open to the warm day, she'd been close to frantic, the sedate calm with which she usually endured these family affairs shredded. She needed him, and she'd grabbed him, determined not let anyone interrupt. But really! These jocks! He wasn't a college athlete, he was a member of a crack military team with an animal name. Navy SEALs, Miami Dolphins, what was the difference? She recognized the type.

They crowded her Understanding Ecology class, a Biology elective for non-majors, and thought she should be flattered. They assumed everything with a vagina was interested in them. They only had to choose which one they wanted. They walked the earth with a sense of entitlement, sure that their place in the universe guaranteed the best.

On campus she carefully kept her professorial distance and made it clear in any interaction, she was in charge. Give them an inch, and they'd take a mile.

She forgot her intention to get on his good side. Knowing the effect was probably ruined by the heat staining her cheeks, she aimed him a don't-mess-with-me glare, "I said what I meant. You know. The *other* four-letter word ending in k. *Talk!*"

Her faced flamed redder. What was the matter with her? She never said things like that!

His grin widened. "Just checking."

He changed the subject. "Why do you call her 'aunt?' You're not kin with this family are you?"

Relief that she hadn't offended him made her expansive. "We're not related, but they *are* my adopted family. Pickett and I were college roommates. Because my parents are missionaries, going home for holidays was out of the question, so I always came home with Pickett. I just got in the habit of calling people whatever Pickett did."

Emmie opened the door into a sunny butler's pantry Pickett's aunt had converted to a home office. "Here we are."

Focused on finding a private place where they could talk, she'd forgotten how small the room was. Hundreds of framed photographs, tiny and large, old sepia-tone portraits and bright clowning snapshots, covered every bit of wall space left by the glass-fronted cabinets. The floor space, occupied as it was by an antique estate desk, left two adults hardly room to stand.

The unexpected intimacy rattled Emmie. He was so close she could see the shadow cast by his golden eyelashes. His eyes, a hazel mixture of brown and gold and green, reminded her of pebbles washed by a mountain stream. Cold and hard. She forced herself to look into them without flinching. Last night she'd noticed the way he looked at Pickett and thought maybe she had an ally. Now she wasn't so sure.

Underneath the sling she tugged the lapels of her jacket together and took a fortifying breath. At this late date there wasn't anyone else she could ask.

"I understand you SEALs are pretty loyal to one another," she said, getting straight to the point. "Does your loyalty extend to Pickett?"

"What are you asking?" In his lazy, liquid drawl the question didn't sound like a question. His voice was deep, sonorous, but damped, as if he saw no need to bring its full power to this situation. Yet the power was there. His voice felt like fur stroking down her spine from her nape to the small of her back.

She ruthlessly slammed the door on the thought. Emmie, child of missionaries, had spent her teenage years with an elderly grandmother. She wasn't opposed to wholesome sex, but the temptations of sensuality were subtle and best avoided. This was for Pickett, but still, his voice, dark as burnt umber and a little gritty, compelled more honesty than she had planned. "I'm asking, are you willing to do a favor for Pickett—no matter what the fallout?"

"Do I have to kill anybody?" He didn't look like he was kidding.

"No, but if we're caught, all hell will break loose. Pickett's sister Grace might kill you."

"And you, I presume."

Emmie dismissed that. “Probably, but I don’t care. Pickett’s the peacemaker.”

“What do you want me to do?”

Emmie took a deep breath and looked him straight in the eye. “We have to switch wedding cakes.”

Chapter 3

Whoa! Miss Emelina might look boring in her all-over beige clothes that matched her beige hair—though bright sun streaming in the window brought out its pretty silver sheen—but she'd just proved she could surprise him.

Do-Lord laughed aloud, the first honest laugh he'd had in days. "I'm getting a vision of a cake exploding like Mt. St. Helens and spewing white frosting everywhere."

Suddenly, he sobered. "Is this a practical joke?"

"I've never been more serious," Emmie gave him one of her cool, spinsterish looks. "But in a way, it is a trick—and unless we do something, the joke will be on Pickett. Grace ordered the cake from a regular bakery."

"Too ordinary, huh?" These people's games in which they displayed their wealth and superiority had stuck in his craw more than once. He couldn't sympathize with their scrabbling one-upmanship when they already inhabited the top of the heap.

"On the contrary. Only the best will do." Emmie flicked her fingers disdainfully. Her tone, loaded with sarcasm, showed her ready comprehension, and he liked her better for it. "And that's Grace's excuse. Sacre Bleu's cakes are the most beautiful and the best tasting to be found south of the Mason-Dixon line. Unfortunately, they're also made with wheat flour."

Do-Lord circled his hand to urge her to wind it up. "And that's a problem because..."

"Pickett has celiac disease, which means she can't eat anything with wheat flour as an ingredient."

When Do-Lord had observed Pickett pretending to eat, but in actuality leaving food untouched, he had assumed she avoided fattening foods. Now he reassessed her restraint. "Does everyone know she has this problem?"

"Oh, yes. You're thinking about the food that's been served this weekend, aren't you?" Again, Do-Lord was startled by her ready comprehension of his thought processes. He must be slipping if she was reading his face that easily. "The roast turkey," she continued, "served on top of dressing and covered in gravy at the rehearsal dinner last night was my personal favorite for least-edible foods for Pickett. Although I must say this morning's buffet runs a close second. There weren't two foods on the table she could safely choose. There's a delicious—you'll pardon the pun—irony in feeding the guest of honor food she mustn't eat, but must smile in gratitude for."

"So you're saying she's not going to be able to eat her wedding cake either." He shrugged. "Nobody ever died of malnutrition from not eating wedding cake." The things these people found important never ceased to amaze him. "Big deal. She'll handle it like she always does."

"You don't understand." Turning away from him, Emmie scanned the wall of photos until she found the one she was looking for. She pointed to a picture of a bride and groom laughingly shoving cake into one another's mouths. "See? She'll *have* to eat it."

The tall white cake served at wedding receptions today was, in previous centuries, the bride's cake, whereas the wedding cake was traditionally a fruitcake, filled with nuts and... When he'd researched wedding customs, he'd passed over the rituals with the cake, assuming all his duties would be over by then. Now he examined the photo more closely.

The tiered wedding cake stood in the foreground of the photograph, a frosting fantasy on fluted pillars. Only the head and shoulders of the bride and groom were visible behind it, and behind them, laughing guests gathered around.

The bride, another cousin he presumed, looked a bit like Pickett. It was all too easy to imagine Pickett in her place, but instead of laughing as the bride in the picture was doing, smiling the strained smile he'd seen again and again on Pickett's face this weekend.

"When Jax feeds Pickett the cake she won't refuse to eat it with everybody watching," Emmie explained. "She'll sacrifice herself rather than ruin the fun for everyone else. She won't want to hurt Grace's feelings and make a spectacle."

A piece of "normal" behavior that crossed all cultural lines was eating whatever was offered. In operations where SEALs had lived with locals, he'd eaten stewed rat—not bad—and goat's eyes—kind of tasteless really—and chili so hot his asshole had burned for a week. Do-Lord understood Pickett's desire not to call attention to herself by refusing. In some places the insult of refusing food could get you killed. At best, refusal branded you forever as an outsider.

"Wait a minute. Pickett doesn't want to hurt *Grace's* feelings? Isn't that backwards?"

Emmie rubbed the spot between her brows, smoothing away the line trying to form there. "Yes, it is, and if you talk to her about it, even *she* sees it. But Pickett is one of the kindest people I've ever known. She always thinks of others first. She's not going to choose a moment like that to stand up for herself." Emmie smiled sadly. "Pickett won't die from one bite of cake."

"What will happen?"

"Her stomach will hurt, but not immediately. It won't start for eight hours or so. Then she'll spend the next twenty-four hours in the bathroom. Her honeymoon will be ruined." Emmie raised her honest blue eyes. Do-Lord had never before considered that honesty might have a color, but if it did, it would be the soft, summery blue of Emmie's eyes. "But it might not be that bad," she finished. "It isn't always."

Do-Lord began to understand how everyone could be aware of Pickett's problem, but pretend it made no difference. They wouldn't have to suffer, or even watch Pickett suffer, the consequences. "The perpetrators will get off scot-free in other words."

"Perpetrator is too strong a word. I don't think anyone means to do Pickett harm—in fact, I'm sure they don't." Emmie countered with a scholarly judiciousness. "Having an outsider's perspective, I can see the family blind spots. They believe a tablespoon or two, or just a bite, won't hurt. All the aunts, uncles, and cousins have gone to a lot of trouble to show their support of Pickett. Grace has worked miracles to pull this wedding off in such a short time. She honestly believes she's making sure everything about Pickett's wedding is perfect."

"And so, *you* think the solution is to bring in a ringer for the cake." Do-Lord struggled against a chuckle that wanted to break loose.

"I would do anything for Pickett. I can't change the people, but with your help, I can change the cake." Emmie paused while she freed her hair from underneath the sling. "If anybody is going to give Pickett at least one moment of unalloyed, lighthearted fun at her wedding, it's going to be me, and, 'should you choose to accept this mission, Mr. Graves,'" Emmie intoned the line from the old *Mission Impossible* TV show, "you."

And they accused *SEALs* of being cowboys! Emmie's means of dealing with it had to be the most overly elaborate solution he'd ever heard tell of.

Laughing, Do-Lord raised his hands and backed away. "Hey, I admire your desire to ride in on a white horse and save your friend from embarrassment or an upset stomach, but this isn't my problem. Not yours either. It's Pickett's and Jax's." He'd bet Jax hadn't given any more thought to the wedding cake than he had. Less, if anything. Jax thought like an officer—meaning he gave orders and expected others to manage the details.

"Then you won't help me?"

Something about the expression in her eyes, some look he could only call loneliness, made him gentle his tone. "You're trying to build a million-dollar mousetrap. All I have to do is tell Jax not to feed Pickett the cake. If Jax knew what was going down, he wouldn't care what the tribal rituals are. He'd put a stop to it."

"If you do, Pickett will wind up embarrassed and tense because somebody—probably a lot of somebodies—will make jokes about why they won't eat the wedding cake. And then, if she attempts to explain, they'll be embarrassed because their jokes called attention to her 'affliction'—"

"'Affliction?' You've gotta be kidding."

"—and then Pickett will be more embarrassed."

She was right about that. Jax would put a stop to any teasing, too—but likely by causing heads to roll.

On the other hand, making an end-run around the system that allowed the problem to discreetly disappear was much more a Chief's approach, especially when everyone needed to respect everyone else in the morning.

Screwball as it was, Emmie's scheme had a certain quixotic appeal—like a reverse practical joke. He'd been pissed by the cousins' sly devaluing of Pickett, and while the remedy didn't administer the justice they deserved, he'd like to know he'd put one over on them.

"I just want Pickett to have the same kind of fun everyone else gets to have, without hurting anybody's feelings or putting anyone in the wrong."

To his surprise, Emmie was winning him over. His irritation with her had vanished as soon as she grabbed his arm. Maybe because in the last few minutes he'd begun to think she was interesting. Plain, yes, but female, definitely. A wedding cake heist was the most entertainment he'd been offered this weekend. Good deeds of this kind were notorious for backfiring, though.

To gain time while he thought it over, Do-Lord pretended to study the wedding cake picture. The photo beside it was of the same couple taken from a slightly different angle. This time the flash had illuminated more of the bystanders. One smiling face, just past the bride's shoulder, arrested his attention.

His heart beat harder, and the small of his back prickled as sweat popped out. His country-boy smile widened.

"Is that Teague Calhoun, the senator?"

Emmie moved closer to see what he was looking at. "Um-hmm. He'll be coming to Pickett's wedding too. His wife is a cousin on Pickett's grandmother's side, I think. Her *mother's* mother," she clarified, as if that made all the difference. She snickered, but not unkindly. "Everybody calls this Aunt Lilly Hale's 'bragging wall.' She's got a president up here somewhere." Emmie reached past him to point out the famous face in a group of men dressed in hunting camo. "I'll bet that wedding photo, while nominally of Aunt Lilly Hale's granddaughter, made the cut because Uncle Teague is one of the richest men in North Carolina, in addition to being a senator."

And she knew him. Do-Lord's heart rate kicked up again. What were the odds? A plan formed in his mind, but he had to know one detail first. "Is Teague Calhoun really your uncle, or just somebody else you call 'uncle?'"

"Not really. I sound like I claim kin to a lot of people I'm not related to, don't I?" Rose color suffused Emmie's cheek, as if she was embarrassed. The touch of color emphasized the blue of her eyes and called attention to the porcelain clarity of her skin. He'd seen a lot of porcelain in the last few days, and now he understood what those romance writers meant. He didn't think he'd ever seen prettier skin in his life. "Calling him 'uncle' is just another habit I got into, but in this case it's because my grandmother was a friend of his. Why are you so interested in him?"

Emmie claimed kin to a host of people she wasn't related to, whereas the only person he knew for sure he *was* related to, didn't claim him at all. It was just one of the many, many differences between them. Do-Lord ignored the relief he felt that she was no relation of Calhoun's.

"Just surprised, is all." Do-Lord decided to give her part of the truth. He was starting to realize that Emmie, unworldly and detached though she might appear, saw a great deal. "My unit was detailed to protect him one time."

"Isn't it strange how no matter where you go, you seem to meet the same people over and over? Or at any rate, people who seem to know the same people you do? Teague Calhoun was executor of my grandmother's estate—not that I think he did the actual work. He has 'people.' I never expected to see him again once the estate was settled, but it turned out he's at all Pickett's family parties. The important ones," she added cynically, "where all the important people will be seen."

Karmic circles, she was talking about. Groups of souls who reincarnate together to work out debts left over from past lives. Reincarnation made a lot of sense to Do-Lord, but he'd never considered that he and Calhoun might have karmic ties that would bring them together over and over until they learned their lessons. Until the moment Calhoun had appeared in Afghanistan, he'd never met the man.

Karma or not, the evidence was in front of him that the unfinished business between him and Calhoun couldn't be ignored. It wasn't going to stay buried even though he'd refused one opportunity to even the score.

He had to think. Do-Lord fought the distraction of her feminine scent. She stood just behind him, still studying the wall of photographs. He wondered if she knew how often she encroached on his space, or what it meant.

In spite of the fact that she irritated him, he was starting to like her. She was abrupt, but he suspected that was because she was as goal-driven as he was, and had as little patience with meaningless chatter. She was as loyal to Pickett as he was to Jax. Where she gave herself, she gave herself completely. Briefly, he wondered what it would be like to tease her into full sexual awareness of him, to stroke that heat he sensed into flame.

The thought was amazingly hot, but he dismissed it. While some SEALs seemed to think wearing the Trident entitled them to sex anytime they wanted, he didn't use women. Sex wasn't hard to come by for any SEAL. There was never any reason to take advantage of a woman who didn't know the score. But that didn't mean he would turn away this opportunity the universe had sent him. She had the background he needed, and the entrée into a strata of society he couldn't touch—yet anyone could see she wasn't one of them.

And right now she needed him. A smart Chief made sure more people owed him favors than he owed favors to. Do-Lord had been wondering ever since Afghanistan how he would get closer to Calhoun in a way that wouldn't implicate other SEALs. Now he knew.

Chapter 4

"I'M IN." A CONSPIRATORIAL GRIN TURNED CALEB'S EYES a devilish shade of golden. "What do we have to do?"

He *was* going to help her. The sudden relief from the tension of the last hour left Emmie almost giddy.

A lot of people thought, because she didn't pay attention to the same things others did, Emmie wasn't observant. She couldn't tell the difference between a Mercedes and a BMW, a Rolex and a Timex, and didn't know why anyone would waste time shopping when slacks could be ordered from catalogs. The surface of things didn't interest her.

She *had* noticed that though he spoke with a country accent, his English was grammatical. He employed an inexhaustible vocabulary of smiles, and despite meticulous courtesy, until these last few minutes, he'd barely tolerated her.

That one may smile, and smile, and be a villain. The quote from Hamlet popped into her head. She didn't think he was a villain, exactly, but she knew beyond doubt he used that particular smile to cover his thoughts rather than to reveal them.

There was more to him than met the eye. A lot more. The thought was a little shivery, but intriguing. He had reasons of his own for assisting her. So be it.

"The cake I ordered is waiting to be picked up at the UPS office. We'll take it to the country club while no one is there and substitute it. Simple, really."

"What will we do with the other cake?"

"Pack it in the box the substitute cake came in. I spent hours on the Internet locating a baker who would make a gluten-free cake identical to the one Grace ordered." And maxed out her Visa to get the cake made and here on time. "I made the plan before I hurt my arm, though. My cake will have to be assembled."

"Haven't you ever heard of Murphy's Law? Anything that can go wrong—"

"Will go wrong," Emmie finished. "Of course, I've heard of it. I find it unrealistically negative." She felt giddy again. Free of anxiety, now she felt challenged rather than pressured. "Really, finding a baker was the hard part. Since you have two good arms, the rest should be—dare I say it? A piece of cake."

On the wide front steps flanked by massive boxwoods they ran into Jax. His normally hard face softened by tender amusement, Jax was watching his small son race around the wide lawn attempting to catch bright leaves as they drifted down from the many old shade trees. Jax had been absent for most of Tyler's short life but was determined to make up for it now.

"Emmie! Emmie!" Tyler caught sight of them and flung himself toward Emmie, arms outstretched wide intending to hug her around the knees the same way he hugged Pickett. Apparently, he had decided Emmie rated the same affection.

Tyler was utterly unrestrained in administering hugs. Do-Lord put his arm behind Emmie's waist ready to catch her if Tyler unbalanced her, but before Tyler could connect, Jax swept him up.

"Easy Tyler, remember? You have to be careful with ladies."

"You said I had to be careful with *Pickett.*"

"Well, you have to be careful with Emmie, too."

"Do I have to be careful with Aunt Grace, and Aunt Sarah Bea, and Aunt Lyle?" Tyler listed Pickett's sisters. He seemed delighted with all the family he was acquiring along with a stepmother and missed no opportunity to name every one. "And Aunt Lilly Hale and—"

"Yes," Jax interrupted the list. Since Pickett's family was large, it could go on quite a while. "You have to be careful with every single one. Now, can you give Emmie a *gentle* hug? She has a hurt arm, so you need to be extra special careful."

Lifted into position by his father, Tyler settled hands weightless as snowflakes on Emmie's shoulders and pressed his cheek against hers. After a moment's hesitation, Emmie brought her good arm up to hold him to her.

"Did the hug make you all better?" Tyler inquired with a child's innocent faith as his father lifted him away. "Do you want another one?"

"Um, maybe later."

"Did you know I'm going to be five soon?" Tyler asked Emmie in the lightning fast shift of attention typical of children. "I'm four now," he clarified, "but *then,* I'll be five."

"Oh." Emmie seemed unsure of what to say, but she gave the child the courtesy of taking him seriously. Do-Lord liked that about her. So many people thought that because children were naïve they were negligible. "When is your birthday?"

"Tomorrow!"

"Not tomorrow, son," Jax corrected. "December twelfth."

"December twelfth," Tyler parroted. "That's *soon,* right? Did you know after we get married tonight, Pickett's mother will be *my* grandmother?"

Emmie's eyes turned to Do-Lord in momentary confusion. She must not have much experience with little kids. Do-Lord nodded. "Yes." She turned back to Tyler. "I knew that."

Before he could start into another *did you know* Jax hung Tyler upside down by his hands. Tyler executed a backwards body flip to the ground.

"Hey, Tyler, go get us five more leaves to take to the hotel, okay?"

Tyler held up a hand, fingers spread wide. "Five?"

"Right."

When the little boy was out of earshot, Jax turned to Do-Lord. "Listen, I just found out his other grandmother, Lauren, is coming to the wedding. Pickett insisted on inviting her."

Do-Lord whistled softly. Lauren was the mother of Jax's ex-wife, Danielle. Tyler had stayed with her until Jax could return from Afghanistan. There had never been any love lost between her and Jax, and now she was trying to take Tyler away from him. The wedding wouldn't have been rushed if not for the need to head off any possibility of her getting Tyler.

"Wait a minute," Emmie interrupted. "You make it sound like that's a bad thing. I understand where Pickett's coming from. Lauren might not be the best custodian for Tyler, but she's still his grandmother. He needs the link to his mother and his past that Lauren can provide."

"I understand what Pickett's saying, too. Inviting Lauren was her call, and you know I'm going to back her. I had hoped Lauren wouldn't accept. Pickett doesn't know what Lauren is capable of. She hasn't ever had to deal with her."

"Don't sell Pickett short. She's a lot tougher than she looks. She can deal with anything Lauren can dish out. She'll protect Tyler if she needs to, but she says it's best not to protect children from knowing their parents and grandparents."

Do-Lord laid a careful hand on Emmie's good shoulder. "You don't have to defend Pickett to Jax. He's on her side. She shouldn't *need* to handle Lauren on her wedding day. No worries, boss," he added to Jax. "Nothing's going to happen."

Jax nodded his understanding. "Thanks." He gave Do-Lord and Emmie a considering look, his light-colored eyes flicking between them. "Where are you two off to?"

"Emmie's ready to leave. I said I'd give her a ride. She can't drive with her arm in a sling."

"Is there anything else I need to know?" Jax's tone was bland, disinterested. Like hell. He knew something was up. Do-Lord wondered what stray flicker of body language had given them away. Do-Lord would just as soon have stayed out of range of Jax's radar. It would be better if Jax had no foreknowledge of Emmie's quixotic scheme or Do-Lord's reasons for agreeing to help her.

"Nah. I've got everything handled." Do-Lord matched Jax's casual tone perfectly, knowing he didn't need to add *trust me*.

"I got 'em. I got the leaves." Tyler ran back to the adults.

Jax slung his son across his shoulder in a fireman carry. "I'm going to take him back to the hotel so we can swim for a while. Maybe I can drain off a few gallons of excitement and get him to nap."

Tyler twisted around on his father's shoulders to regard Do-Lord and Emmie with a look eerily like his father's. "Don't forget," cautioned Tyler. "You gotta be extra special careful when you hug Emmie."

Do-Lord grinned and noogied the kid's hair. Tyler was going to need some fine-tuning before he had his father's ESP. Do-Lord didn't think any hugs would be needed. Doing a favor would accomplish his goal. "No problem, big guy. See you later."

Chapter 5

THE MUSCULAR PICKUP, PARKED ON THE GRASSY EDGE of the tree-lined drive, had to be the biggest truck Emmie had ever seen. Do-Lord unlocked the door on the passenger side and held it open.

"This is a new truck, isn't it?" Emmie stalled for time. "What kind is it?" She had no interest in trucks whatsoever, but she needed a minute to gather her courage to face the pain of climbing in.

"A Silverado 250," His narrowed eyes traveled over her in cool, deliberate assessment. Though there was nothing sexual about the way he sized her up, her breath stalled in her throat. She had never felt so *looked at* in her life. His lips pursed, as if he was fighting a smug smile. "You need help getting in."

She stiffened. "Are you asking me or telling me?"

He ignored the question. "Do I need to be careful of anything besides your shoulder?"

"Everything else works fine. Really, I can do it."

Again, he ignored her. "Brace your good hand on my shoulder for balance—" When she didn't comply, he took her hand and set it on his shoulder. "When I pick you up lean toward me slightly. Don't want to bump your head." Not waiting for her agreement, he placed two hard, warm hands on her waist and lifted.

The sheer novelty of the experience streaked in a shocked tingle down her legs and up her spine. She wasn't the kind of dainty little thing men picked up, and even if she was, she didn't hang around the kind of jocks who showed off their muscles by picking women up.

Emmie hardly had time to absorb the feeling of his shoulder under her hand before her butt was in contact with the passenger seat, her legs dangling sideways.

She shifted in the seat attempting to swing her feet into the car. Her cheeks turned white. She bit her lip, but she didn't groan.

"Stop. Don't twist," he commanded, anticipating her. "I'll straighten you up. If the Cargo is already injured, it usually works better if the Cargo lets me do everything."

One arm around her back steadied her, while the other went under her knees to lift her legs. Dragging on panty hose had been out of the question this morning. His hand brushed the naked back of her legs just above the knee. For one breathless second, she thought it lingered. Then, so smoothly she thought the tiny hiatus hadn't happened, she was facing forward.

She hastily tugged at the hem of her skirt. Turning had twisted it, baring her thighs. If she'd ever been one to swear, she would have sworn now. Covering her legs, one-handed and with no leverage, was impossible.

"Raise up a little." His voice, suddenly deeper, grittier, was so close she felt the moist puffs of his breath. "I'll straighten your skirt."

Efficiently, but with no trace of hurry, he ran his hand under her buttocks to free the bunched material. When that was done, he firmly and totally *un*necessarily, smoothed the wrinkles from the cotton twill.

"Are you done?" Emmie tried to snap but wasn't sure she succeeded.

"Almost." He extended the seatbelt, and she realized he intended to buckle her in.

"Enough!" She caught the hand in which he held the metal tab. "I'll do it, thank you."

He didn't release the tab. He just looked at her. Patient. Implacable.

His head was level with hers, so close she could see the gold and brown flecks in his irises. His eyes weren't cold and hard now.

She had never been on the receiving end of a will so focused it was palpable.

She gasped and drew his scent deep into her lungs. Wool, starch, spice, and some ineluctable, masculine essence. She could still feel the impression his hands and arms had made on her body—the smooth, casual strength with which he took control.

With the same strobe-like intensity as when she had realized one couldn't judge his personality by his good-humored smile, Emmie suddenly understood this man wouldn't give up. He never gave up. The knowledge shuddered through her like a gong that had been struck. Without a word spoken she knew she had been warned: let go of the belt or he *would* do more.

One pointed eyebrow quirked. "Are you going to let me do it now?"

What was he talking about? Stunned by insights, overcome with sensory surfeit, Emmie found the question baffling. As if she could find the answer there, her attention fixated on his mobile mouth. His lips reminded her of Brad Pitt's, she thought, too bemused to notice the irrelevance. The upper curved in a perfect bow, while the lower poked out as if he knew a secret that poised his lips at the beginning of a smile—or the beginning of a kiss. "Do it?"

"Buckle the seat belt." This time the grin was outright, genuine, and so steeped in amused arrogance Emmie wanted to writhe in mortification for letting him make her think about kissing, even momentarily.

Heat flooded her face and spread down her chest in a fire that threatened to consume her entire body. Her torso tightened in a weird reflex that included her nipples.

He was so proud of his little display of masculine dominance she wanted to hit him, and *that* made her writhe because she didn't believe in violence. *And* she wanted to run her finger tips over the short velvety-looking hair on his nape—and that made her writhe even more.

Emmie wasn't naïve about sexual attraction. No one who worked on a college campus could be. If the massive distraction of sex could be eliminated, the test scores of her students would rise one whole letter grade. But she wasn't the kind of girl who'd ever needed to be warned against bad boys. She wasn't the kind who lost her head—but more to the point, she wasn't the kind bad boys gave a second glance. Or, for that matter, a first one.

And bad boy he was. It didn't show through anything as clichéd as a leather jacket or a sullen attitude. He'd been all polite, deferent charm to Pickett's mother and sisters and aunts. He dressed with military polish, and his hair was cut shorter than Jax's. And yet she was sure he never played by the rules—not unless he fixed them first.

If she could, she'd get out of the truck right now. She'd had all she ever wanted of masculine disdain for her plainness. If he knew what she was thinking, he'd probably laugh.

Thank God, once the seat belt clicked into place, he withdrew without further comment.

Do-Lord shut her door. His fingers left a film of moisture on the chrome handle. Sweaty palms. Shit. When was the last time his hands had sweated from being close to a girl?

He'd been pleased—he'd admit it—when he'd realized Emmie couldn't climb into his truck without his help. It freed him to take charge, and SEALs liked to be in charge.

For the last two days he'd fought the urge to put himself between her and movement that would cause her pain. No more. She wasn't going to hurt herself—not on his watch.

But when he'd gone to straighten her up on the seat, his hand had encountered the moist, silky smoothness of her thighs and their soft weight. Turning her had twisted her skirt, exposing her legs to the top of her thigh, allowing him a whiff of her warm, secret woman essence.

It blindsided him. In the way of odors, it bypassed his cerebral cortex and zoomed into his most primitive instincts to survive and to mate. With craving close to pain, he had wanted to bury his head in her lap, press his nose against the source, and draw it deep into his lungs.

If he thought she was the least bit willing, he would lay her down right her beside the sandy driveway. He would have her on the golden leaves beneath the pecan trees in the thin November sunshine.

His unit had been stateside not quite three months, and he knew himself to be still more than half-wild, his senses tuned to register every nuance of his environment. In the aftermath of combat most guys were sexually charged. He was no exception. But God. He hadn't expected this.

Apparently he needed a lot more R and R than he'd had.

He'd willed himself to keep his movements slow and nonthreatening while he'd pulled down her skirt. He wasn't going to go caveman on her. He'd never forced a woman and never would.

Still, invading her space by reaching across her body to buckle her seat belt had been an act of pure male dominance—primitive, atavistic, aboriginal as hell, and damn satisfying. It made getting sweaty hand prints on his new truck almost worth it.

Focus. Knee-buckling lust had thrown him for a minute, but there was a bright side. He drew a deep breath and consciously made his shoulders relax. At last, he'd figured out what irritated him about her, and why he couldn't stop watching her. Had they not had their battle of wills over the seat belt, had he not been looking straight into those kitten-wide, blue eyes, he wouldn't have seen them fix on his lips or noticed the flare of her delicate nostrils. His little, spinsterish professor had been turned on too. Now that he could see it, he couldn't believe it had taken him this long to connect the dots.

He rounded the front of the truck, shrugging out of his sport coat. Since social time was over, he no longer needed it to make the correct impression. Now that he knew what was going on, he had another impression in mind…

Subliminally, he'd probably been picking up the same arousal cues, autonomic nervous system telltales that she couldn't control, for days. And yet, she didn't put out a single indicator that she was available or interested in him—consciously or unconsciously.

She didn't pat her hair, or tilt her head, or cock her hip. She didn't swing her hips, or thrust out her breasts, or lick her lips, or glance over her shoulder. With body language that locked down, he'd bet she hadn't had much sex in her life. In fact, combined with her godawful clothes, she'd might as well be wearing a sign that said, "I'm not getting any."

Well, he could do something about that. He wasn't so ego-swollen that he thought every woman should find him irresistible. He had better luck than average though. He understood that he had the most potent charm of all: he liked women for their own sakes. Short ones, tall ones, hefty ones, skinny ones. SEALs were an all male force, but it took a lot of support to keep a team operating, and some of those people were women. Many he counted as friends. If he got her to loosen up and enjoy herself as a woman, he'd be doing her a favor. She probably didn't know what good sex was.

In spite of his irritation, he'd already found himself liking her quirky take on life. She was completely comfortable in this world of wealth and privilege. She called a powerful U.S. senator "Uncle Teague." Some sort of sexual chemistry was going on between them. He was too much of a SEAL not to use any advantage that came his way.

He draped the coat on a hanger he kept in the backseat for that purpose and methodically folded back his shirt cuffs to reveal his forearms. Hey, he'd read *Queer Eye for the Straight Guy*. There was stuff in there he wasn't going to do—like waxing his nuts for instance—but some of the advice, like rolling up sleeves, made sense.

A woman's pheromones were airborne, but a man's were on the skin and best transferred by touch. He could show a little skin and make it easy for her. He loosened his tie and undid the button at his throat. For good measure, he loosened another one.

He smiled. "Where to?"

Chapter 6

THE COUNTRY CLUB GLEAMED IN THE GOLDEN AUTUMN light, a Tara-dream of white columns, sitting atop a small rise and flanked by glossy-leaved, deep green magnolias.

They had retrieved the cake from the UPS office, and it sat on the backseat of the king cab. All they had to do was carry it in and set it up.

Do-Lord pulled the truck into a parking space and killed the motor, his movements smooth and flowing. He studied the building with narrowed eyes, first tilting his head one way, then the other.

Emmie chuckled. "Yeah. I always have the same reaction. Is it impressive, or is it just plain pretentious?"

"Where I grew up, some rich people lived in a house like that. I don't think you can call it 'plain' anything. Why don't you vote for impressive?"

"I'll grant you it's well-done, but the reference is to a plantation lifestyle that never existed in North Carolina. Most plantation houses in Eastern North Carolina looked more like Pickett's house in Snead's Ferry."

"I've seen it. She called it a farmhouse."

"Precisely. This is the glamorized Hollywood version *of* the myth *of* a golden age *of* the Southern Aristocracy."

"You don't think there *is* a Southern Aristocracy?"

"I think," Emmie quoted the sentimental Stephen Foster song, "'de massa's been in de cold, cold ground,' a long time. And any sort of privilege based on lineage went with him. The right family name and enough money will buy you a membership here, but money by itself will work as well. This isn't a temple of ancestor worship."

"And that's what makes it pretentious?"

"Right. If anything, it's a temple where money and power are worshipped."

Do-Lord turned eyes that gleamed with amusement toward her. In the bright sunlight spilling through the windshield his irises were bright green. "You think a country club would be less pretentious if it looked like a bank?" he enquired in a dry drawl.

Emmie laughed then clutched her shoulder when her chuckles jostled the abused joint. "This really is a silly discussion, isn't it?"

The surprisingly robust sound of her laughter did something strange to Do-Lord's insides, as did the gasp of pain that cut it off. With her laughter the severe, dowdy image disappeared. He'd had his hands on her shapely curves, and now he saw them rather than the boxy jacket intended to hide them. The ways of sexual chemistry were strange, but now the reaction of Old Stupid didn't seem quite so stupid. Who cared what she wore? There was no doubt she was a real woman—and when she was where he wanted her, she wouldn't be wearing clothes at all.

And no doubt, she was fighting considerable pain. "You ought to be home resting that shoulder with an ice pack on it." He released his own seat belt then felt for hers on the other side of the console. His fingers encountered her heat, brushed the soft top of her thigh.

Quite deliberately, he let his hand linger a second longer than it had to before his thumb found and released the catch. With certainty, he knew he would eventually run his hands across every inch of her.

No sooner did he think that, than just for a moment he could see his hand traveling over the white skin of her belly. Not in a wish-fulfillment type fantasy—it was a transposition in time. Every sense he possessed told him it was real. As quickly as it flashed before him, the image was gone.

Some people had flashbacks. Sometimes *he* had flashes of how things were—or how they might be. Flashes forward. It was more than a canny ability to extrapolate from minimal facts. It was knowledge he shouldn't have known, but he did. Do-Lord wished he could talk to someone about what had just happened.

Jax knew about his talent. Shoot, Jax knew because he had talent of his own—he knew what people could do. Jax didn't plan a mission without asking Do-Lord to "take a look at the map." Sometimes he saw more than the map showed. The synergistic interactions of their skills had cemented their unlikely friendship, and yet they had never discussed it. Jax didn't deny it, he just had zero curiosity. Other guys in the platoon got a little weird if he tried to talk about it.

Ah! Suddenly he knew what the flash was trying to show him. The plan was taking shape in his mind. He'd agreed to assist Emmie only knowing: *you do a favor, you're owed a favor.* And she had access to the man he was looking for. Now he saw the plan more subtly and longer-term. He saw himself and Emmie giving off body signals that they were a couple.

He didn't have to settle for just an introduction to Calhoun. Once upon a time, he'd been defeated by the layers and layers of people who insulated men like Calhoun. As part of a couple with Emmie, he could bypass all the sentries and be taken straight into the heart of Calhoun's intimate territory.

Once he was an insider, he would find the areas of Calhoun's vulnerability, what it would hurt him most to lose. Then he would strike. It would take time, maybe a long time.

Not a problem. He had time. He was seventeen when his mother died. He'd already waited fifteen years.

He glanced at the Tara look-alike. He was going in, and she was his passport. That he knew he would enjoy going in with her was icing on the cake. Long-term payoff plus intermediate rewards. That was the kind of plan you had to like.

Do-Lord opened the truck door and turned back to Emmie. "Wait here. That sling makes you plenty memorable, and a big, heavy box will really make us stand out. I want to do a sneak and peek. I'll find a side entrance where we're less likely to be seen coming and going."

In a moment he stood underneath a high coved ceiling from which depended a massive chandelier in the country club lobby. This was Calhoun's natural habitat. Slender Doric columns marked the openings to wide lushly carpeted hallways. Groupings of wingback chairs and satin-covered benches with curly legs dotted the area.

A temple of money and power, Emmie had called this, and he had to grin at the accuracy of her observation. There was a hushed reverence hanging over the heavy formality, and as evocative as incense, some subtle aroma of wealth filled the air. Emmie might be an inhabitant of this world, but she looked beneath the surface. She understood its rules but didn't accept them at face value. And she was proactive. In addition to sexual attraction, the more he knew her, the better he liked her. Really, he couldn't have chosen better.

No one was around. Discreet signs directed visitors to card rooms, lounges, and dining rooms. This time of day it was apparent that all activity was in the opposite wing. A poufy white bow decorated a pedestal sign: Sessoms-Graham Reception—Crepe Myrtle Room.

The door to the Crepe Myrtle room was locked. He took a thin piece of plastic from his wallet and sprung it.

"All right," Do-Lord said as soon as he returned to the truck. "Let's get this show on the road—no, don't move." He forestalled her reach for the door handle. "I'll come around and lift you down."

"I don't like this." Emmie, her chin at a stubborn angle, glared at him, when he'd opened the door on her side. "I don't like feeling helpless."

Do-Lord resisted the urge to laugh. She looked so cute, with those wide uptilted eyes like blue lasers aimed at him by a ferocious kitten. If he laughed though, she'd probably spit and claw. He tilted his head to one side and accentuated his drawl. "If you're shoeless, you don't have shoes. If you're heartless, you're without a heart. I've never understood how *receiving* help makes people feel help*less*."

"Then I don't suppose you've ever felt helpless."

"You're wrong. I've felt it." The ice-cold burn of it lingered even now. "I needed help and didn't have it. I was truly helpless." He clamped down on the memory. He had almost revealed too much. He smoothly shifted the focus back to her, choosing his most understanding smile. "You, on the other hand, are feeling vulnerable. There's a difference. Don't worry. I'm going to take care of the Precious Cargo."

"Precious Cargo?"

"What SEALs call the people they're tasked to rescue."

She blinked in surprise. "I guess you are rescuing me." She didn't look happy about it.

"Yes, ma'am, I am. And the more you just let me do it, the easier it will be. Put your arm around my neck." He slid one arm under her back, one under her knees. "Is your shoulder okay with my hand here?" He wiggled the fingers of the hand on her rib cage to show her which hand he meant. His thumb brushed the soft underside of her full breast. His lower body tightened. It just kept getting better and better. With her chest covered by the sling and further concealed by the boxy suit jacket, he hadn't guessed, but Miss Emelina Caddington was stacked. Much as he wanted to, he couldn't bring his hand up to cup the generous weight he sensed. Not now.

Emmie cursed the fact that she hadn't put on a bra no matter how much it would have hurt to hook the clasp. She'd worn a bust "minimizer" since she was fourteen, ever since she realized boys, who didn't want to be seen talking to her because she wasn't cool or popular or pretty, snickered about her behind her back.

As soon as he set her down Emmie sidestepped to put space between them. Between the time he'd agreed to help her and now, something had changed. The distance he'd held her at literally and figuratively had disappeared. She had a hard time believing he was trying to seduce her, even if that's what his not-so-innocent touches and warm looks pointed to. She must be reading too much into it. In the past she'd made the mistake of believing a man was more interested in her than, in fact, he was.

She'd known Blount, a colleague at the university, for months before they began getting together regularly, months longer before they'd had sex, and still she had read his intentions all wrong. And she'd certainly had reason to believe Blount, with whom she shared research interests, would find her more desirable than a Navy SEAL.

Emmie shook her head and her hair, which had worked its way under the sling again, and tugged her scalp viciously—reminding her that thinking about Blount only brought pain. She freed her hair with a sigh.

Caleb was probably right. She was just feeling vulnerable because she couldn't deal with him from a position of authority. So what if she didn't like feeling rescued? She needed his help, and he was generous enough to give it to her. Her grandmother would tell her it was her duty to accept it graciously without reading anything into it. She had to get the cake taken care of, and the sooner the better. This situation was affecting her judgment.

It was time to remember her purpose for asking him to help her. This was for Pickett.

Emmie didn't know what she would have done if Pickett hadn't come into her life. When she tried to imagine it, she'd get a mental picture of herself becoming flatter and flatter until she became completely one-dimensional and then turned into a design on the wallpaper.

She had been caught in a positive feedback loop. The child of missionaries, she had been sent "home" when she was twelve to a place where everyone was a stranger. At an age when kids crave acceptance like oxygen and want more than anything to fit in, she had been an oddity. She didn't wear the right clothes, understand the slang, or follow their code of behavior. She had been homeschooled by her mother far beyond her classmates. Inevitably, she gravitated to the one area where she shone, her schoolwork. The more she succeeded intellectually, the further she moved from kids her age. Still living at home with her grandmother, Emmie entered college at fifteen and graduated two and a half years later.

At eighteen she went to another university to begin her Ph.D., and that's where she got lucky. Her grandmother insisted she live on campus in a dorm, and since Emmie was eighteen, she was assigned a freshman roommate—Pickett.

Pickett had a kind heart and a gift for listening. With gentle and inexorable patience, she drew Emmie out. Emmie's inability to carry on teenage chatter was no barrier—in fact, Emmie thought she had offered Pickett a challenge to sharpen her fledgling therapist skills on.

Pickett grasped that Emmie was uniquely suited to a scholar's life but insisted Emmie had to develop herself in other areas. Emmie had a nice soprano voice—Pickett alternately cajoled and nagged her until she joined a choral group. Emmie could sketch—she needed electives in art. What Pickett didn't say, but Emmie now knew, was that both disciplines had a long tradition of respecting the dedicated amateur, and both were tolerant of nonconformists.

Pickett took Emmie to Shakespeare festivals and bluegrass festivals. Emmie developed a passion for Shakespeare, an interest in antique musical instruments, and a slight proficiency on the Autoharp. And when Emmie's grandmother passed away halfway through that first year—from then on, Pickett took Emmie home with her.

Whenever Emmie remembered those years of exploration, she feared Pickett had been a better friend to her than she had been to Pickett, even though Pickett disagreed that the relationship was one-sided. There was one way Emmie had changed Pickett's life for the better. She had recognized something was wrong with Pickett physically. She was only sorry that it had taken so long for her to put all the clues together. She might not have if she hadn't read an article on gliadin proteins that mentioned celiac disease. Researcher that she was, she immediately looked it up—and recognized Pickett.

Only she understood how much of Pickett's self-concept had been eroded by not having the energy, the stamina, and the vigor expected of a person her age. Her high-achieving family had believed Pickett had a character flaw that kept her from doing her best, and so had

Pickett. Watching Pickett blossom and begin to assert herself once she had energy to burn had been the single most satisfying experience of Emmie's life.

Celiac couldn't be cured, but a person could become symptom-free by avoiding *all* wheat and wheat products and all the botanical cousins of wheat, like rye and barley. Completely. Always. For the rest of her life. Until a person tried to eliminate it, he or she had no idea how ubiquitous wheat was, and how often it was a hidden ingredient. Whenever she was with her, Emmie didn't eat anything that Pickett couldn't eat, so she understood how often Pickett couldn't participate in that most basic human bonding ritual: the sharing of food. And probably, only she understood how much sharing the cake with her brand new husband would mean to Pickett.

So whatever strange vibe Emmie was getting from Caleb—she didn't have to worry about it. She didn't have to worry that he kept helping her more than she wanted to be helped. This was for Pickett, and all *she* had to do was stay focused on her goals.

"Grace was here all morning with the decorator," she told Caleb as he hefted the large box weighing over sixty pounds onto his shoulder, "putting on the finishing touches. The catering staff won't begin setting up until later. A quick in and out to switch the cakes, and we're done."

They entered through the side portico-covered entrance he had discovered, and a short walk down the thickly carpeted hall took them to the reception room.

"The room is this way." He urged her forward with a fleeting touch on the small of her back. It was the kind of touch men gave women they were *with,* but she had her head on straight now. She refused to read anything into it.

Balancing the box on one shoulder, he opened the door. Emmie got her first look at the reception room.

Grace's taste was exquisite. Even though she'd hired a decorator, she'd done a lot of the work herself. To Emmie's surprise, Grace had eschewed the traditional bridal white and instead filled huge urns with lush arrangements of autumn flowers, seedpods, and even shocks of corn and fluffy white cotton bolls. The result was lush and elegant, and yet as warm as Pickett herself.

Emmie's heart warmed toward Grace as she surveyed the evidence that Grace appreciated her sister as she was.

Right behind that thought came a chill. The cake she'd had copied was exactly the towering white confection she would have expected Grace to choose. She felt the blood drain from her face.

"What's the matter?" Do-Lord swung the large box from his shoulder onto a table covered with a bronze green (*not* white!) cloth.

"The cake. The cake I brought doesn't go with this." She waved her hand to indicate the room's decorations. With her usual flare Grace had melded a harvest theme, suitable for the Saturday after Thanksgiving with the gaiety of a wedding celebration. Urns and tables sported large fabric bows with ends allowed to trail whimsically.

Frantically, praying Grace had reverted to type at least in the matter of the cake, Emmie scanned the large room for the cake table, which would have been set up separate from the buffet. At last she saw the cake on the other side of the room, flanked by more harvest still lifes.

"Oh no. That's not the cake."

Chapter 7

WHITE-FACED AND SHOCKED AS A PERSON DRAWN against her will to look at a car wreck, Emmie wove through the tables, each with a still-life centerpiece, to get a closer look.

"I don't understand it. A picture of the cake Grace ordered was on the bakery's website. She must have changed her mind at the last minute… but I don't see how."

Emmie looked dazed, stricken. Shoulders slumped in defeat, she cradled the arm in the sling. When she swayed, Do-Lord shoved a chair at her back.

"Sit down," he ordered, and pressed her into it firmly enough to show he meant business. He knelt in front of her and took her wrist to check her pulse. Her fingers were icy, but the throb he felt under the silky skin of her wrist was strong and steady. He curled her fingers into her palm, and cupping her hand in his much larger one, he blew on the fingers to warm them. "You looked ready to collapse. Don't you think you're taking this too seriously?"

In a moment the stunned look left her eyes, and she withdrew her hand almost apologetically. "It's just that I wanted to do something for Pickett. Everything about this wedding is for her family, not her. If she had her way, she and Jax would be married in her mother's living room with only her closest family present. But they howled at the notion. Said this or that cousin's feelings would be hurt. Said it was bad enough she was getting married after only being engaged a month. Said it would be like the wedding was something they were ashamed of. In the interests of family harmony, she gave up all say-so about her own wedding. I wanted one thing about this wedding to be special because it was about her.

"You want to know the irony? Grace has done a beautiful job. This isn't *her* taste." Again, Emmie waved to indicate the room's decorations. "Everything, including the cake, *looks* exactly right for Pickett."

She had told him she wasn't playing a joke on Pickett, and he'd believed her. Still he'd persisted in thinking this whole caper was a prank, a way to spit in the eye of Grace and others. She really cared about Pickett though. Despite how different they appeared, genuine loyalty and affection existed between them. He'd gone along with her, because although he had no particular desire to get involved in this family's weird dynamics, he'd wanted Emmie in his debt. She wouldn't renege even if they didn't fulfill the current mission objective. He already knew that much about her.

"So what do you want to do?" He'd made all the progress necessary for now. There was too much heat between them for him to doubt the final outcome, but Emmie wasn't used to a man's attentions. It would take patience and skill to get her where he wanted her.

"There's nothing *to* do. If we switch the cakes now, we'll ruin Grace's decorating scheme. Even if Grace knows I'm the one who did it, Pickett will catch the fallout. I couldn't let that happen."

The color had come back to her cheeks, but he hated

the bleak, defeated look in her eyes, the downturned curve of her mouth. "You're giving up?"

"What else can I do? I tried."

"Is no try," he intoned with Yoda seriousness, "is only do, not do."

"Oh, please. I don't buy Hollywood philosophy anymore than Hollywood history."

"For SEALs, that's not Hollywood. That's the real world." Do-Lord produced a pocket knife and slit the packing tape.

Emmie gave him a baleful look and rose from the chair. "Okay. I tried. I failed. Is that good enough for you? We might as well get out of here."

"Nope. Before we go, I at least want to see this cake you went to so much trouble to get." Inside the box were several smaller boxes, as well as plastic pieces with functions he didn't recognize. He pulled out papers enclosed in a plastic zip-bag. "What are these? Instructions?"

"Yes, they said they'd include directions for assembling the cake," Emmie answered impatiently. "Come on, let's go."

"In a minute," he kind of liked that she was ordering him around again, assuming she was in charge. He liked it better than sad and defeated anyway. He was also curious about how a cake the size of this one was put together—something he'd never had occasion to wonder about before.

He studied the diagrams and the photo of what the finished product would look like. He held up the photo. "You know, Emmie, I think this *is* that cake. See that pattern of leaves, and those vertical stripes?"

❖❖❖

"Okay, it *is* the same cake." Once Caleb had pointed them out, Emmie could see that Grace had used the restrained, classical proportions and embellishments of the original to form a background for the fruits and flowers. "And it's brilliant. She has symbolized Pickett's warmth and cheerfulness, her nurturing and generous nature supported—even enriched—by resting on very traditional values. It's beautiful, and you can see Grace isn't trying to make Pickett over. She understands who Pickett is."

"Brilliant analysis," Caleb pronounced with a dry snap. "The only trouble is, Pickett can't eat this cake."

"I'm trying to look on the bright side. See the glass half full and all that."

"I wouldn't have figured you for a quitter. All we have to do is take the decorations off that cake and put them on this one."

"I'm not a quitter. I'm a realist. Whatever that woman's touch thing is, I didn't get it. Even with two good hands, I couldn't come close to making my cake look like Grace's. Could you?"

"I don't know about having a woman's touch, but yeah, I can do it. It's just a matter of deconstructing it, understanding the components, and reassembling."

"Oh, yeah. Right. That's all we have to do."

"Trust me." He pulled his cell phone from an inside pocket and handed it to Emmie. "Do you know how to use the camera? Okay, get pictures from as many angles as possible, while I retrieve my laptop from the truck."

"Laptop!"

"Um-hmm. The phone pictures will be too small to give us the detail we'll need. Plus I'm going to want to graph it into sectors." He stopped visualizing the steps he would need to look into her eyes, where hope warred with incomprehension. They were such pretty eyes, but strained-looking, and tinged violet underneath. She was exhausted from being in constant pain. With one finger he smoothed the pleat that marred the silken perfection of her brow.

"Trust me," he urged again, and dropped a kiss on the place he had smoothed. He hadn't intended to kiss her yet, but having felt that incredible skin with his finger, he wanted to explore the texture with his lips. He wrenched his thoughts away from images of sampling the taste of her breasts and inner thighs.

Right now, he honestly wanted to help her give her gift to her friend. Quixotic though it was, the task of re-decorating a wedding cake grabbed his interest. Ever since he had embarked with Emmie on this quest, the boredom that had been his constant companion, the sense of being one step removed from everything, had disappeared. And it wasn't just the prospect of getting some sex that had galvanized him. He could switch the cakes by himself, but if he could convey to her his enthusiasm, and instill his confidence, it would be even more fun.

"I can tell you're exhausted. But I know how to do this. I've never reverse-engineered a wedding cake, but it's the kind of problem I solve all the time."

"Okay." He could almost see her pull herself together, reach inside herself for her reserves, but when she unconsciously tried to square her shoulders, she winced.

"Do you have any pain meds?"

"I'm taking the anti-inflammatory they gave me, but the stuff for pain makes me goofy."

"All right. Let's get this op over so you can rest until time for the wedding."

Resting wasn't really an option. As soon as they finished here, she had to go to Pickett's mother's house where Pickett's sisters would dress her in her maid of honor outfit. Grace and Sarah Bea and even Lyle, who usually maintained a hands-off attitude, had made it clear that even if she had been capable of hooking a bra or zipping a dress, they wouldn't have trusted her to dress on her own.

She'd resent their bossiness except they were right. She wasn't ugly. She was just plain, and really that suited her fine. When she'd tried a few times to put together outfits that looked like what other girls wore, the results were disastrous. And makeup? She'd bought eye shadow and blushers but had no idea what to do with them. She had no problem with her lack of feminine skills except for occasions like this, which were fortunately rare.

But for an occasion like this, even Grace didn't depend on her own skills. She'd hired a hairdresser and makeup artist to primp and paint them. Emmie hoped she wouldn't hate the results, but she figured she probably would. She'd had it with frizzy perms and fussy "do's" she didn't have a prayer of maintaining without using enough hairspray to cause an air quality alert.

The phone in her hand vibrated, and she handed it to him.

While he answered, for the first time Emmie took a mental step back and asked herself what was going on here. Nobody had kissed her like that in longer than she could remember. She didn't have a word for what it had felt like. He apparently had moved on, but she was still trying to understand why he had done it. Still bemused by the kiss, Emmie wondered when he'd become the one in charge.

She'd been ready to give up, and though she didn't see how he thought they could succeed, his confidence was contagious. She was willing to shift the problem to his capable shoulders. Intent on her goals, she had tried to ignore the fact that he rocked her off balance over and over. Now she had to face the realization that he interested her as a man. He had eluded her every attempt to categorize him.

The truth was relationships were few and far between for Emmie because except on an cerebral level, most men bored her. And without any false pride, it was simply true that few men could keep up with her intellectually. Choosing her career over any relationship had entailed no sacrifice.

She'd assumed the sexual interest she felt from him was a male reflex. According to something she'd read recently, the attractiveness of so-called ideal women amounted to fitness for childbearing. Even the famous preference for blondes boiled down to the fact that they had more estrogen. This made her as attractive as the next woman since she was healthy, and her hair was dark ash blonde. As for her attraction to him—well, she was a woman, and biology was biology. He was an excellent specimen by any measure. A man who would be able to keep her and her babies safe.

No. She wasn't going to think about it. She wasn't going to think of it at all. For a minute, when he'd placed that kiss on her brow, she'd gotten the idea there was something about her, rather than her estrogen quotient that he responded to. Which was ridiculous. She was probably kidding herself, and she had sworn she wouldn't do that again.

"Good news." Do-Lord pressed the end button and turned back to her. "That was two of the guys from the unit who have come for the wedding. They're already in town, and they'll be here in a few minutes. With their help we'll have this cake dismantled and reassembled in no time."

Emmie looked up from her picture taking to see two men glide into the room as Do-Lord opened the door.

"This is Senior Chief Lon Swales." Do-Lord indicated the older man in his forties. "And the ugly one is Davy Graziano."

As Emmie shook hands and responded to their "pleased to meet you's," she had a fleeting impression that Do-Lord and the senior chief were related. No, she'd spent too much time in the last few days noticing family resemblances. On second glance, except for a similarity of coloring, they didn't look that much alike. It must be something about their stance, the way they held their heads. They were all members of the same crack SEAL unit and undoubtedly spent a lot of time together.

The younger man with his black hair, olive skin, and the sexiest brown eyes she'd ever seen, was Greek-god handsome, and unless she missed her guess, he was well aware of it. Blessed with every advantage nature could provide, he was undoubtedly used to women salivating over him. He flicked a glance over her and dismissed her. It was a reaction she was used to, had encountered so often she hardly noticed, but for the first time in her life, something about it amused her.

She cut her eyes to Do-Lord and found him watching her, assessing her reaction to his astonishingly good-looking friend. She felt him read her amused look, and though his face didn't really change, she had the oddest feeling he was smiling at her. Really smiling.

Women of all ages went all fluttery and melty around Davy. Wherever he went, they circled and fluttered around him like gulls around a shrimp boat. Introducing Emmie to him was a calculated risk. Not that he worried about Davy. She didn't have the obvious kind of prettiness Davy went for, but he hadn't expected her reaction to him to be amusement. He felt… he tried to identify the warm feeling that spread through his chest… good.

Lon quirked a two-toned eyebrow. "So what's the plan here?"

Do-Lord ginned at the skillful double entendre. A man who'd been a chief as long as Lon didn't miss much. Yes, indeedy. The vibe that he and Emmie were an item was already working. Emmie didn't know it yet, but she was toast.

Chapter 8

"PICKETT'S NOT GOING TO EAT THE WHOLE CAKE, IS she?" Lon asked once Do-Lord had explained their rationale for switching the cakes. "Which tier will she take a slice from?"

"The second one." Emmie supplied.

"Then we don't have to dismantle the whole cake. We lift off the top, slide the new layer in, transfer the decorations, and we're done."

"That's brilliant."

"Right. That's why I'm the senior chief." Lon grinned.

"If I'd realized it, I could have saved a lot of money."

"What does a cake like this cost?" Davy asked.

"A couple of thousand."

Davy looked at the cake and then Emmie with new respect. "You spent two grand to keep Pickett from eating something she shouldn't?"

"I didn't pay that much. I found a specialty baker who's trying to get started. But it still cost plenty."

"Let's get to work." Lon shed his sport coat, and the other men followed suit.

In a minute the men were gathered around the cake, examining it from all angles and analyzing its construction. Laughing but serious, the air around them shimmered with the intensity of their focus. They were all men for whom leadership was natural, and though there was a competitive edge to the freely traded joking insults, they tossed leadership back and forth as if it were a basketball.

"Well?" Emmie asked, "do you think you can do it?"

Lon propped an elbow in one hand and stroked his chin. "There's good news and bad news. The good news is we don't see any trigger mechanisms. This cake's not going to explode if we dismantle it."

Emmie grinned but played the straight man. "What's the bad news?"

"It won't be near as much fun to take apart."

The other men shared the joke, but the way their eyes gleamed with almost wolfish intensity made her think they weren't entirely kidding.

"What do you want me to do?" Emmie asked when they finished laughing.

"This is an immobilization sling." Davy pointed to the band that went around her rib cage and anchored her arm close to her chest with Velcro. "How did you hurt your shoulder?"

Talking about it made her uncomfortable. She preferred to let people think she was a just a klutz. After all, it was the truth. She offered the simple version.

"A student slipped, and I grabbed her to keep her from falling. She fell anyway, and my arm got jerked out of the socket."

"But you hung on, anyway? That must have hurt like hell. You didn't let go?"

"I couldn't. It was a twenty-foot drop onto concrete. She might have been killed."

"And you might have gone over with her," Caleb said in flat disapproval.

Emmie didn't know who he thought he was to take that tone with her, but she wanted the topic to go away, so she agreed. "Yeah, it was pretty stupid. I just reacted. Two of the male students saw what was happening and lifted her up before she fell all the way."

The three men traded a look Emmie couldn't interpret.

"How long ago did this happen?"

Emmie's cheeks felt on fire. She wished he would stop with the questions. "Almost two weeks ago."

He made no pretense that he wasn't visually examining her. In that odd way they had of passing leadership around, she understood that Davy was in charge, and the other two would back him up.

"You know, you're going to need physical therapy and exercises to strengthen the shoulder, or it will be likely to happen again."

Finally coming to Emmie's rescue, Do-Lord explained, "Davy's our hospital corpsman. He's not happy unless he investigates every injury and hands out advice. He'll leave you alone if you promise to do everything he says."

Emmie threw him a grateful look and solemnly promised.

"All right." Davy grabbed a chair. "You can sit here." He meant it kindly, but there wasn't any doubt she had been excluded. A wistful sigh stabbed a red blade of pain into her shoulder, and she cradled her arm closer. She had no share in the bond these men experienced.

Because she had been out of the country, she had missed being in on all stages of Pickett's romance. She and Pickett had talked late into the night on Thanksgiving, but it wasn't the same. Since then, the days had been crammed so full they'd had little time together. Nothing could alter the love they had for each other, but there was no doubt henceforward their relationship was changed. To her surprise she missed the togetherness she and Do-Lord had established. It had been nice for a while to feel as if she were sharing something with someone.

Do-Lord listened to the other men as they verbally rehearsed while a portion of his mind stayed with Emmie. The version of her injury was a lot different from the impression he'd gathered listening to gossip. Apparently, Emmie preferred people to think she'd hurt herself through clumsiness rather than heroism.

He reassessed her extreme plainness and her cool stiffness. She was an odd combination of assertiveness and shyness. Except when displaying her formidable intellect, she didn't like to call attention to herself.

In a way her contradictions made her a more interesting challenge. She was neither cold nor disinterested in him, but a frontal assault wouldn't work. A woman who didn't find his attentions flattering was a novel experience. Women came easily to him. In truth, he hadn't encountered many women who interested him enough to pursue them.

Everyone has a secret fantasy. There's a cliché of the bad boy in black leather who longs for the school princess. That wasn't Caleb. He'd had a chance at the princess and turned it down. She collected boys the way other girls collect charms for their bracelets. He hadn't been naive enough to believe he meant anything to her, and he hadn't been flattered.

His fantasy lay outside the bounds of possibility. For a girlfriend, he had wanted one of the serious, studious girls with their books cradled beneath their soft breasts. Clean girls with shiny hair, who smelled of innocence, for whom an evening in the library was a date. The girls who asked the thought-provoking questions in class. Girls who were president of the honor society and the science club. These were the girls he couldn't have. A girl like that you'd have to go out with for a couple of weeks before she'd let you hold her hand. The teenage fantasy had dwelt so far beneath his consciousness he'd scarcely acknowledged it at the time and forgotten about it since. A boy from the wrong side of the tracks, from the wrong side of everywhere, who worked the hours he wasn't in school, didn't dream those dreams.

Those girls had always been off-limits. He had no place in their lives, nor they in his. It wasn't that he thought they were above him in the great scheme of things. Some essential part of him had always rejected the surface divisions of class. The problem was that girls like that required time, and time was exactly what he didn't have—either then or now.

And though he had felt the tug of attraction when he met them, they couldn't offer him what life as a SEAL did.

These girls symbolized what he sacrificed to stay on the course he had chosen. He wasn't one to whine about playing the hand he had been dealt. He accepted his choices and all that went with them. And there were compensations. At an age when most boys are permanently horny he had all the sex he wanted.

But not with girls like Emmie.

Hot longing surged under his breastbone, rocking him.

"This is your gig, Do-Lord." His attention snapped back to the present and the senior chief's curious look under shaggy eyebrows. "Don't go to sleep on us."

Quickly, he replayed all that had been said while his thoughts were elsewhere, a skill he'd discovered early and found useful, especially after he learned other people couldn't do it.

"The two of us lift off the top layer." Do-Lord summarized their strategy. "I hold the bow ends out of the way. Davy removes the second layer and replaces it."

"Right. Davy's got the best hands," Lon went on, "so he will transfer the little fruit doodads."

"The marzipan," supplied Emmie, speaking from where she sat observing the process.

"What *is* marzipan?" Davy asked.

"A paste made from ground almonds, sugar, and a binder like egg white," Do-Lord answered, still visualizing the steps needed, "which can be modeled and painted with food dye. Come on, let's get into position."

Still surveying the cake from all angles, Do-Lord wasn't aware he'd spoken aloud until Davy laughed. *Crap.* Jax knew he had something close to an eidetic memory, and Lon suspected. With the others he carefully maintained his slow-talking, country-boy disguise. Over the years Do-Lord had relaxed his vigilance, but still he shouldn't have let something that… frivolous… slip out.

"How the hell does he know these things?" Davy asked Lon, his bland tone belied by the wicked sparkle in his brown eyes. Among SEALs, teasing was an art form and a lubricant, a sublimation of the natural aggressiveness of alpha males forced into a cooperation that wasn't wholly natural.

A muscle in Do-Lord's cheek tightened. Do-Lord had been hiding his brain power since he was ten years old. Duty demanded that if he had data impacting an operation, he had to share it, so most of the guys like Lon, who'd worked with him for years, had some idea. He didn't make a big deal of it, and neither did they. SEALs were expected to be competent within their area of expertise. He didn't usually let that kind of factoid, which his brain picked up as effortlessly as stuff he *tried* to learn, slip out. Davy was as friendly and eager to interact with everyone he met as a puppy. The marzipan story would be all over the base by lunchtime Monday. He'd be lucky if everybody didn't start calling him "Marzipan."

"How do *you* know he's not making it up?" Lon continued to study the construction of the cake. He indicated a marzipan apple. "These could be made of molded pigeon shit."

Saved. Do-Lord let his diaphragm relax as he made a mental note to return the master chief's favor. He sighed gustily. "I shoulda known I couldn't put one over on you, Lon."

Uncertain if he was the one now being teased, Davy looked from one to the other, then at Emmie, who had stopped taking pictures to listen. "Do you know what these things are made of?"

Emmie. She'd probably *eaten* marzipan. She could blow the whole thing sky high. Do-Lord held his breath.

With the compassion of someone who must tell a child there is no Easter bunny, she nodded to Davy.

"Lon guessed right. I believe they are made of pigeon shit. Refined, of course. But Caleb was partly right—they have been painted with a food-grade dye. So don't worry. They're still edible."

"Come on, come on, everybody in position." He pretended to ignore the byplay. "We'll pick up on three." He didn't see the intrigued look that widened Emmie's eyes.

Lon studied the photo of the cake taken before they'd dismantled it. "If we move the pumpkin three degrees to the left, I think we can cover the dent."

"That's going to widen the angle to the peaches."

"Right. But if we rotate the entire cake, the shift in triangulation will move the discrepancy into occlusion."

Davy carefully placed the marzipan pumpkin where Lon indicated using forceps from his medical kit.

"That's it. Now we rotate the cake. Three degrees. Everybody get in position and mark."

The three men stationed themselves around the cake. Coatless, the extraordinary depth of their chests was apparent. All three had a smoothness about the way they moved, totally at one with their bodies and each other, which gave their every action a balletic choreographed feeling—although Emmie was willing to bet they'd never done anything like this before.

Their coordination really was supra-human, transcendent of human limitation, and when separated they must feel—she couldn't really imagine how it would feel—truncated, even oddly crippled to be back in mundane reality.

This was the source of their arrogance. They really had experienced something beyond the capability of most people, and she suspected it bonded them more than a taste for danger and a love of living on the edge.

They were jocks. She didn't doubt it. All three were well-built, extraordinarily good-looking men, and the irrepressible Davy was certainly full of himself. Jocks though, who had taken their physical gifts from competition to purpose. Lon's attitude contained mountainous dependability. His very presence offered shelter and sustenance. Wherever he was you knew everything was going to be taken care of. In cocky, uncomplicated Davy she sensed a sweetness that was the true source of his charm. Larger than life though they were, what you saw was what you got.

Caleb. Caleb was different. He matched them, and yet, he didn't. He was several inches taller than the others. Every bit as well-muscled, his build was more rangy than compact. He erected a persona that would fool many into believing he was the least complicated of them all.

Had she not spent time in the company of men who were *like* Caleb, she probably wouldn't have seen that his wily charm was only one layer of his personality, not the whole. Emmie loved discovery. She loved to push to the very edge of what was known, then take that edge further. Now she knew there was more to learn about him. She could not turn back.

"Gentlemen, I think our work is done. Bump up!" The men knocked their fists together in mutual congratulation.

Davy returned the forceps and other tools he'd pressed into service to his medical kit that looked like a large tackle box. "Hey, Do-Lord," he said, "I've got everybody's blood samples to send to the donor registry but yours. Forty-three. Pretty good work for three days, but you've been here all week."

Lon grinned. "If you're going to get a sample from him, you'd better do it right now, while I'm here to hold him down."

Davy frowned. "This is strictly voluntary. I'm not pressuring anybody. It's a serious commitment that has nothing to do with the Navy."

"That's not what Lon meant." Caleb halted in the act of pulling on his sport coat. "I hate needles. Won't face one unless I absolutely have to. So yeah, you'd better stick me here and now, before I think about it." Caleb unbuttoned the cuff of the sleeve he'd just buttoned and rolled up his sleeve.

Davy snapped on vinyl gloves. "I'll do the blood draw now. Then you can fill out the paperwork. You know you have to pay for the test yourself?"

"Yeah, yeah." Caleb took a seat and stretched his arm out on a table.

Davy snapped a tourniquet around Caleb's bicep. Ropy veins stood out under the deep golden tan of his arms. Davy palpated a vein in his forearm. "You're not going to faint on me are you?"

Caleb looked at the ceiling. "No. But I'm not going to watch, okay?"

"Because if you're going to faint, it would be easier just to put you on the floor now."

"Shut up, and get it the hell over with."

"Do what he says." Lon watched the proceedings with cool interest, arms crossed over his chest. "I had to threaten to write him up to get him to take his last set of vaccinations."

"What are you doing?" Emmie asked, hoping to distract Caleb.

The men explained about Carmine, a SEAL recently diagnosed with leukemia.

"He's getting chemo, which should buy him time," Davy added, "but his only chance for a cure is a bone marrow transplant. All of his family have been tested, but no one in his family is a match."

"So you don't know whether you will match or not?"

"That's right. It's an odds thing. The more who volunteer to donate, the better the chances a match will be found. If not for Carmine, at least for someone. You doing okay?" he asked Caleb who had turned several shades paler under his tan.

"Do you have to be a SEAL to volunteer to be a marrow donor?"

"The samples will be sent to the National Donor Registry. Any healthy person between eighteen and fifty-five can donate."

"All right. I'll donate too."

Davy smoothly withdrew the vial from Caleb's vein and folded Caleb's forearm up. "Don't you need to think it over? This is a commitment. It's not as serious as donating a kidney, in fact, for a healthy adult there's little risk—but not *no* risk."

"No time like the present." One-handed, Emmie attempted to pull her blazer away from her shoulder and grunted in pain.

"Hey, I'll help you—" Davy said.

"Sit still!" Caleb ordered Emmie. He threw down the

cotton ball he'd been holding to the tiny puncture. "*I'll* help you with your jacket."

In two steps he was by her side. He freed the jacket from her shoulder. "There. Now turn sideways and let your arm dangle behind you." Rather than pushing the jacket down, he gently tugged on the cuff to free her arm.

Emmie knew her pale skin was revealing her blush to all. "It's actually harder to get off than it is to get on." She held out her arm. "You'll have to roll up the blouse sleeve too," she added apologetically.

The sensation of his warm fingers at her wrist, undoing the button, folding back the cuff, mesmerized her. She couldn't tear her eyes from the sight of her bare forearm emerging under his long-fingered hands. With every roll of the cuff, his thumbs stroked the tender skin of her inner arm.

"Are you sure you want to do this?" he asked. His thumb lazily played across the crook of her elbow. "You don't have to."

"Um, sure," Emmie had to wrench her mind away from his hands to remember what he was talking about—and devil that he was, he knew it! But his changeable hazel eyes, a gentle brown color right this minute, looked sincere. "I never realized that it was something just anybody could do. Needles don't bother me. Now, if you were asking me to jump out of an airplane, that would be different."

Caleb folded her sleeve one last turn past her elbow, but his hands didn't leave her arm. "Nobody likes every part of what we do. Jax hates to jump."

"*No!* Really?" Emmie laughed in disbelief. "Did you know he made Pickett jump off a pier?"

Caleb's mobile lips tucked sideways, causing Emmie to catalog yet another smile: the understatement-smile. "I heard about that."

"She's terrified of heights. She said that was when she knew she loved him."

"Hey, Do-Lord!" Lon's amused voice interrupted them. "If Davy's going to do Emmie's blood draw, you gotta let him get close to her."

Chapter 9

DO-LORD ROLLED HIS TRUCK TO A STOP IN THE DRIVEWAY of Pickett's mother's house where the female half of the wedding party assembled to get dressed for the wedding.

"Uh-oh. Grace and Sarah Bea are already here," Emmie said, looking at the cars parked there. "Fixing the cake took longer than I planned. Finding a minute out of their earshot to tell Pickett what we've done is going to be tricky."

"I'll tell Jax, just in case."

Emmie turned to face Do-Lord, ignoring the pain twisting her upper body brought. "Thank you. I couldn't have done it, even with two good arms. Once y'all were done, no one would ever guess the cake had been… altered."

Now that the mission was accomplished, Emmie showed a playful mischievous side of her personality, and although she didn't have much accent, her speech was peppered with southern colloquialisms. "You and Lon and Davy saved the day. But you know, y'all mustn't breathe a word to anyone."

"Don't worry. Not being able to talk about what we do is a fact of life for a SEAL."

"Pickett told me. She said most of the time you can't say where you've been or what you did there. It must make you feel out of sync with the rest of the world." Her wide eyes grew thoughtful. "It's a hard way to live."

What she said was true. SEALs tended to be insular, to socialize only with each other, for that reason. Only another SEAL could understand things they couldn't put into words. Lately, with his terrible secret weighing upon him, a secret even another SEAL wouldn't understand, he had felt out of sync even with them. The real world, the world of operations, was harsh and unforgiving. Any man who wasn't one hundred percent on board with a mission endangered them all, and other SEALs were likely to be harsh in dealing with him. Hell, he agreed with them. He knew how they would feel about his lapse because it was how he felt.

The real world was a world closed to women. He'd enjoyed this afternoon with her. He'd enjoyed the respite of a couple of hours with her in a world outside the real one. She wasn't unattractive. He once read that to people unable to perceive magic, fairies appeared as plain, colorless, negligible creatures. Some would say that was Emmie.

Not him. He liked the way her looks were composed of the simplest ingredients—magic that required no adornment. White skin so perfect it didn't look real, wide blue eyes the color of honesty, and hair that sometimes wasn't a color at all. It seemed to be made of skeins of light. He liked to watch thoughts flicker across her face. He was on the point of asking her what she was thinking when she sighed. "Well, I'd better go in. Someone has seen your truck by now."

"Are you going to be okay?" He unhooked her seat belt and swung her knees around. He didn't know why he asked that. Yes, he did. Turning Precious Cargo over was sometimes hard. Not usually, but sometimes under extreme conditions people showed how special, extraordinary, and courageous they were, and it could be hard to yield responsibility for caring for them.

He could get her in and out of a car without jolting or jarring her shoulder, but he didn't trust anyone else would. She accepted his help now without comment. When he spread his hands around her tiny waist, she no longer tensed; instead, she leaned into him. He didn't want to let her go once her feet touched the ground, he wanted to pull her closer.

He didn't like the complexity of his reactions to this woman. He needed to get clear and stay clear about his objectives. Sure, it was a plus that he found her attractive. He wouldn't have to fake his interest, not at all. He sank his fingers deeper into her soft-firm flesh and rubbed his thumbs across the feminine curve of her stomach. But he had to remember at all times he was on a mission, a private mission that had been too long coming.

He wondered if it was too soon to kiss her. She accepted his right to touch her, a right he was willing to bet she accorded few others. He could tip her head up, and he didn't think she would stop him. Out of the corner of his eye he saw a curtain on an upstairs window move. Reluctantly, he dropped his hands from her waist. Not now. He would wait until she showed him she wanted it.

Unless she took too long. He wanted the signs to be unmistakable that they belonged together and he had admittance to the family circle when she introduced him to Teague Calhoun.

❖❖❖

"Where on earth have you been?" On the second floor landing, Pickett leaned over the polished balustrade of her mother's two-story colonial. The same terry bathrobe Emmie remembered from their college days was clasped at the throat with one hand, but her golden curls were drawn up in a knot, both artless and sophisticated, and her makeup had been applied by a master. Emmie's breath caught to see her friend looking as beautiful on the outside as Emmie already knew she was on the inside. "Grace is about to have a cow. You didn't answer your cell phone. What happened to you?"

Still stunned by her friend's beauty, her heart overflowed with love. Bemused by the thought that Do-Lord had been about to kiss her there in the driveway and confused because he hadn't, her mind went blank. Emmie never had been able to lie worth a damn.

"We drove around for a while, then Emmie showed me how to get to the country club," Do-Lord answered, placing a comradely hand on her shoulder. Now, why hadn't she thought to say that? It was even the truth, if you didn't count the parts that were left out. "Jax knew where we were. Haven't you talked to him?"

Pickett's peachy skin took on a coral tinge, then her eyes lit with her ever-ready humor. 'We, um, we didn't talk about Emmie."

"Emmie, you're finally here." Grace, also in a bathrobe (only hers was silky pale blue with white piping on the man-tailored collar and cuffs) appeared from one of the bedrooms to stand beside Pickett. Her hair and makeup were also perfect, but then Grace always looked perfect. "Trish has already finished everyone else's hair and makeup." She lifted her wrist to check the diamond encrusted watch she wore. Grace was well-named. Unmarred by any trace of jerky impatience, the gesture was fluid and elegant, and unmistakably chiding.

An apology was clearly expected, but Emmie would choke on the words if she tried. She *wasn't* sorry. Furthermore, it was Grace's blind spot that had necessitated her actions. After they had finished with the cake, they'd been further delayed while Emmie sought out the country club's chef. A plate of gluten-free food would appear at Pickett's place at the reception.

Do-Lord's fingers tightened on Emmie's shoulder in a soft squeeze. "Let *me* be the one to apologize," he urged her, as if he didn't know hell would freeze over before the words passed her lips. Only she could see his eyes dancing with devil lights. To Grace he said, "We were enjoying ourselves and didn't think about the time."

He brushed a kiss across her temple—the second time he'd kissed her like that, and she knew no more what to think than the first time. "Go get beautiful. I'll see you later."

"You haven't said a word since you walked in the door," Pickett whispered as she herded Emmie ahead of her sisters toward their mother's master suite. They had commandeered the humongous dressing area as the only space large enough to hold them all. "What's going on?"

"Tell you later," Emmie whispered back as the Sessoms "girls," Grace, Sarah Bea, and Lyle, crowded in behind her.

Pickett's mother had been examining the back of her hair when they entered. She laid the hand mirror down. "I see you've located my prodigal, adopted daughter. All my girls together, and the Baby is getting married. Do you realize this is the last time we'll be together like this?"

There was one of those little silences, no longer than an inhale, in which whole pages of things go unsaid. Whether accidentally or deliberately, Mary Cole Sessoms had omitted her unmarried daughter, Lyle, from consideration.

Lyle had never officially come out to her family. It was one of those things everyone knew and no one talked about. Lyle was next in age to Pickett, and maybe because so many years separated them from their older sisters, Grace and Sarah Bea, she and Pickett were closer to each other. As a result, in private (and with Emmie) Lyle and Pickett had discussed Lyle's lifestyle. Pickett had urged Lyle more than once to assert her right to be who she was. Lyle, though, chose to live in New York City rather than face sticky moments—like this one—over and over.

Emmie with her insider-outsider point of view could tell that everyone did love Lyle as she was, and in their own way, showed their acceptance. They politely inquired about Lyle's significant others, and had Lyle been involved with anyone at present, would have invited her to be part of this wedding. On the other hand, no one saw Lyle's relationships as cause for celebration. Whenever Emmie was invited to a family party, the inviter always added, "And isn't there a nice boy you'd like to bring with you?" Nobody asked Lyle whether she wanted to bring a nice girl.

Pickett got that *I'm taking over now* look in her eyes. Uh-oh. When Pickett looked like that, she was getting ready to set people straight. Emmie had seen it enough times to read it easily, but she wasn't sure how often her family had. As she'd told Caleb, Pickett didn't assert herself around her family. When she disagreed, she subtly moved away from them.

"Don't y'all wish," she asked brightly, "same-sex unions were legal in North Carolina, and we could all come together like this for Lyle?"

Emmie didn't think Pickett's relatives wished anything of the kind. Their denomination was not so vocally anti-gay as some, but conservatism in the area ran deep. They had come to terms with the fact that Lyle would never marry, and to the community, they presented a united front of support. That might be as far as they could go.

"I wish," said Mary Cole in the tone of someone settling an argument, "for *all* my daughters to be happy. It isn't possible to treat all one's children the same. Each child is different and has different needs."

"Then trust me. I'm happy the way I am! I don't want to get married to anyone. Pickett's starry-eyed right this minute—she doesn't know what she's getting into."

"Yes, I do," objected Pickett.

As one, all her sisters and her mother turned to her. "*No, you don't,*" they said in unison.

Everyone laughed longer and harder than the moment called for. Laughed until they had to grab tissues. Mary Cole cautiously dabbed under her eyes then looked up to catch Pickett's laughing but slightly affronted expression. "Oh honey, we're not doubting your competence.

It's just that nobody knows what the future will bring. Now, I need to check on some last minute things, and y'all need to concentrate on getting Emmie fixed up."

Extra chairs had been added at the long vanity with its ceiling-high mirror, where the stylist, Trish, stood surrounded by the implements of her trade. Beyond scissors, comb, and hair dryer, Emmie didn't recognize most of them.

The closet doors opposite were also mirrored, and with the women doubled and tripled by reflections, Emmie felt like a mud hen surrounded by a hundred birds of paradise.

The bird of paradise was, strictly speaking, a flower, not a bird, which somehow made the simile more apt. And more depressing. She wasn't even the same species as these women. No, not species, *phylum.* She visualized the taxonomy charts she'd studied in Biology 101. No, plants and animals were a different kingdom. Her evolution had diverged from theirs so long ago, they weren't related at all. The degree to which she didn't belong among these exemplars of the feminine arts was inescapable. Nor did she wish to belong. She had found her place among the utilitarian desks of the classroom. Against the institutional beige of her natural habitat, she blended in perfectly.

"Since we don't have much time to get Emmie ready," Grace broke in on Emmie's contemplation of the forces of natural selection, "we will have to be efficient. The best way for someone to shampoo her hair is in the shower, don't you think?"

"What are you talking about?"

"Emmie was in absent-minded professor mode," Lyle, torso wrapped in a fluffy white towel, explained to the others from where she leaned, nonchalant in her partial nudity, against the vanity. "Come out of your ivory tower," she admonished Emmie, not unkindly, "and try to focus on the mundane matter of getting this show on the road."

"Your hair, Emmie. Trish wants it washed. The easiest way will be for someone to shampoo it for you while you're in the shower."

Emmie's heart thudded heavily in her chest, and her shoulder throbbed with each beat. Though they had roomed together for four years, even Pickett had never seen her naked. She hated to be looked at.

"That won't work, Grace," Pickett spoke up. "Emmie is modest. We can't ask her to—"

"Well, she can't bend over a basin. It won't take but a minute."

"Okay, *I'll* do it then," Pickett put in. "You won't mind too much if it's me, will you?" she asked Emmie.

Emmie swallowed her rising panic. "I can do it by myself. Really." Her arm wasn't useless, just painful.

Grace ignored her. "Trish has worked a miracle with your hair, Pickett. I'm not going to let you ruin it. You know how your hair gets in humidity."

"Well, I'm not going to let *you* make her uncomfortable." Pickett's ocean blue eyes turned stormy. Pickett too frequently let her sisters take advantage of her good nature, but in defense of her friend she became a tiger. "Emmie doesn't have to do anything—"

Lyle, the sister next in age to Pickett, opened the door to the bathroom. "Come with me, Emmie. The rest of you, give us ten minutes."

Lyle waited for Emmie to pass in front of her, then closed the door behind them. She sat on the turquoise tile rim of the huge whirlpool tub massed with tropical foliage. She tucked the large Turkish towel she wore more securely over her breasts then held the free ends together while she crossed her long slender legs.

"I have three words for you: Suck. It. Up. I don't know what you've been off doing with that homage to the power of testosterone, but we've got forty-five minutes until we have to be at the church. My baby sister wants you in her wedding. You, *your participation,* is the only thing she has insisted on. But I was watching her face. She was one inch from telling you that you didn't have to be the maid of honor—all because you don't want to accept help getting dressed. You're not going to ruin Pickett's wedding by looking like you were dressed by chimpanzees."

"Dressed by chimpanzees!" That was a little harsh. She was always properly covered, and nothing clashed. Still, the glimpse she caught of herself in the dressing room mirrors surrounded by Pickett and her sisters had accused her. Even in various states of undress, they looked sleek, soft, yet sculpted.

Lyle went on as if Emmie hadn't spoken, "And you're not going to give her cause to feel guilty by further injuring your shoulder."

"I can do it. I'm only a little slow—"

Lyle cut her off with a look of compassion, respect, and irritation. "Oh, you're courageous enough to try hooking a strapless bra with a dislocated shoulder, I'll grant you that. But sometimes love requires the sacrifice of our shortcomings."

"Strapless bra?" Emmie's cheeks grew numb as she felt the color drain from her cheeks. Visions of people pointing at her breasts, boyish sniggers, and crude gestures assailed her.

"What did you think you would wear under a dress styled like that?"

"I don't know. I didn't think." When she'd agreed to be Pickett's maid of honor she hadn't thought further than being expected to wear a dress of Grace's choosing and stand in place. How she would look had seemed immaterial, since all eyes would be on Pickett anyway. Too tired to stand any longer, Emmie sank down on the rim of the tub beside Lyle.

"Grace and I disagree about a lot of things,"—in a rare, kindly gesture Lyle laid her hand over Emmie's—"but I will say this, her taste is infallible. She wouldn't put you in anything unbecoming. Or immodest," she added, coming closer to the source of Emmie's distress.

Emmie saw girls all the time on campus boldly wearing little breast-hugging tank tops that left no doubt about the precise amount of their endowment. When she emerged from her scholarly daze for long enough to notice these girls, their unrestraint amazed her. She knew she could never wear anything like that. She would die.

However, faced with displaying her breasts for three hundred wedding guests to stare at, the prospect of one woman seeing her naked in the privacy of a bathroom seemed almost negligible—proving that even total mortification was relative. The gallows humor wrung a pained laugh from her.

Misunderstanding the cause of Emmie's laughter, Lyle stood. "I don't have time to convince you everything is going to be okay. It really boils down to this. You're going to have to trust us, and let us help you."

It was close to something Caleb had said. She was caught up in forces beyond her control, about to be thrust into a spotlight on a stage she had abdicated many years ago. She wasn't helpless though, unless she refused assistance when it was offered.

The shortcoming she'd had to sacrifice to accept Do-Lord's help was temporary. Her arm would heal, and she would be normally competent again. The shortcoming she had to sacrifice *now* was her bone-deep incompetence in the feminine arts.

The insights were rushing at her faster than she could assimilate them. The best way to fight off a sense of being overwhelmed by an enormous task was to choose one short-term goal.

Emmie stood and faced Lyle. "What do I have to do right this minute?"

"If you like, I'll leave you alone so you can undress and get in the shower. You can even cover yourself with a towel while I soap your hair."

Emmie almost grasped the opportunity to avoid the small mortification. With Lyle's cooperation she could probably keep a towel draped around her throughout. Then she remembered gym class and the contortions she'd used to dress and undress without ever baring herself. Would letting someone see her naked for a few moments really be more agonizing?

"Or, I can stay here and help you with all of it."

Emmie kicked off her low-heeled pumps and reached for the Velcro tabs that secured the sling. "I could use your help."

Chapter 10

"You know, if I took some weight off," Trish remarked, running her comb through the long wet strands of Emmie's hair, "I think your hair would have some natural wave."

In the shower, letting Lyle's cool, impersonal, but always gentle, fingers free her from her clothes, and following Lyle's cool, impersonal, but always gentle, commands to turn around or bend a little, a feeling of unreality had come over Emmie. She had waited for the dreaded hot, sick feeling of being looked at, steeling herself to bear it, and it had never come.

Now she felt as if deep inside, a strut that supported all the internal fabric of her existence, had lost its steel. On the inside she wavered and fluttered as she never had before. She didn't like the feeling very much, but it made her reckless.

"Cut it," she told Trish.

Trish traded an amazed look with Grace that let Emmie know they had been talking about her. Probably what a lost cause she was. Grace looked stunned, but hopeful.

"Are you sure?" Trish asked.

Emmie wasn't, but she nodded anyway. She wasn't sure about anything. Emmie was wearing thong panties chosen by Grace and a strapless bra that mounded her breasts together and pointed them at the world like bazookas—both things that had never before entered the realm of the possible.

"I'm going to bring it to where it will just touch your shoulders and add some layers." Trish reached for her scissors and smiled at Emmie in the mirror. "I'll bet you wear it long because you can't be bothered with regular haircuts. Don't worry, this will be almost as easy, and hair won't get caught under your sling."

"I brought your medicine from the other bathroom." Pickett handed her two capsules. "And you're supposed to take it with food, so I fixed you a snack."

Unable to take her eyes from the scissors flashing and snipping around her head, Emmie swallowed the pills and chased them with the milk Pickett placed in her hand.

Her head felt oddly weightless twenty minutes later when Trish turned off the blow-dryer. She turned her head back and forth, and as Trish had promised, strands no longer snagged in the sling. Her head moved easily, uninterrupted by constant painful tugs. Miraculously, since Trish had started work on her, even the pain deep in her shoulder joint had abated. If for no other reason, the haircut was worth it.

Trish moved a couple of strands a quarter inch and stood back. "Do you like it?

She giggled.

"What's so funny?" Pickett smiled at her affectionately in the mirror.

"That there could be anything practical about all this." Emmie waved at the feminine impedimenta—electrified wands, bottles and sprays of what Trish called "product," brushes, huge round things and short ones that looked like paint brushes, tiny pots of color, a case that had to contain fifty lipsticks. She didn't slow herself down worrying about any of this stuff.

She broadened the gesture to include her dress that someone had hung on a closet door. The dress fit so snugly, a thong was required so panty lines wouldn't show. It was silly to need special underwear, when all you had to do was buy loose-fitting clothes.

The thought was more complex than she felt up to explaining, what with her head bobbing like a helium balloon. "If I'd known a haircut would make my shoulder stop hurting, I'd have done it days ago."

Everybody laughed.

Finally, Grace touched a tissue carefully to the corners of her eyes. "Emmie, you are priceless!"

"Now, do you see why I love her?" Pickett chuckled.

"I've always seen why you loved her," Grace averred.

"Me, too," echoed Lyle and Sarah Bea.

"She's special and courageous, and the perfect antidote to Grace's perfectionism," Lyle told Pickett. "We're lucky you adopted her into this family."

"I may be a perfectionist—though I prefer to think of myself as having high standards,"—Grace grinned—"and y'all think I'm the bossy big sister, but you have to admit I was right to bring in Trish."

"I'd like to take credit that you're out of pain," Trish said, focusing on her professional duties, "but more likely, your pain meds have kicked in. Now is probably a good time to wax your eyebrows." She pulled a small Crockpot from the back of the vanity. "Close your eyes."

Chapter 11

DO-LORD WAITED BESIDE JAX AT THE FRONT OF THE church. Behind them the nave glowed with the light of many-branched candelabra. Before them the last long slants of the setting sun through the massive windows lit the very air with jewels of ruby, emerald, and topaz, and dabbed bits of magic here and there on the well-dressed guests packed together in the pews.

He breathed a heady mix of greenery and potted ferns, sweet moist smell of roses, carnation spiciness, woodsy chrysanthemums, layered over the odors of furniture polish, wood, and the slight mustiness of a room that's often empty. The components didn't smell all that different from a funeral. And yet the odor was unmistakably *not* a funeral. Emotions affected the chemical balances in the body, and the church was filled with smiling people. He wondered if there was some exhalation of joy and celebration that could be measured in parts per million.

Do-Lord had a military man's appreciation of the value of ceremony, tradition, and panoply. The word panoply originally meant a full or complete suit of armor. Now it meant diverse elements gathered together into a complete collection and intended to impress. While the organ dripped the serene majesty of the Pachelbel Canon in D one note at a time, Pickett's sisters, beginning with Grace and ending with Lyle, processed to the altar in measured steps.

Do-Lord didn't have to look at Jax to feel the electrical thrumming of his anticipation. Between them Tyler in a navy suit rocked side to side in his little black shoes that Do-Lord himself had polished.

At the very back of the sanctuary Emmie appeared. She came down the aisle with slightly wobbly composure in a slim brown column of a dress, simple to the point of plainness. His heart banged against his ribs as if he had jumped from twenty-thousand feet. Her eyes, those wide, guileless, intelligent, curious, summer-sky-blue eyes, met his, and he had the crazy idea for a minute that she was coming to him, coming for him. And just when he could have reached out and drawn her to him—she turned aside, of course, to join the ranks of bridesmaids.

Then the music changed, and Pickett in a dress that looked like it was made of whipped cream and candlelight appeared in the aisle, her face and golden hair obscured by antique lace. He felt such a lift of incandescent joy come from Jax, he had to blink the sudden wetness from his eyes.

Tyler piped in discovery, "That's *Pickett,* Daddy! *Our* Pickett. There she is!"

A discreet chuckle bubbled through the assembled crowd. Only he saw Jax's hand cover his son's head in wordless caress and heard him murmur, "Our Pickett."

From now on, and in a new way, Jax and Tyler were going to be all right.

Jax and Do-Lord got along because they were strong men who respected and even depended upon their differences. Though Jax was Do-Lord's commanding officer, neither thought Jax was Do-Lord's superior. Do-Lord had been offered officer training and turned it down more than once. His path had always been different from Jax's, and he knew it. This day he rejoiced with Jax and knew he had never loved him more.

Pickett came down the aisle and put her hand in Jax's, and for the first time ever, Do-Lord knew what it felt like to envy Jax.

Chapter 12

By the time the wedding party finished with the photographs at the church and arrived at the country club, the guests were already enjoying hors d'oeuvres and cocktails, filling the large room with well-bred din and the mingled scents of cologne.

Grace's beautiful decorations lent importance to the occasion. Emmie adjusted the sling that Sarah Bea, the only Sessoms girl who sewed, had made. She had been up most of the night, after scouring fabric shops on Friday to find the material that matched her dress. Say what you would about the Sessoms' belief they had a right to run Pickett's life (and by extension, Emmie's), they also spared no effort to make every detail of their sister's wedding perfect. No ugly blue sling would be a jarring note in the wedding photos.

It allowed her arm to swing though, and Emmie cradled her elbow in her opposite hand as she worked her way along the edges of the crowd. Pickett and Jax and the others were immediately surrounded by well-wishers eager to exclaim over the beauty of the ceremony. She needed to reassure herself that the cake really was okay.

Senior Chief Lon Swales blocked her path. "Don't be too obvious about looking at the cake," Lon advised, having read her intentions. "We don't want to call attention to it."

He looked impressive in a blue uniform decorated with rows of gold braid on the sleeves and his massive chest loaded with insignia. His light green eyes swept over her, and the crow's feet around them deepened. There was something kindly about his appreciation.

"Hel-*lo,* Emmie!" The lingering perusal Davy gave her cleavage when he appeared at the senior chief's side a moment later wasn't kindly at all. The glistening brown of his eyes was deepened by his Navy uniform, and his expression was decidedly wolfish. It was so different from his dismissal of her earlier, she was taken aback. If not for the senior chief's comforting presence she might have been either alarmed by Davy's distinctly sexual appraisal or offended. As it was, an unaccustomed swell of power made her straighten rather than cringe. She might even be tempted to test the extent of that power, if she didn't have more important things on her mind.

"Have you looked at it?" she asked Lon. "Does the dent in the frosting look too bad?" Even with three pairs of hands, removing one tier and substituting another hadn't gone quite as planned. The marzipan decorations weren't placed exactly as they had been on the original, and it had been necessary to stick the cascading ribbon into place with surgical glue supplied by Davy, who didn't travel without his medical kit.

"Remember, nobody but Grace knows what it was supposed to look like." Lon's expression changed in some way she couldn't quantify the same instant that Caleb materialized at her side. She couldn't imagine how they'd accomplished it, but she was suddenly sure that Lon intercepting her had been no accident.

Caleb and Jax, since the wedding was formal, were wearing ceremonial or dress uniforms—the Navy's equivalent to a tuxedo. Gold braid slashes on the sleeve indicated his chief petty officer rank and more insignia than she could identify dotted his chest. She recognized the Trident, nicknamed the Budweiser because of its resemblance to that famous trademark. Fully one-third of his chest was covered with bright gold medals. The sight was intended to impress, and it did. "I stopped by the bar to get me a beer and brought you a glass of champagne—I didn't know what you like," he said, offering the flute.

Emmie accepted it eagerly. "I'm not much of a drinker. But I do like champagne." She took a sip, relishing how the tart zing soothed the dryness of her mouth. She also liked the warm weight of his hand on her waist, though she didn't know exactly how it got there. She snuck a look at his face. Against the deep blue of his uniform, the golden tan of his cheeks took on a burnished look. His eyes appeared more gold than green. Underneath the perpetual lazy amusement he regarded the world with, something gleamed hot. The steady rhythm of her heart stalled before shifting into a slow, heavy thud. She took another, larger swallow.

"Go easy on that. It will go to your head if you're not used to drinking." His eyes left hers to flick over the crowd.

"Are you looking for someone?"

"Not now." The fire was banked when his gaze returned to her. "Later, you can introduce me to Senator Calhoun."

"Why?" Emmie gasped before she thought. "I wouldn't have thought you were a celebrity chaser." His hand left her waist, and he gave her a look as cool as the one a minute ago had been hot. "I'm sorry," she apologized. "That was pretty graceless. I'll be glad to introduce you."

"You don't like Calhoun very much do you?"

"He's okay, I guess. He has a politician's gift for seeming genuinely delighted to see one. He'll say all the right things. You watch—he'll even ask about my mother—but whenever I'm around him, I always wind up aware of how unimportant an academic is in the greater scheme of things. I shouldn't blame him or take it personally though. Not many people try to get to know me. I'm pretty dull."

"Oh no, you're not."

"Yes, I am. Most people think someone who loves to teach, who's perfectly happy with life as a teacher, is dull. I guess it's because they found school boring when they were kids. Anyway, few eyes light up when I tell them I'm a professor. Unless they're academics too."

If she looked like she did tonight, people's eyes would light up if she said she was a sanitation worker.

"The conservative media has combined *effete* and *intellectual* so many times, most think the words are synonymous. God forbid we think those with knowledge have a contribution to make."

"So you stay in your ivory tower?"

"See, that's an example of what I'm talking about. People say 'ivory tower' with disdain. Few grasp the exhilaration of intellectual daring or respect the discipline of intellectual rigor. What on earth makes them imagine that teaching young people has no value?"

"You're overstating. People do understand the value of knowledge. The Navy does."

"You're right. The largest marine biology research grants come from the Navy. I'm not talking about knowledge. I'm talking about how people who gather it are perceived. Biology professors don't appear on reality TV. Nobody thinks we are the stuff that dreams are made of."

"*A Midsummer Night's Dream.*"

"You know Shakespeare?" The delicate arch of her eyebrows lifted.

"I recognize the quote." He didn't know why her surprise irritated him. She had bought his country-boy disguise—which was, after all, his intention.

"Did you know *A Midsummer Night's Dream* is set in the New World? The 'vexed burmoothes' where the play's shipwreck occurs is a real place—the Bermuda Islands, which had recently been discovered. All his audience knew about the burmoothes was that terrible storms struck it, and shipwrecks in the area—Bermuda is off the coast of North Carolina—were common."

"So Shakespeare was getting his audience to buy into the fantasy by using a setting that was 'real' but unexplored. Like Edgar Rice Burrough's *A Princess of Mars.*

"Exactly." She smiled a teacher's smile at the quick comprehension of the student. "'Vexed' refers to the hurricanes common to the area. He is making use of his audience's expectations about romance and adventure in the New World to establish a point of departure for his story. Uh-oh. I went into lecture mode. Sorry."

"We've wandered away from our topic. Why don't you think you're the stuff of dreams?"

"I'm a college professor—actually, not even that. I'm a junior instructor. What's that Latin phrase that means the point proves itself? My brain seems fuzzy tonight."

"*Ipso facto,*" Caleb supplied.

"Right. Let me put it this way. I'll bet a lot more romances have been written with SEALs as heroes, than ecology professors as heroines."

Emmie peered into her champagne flute as if she wasn't sure what was in it. "There seems to be more *veritas* than usual in this *vino.*"

Do-Lord laughed at the look of consternation in her wide, innocent eyes. And at the way she inverted the Latin epigram *in vino veritas,* there is truth in wine.

Other members of the unit came up, some in uniform, some in civilian dress. He introduced Emmie, but he kept his hand on her waist. The conversation became general, and Emmie's gaze became unfocused as her mind wandered.

"Emmie!" Sarah Bea's voice penetrated Emmie's brain fog. Her head felt disconnected from her body, and she had given in to the confusing babble and constantly shifting crowd. "Pickett's going to throw the bouquet now instead of later. You and Lyle are the only unmarried bridesmaids. Don't you know the one who catches the bouquet will be the next to get married?"

"Don't think *I'm* going to catch a bouquet," objected Lyle. "I don't believe in that superstition, but I also don't believe in taking chances."

Sarah Bea rolled her eyes. "You're impossible," she said without heat. "Emmie, you go on now."

Emmie finished the last of her champagne and rose to join the women who thronged at one end of the large room. Hobbled by the long narrow skirt of her bridesmaid dress, she teetered a bit on the high-heeled shoes that amounted to little more than straps.

A little girl, one of the several running in from the side room where the children were having a separate party, caught her hips and steadied her. "Here." She offered a hand with very, very short polished nails, "I'll help you get to the front."

"Do *you* hope to catch the bouquet?" Emmie had already seen Cousin Annalynn, sixty if she was a day and twice widowed, jockeying for position. "Aren't you a little young?"

"I'm ten." The little girl grinned to reveal teeth too large for her face. When the rest of her bone structure caught up she'd probably be striking, but right now, with her dense freckles and dancing eyes, she had a rather appealing homeliness. "I just like to be where the action is."

The child radiated an intensity that made it easy to believe. "You go to the front where you can see then. I'll catch up."

The child scooted between two adults, using her smaller size to find openings in the crowd.

"That's Teague Calhoun's little girl," a thin woman in an exquisite petal pink gown informed her. Like Emmie, she was making no effort to squeeze closer to the women surrounding Pickett. No longer young, the woman had classically perfect features that would have made Emmie feel more like a mud hen than usual—indeed, her beauty would have made most women feel that way. But in her oddly disconnected state Emmie reacted mostly to the wide and fixed look in the woman's eye.

Emmie knew that look. Like the person was watching a scene of unendurable darkness and couldn't find the energy or the will to tear her eyes away. She had seen it in refugee camps on the faces of starving people. It was one of the few clear memories she had of early childhood. Her parents had taken her to so many disparate cultures that when snippets surfaced, she had no idea when they happened or where. She thought she remembered the camp because the suffering was intelligible even to a small child. It transcended all considerations of skin color, language, religion, or sex. And that expression had been on everyone's face.

This woman wasn't starving. Her lovely dress and the diamonds at her ears announced she lived at the other end of the bell curve from those who couldn't afford one cup of meal. She smiled in a way that didn't change her eyes at all. "That little girl will never be a beauty, but in a few years most people will think she is."

This woman obviously knew a great deal about beauty. A week ago, Emmie would have found the remark shallow. Now she was interested. "Why is that?"

"Well, her mother knows how to dress her and fix her hair. She'll teach her how to use makeup, walk in heels, and all that—that's fifty percent. The other fifty percent is attitude. Confidence. Fearlessness. And *joie de vivre.* Nothing is more attractive."

Emmie nodded. Caleb had the same qualities, older, hardened, expressed in a masculine way. That must be the reason the child had seemed oddly familiar. She reminded her of Caleb. That, and she'd probably seen the child at some family gathering.

"Don't you want to catch the bouquet?" the woman asked.

"Pickett can't throw, and I"—Emmie indicated her useless arm—"can't catch."

"Oh, that's right. You're Pickett's college friend, the professor. Sit down and have a glass of champagne. The toasts won't start until later, but I talked a waiter into opening a bottle for me and leaving it at the table. I should introduce myself though—before you commit yourself to speaking to me. I'm Lauren Babcock." Lauren's daughter had recently died, which accounted for the tragic look in her eyes. That she had died of minor, elective surgery must make her death seem even more tragically pointless and hard to come to terms with.

Lauren's smile twisted. "I'm Jax's ex-mother-in-law. I feel like Banquo's ghost."

Emmie took a chair. "Attending the wedding of the man who was once married to your daughter, albeit briefly, and many years ago, must be unspeakably poignant for you—in the light of your daughter's recent death."

Too late. Emmie remembered that was hardly the way to refer to loss in polite company. In America there were as many euphemisms for death as there were for sex. Fortunately, Lauren didn't seem to be shattered by Emmie's unvarnished acknowledgement of who and what she was. In fact, for a moment her eyes focused on Emmie's face. Emboldened, Emmie went on with what she really wanted to understand. "But why do you call yourself Banquo's ghost? He was the symbol of Macbeth's guilty conscience, wasn't he? Have you come here to accuse someone? Nobody here murdered your daughter."

"No, of course not. I didn't mean it that way. I was thinking about how unwelcome the ghost would have been to the people at the feast, and how it felt to him to be invisible."

Emmie could just imagine how many people had pretended not to see her, while whispering about her behind their hands. Lauren, widow of a successful and well-known businessman, had been a society leader. Many of the guests probably knew her and would prefer not to offend her. But they also knew Jax and Pickett had to marry quickly in order to shut out Lauren's bid for custody of Tyler in the wake of his mother's death. They thought it was terrible that Lauren would try to take his child away. It made for an awkward social situation at best.

Emmie was on Pickett's side, but she didn't see Lauren's bid for custody as quite so black-and-white. Emmie was the child of people whose dedication had warred with their duty as parents. They had sent her to her grandmother to raise—a woman who did her duty but resisted emotional involvement.

After his mother died, Tyler had needed someone to care for him full time, and Lauren had been more able to do that than his often absent father. If Pickett hadn't entered the picture, for Lauren to have custody would have been logical. Although she didn't agree, Emmie could understand why Lauren thought she was doing the right thing. At least in years to come, Tyler would know that *his* grandmother had wanted him.

"Pickett wanted you here," Emmie told Lauren. "I know it's hard for you, but I'm sure she appreciates that you came. She feels strongly that Tyler needs to have you in his life."

Lauren swirled the champagne in her flute. "On that, she and I agree. But this topic is too solemn for a chat at a celebration."

"Oh, that's okay. I don't really like social chitchat, and I'm not very good at it. I'm never sure what people are talking about—or why. At least I understand what you're saying and why it means something to you."

Lauren gave her a long sideways look and laughed. Her laugh had a rusty, creaking sound. "Mendacity. You have a dearth of mendacity."

"You mean I'm a lousy liar? You make it sound like a bad thing."

"You don't know how to natter on and on about meaningless topics in order to avoid saying all the truths most people are hiding from," Lauren clarified. "Still, mendacity is a useful skill, and you'd do well to learn it."

Emmie grinned. "You're saying I should at least learn to suck up?"

Whatever Lauren might have replied was interrupted. "Over here, Pickett!"

"Throw it this way!"

The feminine yells sounded above the babble of the crowd, which grew silent in anticipation.

Pickett was so short she was completely hidden from Emmie by the women grouped around her, but she must be ready for the bouquet toss. Suddenly, the bunch of lilies and roses arced high over the heads of the women and descended straight toward the table where Emmie and Lauren sat.

With athletic grace, Lauren shot up an arm and caught it, before it hit her in the face.

She frowned at it in consternation and shoved it into Emmie's hand. "Here! You need this. I certainly don't."

"*You* caught it." Emmie tried to shove it back.

"Only to keep it from hitting me in the head."

All around Pickett women clamored, "Where is it? Who caught it?"

Lauren squeezed Emmie's fingers around the wrapped stems of the flowers, her mouth in a grim line. "If I have to try to look thrilled, or engage in banter, or tolerate a bunch of barbed jokes, this evening will go from difficult to unbearable. *Take* it!"

"Oh look, everybody!" Someone standing at the very back of the crowd around Pickett finally thought to turn and look behind them. "Emmie caught the bouquet."

Annalynn's pink face appeared. "Oh Emmie, you're the next bride. I just knew it!"

"I didn't—"

Lauren winked. "Mendacity."

Pickett's uncle Mason tapped the microphone in front of the bandstand, and in spite of the deafening clacks that rocked the room, enquired several times if it was on. Finally accepting the heartfelt assurances that it *was,* he announced, "If you'll all find your seats, Reverend Lanier will say a blessing, and we can begin dinner."

Emmie had experience with Reverend Lanier. He wasn't the Episcopal priest who had performed the ceremony or the minister cum surrogate father to Jax who had co-officiated. He was a relative on the other side of the family whose calling and spiritual authority had to be acknowledged, since he hadn't been asked to take part in the ceremony.

When he asked a blessing he didn't stint, and he wouldn't stop until he had requested the Lord's favor in great detail on everyone in the room. He would also take it upon himself to remind God that Jesus' first miracle happened at a wedding, when He changed water into wine so that the party wouldn't have to break up (Emmie's words not the good reverend's), signifying His approval of marriage and of making a wedding a festive as well as a solemn occasion—thereby justifying Lanier's request for the Lord's blessing upon a party where drinking would go on, which everyone knew his denomination didn't condone.

Emmie had needed to use the restroom for an hour, and there was no way she could wait until he was finished. She either had to slip out now before he started praying or face the possibility of embarrassing herself. While people found their way to their tables, as unobtrusively as possible, she headed for the large double doors.

"I've been looking for you." Caleb appeared suddenly at her side. "We're supposed to sit at the bride's table. It's this way."

Since neither she nor Caleb had dates for the wedding, it was inevitable that they had been paired, and he took his duties seriously. He hadn't glued himself to her by any means, but he'd come over to where she was several times to ask if he could refill her glass or bring her some hors d'oeuvres. Attentive.

That's what he'd been. Now with old-fashioned courtesy, he intended to escort her to their table, a nicety almost no one remembered anymore. In fact, Emmie herself had forgotten it. Despite his country-boy air, the man really knew his etiquette.

"I've got to go to the ladies' room—no, I can't wait—I've got to go right now."

Caleb chuckled at her imperative tone and obligingly reversed direction to lead her toward the hall. "You okay alone?"

"Of course. Go ahead and be seated. Tell everyone to start without me. I'll be right back."

Emmie let the door to the ladies room swing shut behind her. And realized she'd made a major miscalculation.

"Oh cripes." She squeezed her eyes shut, hoping the effort would transfer to the relevant sphincter.

"You're not supposed to take the Lord's name in vain." The remark's tone was more instructive than chiding and came from one of the large upholstered chairs set in an alcove, adjacent to the lavatories.

"I didn't." Emmie looked around, seeking the owner of the voice, and saw the little girl, Vicky. She'd spoken to her earlier. "I said 'cripes' not Christ."

"What does 'cripes' mean?"

"I don't know."

"Then why did you say it?"

"I said it because I've got to pee *so bad,* and I just realized there's no way I can pull up this dress." The slim column of taffeta fell straight from her hips to the floor. A kick pleat in the back made walking possible, but it wasn't the sort of dress that could be reached under—not with one hand.

It was the final indignity, the final assault on any notions of independence she still clung to. Today she had submitted to: help into and out of her clothes, help to disguise a subversive cake, help to climb to and from automobiles, *and* help to bathe herself and shampoo her hair. Now she was trussed up in a dress that made her helpless even to manage bodily functions.

Vicky left her chair and came over to study the dress. "I see your problem," she said, her reddish-gold head bobbing as she looked Emmie up and down. "I could help you. I could push it up for you. At school we had a play, and Kelly was a beaver, and I had to hold her tail out of the way when she had to go."

*You're only help*less *if no help is available.* Emmie could almost hear Do-Lord's slow drawl. Was she really going to have to accept help from a child? Everyone else was sitting down to dinner, but *Vicky* was here. And despite her youth, she evidently had more experience coping with impediments than Emmie did. Emmie mentally threw up her hands. *Why not?* "Obviously, you have strong qualifications," she said, surprising herself with how unfazed—even amused by her predicament—she sounded. "How do you suggest we go about it?"

"We better get you as close to the toilet as we can before we start. It was pretty hard for Kelly to walk with her panties down and her tail up."

The picture that made had them giggling as they as they turned toward the stalls. "Oh, and we probably should use the handicapped toilet," Vicky added.

"Yeah, that fits," Emmie laughed.

Vicky colored a little. "I meant because it has more room, not because you're..."

Emmie was immediately contrite. Inevitably, as Pickett's best friend, Emmie had picked up a good bit of theoretical understanding of children, but she hadn't spent a lot of time around them—not even when she was a child herself. She needed to remember, despite her air of competence, Vicky was a child. She couldn't see things from as many perspectives as Emmie could. "I wasn't laughing because you said the wrong thing," Emmie reassured her. "I was thinking, if having to wear *this dress* when I can't use both arms isn't a *handicap,* I don't know what is."

Emmie's heart warmed to watch Vicky's freckled little face flit from puzzlement to comprehension, and her eyes light up when she saw the double meaning, got the joke, and laughed too.

When Vicky had Emmie positioned in front of the toilet, she placed both hands just below the top curve of Emmie's hips and pushed the stiff fabric up. "Don't you wish you were a boy sometimes," she asked as she eased the material over Emmie's hips, "and you didn't have to pull things up and push things down to use the bathroom?"

"If I were a man I wouldn't be wearing this dress, that's for sure."

Vicky settled her hands to push up another section of material. "Even if you're wearing jeans, it doesn't help. You still have to get half undressed, and it so embarrassing, if you have to go in the woods or something." Vicky worked another section of material up. "And you have to be careful, or you'll pee on your shoes."

Emmie stifled a bubble of laughter at the little girl's artless prattle. "True. I guess I never thought about how lucky boys are. They can stand up. All they have to do is lower a zipper, and they can see what they're doing." The hem of Emmie's dress was above her knees now, and as soon as the top of the long kick pleat passed her hips, all constriction eased. "I think I can take it from here, Vicky. I can reach now."

Vicky examined her handiwork. "Okay," she nodded. "You can call me if you need me." She backed out of the stall and even pulled the door closed behind her, although, of course, it couldn't be latched. "I won't let anybody walk in on you," she promised earnestly.

Emmie sat on the toilet for a minute when she was done, conscious of a relief not wholly due to having eased the pressure on her bladder. And it wasn't only that she, at last, had a moment alone with her thoughts. It was something else, like a problem or a weight had disappeared, but she couldn't classify whatever it was.

"Now we need to reverse the process," she told Vicky as she exited the stall, the skirt of the dress still bunched around her waist. She probably could have pushed it down herself, and almost had, until she thought that Vicky might like to see her job to completion. As soon as she said it, she knew she had guessed right. Vicky knelt in front of her. With her golden freckled face a study in grave concentration, she drew the hem back to its proper position.

Vicky smoothed reverent, gold-dotted fingers over the bronze taffeta and rose. "I don't think we wrinkled it much."

"Thanks."

"Don't mention it."

Emmie went to the lavatory and waved a hand over the sensor to start the water flow. She caught Vicky's eye in the mirror. Vicky sat once again in the large wingback chair where she had been when Emmie came in. Her head leaned against one of the wings as she watched Emmie. "Vicky, everyone else is sitting down to dinner. What were you doing in here when I came in?"

"I got tired of playing with the other kids. All they wanted to do was run back and forth between the kids' room and the big people's room."

It didn't square with Vicky's earlier announcement that she liked to be where the action was. Emmie wondered if something had happened to make Vicky want to avoid the other children. Before she could ask, the door sighed open, and Grace, her heels tapping lightly on the tile floor, entered.

The evening gown Grace wore was of some filmy material coaxed to drape in a waterfall of pleats through the bodice and float around her ankles where tiny crystals sewn into the hem added an elusive glisten. Emmie had never given a great deal of thought to what made a dress look as it did. Now she was struck by how much more mature Grace's gown looked. Not like an old-lady dress, but still, vastly more sophisticated than hers. This evening she was noticing nuances of dress she had formerly been blind to—no, not blind to, willfully ignorant about.

"Oh, good," Grace said when she saw Vicky. "I've found both of you. Vicky, your mother is looking for you. Run on now. She was alarmed that you weren't with the other children."

Behind Grace's back, Vicky flicked her fingers in a secret wave as she disappeared out the door.

Grace laid her evening bag on the counter and turned her attention to Emmie. She whipped tiny boxes, brushes, and tubes from her purse, and filled a paper cup with water, saying it wouldn't take more than a minute to fix Emmie up. Emmie didn't put up one word of protest.

Chapter 13

Careful not to stare from the dais where he sat at the bridal party table, Do-Lord kept the wavy white hair of his quarry in his peripheral vision. It wasn't as easy as it should have been. Not with Emmie right here beside him. He had kissed her on the cheek and told her to "go get beautiful," but he hadn't expected her to do it.

Do-Lord had never put a great deal of thought into what made a girl pretty. They either were or they weren't, and in his experience, most were. His challenge was to find one he thought was interesting.

From the first, his attention had locked in on Emmie like a heat-seeking missile, despite her general frumpiness. Now, no matter how hard he tried to track Calhoun's progress as he worked the room, Do-Lord's eyes didn't want to cooperate. They constantly drifted back to Emmie, transformed almost past recognition. The shimmery bronze material of her strapless dress traced her every curve and fascinated him by changing color subtly every time she crossed her legs or shifted in her chair. Shit, every time she *breathed.*

As servers removed the dinner plates, the well-bred din of several hundred guests increased.

"Change places with me," Emmie whispered urgently. "I need to talk to Pickett."

"Everything okay?" Do-Lord rose and helped with her chair.

"Yes, well, no. I forgot to tell her where to cut the cake."

Emmie put the cool, milky whiteness of her cheek, which glowed with only a hint of rose, next to Pickett's warm, peachy one. They looked like moonlight and sunlight whispering together. As she listened to her friend, Pickett's eyes rested on him speculatively. By the time Emmie got to the end of her recital, Pickett was laughing. She tugged on Jax's sleeve to get his attention. With a smile, he leaned closer.

Do-Lord put his arm on the back of Emmie's chair and leaned over her shoulder to hear what they were saying. His body's relationship to Emmie's exactly mirrored Jax's *vis-a-vis* Pickett. Jax's light-colored eyes narrowed. In the wordless communication he and Jax had perfected over the years, he read that Jax noticed the same thing.

The body language of both men said *this* woman is mine.

Jax's eyes narrowed a bit more. Emmie was (a) female and (b) Pickett's friend. Alpha male to the core, that made her Jax's to protect from any male's encroachment.

Do-Lord met Jax's eye in direct challenge. Emmie would be offended to her liberated core if she had any idea Jax thought he had the right to give her to someone. She'd be even more upset if she knew he was offering Jax a fight, if he wanted it, because he intended to claim her for himself.

One eyebrow lifted, he grinned a grin that said, *What's it gonna be?* until with a tiny smile Jax ceded Emmie to him.

From now on, the lines of territoriality would be

drawn with a subtle difference. Jax would still defend Emmie, but he would be defending Do-Lord's territory rather than his own.

"Whose idea was it to switch the cakes?" Jax asked now, a slow smile taking over his face.

"Emmie's. I just carried out orders."

"Huh!" Emmie objected. "He did a complete save, that's all. And Grace will never find out."

Jax stood a table knife on its end, ran his fingers down it, flipped it. Did it again. "Oh, Grace will know."

At the sudden grimness in his tone, Pickett squeezed his hand. "Jax. Let it go. It doesn't matter."

Pickett accepted the tender smile and the reassurances Jax gave her at face value. Do-Lord knew better. SEALs believed in accountability. Grace was going to find out that from now on there would be consequences, swift and painful, anytime she didn't treat Pickett with care. And if she didn't demonstrate she could be trusted, Jax would see to it that she never came near Pickett again.

Somewhere in this room was a man who had avoided the consequences of his dereliction for fifteen years, insulated by money and power. Do-Lord skimmed his hand across the cool silk of Emmie's shoulder. He traced his finger over the little point where her collarbone ended.

Fate had put in his hands the means to penetrate the layers with which men like Calhoun guarded themselves—the layers which had once defeated him. Do-Lord felt a new surge of satisfaction. When the time came, Calhoun would know exactly who was holding him accountable, and for what.

At his touch Emmie turned toward him, a small inquiring tilt to her lips, the pupils of her wide summer-sky eyes huge—an autonomic nervous system sign of interest over which she had no control.

She also ran her fingertips through the ends of her hair, calling attention to its silky shimmer, and tilted her head toward him. Do-Lord could hardly believe it. Those were the very behaviors he'd noted this afternoon that she *never* did. Tonight she looked like a different woman. Her eyes looked larger and more tilted at their outer corners, and the strapless dress revealed a form that would stop traffic.

She was ready to move to the next stage.

His scrotum tightened. This was going to be good.

She took a sip of her champagne and smiled at him over the rim of her glass in shy invitation. Nothing improved a man's mood like the prospect of getting laid, but the updraft of sexual anticipation he'd been riding suddenly died. She not only looked different tonight, she was acting different. He looked again at her eyes. Not only were the pupils large, they looked bleary and unfocused. Her gestures were larger, and she smiled more frequently.

"What kind of drugs are you doing?"

There was a small, but significant, lag as she processed his question. The first thing he'd noticed about her was how quick she was.

"No drugs," she denied. "Except for the anti-inflammatory."

"Don't lie to me." Cold disgust filled him. To think he'd been taken in by her air of primal innocence. "You're on something."

"No. I'm not."

"Yes, you are," Pickett contradicted, overhearing their exchange. "You took Vicodin too."

"No, I *didn't,*" Emmie objected. "It makes me"—she waved her hand helplessly—"strange."

"Oops." Pickett made a Charlie Brown chagrin-face. "I'm sorry, but you did take it. I gave it to you when Trish was cutting your hair. It should have worn off by now though—that was hours ago." Pickett eyed her friend more closely. "You are acting kind of smashed. How much champagne have you had?"

Emmie ignored the question. "If you gave it to me *then,* what did Grace give me?"

"Grace gave you something?"

Emmie nodded. "When I went to the ladies' room. She fixed my makeup and gave me my medicine."

Pickett leaned past Jax to tap Grace's shoulder. "Did you give Emmie her medicine?"

"Yes. I brought it with me because I knew she wouldn't remember it. *You* didn't need to try to keep up with it. I intended to give it to her when we sat down to eat since she's supposed to take it with food. But I found her in the ladies' room, so I went ahead and gave it to her. Is there a problem?"

Do-Lord caught Davy's eye, and in a minute he excused himself from the well-endowed young lady he was charming. He dropped to a squat beside Do-Lord's chair. "What's up?"

With Grace and Pickett chiming in, Do-Lord explained the sequence of events and their concern about Emmie.

Davy grinned when he heard the story. "I think I know what happened. She was fine during the wedding, right? Then she had a couple of glasses of champagne, but she was still fine because the first dose was wearing off. Then Grace gave her more Vicodin, and it combined with the alcohol already in her system, and *voila,* snockered."

"I never thought to warn her not to drink. Emmie *doesn't* drink." Grace threw up her hands. "You've been drinking on top of taking pain pills. Emmie, don't you know anything?"

Emmie thought the question over carefully. "I know the periodic table of elements," she announced solemnly. "I know how to conjugate all tenses of all English verbs and many Latin ones. I know how to calculate a chi square distribution. And," she added with the superior smile of someone clinching an argument, "I know I like champagne."

They were still kind of unfocused-looking, but Do-Lord thought he caught a mischievous gleam in Emmie's oh-so-innocent eyes that said she was more sober than she appeared and was playing to her audience. She confirmed his hypothesis by grinning outright when everyone laughed. He had several times today relished her dry, slightly subversive wit delivered with bland innocence. He'd bet people who weren't quick on the uptake thought she didn't have a sense of humor.

Davy slapped his thighs and stood up. "I don't think she needs medical attention. If more than one person manages her meds, get one of those pill-minders to keep from accidentally overdosing. In the meantime, I wouldn't worry. You're not going to let her drive, and she's not operating heavy machinery." He gave Emmie a warning look. "I'd go easy on the champagne, though. You're sucking that stuff down."

"I'm thirsty."

"The codeine in the Vicodin dries up secretions and makes your mouth feel dry, but alcohol itself is dehydrating. The more you drink, the thirstier you'll feel."

"You're cut off." Do-Lord lifted the champagne glass from her hand. He thanked Davy with a nod. He helped Emmie to her feet and aimed her toward the non-alcoholic drink table, where an ornate silver punch bowl, big enough to bathe in, lent dignity to the choice not to imbibe in spirits. He guided her wobbling steps with an arm around her waist. "Walk straight," he whispered, trying not to laugh. "You're not that high."

The relief he felt was way out of proportion, and he knew it. He had no moralistic aversion to drugs or those who used them. Where he came from drugs had been a fact of life and dealing the surest source of money, although he'd never dealt himself. He'd watched his mother drift into a fog of drugs that did a better job of supporting her fantasies than the real world did. He'd steered clear of drugs because *someone* had to be responsible, someone had to foresee consequences. The penalties for possession were severe, and even from a young age he'd realized no one would look after his mother if he wasn't there.

He'd land like a Humvee dropped from a transport helo on anyone under him who showed signs of using. SEALs had to be able to trust one another, and there was no trusting someone on drugs. As for the rest of the world—he didn't have to trust the rest of the world. Drugs existed, and people used them. But he didn't want Emmie to use. When he'd recognized the symptoms of being stoned, something within him had howled with a total-body fury that had left him momentarily weak.

"Drink this." He handed her some of the fruity mixture dipped from the ornate silver punch bowl.

Emmie accepted the punch and sipped it, looking around. "Uh-oh. There's Uncle Teague." She grimaced. "I guess I have to speak to him—unless," she added hopefully, "you think I really am too tipsy and probably shouldn't, lest I make a fool of myself?"

"'Fraid not, kitten." Do-Lord tapped her softly on her small, straight nose. He'd been tracking Calhoun the last couple of hours, as politician that he was, he worked the room. He would have gotten Emmie near him sooner or later, but to have Calhoun approach him was perfect. Still, he wasn't faking his commiseration. He liked this playful, uninhibited Emmie, and now that he knew it wasn't entirely chemically induced, he would have liked a little more time with her. Knowing it would be seen, he tightened his arm around Emmie briefly. "Too bad, but I think he's seen you, and he's heading this way."

"Emmie, little Emmie!" Calhoun outstretched a tanned hand. His prematurely white, wavy hair and tanned, unlined face gave him a look of solid, mid-life vigor. His wide, sparkling white smile made it clear that nothing could have delighted him more than seeing Emmie, and he instantly fulfilled Emmie's prediction. "You look just like your mother. How are you darlin'?"

Emmie rolled her eyes at Do-Lord as she accepted a kiss on the cheek from Calhoun. "Hello, Uncle Teague. Uncle Teague, may I present Chief Petty Officer Caleb Dulaude? Caleb, this is Senator Teague Calhoun and his wife, Charlotte."

They shook hands all around. Calhoun's hand was dry and firm, the clasp quick.

"Where are you from, son?"

Do-Lord didn't like anyone to call him son. It was usually a power play, disguised as concern. It was a way of saying, "I'm the big guy. You're the little guy." Anybody who doubted it should try responding, "Well, *Dad*..."

"Alabama," Do-Lord said aloud. He offered only the slightest inclination of his head.

Calhoun's smile widened. "My father was from Alabama. He moved to North Carolina, but I still have relatives there. Where in Alabama are you from?"

"Near Rose Hill. There's a portrait of—I guess it would be your father—in the town library." It was a calculated risk, mentioning the portrait. He didn't want Calhoun to suspect him yet, but he couldn't resist the opportunity to drop a clue. After all, although he and Calhoun resembled each other very little, the portrait had been his first clue that his mother's stories were not entirely products of her imagination.

"Well, well, well. It's a small world, isn't it? You probably know my cousins."

Not likely. Even in a place as small as Rose Hill, people from Calhoun's class moved in orbits that rarely converged with those of trailer trash. He'd known some of them by sight, though. Heard about their doings. Anything a Calhoun did was news in the whole county. Suddenly, Do-Lord's breathing jammed. Those cousins were *his* cousins.

"Caleb and I were saying this afternoon that no matter where you go, you meet people you have connections to," Emmie put in. "In fact, he has a direct connection to *you*."

Oh, shit. Do-Lord jerked back from his daze of memories that were suddenly re-sorting themselves. For one confused second he couldn't remember what he'd told her about Calhoun. Not that, surely. Had she somehow read his mind?

She turned to Do-Lord. "What did you say? You were 'tasked to protect him?'"

Relief made the blood pound in his temples. He slammed the inner door on feelings that kept submerging him. He had to stop lagging behind the conversation and get ahead of it.

"You know, some SEALs saved my life in Afghanistan," Calhoun boomed. "Say, was that *your* unit? I asked to meet them when I met with Admiral Stoner—wanted to have my picture taken with the sharpshooter."

"Active SEALs' pictures can't appear in the media."

"Why not?" Emmie asked.

"'Cause none of his buddies would want to be seen standing next to him." Emmie gave him a blank look. "A lot of SEAL work is covert. The last thing we want is our fifteen minutes of fame. The picture would be everywhere on the Internet in a matter of hours, and terrorist groups would be using it for target practice. Terrorist organizations don't like us much."

"That's what the Admiral told me," the senator affirmed. Charming and charismatic, full of bonhomie, he still didn't let the conversation veer away from him for more than a couple of seconds. The awareness steadied Do-Lord. He was back in the game. "And I guess you can't say whether that was your unit."

"No, sir."

"Well, let me shake your hand again anyway—as a way of saying *thank you* to all our Special Operations."

Charlotte Calhoun held out her hand. "I'd like to add my thanks, too," she said in a soft voice. Turning to Emmie, she asked, "Have you two known each other long?"

"Uhm, no…"

Do-Lord gave Emmie an intimate smile. "Just long enough."

"I've got an idea"—the senator beamed—"Emmie, why don't you bring Chief Dulaude along to our Christmas open house? What's the date, Charlotte, the fourteenth? I'll make sure you get invitations. We used to leave the door open and tell our friends to come on in—just like it says. Now, they've got to have invitations and be checked off a master list. Hell of a world we're living in."

"Uh, I don't know—"

"We'd love to." With a wide smile Caleb forestalled her attempt to think of an excuse. Hot day-umn! He'd known Emmie could provide access to Calhoun, but he never expected it to be this easy.

"Can I refresh your drink, sir?" he asked, pointing to the nearly empty glass in the older man's hand.

"I'd appreciate it." Calhoun handed over the glass, a pale green paper cocktail napkin wrapped around its base. "Bourbon please. Something else for you Charlotte, Emmie?"

Charlotte shook her head, and Emmie admitted she was cut off. Do-Lord left them discussing the need for Emmie's sling and the evils of mixing meds and alcohol.

As soon as he was out of their sight, he carefully inserted the highball glass into the zip plastic bag he had tucked in his pocket for this purpose. Calhoun had even had a napkin on the bottom of the glass, so Do-Lord hadn't touched the glass and risked contamination of the sample.

Do-Lord knew who Calhoun was. He didn't think he needed DNA proof, but it paid to make sure of one's facts. Only Calhoun's DNA would be on the glass, which would make the results indisputable.

As Emmie said, sometimes things went right.

"Can we have a drumroll please?" Jax called out as he placed his fingers around Pickett's on the cake knife. The band's drummer obliged, and when the cake slice touched down on the dessert plate Pickett held in her other hand, he finished with a cymbal ba-dum-dum-CHING! Grace looked on proudly.

Ignoring the advice yelled by some of their audience, Jax tipped a forkful of cake into Pickett's laughing mouth, while she used her fingers to slip a frosting-laden bite between his lips. Pickett reached for a napkin, but Jax pulled her fingers to his mouth. The movement of his mouth against her fingers wasn't blatant, but it was unquestionably sexy. Pickett's cheeks flamed bright coral. The saxophone moaned. The drummer added a slide-whistle. Not to be outdone, the guitarist threw in some hot licks, which the drummer had to punctuate with more cymbal action.

The room erupted in laughter, applause, and a few *whoo-hoos!*

Emmie and Do-Lord shared a secret smile.

"Ladies and gentlemen," the band leader announced. "I give you Lt. Commander and Mrs. Jackson Graham." The band swung into "The Way You Look Tonight."

It was done. Emmie sank into a chair at one of the tables near the dance floor, so she could watch Pickett and Jax take their first dance as a married couple. Tears stung her eyes, but she didn't want to cry. She wasn't sad. She was happy for Pickett.

She and Pickett had seen this day coming for a long time. Planned for it, even. And promised each other that they would never let happen what they had seen happen with some of their other friends. She and Pickett wouldn't lose their connection.

On the dance floor, Jax stopped pretending to hold a dance pose and put both arms around Pickett, letting his cheek rest on Pickett's gold curls. He skimmed his palm down Pickett's arm, and tears heated Emmie's eyes again. Pickett had found someone who loved her, valued her, respected her. The gesture said everything about how he treasured her. It was right that Pickett had found someone to love her this way. Pickett had earned her moment. The scene blurred with tears Emmie refused to let spill.

She wasn't emotional. Really. It was just that the wedding was over, and Emmie felt a little flat. Nothing rose to take its place. Emmie could feel herself fading back into the woodwork now that there was no longer anything she was supposed to do. She accepted her place on the edge of people's lives. She knew how often others forgot she existed. She dressed so no one would notice her in an attempt to make it understandable for people to forget her. Occasionally, she feared she might forget her own self.

She wasn't losing Pickett, but even if she thought she was, she loved her too much to mar her wedding with tears or trying to hold her back.

Her head felt more floaty than ever. Emmie touched the shorter ends of her hair. It was hard to keep her fingers away. Everything was strange. She was happy for Pickett, and they would talk, of course, but the course of Pickett's life was altered now. So was hers. For many years she and Pickett had been not only best friends but each other's emotional support. Emmie had even taken the job at UNC-Wilmington, at least in part, because Pickett lived in the area.

The thought of returning to her soulless apartment and going through the Christmas holiday before classes resumed in January had little charm. She and Pickett had always braved the crowds together for last minute gifts, helped decorate one another's trees, and seen the New Year in together, either because they were at the same party or decided to forego that year's offering.

Emmie had other friends, of course, but most were more colleagues than companions. With the excitement of Pickett's wedding waning, she had time to consider the future, and Emmie's future looked a little bleak.

She had focused on Pickett's needs exclusively for several days. Perhaps it was the sudden cessation of her supporting role that made her see that her life wasn't about her. If someone made a movie of Emmie's life, she wouldn't be the central character.

She lived her life in muted colors, staying in the background. She had thought it was the way she liked it.

But she looked around the beautiful room, and yearning stirred in her. She wanted the sense of color for herself, wanted the surges of sound, the glitter, the rich intensity of feeling a thousand emotions.

And she wanted it more than she needed to stay in the background.

"Would you like to dance?" Do-Lord's question called attention to the fact that other couples were joining Jax and Pickett on the dance floor.

Yes, she wanted to dance. She wanted to feel the rhythm through her bones. She wanted to twirl and soar. She wanted the awareness of herself that quivered across her skin whenever his changeable eyes swept over her. "I don't dance very well," she felt obliged to say.

He nodded, and his eyes left her to glance around the room. He'd taken her apology as refusal. She could let the moment go by. It might already be too late, and the disappointment dragging in the wake of *that* thought stung her into action.

"But I'd like to dance anyway," she said.

Chapter 14

"OKAY IF I CLEAR THIS TABLE?"

Caleb gestured his assent and looked at his watch. The first wedding he'd ever been to was winding down. Apparently, what he heard about people hooking up at weddings was true. Davy had, predictably, left awhile ago with his arm around a girl, and—*big* surprise—*Lon* had gone back to his hotel room with Jax's ex-mother-in-law! Both of them were going to get lucky, which he wasn't, even if Emmie was willing. It was too soon.

Emmie was no live-for-the-moment party girl. Letting her do something she might regret would be the biggest mistake he could make. Inserting himself as a sleeper, an agent who becomes part of a society, able to wait years to strike if necessary, made this his most covert operation ever. He wanted to be in solid and long-term with these people, and that meant he must build slowly. He could wait. He had no doubt he'd have his chance at Emmie, sooner or later, and he intended to enjoy it when he did.

In the meantime, the more they expected to see him around, the better. To that end he approached Grace. With an enlisted man's sensitivity to lines of command he had observed that, without ceding one ounce of her power, Pickett's mother delegated most of her authority to Grace. People more often looked to Grace for direction than to Pickett's mother. Leaning closer to be heard over the band, which was playing to a thinning crowd of dancers, he said, "As soon as she comes back from the ladies' room, I'm going to take Emmie home. Is there anything I can do for you, before we leave?"

"All these presents"—Grace indicated a table piled with boxes, all wrapped in white paper and tied with white bows—"have go to my mother's house. Since you're going there, do you have room for some?"

"I'm in my truck. I have room for them all." He would make sure a couple got "left" in his truck, so he'd have to go back to the house in the morning.

"Would you? That's great. Thank you. And thank you for looking after Emmie. She's a member of the family, you know. And she's been such a trooper." Do-Lord could almost see Grace going down her mental list and checking items off. "Oh, and would you make sure she gets her next dose of medication? Emmie's one of the smartest people I've ever met, but she lives in another world, you know?"

Do-Lord opened the door with the key he took from Emmie. Light glowed through the beveled glass pane of the door, illuminating the tired droop of her shoulders.

"Thanks for bringing me home. Pickett's mother, and Grace, and Lyle, will stay at the country club until all the guests leave, but I admit, I was ready." She stumbled over the threshold, and Do-Lord put his arm around her.

"Here, let me help you up the stairs. Oh, come on," he urged her when she protested, "letting you fall down the stairs would be what we call a career-limiting event."

"'Career-limiting.' You sound ambitious." She leaned into him, tacitly accepting help.

"Where you're concerned, I am. Now, which room are you staying in?"

Emmie directed him to a room to the right of the landing. The wall switch turned on the bedside lamps, spreading pools of warm light across a mahogany bed with a lace canopy. An open suitcase and feminine items laid across a rocker spoke of temporary occupancy.

Emmie slid his jacket from her shoulders and handed it to him with her thanks. She looked around the room as if she was too tired to think of what to do next.

"While I'm here, I'm supposed to make sure you take your medicine. Where is it?"

"The bathroom."

In the medicine cabinet of the adjoining bath he located the two prescriptions. "The label says to take these with food. Why don't you get undressed while I go find you something?"

She nodded absently but continued to stand in the middle of the room looking bemused. "What's the matter?"

"I just realized I can't get out of this dress. The zipper is on the right under my arm. Oh well, Lyle can help me once she gets home."

"That could be a couple more hours. I'll unzip you."

"Um, that's okay… I can—"

"You can what? Sleep in the dress?" Do-Lord began working on the straps that held the sling in place.

"No, really." She tried to step away from him.

"Nothing's going to happen," he snapped, a little testy that she still protested his help. "I'm not going to lie and say I don't wish it could. But it's not going to. Not tonight, anyway."

"It's not?"

Did she sound a little disappointed?

"No." He lifted the sling away from her arm. It had rubbed off the makeup Trish had used to conceal the bruises around her shoulder. He skimmed a careful finger over the discolored skin. "You're not ready, and even if you were, you're not up to it." He turned her to get a better look at the zipper. "How does this thing work?"

"You have to unhook the placket. The zipper is underneath."

He slid his fingers into the hot, moist skin under her arm, bending his head close to see the tiny hook. Her woman smell came to him, and primal need started a slow, heavy thud of his heart. He noted her sudden in-breath and tiny shudder when his fingers grazed the underside of her arms. So she was sensitive there. He filed the knowledge for future reference.

The zipper parted, and Emmie clapped her hand to her breast to keep the dress up. Caleb turned her back toward him.

"Now the bra." He pushed the material of the dress aside, baring her back and the hooks of the bronze bra. Her skin was silk, gleaming over the feminine shape of her back. If he hadn't just promised nothing would happen, he would slide his hands around to cup the fullness he had just released. He let his hands linger only a second longer than he should have.

"What have you been sleeping in?"

"Grace brought me one of her husband's pajama tops.

Something I can get into without lifting my arm. It's hanging on the bathroom door."

"Stay there." Do-Lord found the pajama and the equally oversized robe hanging with it.

He bunched the sleeve together as you would a stocking and slipped it over her hand, then drew it up her arm. Moving behind her, he spread it over her back and draped it over the other shoulder. "Okay, put your other arm through."

"I can't without letting go of the dress."

"Let go. I'm not going to look."

Emmie snorted. "Do you think I believe that?"

Do-Lord reached around her neck and pulled the lapels of the huge garment together. "I'm going to look, but I'm not going to see much, okay?"

Emmie giggled. She released the top of the dress to put her arm through the sleeve. The dress slid down to snag on her hips.

It was the giggle that did it.

The pajama top, having been slept in for several nights, was full of her scent. He had fully intended to help her out of her dress without pushing for more. But with her womanly scent going to his head, he needed a taste of her sweetness. Just a taste to tide him over.

He walked around her. Swallowed in pinstripe flannel, she should have been the opposite of allure, and yet he longed for one taste, just one taste, as a parched man craves the cool replenishment of water. With deliberate fingers he buttoned the pajama top, hiding her from his temptation.

She watched him with the absorbed curiosity of a child. She didn't chat. He'd noticed that before about her. If she had something to say, she said it. Otherwise, she watched and listened.

Loathe to stop touching her when he finished with the buttons, he settled the shoulder seams, then straightened the collar. Her hair was trapped, and he slid his hand under it to free it. His palms encountered the smoothness of her neck while the cool, sleek strands flowed over his knuckles. "I don't even wear pajamas," he told her, his voice a little husky, "but I think I might buy some—just so you can put them on."

The tiny travel clock on the nightstand ticked loud in the breathless silence, and deep inside the house the furnace came on. The long-case clock that stood in the entry beside the stairs bonged once.

She raised those wide, innocent blue eyes, invitation and curiosity in equal parts in their depths. "Are you going to kiss me now?"

"Yes, I think I am." He was a man. It wasn't in his nature not to take what was offered, not when he wanted it with a wanting that clawed his insides and tightened every muscle. Even though it wasn't a good idea. He should stay focused and remember he wasn't looking for a roll in the hay. He needed to make Emmie his ally, and sex would bind her to him. It would work in his favor precisely because she wasn't the kind of woman who casually took men to her body. But she was vulnerable tonight. Exhausted by constant pain, befuddled by unaccustomed alcohol and drugs, she might do what she would regret tomorrow. If she decided her pride was wounded, he understood her well enough to know he'd never get another chance.

He wanted to unsettle her and give her something to think about, but not something to regret. A kiss or two and he would stop. He threaded his fingers deep in her hair and cupped the back of her head. "Come closer." He put his hand at her waist. He wanted to feel the softness of the breasts he had freed crushed against his chest and press himself against the notch of her thighs, but his hand encountered the crumpled top of her dress under the pajama where it had snagged on her hip. "Wouldn't you like to step out of the dress?"

She looked down at the dress bunched around her hips as if surprised to learn she still was wearing it, as if she wondered how it had gotten there. She pushed at it left-handed. "Help me."

He ran his hands under the flannel and tugged, but the dress wasn't going to move. There was nothing to do but peel it away, his hands against her bare skin. He encountered lacy elastic. My god, she had on a thong!

No amount of telling himself to take it easy was going to restrain him. The slightly cooler skin across her hip, even silkier than her nape, called him to explore its textures and test the soft resilience of the flesh underneath.

At last the dress dropped with a silken whoosh to her feet, but not before sweat dampened his armpits and his heart chugged with driving demand.

He took her hand. "Step out of it."

She did, and he pulled her to him. Good idea or not, he was not going to let her go until he'd had some satisfaction.

She came to him willingly, blue eyes wide with feminine curiosity. Just a taste, he promised himself. And if he wasn't going to get enough to satisfy his hunger, he would make it last.

He nibbled at the corner of her mouth just as he used to nibble the edges of the cookies Mrs. McCrea brought to the library, his tongue licking to catch every crumb of sweetness until he found his way to the tender, moist center. He had known he would be even hungrier when the cookie was gone.

Afraid to break whatever spell kept her in its thrall, Emmie held herself very still. For days the big house had been full of clatter and banging doors, footsteps to and fro, excited voices of a constant stream of company. Now it had breathless waiting silence, even the soft sibilance from the heating duct ceased.

Whatever she had expected from this man's kiss, it wasn't this slow careful teasing with tiny touches of his tongue. His lips were soft, yet purposeful, and tiny prickles from his beard abraded her cheek. As if he sought a flavor hidden exactly there, his tongue burrowed deep in the corner of her mouth.

The sensation triggered the ancient primal reflex, present even in newborns, to open the mouth and seek sustenance. But the satisfaction she sought was of a woman's desire. It shuddered through her body, and she fastened on his lips, frantic with the sudden craving to have her mouth filled.

The large, hard hand cradling her skull tightened. With a small groan he obliged her with slow, deliberate strokes and velvety glides along the edges of her tongue, but then he went back to the bites and soft grazes with his teeth that made her frantic.

His other arm had come around her at some point, pressing his unmistakable erection against her belly.

She looped her good arm around his neck and rose on tiptoe to bring their bodies into better alignment. As if they had practiced a hundred times, his hand moved down to cup her bottom and balance her against him. With tender purpose he stroked the lower curves of her buttocks. Butterfly strokes so light she could have been imagining them. Not that she was. Oh, no, those light grazes were landing with far from accidental accuracy and awakening nerve endings across her whole vulva.

She'd always thought sex was for, well, sex, and the structure of interest, the clitoris. Since a woman had to lubricate, and that took time, a certain amount of stimulation was necessary. Foreplay would be better named forework—tasks to be checked off in preparation for the main event. She had never experienced being touched as a pleasure worth taking for its own sake.

The back strap of the thong posed no barrier when his magic fingers found their way into her cleft, questing deeper and deeper into her moist center.

He left her mouth to dot kisses down her neck. "You're wet already." His voice was a rumbly moan. "Do you want more?"

She tried to answer and discovered her voice was little more than a croak. She wanted to scream, "Yes!" She tried again and managed a not-quite-whispered yes.

"Do you want to come?" he asked against her lips. Before she could answer he brought his completely opened mouth over hers.

"YBuTH."

He lifted his lips long enough to teasingly ask, "What's that?" before he deliberately did it to her again, taking shameless advantage of the control he had of her head.

If he could hold *her* head in the place he wanted it, she could do the same to him. With her right arm, she reached for his chin. White hot pain, so intense she saw stars, streaked from her shoulder to her neck.

Immediately, he released her and set her on her feet.

"You're not really in any shape to be doing this," he snapped, his burnt umber voice more gritty than usual. He sounded disgusted, and as if he'd heard himself, he shook his head and offered a rueful, country-boy smile. "I have a hard time knowing what to get a hold of you by. I thought if I supported your head, you'd be okay."

"It *was* okay," she assured him, a little chilled to think he had calculated exactly how to hold her even though she had been the beneficiary of his care. "I moved my arm. Big mistake."

He stepped around her and scooped the dress from where it puddled on the carpet. "Want me to hang this up?" The subject was obviously closed and he was moving on. He held up the dress by the bodice. "What do you hang it up *by?*"

As she showed him the tiny straps sewn to the inside lining and found the padded hanger, Emmie didn't understand how he could be so matter-of-fact and businesslike, when hot, urgent desire still thrummed deep within her. It was like he had a switch he could turn off.

He'd been passionately engaged. Or maybe not. She'd felt his hardness straining through the front of his pants. A man could lie about a lot of things, but not about that. Still, a man didn't have to feel anything for a woman to be aroused. He didn't even need to want *her.* He only had to be horny. Maybe he could act like nothing had happened because from his point of view, nothing had.

"I'll go forage in the kitchen for a snack," he said when he had hung up the dress and evenly spaced the rest of the hanging clothes, "so you can take your meds."

Emmie used the toilet while he was gone. After a minute, studying her face in the vanity mirror, she decided not to wash the makeup off, yet. She still felt a little zip of surprise every time she saw how much different hair and makeup changed her. He wasn't going to hang around long, and she'd like for his last sight of her to be this.

"I brought you some of the pecan pie we had on Thanksgiving," Caleb said when he returned. He grinned. "I brought me some too." He set the food down on the nightstand and piled the pillows against the headboard. "Why don't you get in bed, and I'll eat with you."

Emmie slid under the covers he held for her, bemused. She kept thinking he was going to drop her at any moment. Politely make his excuses and leave, and he kept not doing it. Once their roles in the wedding were fulfilled, no one, least of all her, expected him to stay by her side. But here he was. Which made her think of a question she needed to ask.

"Why did you accept the invitation to the open house? You don't want to go, do you?"

"Why not? Don't you usually go?"

"Not if I can help it. The party is absolutely bottom tier—five hundred supporters who'll be flattered to be invited to the great man's house."

"You're not flattered."

"No, and I'm not one of his supporters."

"I didn't mean to put you in a bind. I—uh"—he forked up a bite of pie—"I wanted to see you again. Accepting the invitation seemed easier"—he shot her a mischievous look—"than coming out and asking for a date."

Emmie's tilt meter hit the red zone. She knew she wasn't at her sharpest right now, fuddled by alcohol and pain meds. A lot of what had happened today was a blur, and those feminine instincts other girls seemed to have in abundance had been left out of her DNA. Pickett and other friends had told her she was unaware when guys were coming on to her—but this was over the top. She was supposed to believe he was interested in her, personally?

She almost choked on her incredulity. "You want a date?"

"Emmie, you must realize we've got something going."

"You don't even like me."

"What do you think that heavy petting session was about?"

She dismissed that. "Even I know a man will take what's offered. I wasn't exactly holding you off—and you sure didn't keep going." She knew she was right, knew there'd been a moment sometime today when his attitude had changed, and it hadn't had anything to do with her. But she couldn't think what it was. She fell back on what she knew. "You don't like me."

"I didn't when I first met you. I thought you were cold and snooty. I've gotten to know you today, and I really would like to see you again."

She wanted him to explain, but her tired brain couldn't form the questions. She clenched her teeth to hide a yawn, but it didn't work. He saw it.

"You can hardly keep your eyes open. If you don't want to go to Calhoun's, we don't have to. I'll call you in a couple of days, okay? Go to sleep now." He stacked the plates together and stood. He bent to give her a careful kiss on the forehead. "I'll bring in the wedding presents, and then I'll let myself out."

With a final good night, he closed the door behind him.

Chapter 15

"EMMIE, ARE YOU AWAKE?" PICKETT'S MOTHER'S VOICE came from the bedroom door.

Emmie rolled over and pushed herself to sitting. "Umm. Come on in."

Mary Cole Sessoms entered, belting a smoky gray all-weather coat that perfectly complimented her stylish silver hair, around her slender middle. "I'm on my way to church for the early service. You don't have to get up if you don't want to, but if you do, there's coffee made and some of Floris's cinnamon buns defrosting on the counter. Lyle's still asleep, and Grace won't be here until later to organize the presents, so you have the house to yourself. Take it easy this morning, okay? You've been such a good sport."

Emmie felt heavy and out of it, aware she'd slept more deeply than since she'd injured her shoulder. Just this once she'd like to stay in bed and snooze, but once Emmie was awake, she was. She'd never been able to laze in bed and rarely needed an alarm clock.

She fumbled for the tiny china clock on the nightstand.

Nine-thirty. She'd slept later than usual. She padded to the bathroom and looked in the mirror. The princess from last night had turned into a hag with hair mashed on one side and standing straight up on the other, and black smudges of mascara under her eyes. *Sic transit Gloria Mundi.* All her worldly glory of makeup and style had indeed passed. Maybe when Lyle got up she'd know how to restore what the night had taken away.

Once she'd washed her face and combed her hair, she didn't look a lot better. Her face was pale, her eyes dull, and her hair was still flat on one side and bumpy-looking on the other. One good change—her shoulder felt stiff, but didn't hurt. Davy had been right when he said that if she took the pain medication on a schedule, she would rest more deeply and heal quicker. He'd also promised that her body would adjust to the Vicodin after a couple of days, and it wouldn't make her so groggy. She hoped so. She had rarely felt so out of it. Her shoulder gave a twinge, letting her know that it *could* hurt if she didn't take her meds.

She pulled on the powder blue terry robe, another item purloined from Grace's six-four husband. Like the pajama top it was roomy enough to slip into without twisting her shoulders. It hung almost to the floor and the sleeves were so long that Grace, who thought of everything, had pinned them back practically to the shoulder seam with safety pins.

Emmie pulled the cobalt blue shoulder harness over the whole and headed downstairs to the kitchen.

The microwave heating her cinnamon roll dinged at the same moment the doorbell bonged. It bonged twice more as she made her way down the hall to the front door, confirming Emmie's assumption that some member of the family had forgotten their key. No one else would drop in for a visit at this hour on Sunday morning.

The fan and sidelights admitted the gray light of the drizzly morning, but when she opened the door no one was there.

She closed the door, and the bell sounded again. Finally, it penetrated her mental fog that she was hearing just one note, not the full Westminster chime. Which meant someone was at the *driveway* door.

By the time she had traversed the hall again, banging could be heard. Without even a thought that she should find out who was on the other side first, she opened it.

Caleb, with Davy at his shoulder, stood there framed by the deep green twining smilax Pickett's mother had trained to cover the stoop.

Both men were dressed in jeans. Davy's were faded almost white along the seams. At the fly, darker blue streaks, where the jeans had worn into permanent folds, pointed like arrows to his package. Davy wore a tee shirt that displayed his chest development and the girth of his biceps. He'd might as well have had a sign that read, "I'm a stud."

Caleb's jeans were newer, not tight-fitting, and ironed. He had paired them with a dress shirt open at the throat of some close-to-white olive shade that brought out the green in his eyes and the same rust-flecked tweed sport coat as yesterday. No one could miss the strong column of his neck or mistake the confident set of his shoulders. He looked exactly right.

Caleb's eyes swept over her taking in the lopsided hair, her pale and puffy face, the shapeless man's bathrobe. His smile was tentative. "Sorry for the banging. Did we get you up?"

"No, I was awake," answered Emmie a split second before she realized if ever there was an occasion to lie, it was this one. Too late, she saw the faint sneer that twisted Davy's too-perfect smile. She should have said she was sound asleep and thinking the house was on fire, had rushed to the door. She should have said an evil witch stole into her room as she slept and turned her into a Simpson refugee. She should have said—anything at all, except the truth. Like a character in a fairy tale, all her gossamer had turned to cobwebs. This was why if she gave herself a birthday party, somebody else would be the guest of honor. She tugged the lapels of the robe together. "May I help you?"

"Grace called this morning to say a whole table full of presents were left at the country club. She asked me to pick them up and bring them here. Can you open the garage door? It's started to rain. Don't want the presents to get wet." He paused, clearly expecting something from her, but Emmie couldn't imagine what. At last he asked, "May we come in?"

"Um, sure." Emmie stood aside to admit them. "I'll open the garage door, if I can remember where the button is."

Caleb walked unerringly to the small button beside the door that opened into the garage. "This it?"

After she'd shown them the formal living room where the gifts were displayed, she placed her hand on the newel post of the stairs. "I'll just go upstairs and get into some clothes."

"Fine. We'll bring in the presents."

Emmie was at the door of her bedroom when she remembered her cinnamon roll still in the microwave. She couldn't take her medicine until she ate it. She reversed her steps and was almost to the foot of the stairs when she heard the men's voices coming from the living room.

"I don't know who I feel sorrier for, you or Lon." She heard Davy laugh.

"What are you talking about?" Caleb asked.

"You know Jax's ex-mother-in-law? She got loaded at the reception. She wound up spending the night with Lon in his hotel room."

"I'd suggest you don't spread that around."

"She's a lush, but at least she's beautiful." Davy pursued the subject, ignoring Caleb's warning. "But you, you were stuck with the dork last night."

Caleb mumbled something Emmie couldn't hear, but that Davy laughed in response to. "I admit," Davy said as he chortled again, "she looked better last night, but *good God,* man, even with great hooters, that's a pity fuck if I ever saw one!"

All the nasty snickers she'd ever heard reverberated so loud she hardly heard Caleb when he rumbled, "Shut up, Davy."

Emmie gripped the balustrade tight enough to leave dents in the polished oak. Her heart beat so hard she was afraid she was going to pass out—or explode. Her fingertips tingled as if she'd had an electric shock.

Then Caleb growled. "Go get the last of the presents."

Oh, God! Davy was going to come into the hall and see her. He was every reason she had preferred to be invisible. Or make sure she only dealt with the Davys of this world from a position of authority. She knew she needed to run back upstairs, but she couldn't make her feet move.

And it was too late anyway. Throwing some remark over his shoulder, Davy exited the living room and saw her at the foot of the stairs.

Who knows what confluence of events makes a turning point in someone's life? Later, Emmie wondered if the fact that she was on the third step from the bottom, which put her head higher than his, was the deciding factor, since it made her literally look down on him. Maybe the flood of adrenaline pounding through her system had burned out something. Maybe it was the fact that she saw in his shocked brown eyes and the embarrassed red of his smooth cheeks just how young—how young and callow—he was.

At any rate, although a second before she would have slunk away to nurse her wounds in private, she wasn't going to do so now. She had had it.

"Go into the kitchen and pour yourself some coffee," she directed firmly.

"I'm sorry—" he stammered.

"Accepted," she snapped. "Go get some coffee."

"Yes, ma'am. Can I bring you some?"

She acknowledged that he was now on his good behavior with a small approving nod, while she said coolly, "I'll get some later, thank you."

Caleb, hearing their voices, appeared in the living room doorway. With a look he dispatched Davy.

In some private corner of her mind Emmie admired the unquestioned power with which he did it, but admiration was not uppermost in her mind. Right now, she had something to say, and she was going to say it.

Chapter 16

Do-Lord watched the slender woman descend the last few steps of the staircase. Her bare feet made no sound, and as the hugely oversized bathrobe dragged on the Oriental runner, it opened with each step to expose shapely ankles and narrow feet. The rich reds and blue jewel tones of the carpet set off the translucent porcelain whiteness of her skin.

He wasn't a foot man.

He thought men who fixated on one or another part of women were strange.

He couldn't believe how those white, almost delicate-looking feet, with toes and sole a shade of pink he'd only seen on the inside of a shell, turned him on. But the steely look in her wide light blue eyes convinced him this wasn't the moment to tell her so.

"A pity fuck?" she enquired coolly, one slender hand resting on the newel post. "That's what I was? Did you think you were doing your good deed for the day?

"Do SEALs get merit badges for sacrificing yourselves to make a girl's day? Oh, no," she answered her own question, "that would be juvenile—*you* get a ribbon, maybe a shiny medal." She descended the last step. "Do you have a ceremony accompanied with backslapping and arm-punching for meritorious fucking above and beyond the call of duty? Or do you just earn enough snigger-rights to keep your arrogance fluffed to maximum?"

Wait a minute. She had a right to be angry—Davy's remark would be insulting to any woman, even if it was true. He was willing to let her get it off her chest, but she had gone too far. "I'm not arrogant."

Emmie stared at him, her mouth open, her wide cloud-colored eyes transfixed. Then she laughed. "If you think that, you're not merely arrogant, you're an arrogant idiot. And a jerk. Or would jerk be redundant? I'm afraid it would. Why don't I ever have a thesaurus when I need one? Wait! I could still use jerk if I used a colon. 'Arrogant idiot colon a jerk.'"

He knew what she was doing. Disappearing into her head. Wrapping herself with the cloak of academe. It accused him as nothing else could have. Having her castigate him like a fiery queen was bad enough, but watching her seem to fade away as if she was turning herself into a ghost was worse.

There was just enough truth in her accusations to heat his cheeks. Not that he had thought she was pitiable, but he *had* thought she probably didn't get much—and yeah, some good sex would probably be good for her. So he didn't need to feel guilty if he seduced her to get what he wanted. She wasn't going to get hurt, and he'd make sure she got something out of the deal—*that* was more his thought. He'd assured himself she'd be willing, and she'd enjoy it.

But he had hurt her, never intending to. He was too much a SEAL to push the responsibility off on Davy's thoughtless remark. It was *his* actions which Davy had interpreted by his own standards that occasioned it.

She hadn't done anything to deserve careless treatment. "Don't."

"Don't what?"

"Don't withdraw. I liked you better spitting erudite sarcasm." He grinned. "Actually, 'meritorious fucking' was pretty good."

Emmie's lips opened in amazement, and a flush of anger returned to her cheeks. "You have the nerve to tell me when you liked me better?"

That was more like it. God, she was pretty with her cheeks glowing and her eyes sparkling. He threw a little more gas on the flames with a cocky smile. "What can I say? Us arrogant jerks are like that."

"Well, I liked *you* better when I didn't know you at all."

For the first time, one of her barbs landed in an unprotected spot. It was amazing how sharp it stung. "That's not true."

In wordless acknowledgement that she had been goaded into saying more than she meant. Emmie looked away. "So," she said, her eyes not quite meeting his for the first time, "You didn't get your fuck, did you? Now, that's a pity. Will you cry all the way to the base? No, you'll probably go beat somebody up. More manly, you know."

Every operation goes to shit thirty seconds after it hits the ground. Staying flexible and remembering the objective was the key. And if you weren't going to reach the objective, but you were going to get your tail shot off trying, the smart course of action was to pull back.

On the other hand, SEALs succeeded by going in where nobody in their right mind would. "Does this mean you're not going to have sex with me?"

Emmie raised her eyes heavenward. "I do not *believe* your audacity! No!"

"Okay, does it mean you won't go to Calhoun's open house with me?"

For a moment Emmie couldn't remember what he was talking about. In her opinion, Calhoun hadn't meant the invitation, and she hadn't meant her acceptance. It was just one of those conversational forms, beloved by Southerners, like "Y'all come back!" She had dismissed it. Apparently, Caleb hadn't. She was tempted to say "no" just to spite him.

Then a better idea came to her. Her heart chugged into a different rhythm. If she was shocked by Caleb's audacity, she was *stunned* by her own. The whole idea behind a pity fuck was that the girl was supposed to be abjectly grateful for being used.

She remembered the dress last night and the way members of Caleb's team had grouped about her. She remembered the rush of feminine power. Her grandmother used to tell her that beauty was only skin deep. Yesterday, she found out her grandmother was mistaken. Beauty was nowhere near as deep as skin. It could be painted on with a brush.

She also remembered the suspicion that Lon and Davy were herding her and that Caleb had acted like he was staking a claim she had never agreed to. Had she not had yesterday's experience, she would have been crushed this morning. Instead, she was mad, and she thought it would be nice to give this SEAL a little taste of his own medicine. It would be nice to have him importuning her. He could beg for her favors—and then she'd make it clear that she knew she could do better. No. Being deliberately cruel wasn't in her. But she *would* enjoy telling him no.

She fingered the bathrobe's bulky lapel. "I haven't decided yet. Why don't you give me a call next week?"

"Are you playing games now?"

"Why shouldn't I? You've been playing some kind of game with me since you met me."

"If I call, are you going to say yes?"

Emmie was tempted to give up the game. She was taking a risk by upping the stakes. He might not call. He might decide she wasn't worth the trouble. If it hadn't been for that arrogant look, that assurance in his lazy, smiling drawl that he already knew the answer, she would have. As it was, she gave him what she hoped was a mysterious smile. "You'll have to call to find out, won't you?"

Chapter 17

Back in the bedroom she'd stayed in so often everyone referred to it as "Emmie's room," Emmie stared at herself in the mirror. She hardly recognized the woman who stared back at her with eyes that glittered dangerously above magenta-splotched cheeks. She couldn't remember ever being so furious. Ever. Fury that made her eyeballs sting and her scalp tighten and made her draw in air in great gulps.

She was angry, and when she looked back she could see she'd been angry a long, long time. She was angry at Davy and Caleb and all the jocks like them who believed she should be grateful they *deigned* to notice her. Angry at her conniving classmates who vied to be her lab partner because working with her guaranteed an A, but who couldn't *see* her in the cafeteria. Angry at her grandmother for not letting her dress like the other girls, for telling her it was only necessary that her dress be clean and modest and pleasing to the Lord, and at all the people over the years who had treated her as if she didn't matter.

She had convinced herself that she dressed to please herself and didn't care what anyone else thought. Her indifference had been a carapace she'd grown to protect her vulnerable inside, to contain her anger, and also to hide it from herself.

And she was angry at herself. For pretending that not taking part in life was her choice. She, who had believed her problem was her honesty and her inability to see the point of pretending—*she* had been lying. She had told herself the beauty game was a competition, and being chosen was an illusion based on shallow values. She had told herself she was above the fray, when in truth, she'd been too cowardly to enter it.

As of this morning that would change. Anyone who saw her from now on would recognize she was a woman to be reckoned with. She didn't lack a girlie gene. That was another lie. She had more than enough intelligence to bring about her transformation by herself. Eventually. She was on a deadline, unfortunately. She had only two weeks, and Pickett was on her honeymoon. Fortunately, she knew a person who had all the knowledge she lacked. Grace.

Emmie never doubted that Grace would help her. Nothing would please Grace more than to make a project of her. Her fear was that if she made herself Grace's disciple, Grace would believe she had carte blanche to completely take over her life. It was a risk that had to be taken.

A couple of hours later Emmie found Grace in the living room organizing the wedding gifts. There was no time like the present. Emmie's newfound nerve would only stretch so far. She ignored the way her heart was pounding.

"Grace, can I talk to you?" Her voice came out a wobbly whisper.

"Sure." Grace answered absently while she carefully numbered the tag on a present, and beside the corresponding number on a ledger, wrote the name of the giver. Pickett would open the gifts in order, and a description of the gift would be entered in the ledger. "In a minute. Just let me get these—"

"Grace," Emmie tried again. "Can I talk to you right now—in private?"

Grace looked up, puzzled. As well she might. Now that she could tell herself the truth, Emmie could admit how much Grace had always intimidated her. She felt "weighed in the balance and found wanting" by Grace, and had been more likely to duck Grace's notice, than to demand it. "I need a makeover."

Grace's eyes lit with joy. Then dimmed with doubt. "But, Emmie, *why?*"

Emmie knew what she was asking. Why after all these years? Why after the discreet hints, carefully worded suggestions, and outright instructions, all of which Emmie had ignored? Emmie couldn't possibly tell her the real reason, so she offered the one she had settled on—a reason Grace would accept and be flattered by.

"The bridesmaid dress you chose for me, the hair, the makeup, was all perfect. I didn't know, if I did what you said, I could look like that."

Grace clearly saw no need to dispute that, but still she gave Emmie a hard look over the little gold reading glasses she used these days. "You're not very good at taking directions. If I agree to do this, will you actually do what I say? Or will you find excuses not to? Will you argue about every step?"

"No excuses," Emmie agreed. "I will put myself in your hands and do as you say."

Emmie regretted that promise less than two hours later when Grace pulled her Lexus into a parking space in front of a lingerie boutique. They'd driven all the way to Raleigh, the nearest large city, to find a place that came up to Grace's standards.

"Um, Grace, do we have to do this? I promise I'll buy anything you tell me to, but I'd rather do it in private."

"Finding the right style for your figure type is all about covering up your flaws and highlighting your good points. Fortunately for you, you don't have any real figure flaws. We're mainly looking for clothes that fit."

Emmie interrupted her. "I don't understand. You didn't mention my breasts."

"What about them?"

"I thought covering up my flaws was what I *was* doing."

"By buying clothes that were too big?"

"The clothes aren't too big. My breasts are."

Grace gave Emmie a long *what planet are you from* look. Emmie had been getting them all her life. She had enough experience to know anything *else* she said would make her look even stupider.

"Fit," Grace went back to expounding on her theme as if Emmie's question never happened, "except for *rail-thin* models, is a matter of having on the right undergarments. In other words, you need bras. With your shoulder, you're not going to last through a lot of trial and error, while we look for the right ones. This shop has the best fitter I know." Grace made her tone a little kinder. "I know you have modesty issues. But you know, you haven't been tastefully covering your body, you've been obliterating it. The fact that you *have* a shape has got to be dealt with. Think of it as going to the doctor—but not as bad. No stirrups."

It was an awful day, but when it was over Emmie was the owner of three bras that were amazingly comfortable. Even she could see that with them on, blouses didn't gape, and suit jackets could be buttoned without bunching under the arms. Even though said blouses and jackets were one or two sizes smaller than what she was used to wearing.

"Intense colors overwhelm you," Grace pronounced, "which is why you've instinctively shied away from them. But that doesn't mean you have to limit yourself to beige. And no, you don't have to wear girlish pastels. What we will look for are muted shades—rose and heather, plum rather than purple, denim blues."

After an exhaustive and ruthless discussion of Emmie's good points and flaws, she laid out her plan. "The most important thing is to emphasize your good points. You have perfect skin—even though you do absolutely nothing to maintain it, and you have good legs. We can't do much shopping right now, because of your arm. But I'm determined to find a cardigan sweater or two, to wear with slacks and skirts. Something that discreetly shows off your bustline. After your arm heals we'll get some pullover tops you can wear under them."

"All right," Grace said at last. "We have as many outfits as it's reasonable to buy until your shoulder is better. The next thing is to decide how to have a few trial runs. I know on TV they do the big dramatic reveal, but that's not really the best way. It's better to try out a new look in a low pressure environment. You want to get comfortable with the unfamiliar clothes and people's reactions so that when it's crucial to look good you won't transmit nervousness. I suggest Aunt Lilly Hale's homecoming. I know she always invites you," Grace added before Emmie could object.

"But it's a family reunion."

"So? You are family," Grace pronounced with sublime disregard for the facts. "Emmie, don't make me get ugly with you. It's perfect. There won't be anyone there you need to impress."

"Let's see if we can find some leftovers in Mom's refrigerator—if we can face turkey again," Grace said as she opened the front door to her mother's house with her key. She had called her husband from the car to tell him to feed himself and their teenage sons. "Mom, we're here."

Lyle appeared in the family room doorway. Emmie took in her skinny-legged black jeans and black tunic sweater with a wide silver fabric belt (to call attention to her small waist—Emmie knew things like that now).

"Mom's not here," she said. "You just missed her. She got a call that her secretary's husband has been hospitalized with chest pains, so she's gone over there." Lyle had declined the shopping trip in favor of a chance to stay and visit with their mother. She didn't come home often, and it was the first private time they'd had. "What did you buy?"

"Let's get a sandwich. Then Emmie can try everything on, and we'll practice makeup."

"Goody." Lyle rubbed her hands. "My favorite part."

"It would be, since you're the artist. I can do my own makeup, but I'm not as good with other people's,"

Grace admitted. "Shall we see if Sarah Bea wants to come over?"

What Grace was asking was, if Sarah Bea came over, would Lyle behave herself? The two frequently squabbled with each other. "Sure, let's call her. She's the best with hair." Lyle smirked evilly. "And the three of us can gang up on Emmie."

"Oh!" Grace laughed. "Do you remember the time she cut Pickett's hair?"

"She thought she could cut out the parts that curled," Lyle told Emmie.

"Poor child looked like she'd caught her head in a paper shredder!"

Emmie had rarely been around the sisters when Pickett wasn't present, and she'd wondered how they would do without Pickett to act as peacemaker and arbiter. But they continued to laugh together even after Sarah Bea arrived and they commandeered their mother's dressing room again.

A few minutes later, their mother, Mary Cole, returned with the good news that her secretary's husband would likely make a full recovery.

They insisted on dressing Emmie in her new clothes, so she wouldn't use her arm too much. Soft, feminine hands buttoned, straightened, folded collars back, and twitched seams into place. Tears welled in her eyes.

Grace saw them. "What's the matter, Emmie? Are we hurting your shoulder?"

"I just remembered something. I was twelve. I was getting dressed to catch the plane to come to live in the States without my parents. My mother came in my room, and she wouldn't let me button my dress or put on my shoes myself. I was *twelve.* I hadn't needed her help with things like that for a long time, but she pushed my hands away and said, 'No. Let me do it.'"

"It must have been hard, going off by yourself like that." Lyle's voice was low, her smile sad.

"And it must have been hard for your mother to let you go," added Mary Cole with a misty smile. "She wanted a few more minutes while you were still her little girl."

Emmie's eyes got wet again. She had never seen that memory from her own and her mother's perspective at the same time.

Warmth filled her chest and merged into an almost visible bond of understanding between Lyle and Mary Cole and her. They were talking to her, but also talking about Lyle's need to leave home, and her mother's need to hold on to her.

After surveying Emmie's purchases, Mary Cole said, "That reminds me. I've got a sweater I bought last year, but I realize it isn't right for me. Would one of you like it?"

When everyone had tried it and all agreed it looked best on Sarah Bea, Lyle showed Emmie how to use the one hundred and fifty dollars worth of makeup she'd bought under Grace's tutelage, while everyone leaned forward to learn the latest techniques. Then everyone wanted Lyle to "glamorize" them, while Sarah Bea demonstrated different ways Emmie could wear her hair.

Mary Cole went downstairs and came back with left-over wedding cake and glasses of wine. They rehashed every part of the wedding and congratulated themselves on how well it had gone, while wishing that this or that had been better.

"I'd better get home," Grace said at last. "I've left my menfolk to their own devices long enough."

"Me too," Sarah Bea stood and stretched. "I'm glad y'all called me though. This has been the best ending to Pickett's wedding I could have imagined. Emmie, I guess you and Lyle will be leaving early tomorrow, so I'm going to hug you good-bye now." She hugged Emmie and then her sister.

Grace came over to hug Emmie. "Thank you, Emmie."

"I should be thanking you."

"No. Thank you for letting me—" Grace, who was never sentimental, swallowed and blinked suspicious wetness from her eyes. "I feel like you really are my sister now."

Chapter 18

Do-Lord turned into the drive of a large white house dripping with gingerbread, and, as instructed, drove around it to the back. There, nestled among huge old camellias and azaleas, their dark green leaves glistening in the bright December sun, sat a tiny, one-story house, formerly a servants' quarters, where Emmie lived. Tall pines shaded it, and a rusty drift of pine needles had piled up along the angle of the tin roof.

Trust Emmie to live in a storybook cottage. He almost laughed aloud. He'd thought about her often in the couple of weeks since he'd seen her. Knowing he wouldn't be content to see her only for the weekend, he'd even taken Lon up on his offer to arrange leave. He had two weeks before he had to return to base the day after Christmas. When Do-Lord said he was going to North Carolina, Lon hadn't blinked. Grinned a lot, but not blinked.

Discovering her connection to Calhoun had been one of the best pieces of luck he'd had in a long time—right up there with the time he accidentally rescued two SEALs.

That had been a major turning point. Until then he had lived on the fringes of society—among the poor and the powerless—all his life. Drifting and aimless after the death of his mother, he just wanted to drive around and see stuff until the three hundred fifty dollars he'd gotten for the sale of the trailer ran out. He could look back and see he'd been on a course that would have taken him from the petty crime of his teenage years to major crime.

He'd been to Six Flags Over Georgia where he rode every roller coaster for a week. He went to Charlotte Motor Speedway, where he lived out of his car and soaked up the aphrodisiacal aromas of chewing tobacco, car exhaust, and beer. The Danville International Speedway was a disappointment. Turned out the little track in the rolling farmland had been shut down a few years before and wouldn't reopen until 1998.

Looking at a map, he saw that from Danville, Highway 58 went straight across Virginia and ended at the Atlantic ocean. Something about that appealed to him—to just get in the car and drive smack-dab to the ocean and finally see that "end of the road" that everybody talked about.

As it happened he arrived in Virginia Beach on his eighteenth birthday. He parked the car in a lot where the highway really did *end,* took the concrete steps down to the beach, and walked on the sand with a nor'easter buffeting his ears under a gunmetal gray sky that spit stinging pellets of rain from time to time.

The bar, The Sea Shanty, looked like a place to get warm and buy himself a beer to celebrate his first sight of the Atlantic and his birthday. It hunkered down, less than a block from the ocean, under a massive freeway that connected the beach to Norfolk. It gave the impression that the highway had simply been built over it—which he gathered, was pretty much the case. It had existed there for forty or fifty years in the same state of stubborn dilapidation. Paint had long since been scoured off by salt winds, and with the freeway overhead it didn't need much roof.

He used the one fake ID (of the five fakes he had) that showed his real birthday—although the year was off a bit, and none of the other facts were right either. It made for a lonely celebration though, since telling anyone why he was there wasn't an option.

He was two sips into his second beer when the fight broke out. It wasn't his fight. Staying clear of swinging fists, he retired with his beer bottle to a short hallway that led past the restrooms to a back door exit and stayed there to watch.

Suddenly, he was grabbed from behind. It felt like being clutched in the arms of a tank. He knew dirty moves. He tried them. The tank effortlessly immobilized Do-Lord with a half nelson forcing his face forward and down. He couldn't see a thing except the way-past-filthy cracked vinyl floor.

"Weed! What the hell are you doing? Leave the kid alone," a voice, that didn't seem to be talking to him, demanded.

"I'm getting the kid out of here," the human tank yelled over the melee, insulted.

"Shit! Are you out of your mind? *Leave him.* We got to get ourselves out. You know what's going to happen if we're picked up by the Shore Patrol."

The shoulder hold didn't let up one iota. "Tha's the *reason* we *gotta* save the kid. Can't let him get picked up. He's underage," Weed explained with drunken perspicacity.

"You are so drunk. Okay, okay! We'll take him with us. Just move!"

Do-Lord was grabbed on the other side by another arm, equally steely.

A thousand thoughts went through Do-Lord's mind. Noticing he was taller than either of the two men who had him now by each arm. How massive were the arms that held him. Whether he wanted or needed rescue, fighting was pointless. He was dragged backwards through a rear exit and yet without unnecessary roughness.

Then they were outside among haphazardly-parked cars in the chilly wet night. Sirens could be heard in the distance. His two drunken Don Quixotes set him on his feet. They were in their early twenties, dressed in jeans and T-shirts, and as he'd already noted, shorter than he. They outweighed him by a good fifty pounds of muscle.

He could have run. He'd been poised to as soon as they loosened their hold the least bit, but Do-Lord had a lifetime of summing up others' intentions in a split second. Whatever they intended, it wasn't harm, although the casual competence with which they had immobilized him said they were no strangers to violence. Being saved was a novel experience. He was curious about what they would do next.

"Hell Tim, my fucking car's been stolen!" Weed roared.

"Locatelli, you idiot, you didn't *drive* your car."

"Did we drive yours?"

"We took a cab. You're the genius that said we'd be too drunk to drive home. You're too drunk, but I'm not."

Do-Lord doubted that. True, Weed acted drunker, but both were in DUI territory. Anybody who had distributed moonshine since he was ten was a fairly good judge of sobriety.

"You know what the Master Chief says. 'A SEAL's gonna git drunk. A SEAL's gonna git in fights. But a SEAL that gits drunk and gits in fights and gits *caught,* ain't gonna be a SEAL for long.'"

"Too late now." The more sober of the pair pulled his buddy by the arm. "Come on, time for us to become one with the shadows."

"What about the kid?"

"They catch him with us, and they'll nail us for contributing to the delin… the lelinq… the you know, of a minor."

Light bulbs went on in both bleary sets of eyes. "Hey kid, how *are* you getting' outta here?"

"My car."

Tim and Weed looked at each other. The more drunk one spoke. "Did you hear him? *He's* got a car."

Now both turned to him with giant, slightly loopy grins. It was the grins that decided the matter—full of sly goodwill and drunken opportunism, yet innocent of malice.

These were men he understood. They would have fit right in to the world he had come from. A world on the wrong side of the law where men looked to get away with everything they could, and took advantage of any weakness they saw. But they also had a largeness of spirit and a sense of purpose that made them assume—however mistakenly—that they should rescue him. He pulled his car keys from his jeans pocket. "Come on. Looks like it's my turn to save you."

The three scrambled into the car, the older men

crouched low in the backseat. Do-Lord drove away slowly.

They let him spend the night in their digs, and a friendship was born. Tim Johnson and Louis "Weed" Locatelli. Weed was so called because someone once remarked he was crazy as a horse who had been eating Loco Weed. It quickly got shortened to Weed.

They were tougher, smarter, and more streetwise than anyone he'd ever met. They had every quality life had taught him to respect. They were exactly who he wanted to be. They weren't criminals. They were SEALs.

Now he was at another turning point. With Emmie at his side he could enter into another area of society. A kind of society that lay at the other end of the bell curve—that of the rich and powerful. "The rich are different" as F. Scott Fitzgerald had said. Emmie understood them, got their nuances. And best of all, despite her insider status, she wasn't one of them. And if there was the added possibility he might get laid, well, that just meant he might get lucky indeed, so the smile spreading over his face every time he thought of Emmie was explained.

She had been just what he was looking for—although he hadn't known it.

He killed the engine and checked the dashboard clock. He was early.

Emelina was ready early. Twenty-eight minutes early by the clock on the computer, the only clock in her tiny house that displayed the correct time. Emmie caught sight of the woman in the mirror over her dresser. She felt like her home had been invaded by a doppelganger. She couldn't connect any feelings about herself to the woman she saw. Anxiety about how long it would take had made her get dressed far too early, and now she wasn't sure what to do with herself. To top it off there seemed to be a strange woman in the house.

The absurdity made her laugh out loud. The woman in the mirror got the joke and laughed too.

Though she'd already memorized it, she studied the checklist Grace had given her. "You'll start thinking about some arcane theory and forget to fix your hair or put on mismatched shoes," Grace had said.

Emmie would have been insulted if it weren't true. But at least this once she hadn't forgotten anything. Hair, makeup, dress, shoes—even her lingerie coordinated with the total picture. Total picture. That's what Grace had insisted on. "Don't look at your waist or hips or fixate on one area. That's the mistake so many women make. Look at how the proportions and all the elements go together."

She'd also said, "You don't have to look trashy and cheap in order to look sexy. This is about strategy. Men only want an easy woman if they don't want her much in the first place. It's in your best interests to eliminate the men who don't want you much. Trust me. You want to send a message that any man who wins your favor will have to come up to *your* standards."

This way of thinking about man-woman interactions was new to Emmie. In the past she'd never thought about it at all. She'd dressed to make sure no one would notice her.

Her heart beat a little harder every time she caught sight of herself in the mirror in the cherry red dress Grace had picked out. Long-sleeved and unadorned, its simple wrap design outlined the shape of her breasts and fastened with just two buttons at the waist, before flaring into a skirt that floated around her knees. "Just what we're looking for," Grace had announced. "Demure but not girlish. Trust me, any man will look at those two buttons and the way the overlap of the skirt moves and be fascinated."

She still didn't feel connected to the woman in the mirror, but why a man would want a date with that woman was obvious. She had practiced the posture Grace had taught her. Her shoulders were over her hips. At first it had felt awkward, like she was leaning backwards, but in a day or so, she had realized how much more balanced her whole body was and how much easier many movements were. Grace had showed her not how to "hold" her head but how to balance it on her neck so that it pivoted, turned and tilted—able to move with the slightest effort.

She was ready early, and she couldn't keep staring at herself in the mirror. She needed something to occupy her mind. Otherwise, she'd be a ball of nerves when he arrived.

Her little house consisted of four rooms all in a row. Living room, kitchen, bedroom, bath. In the kitchen, on the way to the living room, she stopped at the stove and set the timer to go off five minutes before Caleb was due to arrive—just in case she got caught up in something and lost track of time.

Over half the living room was taken up by her desk space, and to anyone else's eyes it was untidy. Books, piled four deep, lay open face-down on it. Printouts of Internet articles were tucked between pages. In spite of its disarray she didn't dare tidy it since there was a filing system of sorts in the piles.

The rest of the room was orderly, but now she wished she'd brightened it with some Christmas greenery and a few candles. If Pickett were here, she would have, but it had been hard to think of having Christmas without her. She missed Pickett terribly. It was easier to forget about Christmas and focus on her makeover goals.

She sat at the computer and took it out of sleep mode to study what she thought of as remedial conversational English.

Hello. Did you have a nice trip? Was the traffic heavy? It's nice to see you. Isn't it a nice day? The word "nice" figured heavily. "The purpose *isn't* to share information. It's like saying, 'Okay, I see you. Do you see me?' And you say, 'Yes, we see each other, and we're working on an agreement about whether to keep talking or not.'" Anyway, that's how Pickett explained it in their last phone call.

The doorbell made it's rusty, grinding sound. For one craven moment Emmie considered not answering it. The future was at the door, and in spite of everything, Emmie didn't feel ready. This was the moment that would put to the test all her shopping and primping, trips to makeup counters, and beauty salons. What if she had failed? What if she was still an object of scorn? Her heart pounding, she opened the door.

The sight of him in a slate gray blazer and brown slacks stole her breath and did something funny to her knees, while short-circuiting large parts of her brain. Not one of the phrases she'd practiced came to mind.

Chapter 19

It was Emmie who opened the door, he was sure it was. Nothing could change the wide, uptilted blue eyes. But the hair wasn't beige anymore. It was some shade of streaky blonde that made him think of cream swirled into honey. And the dress. It was a red that made him think of juicy, luscious things. It was as unadorned as anything he'd seen her in, and it exposed only a vee of skin at the chest. It wasn't revealing, but no man could see it without thinking—obsessing—about the body beneath it.

Do-Lord knew clothes. It was the discrepancy between his unkempt, neglected state and his IQ that had caused Social Services to remove him from his mother. He'd been returned to her because there was no real grounds to believe he was in danger, but after that experience, he studied the other kids' clothes. He saw how their clothes told who they were, where they came from, and how much money their parents made. The need for clean jeans and shirts, a haircut, and shoes had led to his first job. He had loved the Navy's dress code. It took out all the guesswork of wearing clothes that fit in. The correct attire for every conceivable job and occasion was prescribed in detail down to the underwear.

Becoming a SEAL had added another layer of understanding. SEALs often traveled undercover. Their clothes, jewelry, and haircuts had to match their cover identity. He still had five different ID's, but they were all passports.

There was much to know about clothes—not only what to buy, but how to wear them. With Lon as his personal wardrobe mentor, he refined his knowledge of cut and fabric, quality and tailoring. He knew the thread count in the cotton of his light yellow shirt and the slate blue blazer he wore was a fifty-fifty blend of pashmina and silk.

In the last two weeks, Do-Lord had discounted the way Emmie looked at the wedding, though he'd enjoyed it. It was a costume chosen by someone else so she could play a part—it wasn't her. He'd remembered Emmie in shapeless beige, and Emmie swallowed by a terry robe with the sleeves turned up with safety pins. He'd remembered Emmie, the shy fairy-spirit, whose magic was invisible to inhabitants of the ordinary world, but who, like all competent fairies, could enchant.

He didn't know how or why she'd changed, but no one could say that the way she looked now wasn't her. The whole outfit made you see the woman wearing the clothes, not the clothes. In some way she was more richly and truly herself than she had been before. He had created his whole game plan to utilize the fact that although she had access to Calhoun's world, she wasn't part of it. Now she was.

His plan had been fair and equitable. A single woman, particularly a plain one, gains status by having a male escort. Emmie would garner more respect accompanied by him, while her obvious brains and refinement would confer status and legitimacy on him by association. In the semi-social, semi-professional gathering they would be joining, their alliance would benefit both.

He'd planned to keep things light, at first. She was leery of being touched. He'd accepted that he would probably lose ground in the interval before he saw her again. He meant to give her nothing to regret, to bind her to him mostly with people's expectations of seeing them together. Then eventually, if she dropped him, he'd be known. He'd have connections of his own.

That plan was toast. She didn't need him at all the way she looked now. In fact, having him in tow would be a liability.

He needed a new game plan. He was going to have to capitalize on the fact that she wasn't indifferent to him. She'd been eager for his kisses. He had to push the timetable forward, to bind her to him with sensual chains. He knew intuitively that where she gave herself, she would be loyal.

Emmie watched Caleb's gaze sweep from the top of her head to her toes and back in undisguised masculine assessment. She'd always hated when men did that, measuring her with their eyes to see if she fitted their standards. The arrogance. It didn't have quite the same effect today. Not when the one doing it was Caleb. There was a pleasurable flutter and an interesting heat. Instead of looking away and frowning, she did as Pickett suggested—she returned his gaze.

The whole sexual dynamic took a quantum jump. With no will of her own, her shoulders went back, and it felt like her bra got tight. Good lord! She hadn't known *that* would happen.

"You look beautiful," he said.

"*Not* a pity-fuck then." Cripes! She hadn't meant that to come out. She remembered now she hadn't even said, "Hello, how are you?"

"I wish you would forget that. Davy is an idiot. He hasn't figured out what makes a woman worthwhile."

"What *does* make a woman worthwhile?"

He braced an arm on the doorframe just above her head and leaned close. She could see the freckles under the tan of his cheeks, a lazy twinkle of appreciation for her challenge in the golden green and brown of his eyes. The whole spoke of a confidence in his masculinity that weakened her knees. He chuckled. "You don't waste time on small talk, do you? May I come in?"

"Are you still mad about what you overheard?" he asked once they were standing in her tiny living room. "Davy really didn't know what he was talking about. He's cocky and full of himself, but don't judge him too harshly. Life will knock that out of him. I never agreed with him. When I look at you, pity is *not* what's on my mind."

As if he couldn't help himself, as if his hand was drawn by osmotic pressure that had to move from high concentration to low concentration, he touched the side of her neck with one forefinger. "Are we clear about that?" He stroked from near her ear down to where her neck curved into her shoulder. "Because if there's any doubt, any doubt at all, we have to remove it."

After a tiny foray under the shawl collar of her dress, he traced the angle of her jaw. "Now, are we on the same page?"

Stark desire gave his craggy features a graven look. A look she'd never seen before, but had no trouble recognizing. No matter what he was hiding from her, and she still felt there was *something,* it wasn't the truth about his attraction.

Emmie could now explain what might have been wrong with previous relationships. She hadn't felt as if she were being swamped by repeated waves of desire. She wasn't sure she liked it. She felt out of control, caught up by vast tidal forces that made her goals seem puny, pale, and insignificant. If she *had* felt this way before, she would have fought it.

But even as she considered that, he wrapped his hand around the nape of her neck, and drew her to him. Without one single thought of fighting the attraction, she moved toward him.

"You didn't answer me." His burnt-umber voice was grittier than ever, and his eyes were close enough to see all the specks of blue and green, gold and brown, in the iris. His breath came in warm, moist puffs against her face. "You know what's happening here. You know what's *going* to happen. Say it."

"Yes." He was going to kiss her. Her heart pounded. Her lips opened of their own accord.

"And you want it. Say it," he demanded.

"Yes."

His lips came down on hers, fierce and hungry, while he laid his hand on the middle of her back and pressed her into full contact. His taste was in her mouth, and his smell filled her head. It made her a little dizzy, and she stumbled slightly when he used his other hand to scoop her hips closer. There was nowhere to go except into him, against his hard chest and his hard thighs. She inhaled his clean, musky smell and relished the total competence with which his arms enclosed her.

He lifted her onto her tiptoes until the notch at the top of her thighs matched the fullness of his erection, which he ground against her with blatant intent.

The kiss went on and on. He groaned. "God, I wanted this," he said as he dabbed kisses and little licks down her neck. No one had ever licked her before. When he reached the juncture to her shoulder, he let her back down on her feet and with one hand opened the buttons at her waist. He pushed the two halves of the dress aside and closed a hand over her breast, kneading it insistently.

The timer on the stove buzzed.

Caleb lifted his head. "What the hell is that sound?"

"The timer on the stove."

"You're cooking something?"

"No."

"Good. How do you turn it off?" He traced the rim of her ear with his tongue, even as he moved her toward the stove.

But forced to think, to allow awareness of time and place back into consciousness, the forward momentum was blocked. The implications of what they were getting ready to do intruded. They had gotten pretty far from her game plan. She'd thought they would get to this point eventually, but not the minute he walked in the door. And by the time they did, she'd have made her decision whether to tell him to get lost or not. Now it was all mixed up.

"Stop… wait…" Emmie pushed against his chest and avoided his devilish tongue, little as she wanted to. "I don't do one-night stands. I don't even do two-, three-, or four-night stands." Caleb finally stopped kissing her. "And I don't do afternoon quickies either."

"Okay, I rushed you." Caleb rested his forehead against hers. "Sorry." Once his breathing evened out, Caleb drew back until he could look into her eyes. His irises were dark green in the afternoon light coming in the kitchen window. Russet color rode high on his cheekbones. His eyebrows drew together in a frown. "Wait. Are you saying 'no sex?'" He looked perplexed. Stunned even. "See each other and never have sex? I don't want that. In fact, I don't think I could."

Emmie pushed a little further away lest she succumb to the desire to soothe away the lost, bewildered note in his voice. And she couldn't look into his eyes either, because of the distracting way her heart pounded whenever she did. She needed to be rational, despite the fact that she was feeling more than a bit bewildered herself. From the moment she'd seen him at the door, nothing had gone as she had planned. He was supposed to court her and realize just how desirable she was and when he was smitten—oh, she liked the sound of that—she would tell him she wasn't interested. If she wasn't. She wouldn't cut off her nose to spite her face, after all.

"I'm not opposed to sex," she explained carefully. "Per se." She pushed against the solid wall of his chest, and this time he let his arms drop. Able to breathe a little easier, she tried to organize her thoughts. She brought her fingertips together at her chin. "Sex is an important part of the man-woman bond. But I think sex is too important, too *fraught* with potentially life-altering consequences, to handle casually. I'm not going to enter into sexual congress without some sort of mutually acknowledged relationship."

Caleb did that posture-thing of broadening his shoulders. He pushed back his sport coat from his waist like a gunslinger and hooked his thumbs over his hips. "That may be the stuffiest sentence I ever heard. Sexual *congress?*"

"I know I sound strange." If this conversation didn't send him running, nothing was ever going to. She certainly hadn't expected to discuss a contract minutes after he came in the door, but she'd been blindsided in the past because she'd never had the conversation at all.

She'd drifted into relationships only to discover the man wasn't in it the same way she was. Shared interests had become shared dinners, and eventually, shared beds. But Blount hadn't thought that seeing each other for months and having sex implied they were a couple in any sense of the word. During the past few weeks Emmie had accepted how much of that was her fault. She'd been as willing as the man to substitute shoptalk for intimacy. And she'd also allowed herself to become part of the furniture in his life. There, available, undemanding. Keeping herself in the background even in her own love affairs.

Although she didn't think she went in for casual sex, apparently, men she'd been with didn't have the same opinion of her. Viewed objectively, she could see that she had let men think she'd be around any old time without believing anything was required of them. She had drifted into relationships based on mutual professional goals and drifted into sex that was based mainly on proximity. Never again.

Not being in the background was darn uncomfortable though, and she was sure she was going about it all wrong. "Why don't we quit talking about it? I'm sure you want to forget I said anything as much as I do."

"You haven't weirded me out, if that's what you're worried about. I just don't know what you're talking about."

"Oh. Sexual congress means—"

"I know what it means." He growled between clenched teeth, then visibly got ahold of himself. He relaxed and put on his good-ole-boy smile. She was starting to recognize it. "Sounds like you're talking about commitment. I can do that. Just tell me what you want."

"Exclusiveness, for starters."

"Okay."

Emmie blinked in surprise. "Just like that? 'Okay?' We live in separate towns—separate states, and no offense, but you're... um a..."

"A what?" He crossed his arms over his chest. "A SEAL? A sailor?" His grin shaded into cocky. "A stud?"

"I don't get the feeling you're taking this seriously."

For a second his eyes turned hard and flat in that cold distant look she'd seen before, but it was so quickly supplanted by a bad-boy gleam, Emmie wasn't sure she'd seen it. "Now that's where you're wrong, Miss Emelina," he drawled. "Just how serious do you want me to be, darlin'? Marriage?"

Her heart rate, which had finally settled down, doubled. It was a dare. She knew it was. And just for a second she had a vision of herself as a gum-popping, curl-twirling, pouty-lipped chick who could be dared into doing outrageous things and double-damn-dare him right back.

And for one don't-look-down moment she wanted to say *yes*. She was *that* curious to see what he would do *then*.

But, of course, she didn't. Cliff-walking just wasn't her style. She took a step back. "No... no, I'm not ready to say ''til death do us part.' I might not ever be."

Honesty, just in case he *wasn't* kidding, compelled her to add, "If I'm not ready, I certainly don't expect *you* to be."

"What are we talking about then?"

What had been missing in the past? What galled her was that she hadn't even noticed anything was missing, until she mentioned a department dinner, and Blount told her he'd accepted an invitation from one of her colleagues. A woman. And been surprised when Emmie was upset. It was true they hadn't made any formal declarations, but didn't she at least get first dibs? "I guess you could call it loyalty," she told Caleb. "Yes, that's the word. For as long as we're together, I want loyalty."

Caleb nodded, almost as if he approved. "I'm pretty good at loyalty. That's not a problem. Anything else?" His dark, slightly gritty voice felt like it lapped at her skin.

"No." Actually, there were *lots* of other things—if only she could think of them. Somehow, in the couple of weeks since she'd seen him she'd forgotten—or maybe discounted was a better word—the effect he had on her senses. The trouble was she hadn't expected to have this conversation on the first date, heck, before the first date got off the ground! All her brain synapses were scrambled from sensory overload.

Do-Lord waited for her to say more, and when she didn't he said, "Okay, you want commitment? You got it." And the funny thing was, he wasn't lying. He didn't think there was a snowball's chance she'd want anything long-term, but if she did, he could be up for it. Set aside the pyrotechnics that exploded every time they touched, life around Emmie was interesting. She had a focused dynamism he could respect. He'd always been able to set a goal and then do whatever it took to reach it, and he suspected she could too. Even the dull clothes hadn't completely hidden her dry, subversive sense of humor. Being able to call her his, even for a little while, satisfied some primal desire for possession he hadn't known he had. "This commitment to be faithful and loyal—it goes both ways, right?"

Emmie pushed her hand into her hair and pulled the long strands through her fingers as if she relished their silky softness. It was a wholly feminine, utterly sensuous gesture he'd never seen her make before.

"When you put it that way, it makes us sound like a pair of hounds." She laughed, then gave him one of her direct looks. "But yes. I wouldn't ask you for a promise I wasn't willing to keep myself."

He looked deep into those wide innocent blue eyes. She meant it. He could count on her forever and beyond.

"Kiss me." He slid his hand under her hair at her nape again, wanting to relish the silky sweep across the back of his hand, while his fingers stroked the warm softness of her skin and traced the vulnerable little groove at the base of her skull. "*Kiss me.*"

Emmie pulled back. "Wait. It's not a done deal that I *will* have sex with you. Only that if we do, a commitment is implied and agreed to by both parties." She glanced at the clock on the stove. "Now, if we're going to make it to the open house before we're insultingly late, we need to leave."

For a second, Do-Lord couldn't reference what she was talking about. Holy crap. When had this gotten completely out of control? He'd been ready to blow off his objectives for a quick fuck. No, he corrected himself. He wouldn't have made it quick. When he had Emmie Caddington under him in bed he was going to make it last a long, long time. His mistake was that he'd been trying to convince himself that Emmie wasn't a priority. She was an extra on the side.

His body disagreed. If he'd never heard of Teague Calhoun, he'd have wanted her. He had two objectives. The good part was that they were compatible, even complementary.

Two steps took her back to the living room, where she picked up a purse resting on the arm of an easy chair, then walked to the door. "Ready?"

Her lipstick was blurred from his kisses, her dress was partly unbuttoned, and the smooth fall of her pale, silver-washed hair was hanging over her cheek in a way he didn't think it was supposed to. In other words, she looked like he'd had his hands all over her.

As far as he was concerned, she looked just right, but it was clear she hadn't given a thought to her appearance and whether she could go out in public like that.

She'd obviously gone to a lot of trouble to get all dolled up for their date, yet her concern for her looks was only skin deep. There was a simplicity about Emmie, a clean, transparent innocence that made him ache for her in tender amusement.

"Emmie, Emmie, Emmie." Do-Lord shook his head. "Go look at yourself in the mirror."

She threw him a questioning look, but obligingly made the short trip to her bedroom.

When he heard the soft "eeek" he let himself laugh, but quietly, so she wouldn't hear him, while he brushed crumbs from the desk blotter into an empty coffee cup and carried the cup to the dishwasher. In spite of her lawyerly little speech, whether they would make love was a done deal. The thought warmed him clear to his toes.

Chapter 20

"UNCLE TEAGUE'S HOUSE IS ONLY A FEW BLOCKS AWAY in the direction of the river," Emmie said. When she returned to the living room, her hair and makeup had been restored to their former perfection, and the flap of that flirty red dress was buttoned, but it still threatened to open with every step. "It's a beautiful day, and it will be easier to walk than to find a parking place."

Their walk took them through the historic section of Wilmington, where block after block of lovingly tended nineteenth-century houses, many restored to the ebullient reds and blues the Victorians had favored, faced the street with gracious porches and hid their interiors with lace curtains. Every door boasted a wreath, and lampposts sported red bows and sprays of greenery.

Sidewalks that buckled over roots of ancient oaks presented a hazard to someone unaccustomed to high heels, and after Emmie stumbled the second time, Caleb took her arm and kept it. He did it just right. Not holding on to her or making her feel fettered. He simply offered her his strength and stability, while adjusting his steps to hers. Her heels tapped the concrete with every step. His made not a sound.

The sun was warm and the bare branches of immense oaks threw a graceful tracery of shadows on houses, lawns, and streets. "I love to walk these old neighborhoods when the shadows look this," Emmie remarked.

"I like to fancy that the ancient trees have drawn delicate lines between things to point out to us that everything connects everything to everything else."

"I'm surprised a biologist would be prey to the anthropomorphism of believing trees have intentions, much less a philosophy."

Emmie gave him one of her dry looks, only this time she did it out of the corner of her eyes. Holy crap. Where had she learned to do *that?*

"Empirical materialism is as likely to limit understanding as expand it," she commented quietly. "Now. Before we get to Uncle Teague's house, tell me what's going on with you. What's your interest in him, really?"

"What makes you think I have any particular interest?"

"Well, you agreed to help me with the cake after you saw his picture, you steered me toward him at the wedding reception, and you accepted his invitation for both of us before I could say a word. Finally, and most telling, you were willing to put off sex in favor of this open house."

Note to self: Emmie is an astute observer. Don't be fooled by the wide, innocent eyes and otherworldly air. "Would you believe I was looking for an excuse, any excuse, to see you again?"

She peeped at him out of the corner of her eye. She chuckled. "No."

He stepped in front of her, forcing her to stop walking so that he could look directly into her eyes. "Well, you'd be wrong, because I was. I want to see you again and again." She had no idea how close he had come to forgetting his objective.

"Okay, you have *two* reasons," she conceded, without backing down one bit. "And one of them has to do with

Senator Teague Calhoun. I'm being made a party to something. I'd like to know what it is."

He didn't have a lie prepared, but even if he had, he wanted to tell her. Wanted her to look at the facts with her cool, spacious innocence. "There's something nobody knows. Something that wouldn't do either my career or Calhoun's any good if it were revealed. I believe Teague Calhoun is my father."

"You mean—"

"I'm a bastard, illegitimate, a love child—that's what my mother said I was."

"And Teague Calhoun is your father. Humph! That hypocrite. That anti-birth control, anti-sex education, assistance-for-women and children-program-cutting, just say no, Bible-thumping, moralistic, 'family values' hypocrite! Teague Calhoun is a fornicator and a dead-beat dad."

"Hey, hey. Calm down." He stroked her shoulder. She was like a spitting-mad kitten with its fur all ruffled. It wasn't the reaction he'd expected. A corner of his heart warmed as if the sun had finally reached it.

"It just infuriates me that men can father children that they take no responsibility for. Pickett and I used dream up ways to make it impossible for men to get away with it."

"Like..."

"Pickett's idea was to take DNA samples of all males, creating a database—kind of like the FBI's fingerprint database. The father of any child needing support could be identified. The government would also have his tax returns, and he could be billed on a sliding scale for the child's support."

"What was your plan?"

"Unless men are in a stable relationship, they can't connect their actions to a child appearing nine months later—that's the real problem. Nothing forces them to look at the consequences of their actions *before* they take them. The biological fact is that people can have children regardless of whether they want them, whether they are willing to be responsible, whether they are mature enough, or whether they are healthy enough to raise a child. Biology trumps. Strictly from a biological perspective, people have only one function: to pass on their genes. Left to itself, natural selection would favor the strongest children born to the best parents. Since children are helpless for a long time before they are capable of reproducing, the best parents would have the best chance of having their genes passed on. Society interferes with natural selection, though. We don't believe children should starve just because their parents abandon them, are too young to have any idea how to raise a child, or are strung out on drugs. I think it's time human beings loaded the biological dice in favor of society. I would propose that as soon as boys reach puberty, sperm samples would be taken and placed in cryonic storage."

"Their sperm would be frozen? Uh-oh. I'm a little afraid of where this is going."

Emmie's head bobbed in a scholarly little nod. "Then they would be given a vasectomy. When they wanted a child, they could go to the sperm bank and make a withdrawal. Society could be as restrictive or as lax as it wanted to be about who would be allowed to procreate. Wouldn't matter. Natural selection would favor men and women who had at least some good parenting traits. Only people who consciously wanted children and were able to plan for them would have them."

"You would do this just to give natural selection a leg up?"

"There would be other benefits. Abortion, except for medical reasons, would be a thing of the past. No woman would ever be accused of 'getting herself pregnant'—don't you love that phrase?—to trap a man into marriage. No woman could get pregnant through rape. No teenagers, boys *or* girls, would find themselves saddled with a child they were not mature enough to be responsible for. Above all, every child born would be wanted and planned."

"But wholesale vasectomies? Isn't that Draconian?"

"I'm not proposing *killing* boys or even hurting them. It's a simple out-patient procedure performed under local anesthetic."

Her wide blue eyes were guileless, but he was beginning to recognize the smile lurking at the corners of her mouth.

"And you look so harmless." He stroked his knuckles against the underside of her chin. The breeze was stronger now that they were nearer the river. It lifted shiny silvery strands of her hair. A strand blew across her face, so he carefully hooked it with a forefinger and tucked it behind her ear.

When they resumed their steps along the shell-embedded sidewalk, they were hand in hand, like lovers. "You said you believe Calhoun is your father," Emmie spoke, returning to the previous topic. "You're not sure?"

"My mother told me he was, and for years she waited for him to come back. But you had to know my mother.

She was imaginative. She lived in a dream world most of the time. Her relationship with Calhoun could have been her imagination."

"Imagination? Thirty years ago, why would she pick *him* to fantasize about? He wasn't well-known then."

"Calhoun hasn't always lived in North Carolina. His father and grandfather were from Alabama. The family is known there—sort of the local aristocracy. I know you don't believe in a Southern aristocracy, but the people there did. You should have seen the house they lived in."

"The one that looks like the country club."

Do-Lord had forgotten he had told her that, but she remembered the minute detail and unerringly put it together with what he was telling her.

"So your mother said Teague Calhoun is your father, but her word isn't trustworthy. Do you have any other evidence?"

"When I was sixteen I went into a public library endowed by the Calhoun family. I saw a large portrait of the library's benefactor, Calhoun's father."

He had gone in mainly to get warm. The Trans Am he drove had a rebuilt motor and good tires, but the heater hadn't worked since before he bought it. He had a couple more bootleg deliveries to make and an hour to kill before he could make them. A library was a great place to hang out. Spending an idle hour there wouldn't put him on the "watch" list of the police the way hanging around a gas station would. Besides, anytime he had an hour to spare, he'd rather satisfy his reading mania.

Once he had been limited by the range of a bicycle, but after he had a car, he could travel further to make his deliveries. His route that day had taken him to a neighboring county and a library he'd never been in before.

Built circa 1950, the library was a squat, ugly red brick homage to utilitarian architecture. On the inside it was hushed and stuffy, but warm enough to make his cold, red fingers sting. And filled with the wonderful dusty mustiness of a thousand books in one place. His wet sneakers squeaked on the gray vinyl floor as he made his way to the periodicals.

The life-size portrait hung on the back wall of the periodical room. The man in it, clad in a dark suit with the wide lapels of a bygone era, was a few years older than Caleb, and had dark blond hair and blue eyes. Other than that, he looked just like Caleb.

"I had stopped believing my mother a long time before. I knew he wasn't going to come for us. We were on our own, and he wouldn't be proud if I made good grades. I figured that Teague Calhoun was just part of the fantasy she'd constructed—the way she made up our name."

"Wait a minute." Emmie craned her neck to look into his face. "She made up your last name?"

"Yep. She said it was French, meaning 'with honor or praiseworthy.' I couldn't have my father's last name like other kids did, but my birth was honorable just the same."

"That's really creative. Did you encounter a lot of teasing about being illegitimate from the other kids?"

"Not a lot. I wasn't the only one in the trailer park."

"And you grew up poor." Emmie was checking her assumptions and assembling data.

"Movie stars notwithstanding, children of unmarried mothers generally do," Caleb answered with dry understatement.

"And she named you Caleb, after the Israelite spy in Exodus who was allowed to reach the Promised Land, although the older generation was not. They would die in the Wilderness."

"How did you know?"

"I'm the child of missionaries, remember? And the grandchild of the president of the women's society of our church. I was fed Bible stories with my cereal."

Emmie was silent for a while. Do-Lord had already told her more than he revealed to most, and he'd seen how much information she could extract from a few facts. He didn't think she'd let the subject drop though, and her next question proved it. "So when you saw the portrait of what would be your grandfather, you realized your mother's stories might be true. What did you do?"

"Well, I was in a library. What would you do?"

Emmie's eyes lit with scholarly fervor. "Research!"

"I read old newspapers—anything a Calhoun did was newsworthy in that county—and learned Teague Calhoun had settled in North Carolina after attending the university here."

"Did you want to meet him?"

This was the part he had to be careful with. Emmie had already demonstrated she remembered and made inferences from everything he said. She didn't seem to like Calhoun much, but he was an old family friend, close enough to be called "Uncle Teague." She wouldn't want to be part of bringing Calhoun down.

"My mother died not long after that. I was on my own then. I got out of there, and I didn't look back."

"How did your mother die?"

"Myocarditis."

Emmie made a sympathetic sound. "You were so young, and she must have been young too."

"Thirty-four. She was seventeen when I was born."

They were both silent for a minute, contemplating a life cut short, a boy-man cut adrift.

"I'd see something about Calhoun in the news every now and then. I'd be a little curious. But the life of a SEAL is intense, all-absorbing."

"And then you met him face-to-face in Afghanistan."

Did she forget nothing?

"Face-to-face would be stretching it. He was 225 yards away. I could see him, but I'm pretty sure he never saw me."

"And now you're curious. Do you want him to acknowledge the relationship?"

"I got along without him my entire life. I don't need him now. And like I said, if it became public knowledge, it wouldn't do either of us any good."

"The media would have a field day. I understand why it would be disastrous for the senator—the conservative, family values candidate with an illegitimate son, whom he abandoned. And—oh, my goodness—*your* picture would be splashed from one side of the globe to the other! You wouldn't be able to—what do you call it—operate."

"SEALs whose identities have been splashed all over the media are not much use in a covert operation," he told her with dry understatement. In fact, he might as well pin a target on his back. SEALs went to some lengths to maintain the psychological advantage of seeming invisible and invulnerable. As a result, terrorist organizations all over the world would love to claim the coup of assassinating one. "Spin doctors might be able to save Calhoun's career, but mine would be over."

Emmie nodded and then fell silent. While she thought over what he had said, he kept his breathing slow and regular, despite the tightness in his diaphragm. Whether he had said enough or too much he couldn't tell. The tall, limestone Calhoun house, with it's imposing semicircular porch upheld by soaring two-story pillars, came into view. The streets around it were, as Emmie had predicted, clogged with parked cars.

She tugged on the hand she still held and turned her wide blue eyes to him. "When Moses sent Caleb to Canaan to spy, the Israelites needed to know if it was a land flowing with milk and honey, or if the stories of its abundance were fabricated. Maybe it wasn't the Promised Land. Maybe, as some said, they didn't need it. They'd gotten along without it for forty years. You, Caleb, don't know whether your mother's stories about Calhoun and his Promised Land were *her* imagination." She squeezed his hand. "Let's go find out."

Chapter 21

SATISFACTION BURNED HOT AND DEEP IN DO-LORD'S chest as he gazed around the wide entry hall of the imposing three-story mansion overlooking the Cape Fear River.

He was in.

At the base of the tall steps leading to the imposing, tan-colored limestone mansion, a man whose cheap polyester jacket shouted rent-a-cop had taken the card and checked their names against a list. And then he and Emmie had waited in front of the wide front door with its ornately etched glass side panels and large Christmas wreath until another blue-polyester flunky, at some signal from within, had ushered them inside. Somebody here was serious about crowd control.

"Well," Emmie had whispered with heavy irony, echoing his thought, "I guess we know we're being admitted into the presence of a Very Important Person."

Inside the wide red-carpeted entry hall, a discreet velvet rope just like those in museums denied access to the staircase, while even more discreet cameras tucked into the coffered ceiling provided the real security. He'd already noted motion sensors on every downstairs window—but not those upstairs. It was amazing how many people assumed that just because windows were twenty feet off the ground, they couldn't be entered.

A minion with a fringe of gray hair surrounding a shiny pink pate, this one better dressed than the rent-a-cops, nodded to Emmie as if he knew her, then shepherded him and Emmie into the line of people waiting to enter the large reception room separated from the entry by more tall white columns.

The long reception room, which couldn't be mistaken for a living room, despite the groups of sofas and coffee tables, ran the entire south wing of the house. A grand piano set in the center of the room almost looked small. At one end Senator Calhoun and his wife stood in front of a large fireplace banked with poinsettias to greet their guests and have photos made with them.

"Whoever designed this place had no problem mixing styles of architecture," Emmie observed as she pointed to white columns bordering a small alcove where a coatrack had been placed. "See, these are Ionic, but those are Corinthian."

Do-Lord flicked a glance at the columns, then went back to studying the layout of the rooms visible on either side of the hall. This was his purpose. To have a look-see at how the house was arranged and scope out the security. On the north side of the hall he could see a small yellow parlor that looked out on the front of the house and behind it a paneled dining room with a table that would seat sixteen easily. He mentally placed them on the floor plan he was creating in his mind. Other rooms, not accessible to the public, must lie beyond them.

He was having trouble concentrating on his intelligence gathering though. There were too many people too close to him and Emmie. Too many stood between them and any exit. Too many places a shooter could be hiding. A shooter at the top of the stairs that half-encircled the hall in three easy flights would be invisible and could kill everyone in one burst of automatic fire.

Emmie saw architecture, and he saw sniper hides. Do-Lord recognized his state as hypervigilance, common to combat veterans returning from deployment, where the enemy could be anyone, anywhere, and the most ordinary moments could erupt in smoke and screams and spattered blood. He'd been in the crowded lobby of a hotel once, flirting with a pretty woman while waiting in line to check in when a terrorist had driven a truck through the plate glass doors of the entrance. Only seconds before, there had been a busy low-keyed babble overlaid by music from a piano—just like now.

Do-Lord caught Emmie looking at him out of the corner of her eye again. He was aware he hadn't responded to the last few topics she'd thrown out, and she'd fallen silent—as silent as he was. He wasn't having a flashback, not the classic kind. He was completely aware that he was *here* in the senator's house, the pretty girl beside him was Emmie, and there probably was no danger.

Still, he had to get Emmie out of here. He could look after himself. If he was by himself he would handle any threat, but keeping Emmie safe in a crowd this dense was practically impossible.

Guests were being allowed into the reception room in groups of four or five, and then herded into the line to shake the great man's hand. To hell with that. When the flunkie's attention was on a group to be escorted, he looped an arm over Emmie's shoulders. He guided her through the people bunched together in the entry hall and into the reception room. He didn't stop until they were at the back of the room near the long Palladian windows that opened onto a covered veranda.

With a wall at his back and the windows providing easy egress, he felt marginally better. He wanted Emmie where he could get her out.

"What's going on?" Intelligence, curiosity, and something that looked like concern made Emmie's wide blue gaze even more direct than usual. "I thought you wanted to see Teague Calhoun. Why did you take us out of the line?"

He wanted to tell her the truth. All of it. Already she knew more about him than anyone—even his best friend. The thorough background checks required for his security clearance hadn't turned up any of what he had told her. There was something about her—a cleanness, an innocence.

"I don't like to be in the middle of crowds," he said.

"Do you have claustrophobia?"

"No." He might have said more, but hypervigilance made him more conscious of movement in his peripheral vision. A flicker of something out the window caught his attention.

"Did anything happen to you in a crowd?"

"Not *one* thing, no," he answered absently, trying to spot whatever had drawn his attention. He turned his head to see whatever it was more clearly.

Holy shit. What had caught his eye was a rope twitching against the side of the house. Attached to the rope, a small figure dangled beneath a second floor window.

Casually, before Emmie could ask him what he was looking at, he tucked an arm around her shoulders and turned her toward the door to the veranda. "Let's walk outside for a minute, okay?"

"Of course," Emmie agreed. Caleb's behavior had been different in a way she couldn't put her finger on from the moment they had entered the Calhoun house. "Tell me, did you have this problem with the crowds at Pickett's wedding?"

From the veranda, steps led down to a slate-paved patio in back of the house. Realizing he wasn't listening to her, Emmie followed the direction of Caleb's gaze. "Oh, my God! That's Victoria Calhoun!" she told Caleb. "Vicky, what on earth are you doing?"

"Going out the window," replied the jeans-clad figure. "I do it all the time. But I can't..." Vicky swallowed a small sob. "Today, I can't make the swing over to the porch." She sounded more upset over her unaccustomed failure than panicked. The small bathroom window was actually only ten feet or so above the veranda roof and maybe four feet to the side. Emmie could see that anyone with climbing skills—and intrepid enough—would think it possible to reach. Unfortunately, directly below the little girl was a three-story drop to the flagstone-paved patio.

"Vicky, what's the rope anchored to?" Caleb's voice was pitched to carry without being loud. He remained calm—as if a dangling child merited only mild curiosity.

"The radiator in my bathroom. I go out that window because it's closer to the porch."

"Okay, good. That's real good," he told the child as he stripped off shoes and socks. "The window on your left—is that your bedroom window?" She was actually closer to it than to the porch, and since it was larger and longer than the bathroom window, she was almost level with it.

Caleb thrust his shoes and socks into Emmie's hands. "Go upstairs and open her bedroom window. I'm going to climb up and move her over to it."

"You're going to scale that?"

"Um-hmm." The wall wasn't flat or smooth. From a distance the limestone façade of the house almost looked like basket weave. The stones had been carved into roughly convex surfaces, which offered handholds and footholds. Coming down aided by a rope would be easy. Going up without a rope or equipment would be harder, but he could do it. Do-Lord stripped his sport coat off and handed that to Emmie as well. "Go!"

Emmie couldn't believe he intended to climb up a wall. Still, despite her curiosity about how he would do it, she reacted instantly to the note of command in his voice.

With his jacket draped over the shoes she raced back to the veranda door. The warmth and babble of the crowded room when she slipped inside was shocking for its sheer normalcy. Briefly, she wondered if she should find one of the security guards and tell them what was going on. But she had a conviction that if Caleb had wanted her to do that, he would have told her to.

She made her way across the room, trying not to catch the eye of several people she recognized. Being invisible had its uses, she was thinking smugly, when her path was blocked by a man in a three-piece suit.

The cut of the deep navy pinstripe suit was good, the touches of maroon in the tie discreet, and if the outfit seemed a little stuffy and made him look older than his years, well, Blount had always had ambitions to switch to the administration side of the university. Looked like he had decided to dress the part of a senior dean.

"Emmie..." Blount's eyes swept her up and down. "Emmie Caddington, is that you?" To her surprise he held out his arms in welcome.

Emmie sidestepped his hug, but while she tried to think of an excuse to get away from him, he continued talking about people he had seen and spoken to as if she had answered him.

The man loved the sound of his own voice, and now that she thought about it, his habit of talking through everything had irritated her back when they were what, dating? No. Though they had eaten together frequently and spent evenings together, he had never asked her out on a date. A couple? No. Believing they were a couple and assuming a social invitation to one included the other was her mistake.

To be fair, she had preferred not to go out, and if they ran into others, she had stayed in the background. But appearances at certain faculty functions were required. Learning he intended to escort another woman to a function *she* couldn't possibly avoid had been the first shock. The second had been his surprise that she had expected to attend with him.

God, she'd felt stupid. When another faculty member suddenly had to drop out, she'd accepted the trip with the students so that it would be a good, long time before she had to run into Blount again. Now, as he mentioned this or that person he'd talked to, she realized how much she had depended on him to manage social situations.

How easy it was for her to say nothing because he could say everything.

For instance, right now, if she had the right kind of social graces, she'd be able think up a lie to get away from him, but she didn't. She couldn't. Instead she backed away from him while he nattered away.

"I thought I saw you earlier, but it looked like you were with some guy," Blount said. Looking slightly puzzled, he swept his eyes over her again. She could see him take in her new hair, new dress, and new shoes.

Suddenly, being trapped by him wasn't uncomfortable, it was funny. "And you knew that couldn't be me, right?"

He stammered, "No, of course not." But extra ruddiness in his cheeks made her think she'd nailed it. "I just didn't think—if you were with someone—I should interrupt you."

"Well, you were right the first time. I am with someone." God, it felt good to say that. Call her shallow, but it felt especially good to say it to the ponderously self-important Blount. Caleb was someone who held her hand as they walked down the street, unlike Blount who had never touched her unless he wanted sex. Someone who had no need of padding for his shoulders or a vest to disguise a thickening waistline. Someone who hadn't blinked at the mention of commitment. "You'll have to excuse me. He's waiting."

Blount's eyes searched the thinning crowd. "Where?" he challenged.

He didn't believe her. Why hadn't she noticed before that he didn't respect her? That he had often made her defend the blandest observation. Why hadn't she seen that he thought his presence conferred importance on her, and she should be grateful? Whatever lingering traces of attachment to Blount she might have felt dropped away. Any wisps of yearning for the intellectual partnership they might have had vanished like vapor in strong sunlight.

She giggled, then giggled harder at the look of confused affront he gave her for daring to laugh at his challenge. Her inner imp made her give him a saucy wink. "Upstairs."

Still giggling at his stunned look, she waggled her fingers bye and walked away.

The broad entry hall, by the time she reached it, had only a small knot of people at the door and was free of official minions. The crowd for the open house had peaked and was dwindling now. Emmie made for the staircase. The barrier of the wine velvet rope was more psychological than physical. Without hesitation and with her inner imp cheering, she calmly unhooked it, stepped through, and hooked it behind her.

Chapter 22

"Okay, Vicky, I'm coming up. You're doing just fine. I'll be there in a minute and help you in the window. No, don't try to watch me," Caleb said when the little girl craned her head to locate the sound of his voice. "I'm here," Do-Lord made his voice low and crooning. "I'm right beside you. I'm going to put my arm over you. What kind of knot did you use to secure the anchor?"

"A figure of eight."

If she tied it correctly, it would easily hold both of their weights. "Okay, then I'm going to reach around you and take hold of the rope. It might bounce a little, but I've got you. I'm not going to let you fall.

"You're doing great," he said when he had one hand on the rope and her little body pressed between him and the limestone. "I'm going to bring my knees up and make a lap. Let your thighs sit on my thighs. That way we can move together. Now we need to go down about a foot."

When he felt her weight against his thighs, he said, "I'm going to let us down now. Ready?"

"I can't let go," she said in a small voice, for the first time truly frightened.

"That's all right. You don't have to. Just let the rope slide through your hands."

"I mean my fingers—they won't move. I can't move my hands."

"Okay, in that case, we won't go down, we'll go up." The first necessity was to take every bit of strain from her arms and shoulders. The problem was equal parts spasm of abused muscles and fear. Even if she could work against the spasm, the most primitive part of her brain wouldn't let go while she felt like she was dangling.

He grasped the rope and pulled until her hands were below the level of her shoulders. He now supported one hundred percent of her weight. It wasn't much, seventy pounds or so. "Is that better?"

Inside the safety cage he'd made of his arms and legs he felt her draw in a deep, shuddering breath. The worst part about dangling for long periods was that a person couldn't breathe well in that position, which increased anxiety and fatigue. She relaxed against his chest. "How are we going to get down?" she asked at last.

"Don't worry. We'll get down. I promise. Just let yourself rest a minute." He closed one hand over hers, and rather than attempting to pry her fingers away from the rope, stroked firmly from her wrist to her fingertips, encouraging the muscles to lengthen. He felt her pinkie relax first, then her ring finger.

Her whole body settled against his as the security of the human cage he had made around her penetrated her fear. Now was the time to move.

"Emmie, you there?"

"I'm here." Emmie leaned out the window as far as was safe, but they were beyond her line of sight. She'd thrown the window open in time to hear Caleb say, "Then we'll go up," but she couldn't hear what Vicky had said. It seemed like they'd been "up" a long time, but probably it was less than a minute.

Though she couldn't see them, Emmie had been hanging onto the sound of Caleb's voice. From the first time she met him she'd been captured by his voice, it's flexibility and latent strength. Now as she listened to him reassuring the child, she heard the full power of his voice unleashed. Not harsh or loud, it was pitched to soothe, to reassure, and to instill confidence. Gentle, tender, almost lighthearted, yet earnest, she knew he meant with every fiber of his being exactly what he said. He was master of this situation, and Vicky was completely safe.

She wondered if this voice was yet another mask, or belonged to the man behind the mask.

"Okay, Emmie," Caleb's voice floated from above her. "Here's what's going to happen. I'm going to lower us. When we're level with your window, I'm going to work us over to it. Vicky's going to hold out her arm, and you're going to catch it and pull her in head first." His words in his easygoing drawl were backed up by will so focused and implacable, she could feel in her bones the inevitability that she would do what he said. "Do you understand?"

"All right, Little Bit," he spoke to Vicky again, "we're going down. One leg down. That's right. Move with me. There are plenty of good footholds. You've got it. You're doing great. It's no more than two or three steps." Through every movement he talked to Vicky in the same calm, confident voice.

There were rough scrabbling and scuffing sounds, then they came into view, and the sight snagged at Emmie's heart. He had Vicky enveloped in his strength, and moving as if they were one, he kept her back, the backs of her legs and arms in contact with his front.

When he saw Emmie leaning out the window, Caleb's teeth flashed white in a rather fierce-looking smile. "Good girl, Emmie. I want you to keep your weight inside the window though. When you catch Vicky's arm, I just want you to add momentum, understand?"

Emmie drew back. The window's wide aperture was filled with man and child. Before she could react, he ordered, "Put your arm out, Vicky, now."

At the same moment that the little girl reached out, he grasped the waistband of her jeans and thrust her forward. It was a tour de force of strength, coordination, and timing. Almost reflexively, Emmie grabbed the child's outstretched hand and tugged. Vicky tumbled into the room, while Emmie stumbled backwards to avoid being bowled over.

"Out of the way. I'm coming in."

Vicky scrambled to her feet and out of his way. Caleb hooked his hands on the sash above his head and in a smooth pull-up and tuck worthy of a gold medalist, sent his feet and legs through the aperture. With a perfectly timed release, he stuck the landing.

Vicky, her face so white each freckle across her cheeks stood out, grabbed his arm as soon as he was in the room. "Don't tell. Please don't tell," she pleaded.

Without answering her Caleb lowered the window and locked it, then stalked, *prowled,* with the fluid, deliberate, dangerous tread of a big cat, which could be contained but never tamed, to the deep wing chair near the door. Emmie had thrown his shoes and socks there as soon as she entered the room. Grim vertical creases bracketed his mouth. His silence was more shocking to Emmie than yelling would have been. He'd been so confident, so secure in his ability to scale the side of a house, so jaunty as he supported his own weight with one arm, Emmie hadn't realized how scared he was. But now the extreme control of every movement told of the iron clamp he had on his feelings.

He sat down in the chair and brushed his hand over the sole of one foot. Resting on his opposite knee, the tanned foot had a rough-hewn elegance, a marriage between innate grace and slim lines, strength and hard use. The sight of his bare foot, so human, so strong, and so vulnerable compressed her heart. He glanced up and saw her looking, and crinkles appeared around his eyes. He pulled on a brown sock, so soft-looking it must be cashmere.

Then the crinkles disappeared. "Emmie, would you retrieve the rope from the bathroom? Vicky and I," he explained in a voice scrubbed of all emotion, "need to have a very serious talk."

Feeling a little cowardly, Emmie scuttled toward the bath. She wouldn't want to face him in his current state. There wasn't a doubt in her mind that he intended to make Vicky aware of how foolhardy her actions had been. Just because she didn't want to be in the line of fire didn't mean she didn't want to know what was going to happen, though. She was intensely curious. She didn't close the door completely.

"Explain," she overheard him say. Just one word of command in that dead, level, calm voice.

"Mommy said I had to stay in my room and rest," Vicky began, then faltered. A long moment of silence ensued.

"Why did she say that?"

"Cause I had the flu, and she thinks I'm not over it. But I am, and I got so bored stuck up here while the reception was going on."

"So you decided to go out the window?"

"Sure. I've done it lots of times. It's easy. I don't have to belay the entire distance."

"You have the equipment. Someone has taught you climbing. Did they also teach you never to climb without a buddy?"

"Ye-es."

"Now, you know why."

"Nothing ever went wrong before. Really. Please, please, please, don't tell my mother."

"Something can always go wrong." He said it so sadly and so finally, his forehead corrugated with worry lines. "Vicky, when you give your word, do you keep it?"

"You mean, like keep promises?"

"You have to promise me, until you are twenty-one and have your climbing instructor certification, you will never climb alone. You shouldn't climb alone even then, but you will be an adult. It will be your decision to make."

"Okay, I promise."

"Will you keep your promise?"

"Cross my heart—" the girl began breathlessly.

"No. None of that. This isn't about being an obedient little kid. I think you've demonstrated you're not obedient. I'm talking about what you *will* do. Can you decide what you will do and then stick to it? Never forget, and never change your mind?"

"I promise."

"Okay, then I promise not to tell." He bent over to reach his other shoe. "Get out of that harness, and stow it somewhere. Someone will be here any minute. The security cameras probably picked up Emmie's every move."

Galvanized, Emmie released the breath she'd been holding and leapt to the window to haul in the rope. She was stuffing it under the vanity when his prediction came true.

The door opened. The gray-haired man in the gray pinstripe suit—the better dressed one who had shepherded guests into the Presence—burst in. He took in the scene. Vicky perched on the bed, Caleb in the wing chair pulling on a sock.

"I'll handle this," he snapped to someone outside the door. "Vicky, are you all right? Did he touch you?" Without waiting for a reply, he demanded of Caleb, "Who the hell are you, and what are you doing up here? The security guard saw a woman run up the stairs. Where is she?"

"Hey, there's no problem here. Vicky and I were just talking," said Caleb, "while Dr. Caddington used the bathroom."

"Surely you could tell by the rope that this section of the house was closed to visitors."

Caleb shrugged. "Sometimes the need for a bathroom is urgent. We figured we'd find one up here quicker than asking where the downstairs powder room is." On cue, the toilet flushed. Obviously, Emmie had overheard the conversation. "Ah—" He smiled knowingly, man-to-man. "A two-flusher." Water ran for a moment, the door opened, and Emmie appeared.

"Oh, hello, Mr. Fairchild. Vicky, thanks for letting me use your bathroom."

"Dr. Caddington, I'm surprised you would use your acquaintance with the senator to abuse his hospitality," Fairchild said with caustic disapproval. "I'm even more surprised that you would bring a stranger into the private section of the house. One who was making himself at home—to say the least—when I got here."

"Mr. Fairchild, I assure you—"

"Don't apologize," Caleb interrupted. "Fairchild has found out his security isn't very good and is understandably upset."

"Mr. Fairchild," Emmie said, trying to put the situation on a social footing. Fairchild was much more than a factotum in the senator's household. According to gossip, he had masterminded Calhoun's career and was a control freak who let no detail escape him. Although he was close to seventy, it was said he didn't intend to retire until Calhoun had made it all the way to the White House. "This is Chief Petty Officer Caleb—"

"The SEAL." Fairchild's lip actually curled. "How did you get up here? The cameras only showed a woman on the stairs."

The corner of Caleb's mouth quirked with lazy mischief. "And yet, here I am."

Why was he goading Fairchild? Emmie felt her knees get weak again. She was a terrible liar, but she'd already noted that Caleb was a skillful one. If Fairchild questioned her, she didn't know what she would say.

"Dr. Caddington." Fairchild turned flinty eyes her way. "I considered your grandmother a friend, so I can believe you didn't mean to trespass. But if this man comes into this house again, by any means, he will be arrested."

"No, wait!" Vicky, who had been watching the interchange between the adults, protested. "It was all—"

"Quiet, Vicky," Fairchild snapped. "I'm not pleased with you either. I will have to explain to your mother your part in this. You should not have admitted this man to your room, and you know it. You should have informed security there were unauthorized people on the second floor." He opened the door to the hall. "Escort Dr. Caddington and this man to the door," he told the security guard who waited there. "Do not admit him to this house again, and if you see him anywhere near it, inform the police."

"No, wait!" Vicky barred the door with her body. "Please. It isn't fair. I'll tell—"

Caleb touched her lightly on the arm. "Move out of the way, Little Bit." At her mulish expression, he grinned. "You've got guts, but don't get into more trouble, okay? It was nice to meet you."

Chapter 23

"That went well, don't you think?" Emmie, tongue in cheek, broke the silence just as they turned the corner for the final leg of the trip back to Emmie's little house. "That was the first time someone ever saw me to the door *in order to make sure I left.*"

"There's a saying in special operations. Every operation goes to shit thirty seconds after it hits the ground. I'm sorry you got caught in the splash."

Emmie waved his apology away with one fine-boned hand. "If I'm never invited to their house again, I'll be relieved. I told you before, the association was with my grandmother. But it just doesn't seem right for you to be declared *persona non grata* when, really, they should be hailing you as a hero. And we only went so you could see Uncle Teague, and you didn't even get a chance to talk to him."

Do-Lord looked down at the woman walking beside him. The wind, no longer blocked by houses because they were on a street perpendicular to the river, was stronger. The breeze floated silvery pale strands of her hair, emphasizing the fey qualities of her face.

It also played with that teasing, flirty opening down the front of her red dress. He was fairly well convinced it wasn't going to open and reveal her legs, and yet he couldn't stop watching it—just in case it did.

She really was incensed on his behalf. From the first he'd seen her loyalty and her willingness to go to bat for a friend.

It felt strange to have loyalty given to him—especially when he knew he hadn't earned it—strange, but kind of warm, too.

"Forget it."

"I don't want to forget it. It isn't fair."

"In case you haven't noticed, life isn't fair."

"It's true *life* isn't, but people can be. To say life isn't fair when it's *people* who make decisions not to treat people evenhandedly is a cop out. Mr. Fairchild made it clear that he was treating me like I was somebody, and you, like you were… I don't know—" Emmie shrugged impatiently. "A criminal or something."

The sky had clouded over, bringing on an early dusk, and no longer sheltered by houses, they could feel the full force of the breeze from the river.

Emmie crossed her arms over her chest and shivered. "It's getting chilly. It's warm when the sun is out, but as soon as it starts to go down, you're reminded this is December."

Do-Lord pulled off his sport coat and draped it over her shoulders. Curling his fingers into the lapels, he tugged her closer. Her wide blue eyes regarded him with curiosity and more than a hint of feminine anticipation.

The kiss they'd shared earlier had hummed between them ever since, tingling across nerve endings, sharpening his every sense until the importance of anything, *anything but her,* disappeared.

"Forget it, I said. It's not important." It certainly wasn't important right now. For today, he had done all he could in his quest for justice for his mother. His desire for Emmie was unrelated to his pursuit of Calhoun, and from now on, he didn't want Emmie involved.

Compartmentalizing was something every SEAL learned to do. Right now, it took no effort to stuff thoughts of Calhoun away. Desire flowed, hot and thick, deep in his center, and his heart beat in slow thuds. The only endeavor he wanted to focus on at this moment was kissing her.

"I want to kiss you." He outlined her lips with his forefinger. "But the rest of what I want to do could get us arrested, if we do it in public." When his finger brushed the corner of her mouth she… *shimmered.* It was the only word he knew for the tiny tremors of desire he felt flow through her. She was so responsive, as if she was already tuned to his frequency. "Be advised: once I start kissing you, I'm not going to stop."

His words, a promise and a warning, echoed in Emmie's head as they continued down the street. Christmas lights, twinkling red and green on porches, white lights outlining bare branches, punctuated the dusk of December nightfall, and the breeze wafted smells of supper cooking. By the time they arrived at Emmie's house she was shivering constantly, but whether from cold or anticipation or trepidation, she couldn't have said.

She wouldn't have said she had ever taken sex lightly. No one raised by her grandmother could embrace an *if it feels good, do it* philosophy. It hadn't been like this though. Not this heart- pounding, palm-sweating, breathless knowledge that she was diving over a cliff, and she was going to find out she really could fly, or she was going to crash horribly—and there was every possibility she would do both.

A blast of self-honesty showed her she'd chosen men in the past with whom she didn't expect sexual attraction to be part of the equation. She and they had been far more buddies than lovers. She had looked at how little she had asked of those relationships and determined to ask for more. In the past few minutes she had begun to understand how little the relationships had required of *her*.

She had set out very deliberately to attract Caleb, and she had succeeded more emphatically than she had dreamed of, or prepared for. When she had asked him for commitment, he had agreed so readily she'd been suspicious.

However, she had seen at the Calhoun house that he could make lightning decisions, give his word instantly, and then abide by it—even when there was cost to himself. He could have ingratiated himself with Calhoun by telling on Vicky, and some people would say he should have. She'd had a lifetime of watching people who swore allegiance to moral positions, but whose scruples dissolved the instant they had something to lose or gain.

Integrity. That's what she saw in him. He might not be a person who played by the rules, but promises he made, he would keep.

He had pocketed her keys after locking the door behind them when they set off, and now he drew them out as they went up the two shallow steps to her porch. In seconds he had the door open and was drawing her through it, into the deeper dusk inside, and into his warm embrace. At the sudden heat Emmie shivered even more violently.

"I haven't been taking very good care of you," he murmured in his burnt umber voice, as his hands chaffed her arms in long smooth strokes. "I let you get cold. I should have insisted on driving or made you wear a coat."

"I haven't been taking very good care of you," Do-Lord whispered, pulling her slight form closer. That she could use a caretaker he didn't doubt. She seemed so direct and guileless, a real lamb among the wolves. It was hard to imagine how she made her way in the world.

He had surprised himself a little, when he'd suggested marriage earlier. It wasn't the kind of relationship it was ever smart to tease about. Do-Lord was a man capable of learning from other's mistakes. He'd seen for himself that marriage didn't work for most SEALs. He knew men who were paying alimony to as many as three ex-wives. He'd always assumed if he ever got married, and he figured he would, it would be after his twenty years was up. It hadn't been a hard decision to stick to. Some men were prone to fall in love. Some weren't. And yet, when she rejected the idea of marriage, he'd felt as much disappointment as relief.

His whole plan for breaching Calhoun's defenses depended on having other people see them as a pair. Today though, he'd had a small taste of what being a couple with Emmie would feel like, and the funny thing was, he could imagine himself married to her. Where she gave her loyalty, she would give it without stint. He could have her always with him. Always on his side. He could imagine coming home to a house that smelled like her. Logging on at the end of the day and finding an email from her.

He thought he understood now what the attraction to falling in love was.

He slid his hands under the jacket he'd placed around her shoulders and let it fall unheeded to the floor. He found the crook of her shoulder with his lips. "How's your shoulder?"

"A little stiff. I start physical therapy next week. Until then, I follow the rule of: 'Keep your hands where you can see them.'"

"Okay." He moved from the slight coolness of her cheek to the crook of her shoulder on the other side. "So no putting your hands above your head or behind your back. I can work with that. Anything else I need to know?"

"Wait." Emmie squirmed away. "Why are you asking? What's going on?"

"What do you think I mean?" Do-Lord laughed in disbelief, letting her pull away, but not outside arm's reach. "You know where this is going. We've both been ready for hours."

Emmie blushed, her clear white skin suffused with rosy color. "Well, yes, but… You know when you asked me earlier if there was anything else? I knew there was, but I couldn't think of it. But I just remembered. We can't. Really. Not yet."

"Why the hell not?" He sounded testy. Hell, he *was* testy. No meant no. A girl didn't have to have a reason, but he couldn't believe he had read her so wrong. And this was the second time she'd called a halt, when he'd thought all the signals were go.

Emmie gave him her wide-eyed look. "Pickett says women shouldn't have sex on the first date." She thought. Visibly. "I can't remember if she said *men* could have sex on the first date"—her brow cleared—"but I think the rule would be the same for men, don't you?"

All the blood must have left his brain to fill his groin. Pickett, first date—he couldn't even think of where to start. "Pickett?"

Emmie nodded sagely. "Pickett is smart about people. She's usually right about these things."

His mind was clearing. "But this isn't our first date. We've seen each other several times."

"You mean at all the parties before the wedding? That didn't count. We were together there whether we wanted to be or not. It's not like you asked me."

"Could I talk you into making an exception to Pickett's rule? Just this once?"

Emmie looked at him a long time, an expression he couldn't read in her eyes. "Yes, you probably could."

Shit. Why couldn't she be flirty and silly like most girls? Why couldn't she act teasing and sexy and make it clear she was going for a good time?

Because she wasn't like other women, that's why. Over and over he'd watched her react to events in a way that was completely her own. He noticed a warm feeling in his chest and an upward pull on his lips as if he wanted to smile, though only a damn fool would be smiling at a moment like this. He should be acting on the advantage she just told him he had—any SEAL worth his salt would. A SEAL motto was: "Never fight fair."

He carefully pushed a strand of pale hair behind her

ear. For many years he hadn't desired the trust of anyone except another SEAL.

The room was warm and dusky. The last rays of the setting sun coming through the plantation shutters painted gold stripes on the wall, while shadows in the rest of the room deepened.

His hand, which had never left her waist, seemingly without any direction from him, reflexively stroked and kneaded the curve of her hip. The soft wool of the dress slid over the satin lining, and underneath that he could feel the warm supple flesh he craved.

If he won now, she would regret it later. He didn't think he could stand that. Slowly, slowly, he withdrew his hand and let it fall to his side.

Emmie rinsed her hands far longer than necessary before she finally met her own eyes in the bathroom mirror. Her face looked as strange as she felt, which wasn't reassuring. Her eyelids were lower than usual, the pupils large and unfocused. Her lipstick was gone, and her lips looked softer. Color that had nothing to do with makeup glowed under the skin of her cheeks. This business of being captain of her fate wasn't easy. And her timing was atrocious. What on earth had made her decide to become less passive, more self-determined, just when she found a man she could safely turn everything over to? She could let him set the pace, and he'd make it good.

All day long she'd looked at how passive she'd been, and it had made her a little queasy—because she wasn't that way! Not in any area of her life except the most personal. Now that she had seen it, she couldn't go back, though she had no idea where the road forward would take her.

Emmie had doubted her place in the world since the day her missionary parents had sent her "home" to Wilmington, North Carolina, a place she'd never been. No promises to be good or to put the mission work first, either to them or to God, had changed the outcome. On the twenty-eight hour flight halfway across the world, her tears had dried. With her extraordinary capacity for logical thought, evident even then, she'd accepted that their work was essential. She was an extra in their lives.

Consumed with bitter homesickness, Emmie's first year was made hideous by her fear for her parents' lives and her resentment of their dedication, mixed as it was with guilt because she couldn't accept God's will. These feelings were complicated by burgeoning hormones and fascinations she was at a loss to explain. She doubled her prayers and study of the Bible, since her grandmother told her repeatedly all the answers she needed were there. When nothing seemed to change, she added fasting, since that was the method recommended by the Bible.

She grew thin… and then thinner. At first she liked the feeling of lightness, of emptiness. She liked the weakness and lethargy. She could drift through her days caring little about anything.

One day she fainted. There had been a couple of near misses, but she'd always averted them. On this day though, she was walking home from school one hot afternoon in May. Thunderclouds were massing behind the steeple of the Presbyterian church, making it glare white against the purple-black of the sky as if she should read a portent. Her heart began to pound in slow thuds, and sweat dampened her forehead. She pulled off her sweater, and when that didn't help, she unbuttoned her blouse to expose the long-sleeved T-shirt she'd taken to wearing to mask her shape and her thinness.

Drapes of gray Spanish moss, swaying under the approaching storm, dripped from the live oaks that shaded Market Street, intensifying her dizziness. Emmie knew she needed to sit down before her legs gave way. Wrought iron benches were placed at intervals in shady spots along the street, but the next one was too far. And anyway, the thought of passing out where these strangers could see her made her feel even sicker.

Just ahead, in the yard of an old white house, sat a huge hydrangea bush, five feet tall and just as wide. The sapphire blue flower heads, the size of soccer balls, glowed in the greenish light of the coming storm. In Emmie's disoriented state she thought the bush radiated strength and power. Her head spinning and the edges of her vision darkening, she staggered to it.

She couldn't have been unconscious long. Fat drops of rain stung her face and dampened her clothes when she became aware again, but she wasn't soaked. And she must have made it to the hydrangea because its musty-green scent filled her nostrils. Above her head a huge blue flower dipped and bounced with each drop that struck it.

All the anguish of the past year seemed to have dissolved in her last moments of consciousness, and for the first time since her parents had put her on the plane for the States, she simply existed where she was, not wishing she were somewhere else, not wishing for anything at all.

She discovered that the hydrangea blossoms were actually millions of tiny trumpet-shaped flowerets that spread into four blue petals around a lighter blue throat. Each floweret was lifted to its place by a pale blue stem finer than thread. This was her first experience with looking into the heart of life and her first experience of consciously seeing things the way they were, not the way she thought they were or wanted them to be.

A drop of rain pelted her square in the eye and snapped her away from her timeless contemplation, but some remnants of that moment of clarity, when for one instant she had seen past the illusions that dance on the surface of the world, remained.

The connection between fasting and lying beside a bush in the rain was as inescapable as a geometry proof. As an experiment in finding answers, fasting was an abysmal failure. She knew she would not do it again. Whether she would pray again remained to be seen, but she thought not.

Emmie tied her sweater over her head like a scarf and tucked her schoolbooks under her T-shirt, sucking in a breath when the clammy plastic covers touched the bare skin of her midriff. On wobbling legs she walked the rest of the way to her grandmother's house.

Emmie dried her hands and watched the woman in the mirror do the same. She hadn't thought about that day for years. Why had that memory come back now? It had been a wake-up call, a clear warning that she had to deal with problems herself, without help from her grandmother, her parents, or God.

Do-Lord wandered Emmie's living room while he waited for her to freshen up. It was going to take longer than he had thought to win her trust. He looked at the titles of the books open face down on her desk, carefully putting them back in the same order he found them. Her computer was in sleep mode, not turned off, and when he jostled the mouse, the screen lit. A little game he played was seeing if he could guess people's passwords. It was amazingly easy. Birthdays, pet names, favorite color, favorite rock group, birthplace—people mentioned them in conversation all the time. All he had to do was pay attention.

He frowned. He didn't know any of those personal details about Emmie. Where she was born. Where she grew up. What her parents' names were. She knew all the trivia about him, although she was the only person alive who did. He had created a fund of amusing stories, which he could recount by the hour. They were a smoke screen so others wouldn't notice he didn't talk about his origins. And yet, until this minute, he hadn't noticed that private information about *her* wasn't coming through. He doubted if her leaving out facts was as conscious as his. It was like she faded away behind her intellect.

On the other hand, he couldn't accuse her of keeping secrets. If he asked for her password, she'd probably tell him. Just like she'd told him he could get around her no-sex-on-the-first-date rule.

As it happened he didn't need the password to get into her files. A document titled "Remedial Conversational English" was open in the window. *Hello. Did you have a nice trip? Was the traffic heavy? It's nice to see you. Isn't it a nice day?*

Who had she been making this list for? Not herself. She didn't chatter, but she didn't have any problem holding up her end of a conversation. In fact, she was more interesting to talk to than—the thought broke off. Her first words at the door had been, "Not a pity fuck." It wasn't even close to, "It's nice to see you."

The pieces of the Emmie-puzzle he'd been assembling suddenly interlocked. He could see the picture emerging now. He had always seen that she was vulnerable. It had been so easy to see that it had blinded him to the truth. A lump rose in his throat. He understood what kept going wrong. What had been wrong all the time. Why all her signals seemed to be on *go,* and God knows *he* was ready, and then the moment would vanish. Poof. The problem was with him. He hadn't wanted to seduce her.

Not that he didn't want her. He did. Wanting her was like a toothache in his whole body. And it wasn't an excess of scruples that held him back. If he thought seduction would make her his, he'd do it. She was a plum ripe for the picking. He could do it. She was sending out come- hither signals clearly now. Even though she hadn't said an unequivocal *yes,* yet, it was only a matter of time. He had only to keep pushing her. And that's exactly what he couldn't do. Didn't want to do.

The trouble was, he wanted her to want *him.* The longing went too deep to have words to describe it, even to himself. If he pushed her, time's one-way door would swing shut, and he'd never know if *she* would have chosen him.

He knew what the trouble was, but damned if he could see what to do about it.

◈◈◈

Caleb tapped on the bathroom door. "Your phone is ringing."

Not ready to look at him yet, Emmie opened the door a crack and stuck her hand through.

Still regarding her reflection, Emmie flipped the phone open. "Dr. Caddington."

"Hey!" Pickett's voice came over the phone. "Did you turn your phone off and forget it again? I've been leaving you messages all afternoon."

"No—well, maybe yes." Emmie couldn't remember exactly what she'd done with her phone. "What did the messages say?"

"I want you to meet me at Aunt Lilly Hale's family reunion."

"I thought you weren't coming home until Christmas."

"I wasn't, but the last twenty-four hours have turned weird. Tyler's birthday is this weekend. Jax has had to go out of town." *Out of town* Emmie and Pickett had agreed was code for *doing something secret that couldn't be speculated about.* "And there was a letter in this morning's mail from Tyler's grandmother, Lauren—actually, from her lawyer."

"Bad news?" Lauren and Jax had been locked in a custody dispute over Tyler. Pickett and Jax had hoped their marriage would make the question of custody moot.

"I don't know whether it's bad or good. We haven't heard from his grandmother since the wedding. Before then, she was calling him two or three times a week. But the letter says she's gone into rehab. In the event of an emergency, we're to contact the lawyer."

"You mean she's gone for alcohol treatment? That sounds like good news."

"Well, it is, of course, and for Tyler's sake I hope she gets better, but it's too soon to get excited about the prospect. In the meantime, it's Tyler's birthday. His birth mother is dead, and both his father and his grandmother are incommunicado."

That was just like Pickett. She was thinking of how Tyler would feel on his first birthday after losing his birth mother. For Tyler's sake she was more than willing to maintain a relationship with a mother-in-law left over from Jax's first marriage. "Do you think she should have waited until after his birthday?"

"Not really. When a person is finally willing to seek treatment, it's important to act right then. I don't know if he'll be hurt if she doesn't call or send a present. He's really too little to have built up those expectations. The main reason for coming home is that Tyler enjoys having cousins so much, and he doesn't know many children here yet—"

"And you know you can trust your family to make a big deal over his birthday."

"Well, I can. Anyway, will you come too? Aunt Lilly Hale has already asked me if you're coming."

Grace had suggested she attend as a way of revealing her makeover to a friendly audience, but Emmie had let it slip her mind. Deliberately. She hadn't wanted to go if Pickett wouldn't be there. The habits of being unnoticeable were still strong, and she didn't think she could face the crowd, if her presence was about *her*. Anyway, the reveal, such as it was, had already happened.

Everything changed if Pickett was going to be there. "When is the family reunion?"

Pickett chuckled in fond exasperation. "Today, silly. That's why I've been calling you and calling you. I've got to see your new clothes. I've got an idea for a few items I think you should get. Grace's taste is infallible, but, you know, serious. You need some fun clothes too."

"Fun clothes? You mean sports clothes?"

"No. I mean apparel, the purpose of which is entertainment. That's a foreign concept for you, isn't it? I've got to admit I hadn't fully grasped the possibilities myself until Jax," Pickett added with a chuckle that was positively *sultry.*

More than ever, Emmie regretted that she hadn't been around for Jax and Pickett's courtship. This was a side of her friend she'd never seen before. Being in love had evidently brought out new elements in her Pickett's personality. There was a new kind of confidence about her, a deeply personal self-assurance. Emmie was a tiny bit shocked and a tiny bit envious.

"What kind of fun are we talking about here?"

Pickett giggled. "The kind you're thinking about. But also frivolous or provocative things—like you'd look great in high-heeled boots."

Emmie was on the verge of pointing out how utterly impractical high-heeled boots were when she got a picture of standing in front of Caleb wearing them. And nothing else. Her heart did a double backflip.

"Say you'll come, Emmie."

"I don't know. Caleb is here."

"Oh, that's right! So much has gone on here, I forgot today was *the* day. How did it go?"

"We went to the open house, but Caleb got thrown out."

"Is he there now?"

"He's in the living room."

"Where are you?"

"In the bathroom."

"Why are you in the—forget I asked that. This conversation has gone way off track. But now, you've got to come because I've got to hear the whole story, and I've got to tell you what I think sent Lauren into treatment."

Chapter 24

Caleb was in Emmie's big blue velour easy chair reading a book, his tie loosened, his shoes kicked off, his feet in coffee-brown socks propped on the ottoman, when Emmie returned to the living room. He had switched on the standing lamp behind the chair. The light brought out the gold in his reddish-brown hair and dwelt in loving lines along the planes and angles of his face. He wasn't handsome, and he never would be. He was beautiful. Her artist's eye noted the color composition, palest yellow shirt, tobacco brown slacks, deep blue chair.

His legs were crossed at the ankles, his elbow propped on the armrest, his head supported by the headrest. Light, reflected from the open book, limned the underside of his chin and found the golden fringe of his lashes. A buoyant lightness filled her chest as if something she had waited and waited for had at last transpired.

In a way she couldn't define, he had made the chair, the lamp, the corner of the room, *his,* and he looked completely at home there. Except for Pickett, not that many people entered Emmie's space, and as a rule she felt more at ease when they left it. From now on, the room wouldn't look quite right without him.

His eyes lit in welcome when he saw her. He held up the book so she could see the cover. "Asimov's *I, Robot.* I took it from your bookshelf. Hope you don't mind. It's one of my favorites." He moved his legs to one side on the ottoman in a clear invitation for her to perch there.

Emmie sank down on the low footrest. A faint, warm shock traveled through her when her hip came in contact with his crossed ankles. His toes, those long, strong, elegant rough-hewn toes stroked across her buttocks in what might have been an accidental settling, might have been a caress. Emmie was momentarily diverted, but his expression was so innocent she returned to the subject of the book.

"Mine too. I liked the three laws of robotics. I loved them so much I committed them to memory. 'One: A robot may not injure a human being or through inaction allow a human to come to harm. Two: A robot must obey a human's orders except where to do so would conflict with the first law. Three: A robot must protect its own existence except where to do so would violate rules one or two.' In the stories, the robots must make moral choices within a nested hierarchy of values."

"Unh-unh." Caleb shook his head. "The robots weren't acting morally. They're machines. The three rules were a design function to make them harmless."

Again, she felt a stroking movement of his toe near the small of her back. This time she caught the playful gleam that accompanied it.

"True. Nevertheless, as the three rules are weighted, they are a perfect, logical encapsulation of Christian ideals."

His smile left "interested" and shaded into "indulgent." "Do you think anyone lives by them?"

"My parents do. The first law of robotics summarizes the commandment to love one another and the Golden Rule. The second rule is about service. My parents' life purpose is to serve, and their obedience is to the laws of God."

"What happens when Biblical commandments conflict with the first law? The Old Testament requires the faithful to stone people for everything from wearing the wrong clothes to sassing their mama."

"Right. Deuteronomy 22:5 and Exodus 21:17—although your translation is extremely loose." Emmie rolled her eyes. "My parents are *Christians,* not 4000 BC desert nomads. *Christ's* commandment was: 'love one another.' It supersedes all the others."

"How about looking after themselves?"

"They would say self-maintenance is incumbent upon Christians—the body is a temple and all that—but they believe it comes third. The first two are much more important. I think I loved the book because at last I could see the logic on which they based their lives."

"The logic? Not the faith?"

"Faith didn't work for me. I hated that they had sent me to live with my grandmother. I knew they loved me, but it was a paradox. If they loved me, why didn't my happiness matter? If I couldn't stay with them, why didn't they come to the States *with* me?"

"Why *did* they send you to America?"

"Two people with our mission were kidnapped and held for ransom by terrorists. They were targeted because they were Americans. My parents sent me to live with my grandmother for my safety.

"*I, Robot* put the choices they made into a framework I could understand. For my parents, the first law meant they needed to stay and minister, despite possible harm to themselves. However, they could not, through inaction, allow me to come to harm. Anyway, I was a typical self-absorbed teenager. I wanted them to be dedicated to *me,* not to God."

Emmie laughed. Until this moment she'd never seen it from this perspective exactly.

His eyes were gold again. The angles of his cheeks softened, and his lips, those shapely, full, firm-looking Brad Pitt lips, opened in an unconscious smile. He wrapped one hard hand around her upper arm, tugging her forward, lifting her onto his lap. "I don't think you've ever been typical in any way."

He tucked her left arm between them and settled her right hand on his shoulder so that her arm was completely supported when he leaned her against his chest. "Shoulder okay?" he murmured. Instead of kissing her as she expected, with smooth strokes he molded her until she relaxed against him with her head on his shoulder.

Emmie nodded, her eyes suddenly hot and wet. Emmie had encountered his strength before. She'd seen the smooth confidence with which he moved her body when he needed to. No matter that she still wasn't sure how much she trusted him—at some point her body had decided it trusted his. Pickett had told her repeatedly to become more aware of how she was being treated. He wasn't dominating her as he'd done before when he'd buckled her seat belt. She couldn't yield though until she understood… something.

"What are you doing?" she asked.

A soundless chuckled moved his diaphragm. "Holding you."

"Oh. Why?"

"Because I wanted to."

"Is that a good enough reason?"

"*Emmie.* Stop trying to figure out the regulations for what's happening between us."

Was that what she was doing? From the first she'd been a little afraid of him, sensing he wasn't a man who would be easily kept in his place. Time had proved her right. She hadn't successfully managed him. At every point he had been doing what he wanted to, what he saw fit to do, and as she had expected, *she* hadn't been the reason.

"And don't ask me what *is* happening," he said, apparently having read her mind. "All I know is I went looking for my father and found you. That's enough for now."

Enough for now. The words moved around in his mind as if he was deep in a forest, and they were echoes tossed from tree to tree, sometimes right beside him, sometimes impossibly distant. After a while they fragmented, became softer…

Something had changed. Something that defied every bit of her experience (albeit limited) with men. Despite his protests that he had pulled her in his lap because he wanted to hold her, Emmie had expected him to make love. She had waited, and waited, trying not to control what he was doing. But she did like to understand the goal, and his response indicated there wasn't one, which wasn't entirely satisfactory. And then—she wouldn't have believed it if it hadn't happened to her—he had fallen asleep.

Draped across him as she was, the sensation of moving with his breath was almost like floating, and when he didn't do anything… and didn't do anything… she had been lulled into deeper and deeper relaxation. When eventually she had realized that his breath had become deep and regular and he might be asleep, she hadn't known whether to laugh or to cry. She'd had plenty of experience with men who couldn't get rid of her fast enough when they learned she wouldn't put out, but if he could ignore the fact that she was there and go to sleep even with her on his lap, she was insignificant indeed.

On the other hand, she'd noticed how much of the smiling ease with which he approached life was in fact ironclad self-control. He was miles from the swaggering jocks with their sense of entitlement and unwillingness to take seriously anything that didn't directly impact their own egos. She was a little ashamed of herself for ever having thought that of him. This afternoon she'd become aware that there was a price for the seeming ease with which he managed and mastered every situation. Maybe the bill had come due, and he was simply exhausted.

The arm under her was going numb, but she didn't want to move lest she wake him. It was a small enough courtesy to give the man a few minutes of peace. She was mastering his lexicon of smiles, but she'd never seen his face in repose. He'd sighed deeply and expertly shifted her so that the pressure on her arm was relieved. She was disappointed a few minutes later when he removed the hand on her hip to look at his watch.

He opened his eyes. Outside the broad slats of the white plantation blinds, night had fallen. He must have dozed for a minute.

Funny, he couldn't remember the last time he had dozed off, accidentally, without preparing himself for sleep first. He wasn't good at going to sleep, period. He'd never gotten the hang of power-napping, as some guys could, sleeping for ten or fifteen minutes wherever they were, no matter how noisy or bright or uncomfortable.

He'd survived as a SEAL only because he required less sleep than most. Through meditation he could achieve profound relaxation that allowed his body to rest, while he remained alert. He lifted his left arm from where it rested on Emmie's hip to check his watch. He'd only been out a few minutes. That he had done it while holding Emmie on his lap defied imagination.

"Are you awake now?" she asked.

"Um-hmm." He felt ridiculously good, and when he put his hand back down, he felt even better. The flap in her skirt—the flap that had teased him and tantalized him all afternoon—had come open. His hand encountered the silky mesh of her hose. He was instantly as alert, as fully conscious, as he had ever been in his life. And as hard. But there were some particulars he needed to know first. "When's your birthday?"

"February 16." Suddenly, Emmie sat up straight. "Birthday! I forgot."

"Whose birthday?"

"Tyler's. That was Pickett on the phone. I'm supposed to ask you, instead of going out to dinner, would you be willing to go to Aunt Lilly Hale's family reunion? It's like a Christmas party she throws every year."

"Tonight?" All the plans he had made for an intimate dinner to set the mood, a little wine, and then back to Emmie's cottage, disappeared. He couldn't think of much he wanted less than to make conversation with people he didn't know in the huge formal rooms of Lilly Hale's house. He wanted Emmie. Needing to have her was getting close to an obsession.

"Yes. She wants me to meet her there." She looked at his face, which he knew wasn't radiating joy. "Forget it. I'm sure a family party of people you don't know doesn't sound like a fun time. You don't have to go." She started to scoot of his lap. "I hope you'll excuse me from dinner with you."

"Wait a minute," he anchored her hips in place. "Yeah, I'd rather have an evening alone with you—a chance for us to talk—yeah, talk, not the other four-letter word. But if this is what you want to do…"

"Usually, it wouldn't be. But I've seen so little of Pickett lately. We've talked on the phone, but it isn't the same."

"This isn't for Pickett, it's for you? You want to see her?" Emmie nodded. He gently helped her off his lap. "Stand up for a second. I need to get my cell phone. I left it in my jacket pocket." He punched in numbers and in a distant part of the house, Emmie's phone warbled. A look of confusion appeared between her brows. "Your phone is ringing," he told her. "You left it in the bathroom."

Chapter 25

EMMIE PADDED IN HER STOCKINGED FEET THROUGH THE kitchen and the bedroom. She had to turn on the light in the bathroom. The phone was on the lip of the tub.

What kind of game was Caleb playing now? She was asking for a sudden change in plans, and she'd been a little disappointed when Caleb wouldn't go along, but not surprised. Blount had never wanted to do anything that was her idea—blowing her off for the faculty dinner wasn't out of character—she should have expected it. And he'd sneered more than once at what he called her "country cousins."

She and Pickett had sworn they would keep their friendship strong, and if that meant going off and leaving Caleb, she would.

"Hello," she said.

"Is this Emmie?" Caleb enquired, for all the world as if he hadn't expected she would answer her own phone.

Emmie swallowed a surprised laugh and played along. "Yes, it is." Phone to her ear, she started back to the living room.

"This is, your friend, Caleb."

"Yes, Caleb." Emmie suppressed another giggle and added with dry understatement, "I had guessed it was you."

"There's a party at Miss Lilly Hale's house tonight. I'd like to go, but I don't have a date. I was wondering if you'd go with me?"

The sheer sweetness stopped her in the doorway to the living room. If he'd said, "Okay, I'll go with you," never in a million years would she have trusted that he was doing anything but placating her. His back was to her. He was touching items on her desk in one of the few aimless gestures she'd seen him make. "Yes," she whispered past the yearning that threatened to close off her throat. "I'd love to."

He must have known she was there, but he kept his back to her. "Do you want me to pick you up?"

Emmie thought they were done. Why was he carrying it further? "Pick me up? You're standing in my living room." She closed her phone. "Caleb, what is this about?"

He turned around, clipping the phone to his belt. "It's called multitasking. We'll go to the party. We'll go because you want to see Pickett. But I want it to be perfectly clear—you're going with *me* because I just asked you for a date, and you accepted. Even if you spend the whole evening talking to Pickett—this counts as our second date."

"Sit tight." Caleb pushed the gear lever into park and shut off the engine. "I'll come around and get you." It wasn't a suggestion. She had asked for this. Put that man anywhere near a four-wheel drive vehicle, and every alpha trait he had came to the fore. He pressed the latch of her seat belt before she could reach it. In the glow of the delayed turn-off headlights, she thought she caught a trace of a smirk.

He opened her door.

At least a token protest was called for. "I'm perfectly capable of climbing down myself."

"I know you are. Lean forward." He grasped her waist. Emmie was used to the casual strength with which he picked her up, but he didn't set her on her feet. Instead he pulled her flush with his body.

Her breasts brushed his chest as he slowly let her down.

"You're using this as an excuse to cop a feel!"

"Right."

"You're taking advantage of me."

"You sound surprised."

"I thought you were doing the 'man has to be in charge' thing."

He tugged one of her curls. "Think multitasking." The corners of his Brad Pitt lips dug deeper into his cheeks. "The two aren't mutually exclusive."

Golden oblongs of light streamed the promise of welcome and warmth from every window of Aunt Lilly Hale's house into December's early dark. Emmie pulled her coat closer. Damp wind chased leaves across the sandy driveway. Because they were late, Caleb had to park almost at the highway.

He bent and put his lips to her ear. "Look." He pointed to the edge of the field where a drainage ditch divided the field from the road. "Deer. Five of them."

"Aunt Lilly Hale says that during hunting season they actually come onto her lawn, right up to the house, in daylight. They know no one will shoot that close to the house."

One of the larger deer raised its head. In less than one second they vanished so completely it was difficult to believe they had been there.

Emmie slipped her hand into his. Her fingers were

a little cool, the bones tiny. His eyes prickled. He had been the sexual aggressor, and yeah, aggressor was the right word. He'd gone after her without a lot of concern for the impact he would have on her life. She had always responded, but except for the beginning when she'd grabbed his arm and dragged him into the small office, she had never touched him first. An odd pride filled his chest that somewhere in this day she had given him this much trust.

Emmie led him around the house to a back door. "Nobody uses the front door."

"What do you mean? Everybody used it at the breakfast."

"That wasn't a family gathering. That was social. Different rules." Emmie led him up a short flight of brick steps and onto a screened porch. Without knocking, she opened a glass door decorated with a spray of pine boughs gathered with a large red bow.

They entered to cries of, "Hey, look who's here," and an olfactory blast of roasting turkey and sage, tangy cranberry, cinnamon, yeasty rolls, and an oddly refreshing resiny smell coming from pine boughs stuck everywhere. There was also the smell of a lot of people. American people.

Every place had a smell, and the people in a country also had a discreet, recognizable odor. He'd left Afghanistan months ago but he was still was surprised sometimes to smell a bunch of Americans in one place.

"Don't get hung up on expectations," he'd told trainees. "Once you're inserted, it's never the way you thought it would be, and even if you've been there before, it's never the way it was."

He knew better, but he'd fallen for his expectations.

He'd anticipated a low-key, decorous gathering. Not this. The kitchen was a surging mass of people, colors, sounds, and smells, and calls for consultation shouted above the noise of a mixer.

Underneath it all was the smell of the house. He remembered it from before. There was a certain smell all old houses had in common. Old wood, old wool, old dust—no matter how clean. This one had that smell. But he also thought it smelled like stability, lives lived to completion, and kindness, sweet and dark and rich and complex.

At the stove in conversation with other cooks, Miss Lilly Hale, a large poinsettia-printed apron over her sweater and slacks, heard the commotion and turned around. "Do-Lord, I'm so glad you're here!" She held out her arms in clear expectation of a hug.

Do-Lord had one of those "where the hell am I?" moments. Everybody had them. They could be scary seconds of disorientation when waking up in a strange place. Or Zen moments in which the juxtaposition of the familiar into the unfamiliar produces an awakening when you suddenly find it remarkable that *you* are *here.* It could totally derail one's focus, which usually wasn't good. It could also make perception hyperclear. A person suddenly knew how remarkable, special, and singular this particular instant is.

Of all the things he'd ever done, hugging an old lady wasn't one. He wasn't sure what he should get hold of her by. He stepped closer, and her arms came around his middle and squeezed while he tried to reason where he could safely put his hands. Lilly Hale Sessoms was a substantial woman, so he was surprised at how little she felt, and how fragile. And peculiarly soft. Not flabby. But like some crucial binder that keeps flesh together was breaking down. He didn't dare squeeze her. He settled for placing his hands lightly on her shoulder blades until she let go of him.

As she pulled away her gray curls brushed the underside of his chin, and his throat tightened around a strange lump. And the world settled back into ordinary reality.

After a few exchanges of ritual greeting phrases, Lilly Hale twinkled, so obviously sizing him up it was impossible to take offense, and said, "I expect you're a very useful young man."

"Yes, ma'am, that I am."

"I need someone to set up the children's table in the family room. I have to leave it until the last minute. Come with me."

She led him through the crowd spilling into the wide hall. Pickett's sisters Grace and Sarah Bea and their husbands were there, along with others he had met at the wedding. Occasionally, she stopped to introduce him.

"Charles," she said, to a twitchy, hunted-looking young man of about sixteen. "Chief Dulaude is going to set up the tables for me. Will you help him?"

In a few minutes he understood why Miss Lilly Hale had assigned him to the table detail and designated Charles as his helper. In short order, three teenage boys who had been hanging out with teen-angst casualness in the hall, unwilling to align themselves with the children in the family room or the older adults in the parlors, appeared. Two he recognized were Grace's sons, and one, he wasn't sure. That they wanted to hang out with a SEAL was clear. That they didn't want to align themselves with Charles, equally clear.

If there was one thing he knew how to do, it was get a bunch of young guys working together. "Hey, men." Do-Lord waved them over. "Give us a hand."

"Emmie! You're here!" Pickett carried a stack of linen napkins. She dropped them on a table and held out her arms.

"Pickett!"

Pickett held her at arm's length. "Wait a minute—I've got to look at you! Turn around. Oh, my, you look terrific!"

Emmie was glad she'd changed into her new charcoal blue slacks and lavender-blue woven silk sweater. She looked good. She was dressed just right, and there was nothing so satisfying, she suddenly discovered, as sincere compliments from a good woman friend.

Pickett's eyes were wide with wonder. "Emmie, what *happened?*'

Emmie laughed. "I finally noticed there was something missing from my life. Me."

Once the tables were set up and covered with white linen cloths, and chairs were fetched from various places around the house, they were summoned to the large double parlor where a grand piano had been opened.

Lilly Hale called for attention. "James," she announced indicating a scholarly-looking man in his fifties, "is going to read us the Christmas story from Luke. Then I've persuaded Hannah and Emmie to sing."

Children were shushed, and James opened the Bible and began to read. "And it came to pass in those days, a decree went out from Caesar Augustus that all the world should be taxed."

"And they came and found Mary and Joseph and the babe lying in a manger."

Charles took his seat at the piano. Emmie and Hannah, a dark-haired girl about fourteen, stood in the curve of the piano. Emmie squeezed Hannah's hand and nodded to Charles to begin. For all his youth, from the first notes, Charles played with unmistakable mastery. "Away in a manger…" Over the glistening notes of the piano, voices poured like silk, finding silver curves in the fabric of space—tracing them with their song. The simple joy of allowing music to manifest through them shone in three faces. They knew they had been given a glimpse of the mystery from which all life springs.

Chapter 26

"EMMIE," AUNT LILLY HALE DIRECTED, "I WANT YOU and Do-Lord to sit at an adult table. Pickett, you too. There are enough adults to supervise the children. Tyler will be fine with them."

In the double parlors, furniture had been pushed back and two dinner tables spread with snowy linen. To accommodate all the diners, chairs from every corner of the house had been pressed into service to augment the regular dining chairs—another job assigned to Do-Lord and his crew.

Caleb set his plate beside Emmie's, held her chair, and then Pickett's. He was ready to take his own seat when the doorbell rang.

"My goodness! That's the front door. Do-Lord, you're up." Lilly Hale said from her seat at the head of the table. "Would you answer it please?"

On the threshold stood Charlotte Calhoun and Vicky. As soon as she saw him, Vicky threw her arms around his waist. "You *are* here! I told Mother you would be." She pulled back, smiling tremulously. "I told. It wasn't fair for you to get in trouble when it was me."

Aunt Lilly Hale appeared behind Do-Lord. "Why Charlotte!" She quickly mastered her surprise. "How wonderful you could come. And little Vicky too. Vicky, the children are eating in the family room. Run on back."

"I hope we're not intruding," Charlotte apologized to Lilly Hale. "I know we sent regrets to your invitation, but we got free at the last minute. Vicky wanted to come so much."

Lilly Hale waved that away. "You're family. Of course, you're welcome. Let me take your coat, and Do-Lord will show you how to get to the dining room to serve yourself."

Vicky looked to her mother for permission and at her nod ran down the corridor.

"This way," he said, leading Charlotte into the hall. "With so many tables set up, there's only one path open to the food."

When they were out of earshot, she stopped him. "I'm so grateful you were there this afternoon. I had to come and thank you after Vicky told me what happened. I'm sorry you had a run in with Mr. Fairchild. He wasn't speaking for me or my husband. You will always be welcome in our house. Vicky is… she's a handful."

Do-Lord shook his head. "She's resourceful, that's for sure."

"I want to do something for you—"

"Thank you, ma'am. Nothing is required." When he saw she was ready to protest he added, "Really ma'am." He let his voice harden into a command. "The less said the better."

Charlotte acquiesced with a nod that said she was only temporarily agreeing. "I hope you will at least come to dinner. My husband never got a chance to speak to you and welcome you into our home."

"Thank you for making Charlotte feel at home. She is family, on her mother's side, and ever since they moved to Wilmington she's been invited to my Christmas dinner, but she's never come." Lilly Hale was in full spate. Do-Lord let the comfortable sound drift around him and didn't worry about needing to reply. If she wanted him to say something, she'd tell him. "Charlotte told me Vicky insisted they come tonight. I understand that Charlotte and Teague lead busy lives, but I'm glad to see she's finally taking her responsibility to make sure Vicky knows her cousins seriously. My late husband, Garson, used to complain about all the fuss. And I'd say to him, 'Garson, a family is not something that just happens, you must build it.' I started having this party when our children were grown and had moved away from here. I saw that the grandchildren were growing up not understanding how they were related. This is the homeplace."

"Are all these people kin?"

"I always invite some dear friends who have become honorary family members—like Emmie. After all, a family doesn't *begin* with blood ties. A family starts with ties of the heart."

"Aunt Lilly Hale," one of the women working at the sink called, holding up a bowl and saucer all made into one, "can this gravy boat go in the dishwasher?"

"Yes, oh, and Grace, be sure to count the silver before it's put away." Emmie and Grace, who were drying a mountain of silver utensils, traded a secret smile.

"I saw that." The matriarch laughed. "You're too young to remember the Christmas eve we sifted garbage at 10:00 p.m. looking for one of the silver forks."

"Oh, Lord, Mama, I remember." The fiftyish woman married to the James who had read from the Bible, looked up from the leftovers she was organizing. "It was *cold,* and you made Daddy put the garbage barrels—the humongous oil drums we used back then—on the pickup and drive them up to the house where there was enough light. You made every one of us children spread the garbage out in pans on the porch there. Daddy was cussing a blue streak. But you said the fork was in the garbage, and you were right."

"After that I made a rule that no garbage could be carried from the house until all the silver was accounted for."

The exchanges had the well-worn feel of a story that had been told over and over. Strophe and antistrophe, everyone knew the words, knew what came next, and the different voices flowed together so seamlessly it was like a story told in chorus.

"And you made sure you taught all your daughters—"

"And daughters-in-law—"

"And granddaughters—"

"And nieces—"

"And great-nieces—"

"And great-great nephews," said Grace's son, returning a chair to its place at the kitchen table.

"Let me show you the we room we added when my mother came to live with us," Lilly Hale told Do-Lord conversationally.

"Sit down," she commanded in a steely tone as soon as they were in a large bedroom. She took a chair and indicated he should sit on the bed. "It's probably too soon to ask this, but I no longer have as much time as I once did. Old ladies are allowed much more latitude than young women to be rudely inquisitive," she explained. "I take shameless advantage of it."

He didn't like the feeling that he was being called to account for his actions. He didn't like it one bit. Still, Do-Lord had to smile at her charm.

She folded her hands in her lap and leveled him with an uncompromising look. "How serious are you about Emmie?"

"I'm ready to be as serious as she wants me to be."

"And Emmie?" she prodded. "How does she feel?"

Do-Lord decided to push back. "Why don't you ask her?"

"Because I'm asking you." She tapped the upholstered arm of her chair with one gnarled finger. She relented a little. "Emmie is sensitive. I don't wish to embarrass her or make her self-conscious."

She had given a little. He could give a little. "I haven't won her over to my way of thinking yet. But I'm going to try."

She digested that without comment. "Do you have a family?"

"My mother is dead."

A trace of sympathy flickered in her eyes, but her expression didn't soften. "And your father?"

"Was never in the picture."

"He was not married to your mother."

"No, ma'am."

"And you were raised without a father's guidance." He'd never thought of it in exactly that way. There was no need to reply. The facts spoke for themselves.

"People who have been raised without family ties do not always grasp family values. I suspect that new husband of Pickett's doesn't. However, Pickett is quite strong. She understands how a family functions and dysfunctions." Lilly Hale smiled at her little joke. "She'll set him straight."

Do-Lord was suddenly confused. Unless he was mistaken, Pickett's sister Lyle was a lesbian. Jax didn't have a problem with that. "Do you mean like trying to keep homosexuals away from kids?"

"Pshaw!" Do-Lord hadn't heard the old-fashioned exclamation since he was a kid. It made him feel connected to the old lady—like she was somebody he'd known a long time. "Some people act like homosexuals only recently moved into society. They have *always* been among us. Always been one of us. Let me tell you, if congregations eliminated their homosexual members, the music programs of three-fourths of the churches in this state would collapse. It was true seventy years ago, and it's true today."

"So, which family values do you mean?"

"Kindness, devotion to one another's well-being, respect, and responsibility for teaching the children as well as guarding them from harm. And heaping amounts of forgiveness and tolerance. Especially the last. Families are made up of human beings, not saints. We are weak, selfish, and shortsighted much of the time, and we make mistakes as often as we get it right."

Lilly Hale came out of lecture mode and gave him a weary smile. "You are close to the height of your physical and mental powers with the natural arrogance of youth. You don't believe me. You think you're different. My boy—" On her lips the words sounded like a real endearment. "There will be times when you fail the people you love most."

Against his will, he thought of how he had endangered Jax and his team. And of his mother, lying so still, so silent, so beautiful, where the red light of the setting sun touched her hair.

"The values that I'm talking about demand we search our own conscience, not the conscience of others. These are the values that constantly invite us up to a higher standard. And forgive us, and comfort us when we inevitably fail. These are the values that nourish love. They will allow a family to flourish in the good times and survive the bad times."

She had gone back into lecture mode. Still, he was listening. Against his will, but listening. He thought of what he had promised Emmie. "What about fidelity and loyalty?"

"They are good to have," she allowed.

"But?"

"In the bad times, they will not be enough."

They were silent a minute. "We've been absent a long while," she said at last. "Give me your hand. This chair is too low. Always was."

She didn't release his arm even after she was standing. Instead, she leaned on it as they made their way back to the noise and crowd. She halted him in the hallway, behind the stairs. "What is your given name?" she asked out of the blue.

"Caleb."

"What did your mother call you?"

"That. Caleb."

"It's a good name. Caleb was one of the two Israelite spies who told the truth. All the other spies lied because they didn't have the courage to go forward. They didn't want to face what must be faced to reach the Promised Land.

"Caleb," she said as she resumed walking, "I imagine Pickett's mother will want Emmie to come home for Christmas, especially if Pickett doesn't come. If she does, why don't you plan to come and stay with me? My children are all middle-aged and dull and mistakenly believe they're supposed to raise me now. I'll enjoy having a young person around."

Do-Lord put the truck's wipers on their lowest setting to deal with the heavy dew that kept condensing on the windshield. The foil-covered leftovers he'd placed on the floor behind his seat filled the cab with fragrant reminders of the feast they had left.

"Did you and Pickett get to talk?" he asked Emmie.

"Uh-huh. We crept upstairs by ourselves for a few minutes. It felt good to talk. How about you? I saw you and Aunt Lilly Hale go off together," she teased. "Did she manage to have her wicked way with you?"

"I fought her off. Told her I'd promised to be loyal and faithful to you." He took one hand from the wheel to squeeze her shoulder. "Hey, I didn't know you could sing." Do-Lord cut off her disclaimers. "One of Pickett's sisters told me you'd never been willing to sing before. Why tonight?"

"Aunt Lilly Hale is so thrilled to have two great-grandchildren who are musical. I knew she wanted them to perform, but they're both at awkward stages. So I said

I would as a gift to their great-grandmother and asked them to help me. And, of course, they *wanted* to—if someone would make it legitimate."

"If someone would assume leadership."

"Have you ever seen such gifts? Aren't they incredible? Hannah's voice hasn't matured to its full resonance yet, but when it does…"

"Is that why you had Hannah sing the last verse solo?"

"Not entirely. I can't sing the last verse. Literally. When I come to 'Be near me Lord Jesus/ I ask Thee to stay/ Close by me forever/ and love me, I pray' I start choking up—" Her voice cracked. "—just like now. By the time I get to 'Bless all the dear children/ In Thy tender care' I can't croak out a note." Emmie sniffed and laughed self-consciously. "I can't believe I have such a sentimental streak, but there it is. My guilty secret."

Tender laughter threatened to stop his heart. She was so courageous, so unwilling to complain, he doubted if she knew what she had just revealed. She had laughed earlier about wanting her missionary parents to be dedicated to her, not to God. Emmie had been the twelve-year-old exile who begged for someone to stay with her forever and love her. With one hand he stroked the silken softness of her wet cheek.

Emmie laughed again and rubbed away the evidence of her vulnerability.

"Did you see the dishes set on the warming tray?" She changed the subject. "They were all gluten-free dishes prepared for Pickett. Dressing, rolls, gravy, everything! Pickett and I almost had a meltdown over that. We couldn't look at each other, or we'd start bawling."

"How did that happen?" Do-Lord thought he knew. He'd have to ask Jax the next time they popped a beer or two.

"I don't know whose idea it was. Several people said they had brought a dish and asked her how she liked it."

"Okay," Emmie asked after awhile. "Are we going to talk about Charlotte and Vicky showing up tonight?"

"Don't think so."

"Right."

After that they talked about the food. Do-Lord asked about people he had met. Together they wondered about relationships, retold funny incidents that had happened.

Sessoms Corner was about twenty miles off the interstate that would take them back to Wilmington. Theirs seemed to be the only car on the two-lane country road. The heavy moisture in the air thickened to patches of swirling mist and then to a drizzle, and their voices rose and fell against the slap-swish backbeat of the windshield wipers.

A fantasy stole into Caleb's mind. He was driving through a rainy night, driving home with Emmie, sleepy children in the backseat, talking about the party at Aunt Lilly Hale's… suddenly, not five feet from the car, there was a deer in the middle of the road—

He could see the upright ears and wide staring eyes of the deer so clearly. He braked hard enough to cause his shoulder harness to tighten. Time slowed. He felt the antilock brakes sense each wheel's traction on the wet surface and send more or less brake fluid. Things slid around on the backseat.

"Wha—?" Emmie said.

There was no deer in the road. For as far as the headlights could penetrate the silver curtain of rain, there wasn't any hazard on the shiny blacktop. But the feeling of time split in two continued. He ignored the inner voice (that was in what he knew was real time) yelling at him for letting his imagination run wild. He was in the *other* time. No power on earth would have made him let up on the brake, until the truck was stopped.

With a tiny *errk* the truck halted. The second it did, not five feet from the bumper, a large buck bounded onto the highway, followed immediately by two smaller deer. Something thumped onto the floor from the backseat. He hoped it wasn't the tinfoil-covered plate of leftovers.

Time went back to normal.

He had the truck moving again, its big motor purring, the tires swishing on the wet pavement, before Emmie broke her silence.

"How did you do that?" Intense curiosity vibrated in her tone, but not a trace of fear. "You stopped the truck *before* the deer appeared."

He could tell her he had great peripheral vision. She might believe it.

He could tell her the truth.

Some guys in the teams could handle it. Some couldn't.

It was funny. Jax had psychic ability himself. He knew what people could do. Do-Lord had seen it too many times to doubt he was using some sort of extra sense. Jax didn't deny it, but he had absolutely no curiosity about it. When Jax asked Do-Lord to visualize placements, they both knew what he was asking Do-Lord to do—but they had never discussed it.

Lon knew. He, himself, had what he called a *feel* for things. He had a degree of insight into people and their motivations that was nothing short of uncanny.

He'd never talked about it with either man.

From the passenger seat, Emmie mused, "Peripheral vision, with headlights in the front of the visual field and darkness at the sides, is practically useless." *Well, there went that explanation.* "With the windows rolled up and the wipers going, I can't imagine you heard them." *Scratch that one too.* "It wasn't great reflexes. You reacted several seconds before the deer were there."

She didn't sound upset. And he felt the way he often felt afterwards. Athletes called it "in the zone." A feeling of perfection, of surpassing ease—like your life had power steering—ordinary rules and conditions were transcended. One of those moments when you could ask for anything and get it.

Emmie twisted in her seat to look at him. "You *do* know something happened, don't you?"

He laughed. A great, big, free laugh that shook something loose in his belly. He lifted her hand from her lap and brought it to his lips.

He liked the satiny-cool feel, the slight lemon scent. He liked it so much he kept it there and rubbed it against his lips.

"If you're communicating in sign language, you need to know I can't read it." Emmie's dry humor carried a touch of asperity.

Her tone let a bit of the helium out of his balloon. God, he didn't want to blow this. Psychic stuff scared the hell out of some. She was a scientist. She admitted she dealt with logic better than faith. He tried to calculate which way his chances with Emmie were better—talk or don't talk.

What the hell. *Talk.*

"Something happened," he agreed, and suddenly he was laughing again. "Shit. It's almost impossible to put into words. It sounds so ludicrous."

"I was *there.* Remember? Nothing you say will be less believable than what I experienced."

"You've got a point. Okay. I saw a deer in my mind's eye."

"You mean, before you slammed on the brakes. Was this what they call precognition?"

"Precognition is an after-the-fact label. It doesn't describe the experience. When it happens, there's no awareness that I know the future. It's like there's this split in my consciousness, and I'm in two realities, two places in time, at once."

"You've had experiences like this before? This is fascinating." In his peripheral vision he saw her shift in her seat so she could look at him face-on. "How do you know you're not imagining things?"

Whenever he'd tried to discuss his experiences, that question had been asked, usually with a skeptical implication that he couldn't tell the difference between what was imagined and what was real. The inquiry was usually a precursor to dismissing everything he said. Emmie hadn't freaked out yet. And now that he thought of it, people frequently asked him how he did it—just as Emmie had—but no one had ever asked him if *he* was aware something had happened. That was Emmie. Seeing events in her own unique way. He wondered now why he had been worried that she would reject him or his experience.

"There's a feeling..." He struggled to find the words. "I knew there wasn't a deer in the highway in *this* now. But I *knew* there *was* in that one."

"The *now*... where... the deer... *was*."

Caleb grinned at *her* struggles to understand. "See how strange the sentences get? I warned you."

"It's a communication challenge, all right." Emmie shook her head and giggled helplessly. "Here," she held out her hand. "Maybe we should go back to the sign language."

God, she was a darling. Other people freaked out when they encountered something beyond their frame of reference. Wanting her ratchetted up another turn. "Got a better idea." He felt for his phone, unclipped it and touched speed dial. Emmie's phone rang.

Emmie shot him a glance and pulled the phone from her purse from the backseat where she had tossed it. "Hello?"

"Is this Emmie?" he enquired politely.

"Speaking."

"Is it really you?"

Emmie slanted him a puzzled smile. "Um... yes?"

"It's just that I've been waiting for a chance to call you for hours. I can't believe I finally got you. There's something I need to ask you."

She glanced at him again, out of the corner of her eye. "You certainly have my complete attention, now."

"Okay. I've been at this party all evening. I was hoping—I know it's last minute to ask for a date—the thing is I was hoping you would go out with me."

"When?"

"Tonight."

"Tonight-tonight? *This* night?"

"Sure. It's not late. I can be at your house in twenty minutes."

"What a coincidence," she observed dryly. "I'll get there at the same time."

She should have known she couldn't rock him—not at his own game.

"Hey! Perfect timing! What do you say? Is it a date?"

Emmie gasped. She connected the dots. "I get it. If I say 'yes' this will be our *third* date."

"Y-y-y-y-y-ep!" He drew the word out and exploded the p with the self-congratulation of a man popping the cork out of a bottle of champagne.

Chapter 27

Do-Lord played with a piece of Emmie's hair. Once at her cottage, they had agreed they didn't want to go out and opted instead for glasses of Baileys. Now they were ensconced in the big blue chair again. There was only the one chair, so he had pulled Emmie into his lap, which suited him just fine. "What's your favorite color?" he asked.

"Prussian blue."

"What color is that?"

"A deep blue that has no hint of red. The chemical name is iron ferrocyanide. It was the first synthetic paint pigment. Like a lot of discoveries, it was the result of an experiment gone bad. The chemist was actually trying to create a synthetic red. This chair is pretty close to Prussian blue."

"What was your mother's maiden name?"

"Crenshaw. Thank God, my parents don't follow the tradition of giving girls their mother's and grandmother's maiden names—like Pickett's family does."

"Is that how she got the name Pickett?"

"Um-hmm. Her grandmother on her mother's side was a Pickett."

"Is Emelina your first name or middle?"

"First. My middle name is Theodora."

"Emelina Theodora?"

Emmie gave one of those bubbly chuckles he loved. "I'll bet you're wondering why I think Crenshaw would have been worse, aren't you?"

"Emelina, gift-of-god," he translated.

"That's what my mother said. They thought they might be unable to have children."

"Where were you born?"

Emmie craned her neck, attempting to see his face. "What's going on? Are you trying to guess my passwords? I'm warning you, there's not enough in my bank account to steal."

He kissed the top of her head, hiding a smile. As usual, she had kept track of everything he said. "I just realized there was a lot you know about me, and I don't know much about you."

"Okay. I was born in San Francisco. Where were you born?"

"Rose Hill, Alabama."

"That sounds like a nice place."

"The best thing about it is that I don't live there anymore." Enough with minutiae. He had Emmie in his arms, true, but she'd been there twice. Just when he thought everything was a go, there was another condition to be met. Time to ask for the data he really needed.

"Emmie, the last guy you were with. How long did you know him before you had sex?"

"That would be Blount."

"Blunt? Like blunt-force-trauma?"

"B-L-O-U-N-T. It's hard to say. I'd seen him around campus for about a year. After all, we were in the same department. Then our class schedules coincided, and we started chatting for a few minutes sometimes."

"Okay, how long, counting from your first date?"

"We never had a date."

"I thought you said—"

"He never asked me for a date."

What the hell? She had all but insisted on a notarized contract with him. Every attempt to understand her made him understand less.

"We ran into each other fairly frequently, and he liked to talk. And then we'd get together at his apartment sometimes. One thing led to another. "

She went to bed with the joker though, official dates or not. "Okay, count from whenever you like."

"Five months. Six months. Maybe seven."

It was as bad as he thought. A guy lived in her world. Had all the right credentials. Could see her every day. And it took him seven months. Five minimum.

"Did you fall in love with him?"

"Now that I've had time to think about it, strictly speaking, it wouldn't be accurate to say that I *fell* in love. It was more like... *wandered off.*" Emmie chuckled. "Yeah, that's it. I strayed into love. Oh, wait... I *misdialed* into love." Emmie threw back her head, laughing. She would have tipped over backwards if Caleb hadn't braced her with an arm around her shoulders. "Oh! Oh! I've got a better one: I *got on the wrong bus* into love!"

She was adorable. He dropped a kiss on her hair. Thank God, she wasn't nursing a broken heart over the chump. "When did you notice your mistake?"

"There was a departmental dinner. A command performance. We didn't go out together frequently, but I assumed, incorrectly as it turned out, that we would go to the dinner together. Nope. He was going with someone else." Emmie snorted. "Since *he said* our friendship"—Emmie made finger-quotes—"'transcended the man-woman thing,' it never occurred to him he ought to share his plans with me."

Okay, the guy was a jerk. One who didn't know shit about the family values Miss Lilly Hale talked about. Didn't mean Caleb couldn't learn from his mistakes. He was serious about Emmie. To make the most of their time together, they needed to talk over their plans and get on the same page.

"Just so you know, I'll be transferred to San Diego in January," he said.

Confident he would support her, Emmie leaned back to see his face. She pressed against his arm and grinned. "Are you trying to set me up for the great 'been nice knowing you' speech?"

That stung. Mainly because she could joke about it. He'd gotten mixed signals from the beginning, but the one clear signal, that *she* had insisted on making clear, was that if they had sex, a serious relationship was on the table. She was out of line, way out of line, to suggest he was setting her up for the kiss-off.

"No, I'm just telling you *now*. I'm working on a game plan to get things started before I leave in January. I'm saying, Emmie, I don't want to rush you. I'll give you all the time I have, but I don't have time for coffee together two or three times a week and chats between classes for seven months. I need an estimate of how many dates it's going to take.

"And I probably better warn you. I don't think we've got a chance of transcending the man-woman thing."

Chapter 28

"UM... DATES." THE PHONE CALLS TO ESTABLISH A record about the number of "dates" they had. And she had mentioned Pickett's rule about never having sex on the first date. "Are you talking about a timetable for when we have sex?"

"Hell, yeah. You don't think I want a long-term relationship without sex, do you? I've already told you I can't do that. I don't *want* to do that. What I feel for you isn't in any sense platonic."

Emmie said his words over and over in her mind. Her heart chugged violently. Her whole body shook with each thud. Her fingertips went cold. Even after all these years there were nuances other people understood because they were native to the culture in a way she wasn't and never would be.

"Feel for me?" Emmie squirmed on his lap trying to get her feet to the floor.

He helped her to her feet, then stood himself. "Yes, feel for you. You want a declaration? Fine. Write it out. Anything you want. I'll sign it."

"But... you want a schedule?" Frantically, she pawed mentally through Grace's lessons on projecting confidence, holding her value high, not making it too easy. Neither Grace nor Pickett had said anything about *schedules*.

Why did he have to talk about putting declarations in writing? This wasn't romantic at all. He was good at being masterful. What she really wanted was for him to take her in his arms and overwhelm her with kisses—that would be a big step up from what she ever had before. This would be a good moment to sweep her off her feet. And she could just let it happen, without worrying about which date they were on. And pretend she was admitting nothing.

"Emmie, do you want me? You act like you do. Yet you're the one who keeps insisting we can't be swept away by passion. I try to nail down what's on the table, and you look like that deer caught in the headlights."

There wasn't any pretend room here.

He was saying choose.

She could say scrap the timetable.

She could pull his head down and spend as much time on his lips—those mobile, perfectly-shaped, smiling, tender-looking lips—she could spend as much time on his lips as she wanted to.

But the trouble was, she couldn't do either of those things.

All day her anger had been draining away. Once her façade of indifference to herself had been breached by Davy's slighting remark, she had been shocked by the amount of rage she had found dammed up behind it. And the fury had given her the strength to further widen the cracks herself, and let the anger drain faster.

She wasn't angry anymore at idiot jocks, her parents, God, or her grandmother. The last bitter drops had run out while she laughed and laughed at herself over her aimlessness, her willful cluelessness about Blount. Davy's remark had made her mad because it had been true. "Pity fuck" was exactly what Blount (jerk that he was) had thought of her. And who could blame him?

If he hadn't given her much in the way of respect and consideration, he also hadn't asked much. She'd already admitted to herself (and to Pickett this evening) that he had made it easy for her to stay well within her comfort zone. Above all he had made it easy for her to get sex without ever having to admit she wanted it.

Grace had put her finger right on it. She *had* been trying to obliterate her body. She had symbolically tried to get rid of her body over and over. That wasn't possible, so she tried not to think about its desires. *That* wasn't possible, so she tried to pretend that she didn't think about it.

How rational she had pretended to be. How cool and distant to keep herself from knowing what she was doing. Talk about hypocrisy! She had found men who didn't ask her for dates, and that way she never had to wonder if they would ask her for the next one. She called that "freedom from expectations." She found men who liked to hear themselves talk long enough for her to pretend the relationship was significant. She had called that "building on a friendship."

As for the sex they had, she had insisted on hygiene. But otherwise, she hadn't needed to do anything. Sooner or later in an evening, Blount would say, "Time to take off your clothes," or something just as memorable. She could have sex without ever admitting she wanted it.

From the moment he had walked in the door Caleb had demanded that she say it. Say she wanted it. All day long, she had known this moment was coming. Still she had drifted along, pretending that in the end something would happen, and she wouldn't have to decide.

This was where she stopped begging for crumbs from life and stepped up to the table, if she could find the courage.

"Emmie?"

"You called me a 'deer in the headlights'—" She shrugged. "This is the way I get. Totally paralyzed. I have never said what I want. You know all those fairy tales about the person who makes a wish and gets it, and it's terrible—something awful happens?"

"You looking for guarantees? You want me to say everything will be all right for the rest of your life if you do this?"

"No. I'm looking for a way to have what I want without taking the chance of asking."

Chapter 29

SHE HAD LOST HIM. SILENTLY, HE PICKED UP THE TWO glasses they had used for the Baileys. Cradling them between the fingers of one hand, he carried them to the tiny kitchen. People had bathrooms larger than her kitchen. There was only the sink on one wall with a small refrigerator at the end of the cabinet, an apartment-size stove between the doors, and a little table with two chairs next to the window. There wasn't room for two people. Emmie stood in the doorway.

As always he moved nearly soundlessly. At the sink he washed the glasses and set them in the dish drainer. He performed the mundane chore as he did everything—with complete focused attention, no hint of a wasted motion. The glasses made no noise when he set them on their rims in the old yellow plastic drainer. He carefully dried his hands on a towel that had been left on the counter, then hung the towel on its rack, straightened it, and centered it.

The action might have looked finicky performed by anyone else. By him, it simply looked like he did tasks until they were done, and he did them right. He was going to leave, so, of course, he would tidy any mess he'd made before he did.

She was more aware of him as a physical man, a person in a body, than she had ever been. No, that wasn't true. She was as aware as she had *always* been. The only difference was that now, she admitted it to herself. Now, too late, she made no effort to stop herself from wanting to run her hand across his shoulder, down his back, and across his neat buns.

He turned to face her. The color of his eyes was lost in the deep shadow under his brows, while the glare of the harsh ceiling light threw his strong nose and sharp cheekbones into high relief. There was a scar she hadn't noticed before on his left cheek. Small, but scarily close to his eye. Her heart contracted to think of him imperiled, at the mercy of the forces that compel us to consider mortality. Yes, she admitted now, she had wanted to touch him.

She hadn't done it.

He wasn't smiling.

Her art teacher used to say there's never a shadow so dark it doesn't have some light. Though she couldn't make out the color of his eyes in their deep shadow, she could see the transparent glisten of the lens. She could see him looking at her. For once, even as shadowed as his eyes were, there was nothing hidden in their gaze.

He leaned against the counter and rested his hands on his hips. It was a way he stood when he had something to say. She hated that she was just now understanding that. Before she'd only seen that the stance brought out the breadth and power of his shoulders and the strong modeling of his forearms, making the point that he was not a man to be trifled with.

He cocked his head slightly. "There's a line drawn between us," he said in his dark umber voice. "It's a line that *you* made. I didn't make it. And you're the one who has to step across it."

"You're not leaving?"

Now, he did smile, just enough to change the shadows at the corners of his lips. "I'm here, Emmie. Right here. Tell me what you want."

She tried to hold out her arms. He could come to her. He could. He knew how. He could take over now. He smiled a little more, raised one eyebrow. Emmie reevaluated the shoulders and decided she'd been right the first time. Holding out her arms wasn't going to do it.

"This is scary for me."

"Scary for me too."

Emmie hated to confess her ineptitude, but the time for pretense was gone. Nothing, absolutely nothing, came to mind. "I don't know how to say what I want."

"Tell you what. I can't step over the line for you, but I'm right here. I'm not going anywhere. And you don't have to think of everything you'll ever want. Just one thing."

"But I don't know. I don't know how to start."

"Don't treat it like a bunch of moves to be gone through. What do you want? What's the one, next thing you're sure you want?"

"I don't want to be across the room from you."

"That's what you *don't* want. What *do* you want?"

Emmie listened deep inside her body to find what the hunger was, where it lay in her body, what would satisfy it. "I want to be right up next to you. I want to feel your heat against my body."

His eyes flared in what? Surprise? Disapproval? Emmie wondered if, even yet, she hadn't gotten it right, but she didn't care. "It's what I want.'

"All right."

❖❖❖

Emmie had said what she wanted, but he still stood with his back to the stove. Still with his shoulders spread and his hands on his hips. "Aren't you going to *do* something?"

Caleb's eyes crinkled. "I will. When you help yourself to what you want."

Emmie stepped closer. Closer to where his scent, his warmth, came around her. It was wonderful. It was safe and heady and scary. She could feel the power that resulted from intense physicality trained into service of his intellect. It wasn't control so much as a perfectly tuned agreement among his parts. It radiated from him like magnetic lines of force. She had felt it before. More than once it had irritated her because it could not be ignored, nor could it be contained—not by her. What she hadn't admitted was how much she liked it. How it pulsed energy deep inside her to make her feel vibrant and focused as if she'd discovered the most interesting sensation in the world. She was oddly languorous, her hips suddenly looser, her breasts heavy.

There was something else, now that she opened her senses to him. He wanted her. She knew it. She could feel his hunger. And she could feel how he hungered for her to want him. Her own sexual power that she'd first felt a couple of weeks ago had been like a candle flame. Now it felt like the roaring burner of a hot air balloon. It heated her and filled her, and if she loosed the last of her tethers, it would sweep her away.

The more she allowed her senses to fill, the more the hunger intensified. Her throat felt too full, and she needed pressure. She slid her fingers across the crisp cotton of his shirt around to his back, so she could use leverage to pull him and herself closer.

It was wonderful. Her arms felt full at last, and paradoxically she could relieve the pressure in her breasts by pushing against him. In a minute, it was still wonderful, but it wasn't enough. "I want you to put your arms around me. I want you to pull me closer."

His arms came around her, wrapping her in strong, hard heat. She could feel his soundless groan of relief under her hands, where she held them firm to his back.

She couldn't lift her right arm high enough to put her arms around his neck and pull his head down. She hooked her hands around his back and over his shoulders, pulling herself up. She lifted her face as close has she could get. "Kiss!"

A silent chuckle shook his diaphragm.

His mouth came down on hers. Hot. Open. He gave himself for her pleasure.

After a minute the strain on her shoulder intensified into an ache, and she reluctantly let herself down. "I can't do it by myself. I can't do it unless you hold my head."

"We could lie down. You wouldn't have to ask so much of your shoulder."

It was a good idea, but… "Not… yet. I want to feel your front on my back."

She turned in his arms to put her back against him and through the doorway into the bedroom saw herself in the dresser mirror. The bedroom was in shadow, the only light was the reflection. It was like there was a window in the bedroom open to a different reality.

Her face looked as she had never seen it before, her eyes large and dark, the lids heavy, her expression remote, yet intent. He sensed her transfixed attention, looked up, met her eyes in the mirror, and smiled. Just the faintest lateral movement of his lips. The smile of a chess master watching the perfect move to set the game exactly the way he wants it to go.

"Want to see?"

She couldn't answer, because she couldn't take one shred of attention from the woman in the mirror and the golden man beside her.

He smiled his chess master's smile. "Watch."

Slowly, while one hand rested on her shoulder, he moved the other. In the mirror a golden masculine hand, large-knuckled with long tapered fingers, traveled across the blue silk of the sweater over the woman's ribs and with excruciating deliberation cupped the woman's breast then kneaded it.

With the same deliberation he moved to the other breast to give it the same attention. Then he let his hand fall to his side.

She knew what she could do if she wanted more.

Still mesmerized by the woman in the mirror, Emmie brought her hands up to the loops that fastened the covered buttons.

"You're unbuttoning the sweater to show your breasts to me." His voice was deeper, darker, rasping. In it pulsed a triumph he made no effort to hide. "Because you like looking at yourself, and you want me to look at you."

When she had unbuttoned the last three buttons across her midriff, pushing his warm hard hands between her skin and the sweater starting at the shoulders, he peeled it down her arms. The whole time, he watched what he did in the mirror. The sweater dropped to the floor.

He finished with his arms covering her arms, his hands covering her hands. She felt as if she *wore* him now, and in the mirror, the blue lace of the bra made the whiteness of her breasts almost luminous. He looked at them, and as he said, she liked looking at herself when he was looking at her.

"Now what?"

"You decide. One next thing. Have you ever felt your own breasts?" His hands still cradling hers, he brought her fingers to her chest. "Here they are. Feel them. Feel what I feel."

He took his hands away, and she kneaded her breasts as he had, her white hand against the blue lace. She felt him inhale. Saw his intent face in the mirror.

"Do you like that? Watching me touch my breasts?"

"Oh, yeah." He stroked himself against her buttocks.

She felt for his hand and brought it to her breast. His golden hand with the long fingers and scarred knuckles. She put her hand on top of his and pressed hard, watching the breast move.

She made sure she had his eye in the mirror and snapped open the front clasp of her bra. She lifted the lace away. Perky her breasts would never be, but she saw them the first time without judgment. They were white. Even whiter than her upper chest. Faint blue veins crisscrossed under the skin that gleamed with a satin sheen.

Still watching him, she lifted one white globe. She moved her hand until the pink nipple peaked between two fingers. "Touch it."

He smiled at her in the mirror and laid one forefinger on it. She saw the devilish gleam just before he caught it between thumb and forefinger and plucked it. Her knees threatened to buckle.

She turned to face him and felt for the buttons of his shirt. "I want to see you now. I want to feel you."

When her hands went to his belt, he pulled them away. "Now I get what *I* want."

His declaration shocked her and scared her. He had been urging her to take the lead, encouraging her until she had begun to think it was her show.

"Did you think it was all your way? Oh, no, sweet lady. You say what you want. I say what I want."

His hands went to the waist button of her slacks. The zipper hissed. He pushed the slacks off her hips the same way he had the sweater, making it blatantly sexual. It wasn't about removing slacks, it was about touching her. Claiming his right to her.

He skated his hands over her hips, he shaped the curves of her buttocks, squeezed them and kneaded them with strong strokes. He worked his fingers down into the cleft and the moist flesh, moving around her center, but never quite touching.

He pushed the slacks off her hips and dropped to his knees so he could follow with his hands. "Step out," he said when his hand were on her ankles. He tossed the slacks to one side.

Again, he gripped the globes of her buttocks. "Come closer…" She inched her toes forward. "Closer."

The pressure on her buttocks made going backwards impossible, but any closer and she would be… his face would be… "Closer." He dug into her buttocks, and she had to inch forward or fall. She grabbed the only part of him she could reach, which was his head.

He pressed his face to the juncture of her thighs. He inhaled deeply.

She stiffened and dug her fingers through his hair to grip his skull. She wasn't sure if she intended to push him away or brace herself. Her knees went weak.

Strengthening his grip to keep her supported, he turned his face up to her. "Did I shock you? Am I moving too fast?"

She was shocked and surprised, but more by his face than his actions. Emmie wasn't sure when they'd taken the steps that carried them into the bedroom. With the only light coming from the kitchen, his face was in deep shadow. All nuance of expression that created the surface, social man was hidden, only the most basic components of who he was were visible. His words might have sounded sensitive, but his face looked harder and more intense than she had ever seen it.

Suddenly, his teeth flashed white in an unrepentant grin. "I've been wanting to do that for fourteen days and ten hours."

Emmie did the math. "When we went to take care of the cake?" she clarified. All the time he had been acting so arrogant and condescending. Was that possible?

"The first time I put you in the truck," he confirmed.

"Caleb, *no!*"

"Emmie, *yes!*"

"Really?"

He tightened his fingers on her buttocks with frank possession, and his smile edged toward *marauder.* "I wanted to push your shapeless, beige skirt up, pull down your plain, white cotton panties, and bury my face in your woman smell until I had you all over me. And I had been all over you."

Despite his rather prideful declaration, the throb of raw, aching longing in his voice—longing that went far deeper than the need for sexual release—brought tears to her eyes. Desire to succor sent all her sexual craving into something richer, more compelling and more complex than she had ever known. It made her cradle his face in her hands. She relished the faint prickles along his jaw, the subtly thicker feel of masculine skin. She traced his perfect lips with her fingertips. She stroked the silky wiriness of his brows, and when she drew her fingers down the sharp strong wedge of his nose, he closed his eyes, leaving a wet glitter in his lashes.

"Stand up," she whispered, lifting his face to hers as if it were made of glass. Her fingers went to the buttons of his shirt. "You have on too many clothes."

Emmie had the shirt unbuttoned and was nuzzling the tiny flat nipples she found in the springy thatch across his pecs. He trailed his own kisses down the exposed side of her neck, then gently pushed her away.

"I was playing!" she protested.

"You can play to your heart's content in a minute. Let me get out of these clothes. Why don't you get into bed, so I'll know where to find you?"

He switched on the reading light beside the bed and saw the six or eight textbooks, some open facedown on the bedspread. "Are you expecting to need all these?"

"Publishing companies send me advance copies."

"And you use them for bedtime reading?" He was getting himself back under control after nearly losing it in uncivilized, raw, rude, ravenous need, and now this. She had a bed full of textbooks! It shook a place so tender, so protective, his whole insides shivered with it. His diaphragm fluttered in what felt like a chuckle, but not because something was funny. Because something was so inexplicably, perfectly, miraculously right.

"Hand them to me." One by one he took them and stacked them on the floor. Tomorrow he'd have to see about finding more bookcases or maybe talk her into getting a larger place. He hung his shirt on the back of a chair and folded his slacks carefully across the seat.

"Now lean back on the pillows, so I can see you."

She obliged. Her honey and cream hair flowed around her face and lightly kissed her shoulder. The perfect white globes of her breasts, the skin like translucent satin, gleamed in the lamplight. As he looked at them the little pink nipples puckered. Just like that his own desire doubled. "You like for me to look at your breasts, don't you?"

She touched her hair, a delicious combination of shy and wanton. "Yes."

He forgot everything. All the reasons he needed to stay in control, stay focused, stay separate. All he knew was he had to feel those little nipples in his mouth, push his tongue against the hard little tips, and mold the delicious, slightly cool, fluid weight of her breasts in his hands.

With no intervening motion he was beside her on the bed, his mouth fastened on her, his hands full to overflowing, exactly as he'd dreamed. She arched against him and moaned. "Was that a good moan?"

"The best."

"Then let's make love."

And they did… and they did… and they did.

His wonderful weight was on her, her skin so sensitive she was one quivering nerve ending. His hard, velvety length touched, just touched, at her center, and she tried to squirm it to where she wanted it to be.

He pulled back, and she clutched at him, digging her nails in when her strength wasn't sufficient to hold him. "Don't pull back. I need you now."

"I know. I know." He tore open a foil packet and sheathed himself. He lifted her heels to his shoulders and positioned himself.

"I want to hold you!"

"Not tonight. I can't let you put strain on your shoulder. This will be good. I'll make it good. This way you can get lots of leverage with your hips."

The time for careful feather touches was over, and he knew it. He stroked her back to front, front to back. He opened her with his fingers and positioned himself at her entrance.

Four long, smooth strokes, three short ones. Four long smooth strokes, three short ones. Over and over with bodies slick with sweat, straining together in an agony of pleasure and anticipation of the peak.

Suddenly, she was there. It was like hot white light shot from where they were joined, ran up her spine, and exploded out the top of her head, enveloping him in instant, spontaneous answering incandescence.

Yes, she felt it, in *his* body.

It is the human condition that peaks may be scaled, but they cannot be sustained.

Sometime later they drifted back into ordinary time. How or when they had come to be lying face to face, arms around each other, neither knew.

"Did that really happen?" Emmie asked when the world seemed firm enough again to dare speech.

"The light? Yeah."

"I could feel it in your body. I could feel your body feel my body."

"Yeah."

They slept.

Chapter 30

Entre'act

"WHAT'S THE PLAN FOR TODAY?" CALEB SIPPED HIS coffee sitting at the table in the kitchen. When he ran in the mornings he was taking routes through different neighborhoods, learning what was where and checking out apartment complexes and condos. There really wasn't space for two people in this cottage.

What he'd really like would be a house over on one of the barrier islands. A condo was the next reasonable step. The beach house could come after they were married. In the meantime, while Emmie got ready for work, he stayed in one place, and they could talk as Emmie moved from room to room.

"Today. Today is packed," Emmie answered from the living room. "I have two classes to meet. Six advisees to comfort. Then a departmental meeting. That will go on until five-thirty."

"Would you like to do something tonight?"

"Tonight is my choral society."

He laughed. "You belong to a choral *society?*"

Emmie poked her head in the kitchen doorway. "I don't understand your reaction. Should I be offended?"

"It's so academic. So cultured." He raised his mug and crooked a pinkie. "What do you do at meetings of the choral society?"

"Sing together." Emmie disappeared back into the living room. He could hear her moving books around, putting things in her briefcase. "Choral singing is a totally different experience from singing by oneself or singing along with the radio. It's like the distinction between running and playing football. You can practice the moves of football alone, but by definition, if you want to play it, you need other people to play with you." She reappeared in the doorway to look down her adorable nose at him. "*You* can call it 'culture' if you want to. I call it recreation."

He grinned at her *so there* tone. "Consider me chastised."

"And humbled, I hope."

"Don't ask for too much."

She laughed, that rich, robust woman sound that always turned him on. He set down his coffee and closed the distance between them—a matter of two steps. Anyone who could laugh like that deserved a kiss, so he kissed her. "What do you sing?"

"Sacred music mostly. Almost all the great choral music has been written in the context of Christianity. I think there's a deeper meaning in the music about our search for unity and harmony among all our separate parts. We're practicing for the Christmas concert right now."

Finding the room in which the choral society met was easy. He followed the sound down the polished, and not brightly lit, corridor of the recreation center.

He didn't think it was his kind of music—might not ever be. He liked a few groups, but he'd never gotten his identity from popular music and followed certain bands the way some did. He hadn't come to hear the music.

Most of the large rooms in this wing were dark. He didn't like the idea of Emmie walking in this big sinister building at night. He also had a feeling he'd better keep his mouth shut about it.

He located a side door, outside the line of sight of most of the people in the room, and slipped in, keeping to the shadows. He wanted to observe without being seen. It had never occurred to him to wonder how a choir rehearsed, and now he was curious. He wanted to know how rehearsal was done. He could hear in Emmie's voice that it mattered.

After twenty-two minutes he thought a chorus rehearsal was as interesting as watching paint dry. They would sing for maybe thirty seconds. The conductor would stop them, say something usually incomprehensible, and they would do the whole thing over, with no difference he could discern. One positive was that he now understood the musical definitions of words like *allegro* and *staccato*.

He also knew that they were a more disciplined lot than he had seen in any context, except SEAL training. Rarely did the others talk if the director was working with a small group. No matter how often they were stopped, no one grew irritated. Instead, they did it over and over. The director did not have to ask for their attention. Well, except for the times he yelled, "Look up! Look up!" meaning he wanted the attention on him, not the sheet music.

Mostly, he watched Emmie and her shining hair—a look so pure, so full of ardor, and so transcendent of all human emotion, she appeared almost inhuman. He had seen that look on SEALs' faces when they practiced firing drills.

The conductor snapped off the line of music with one whack of his baton.

"You're late!" His eyebrows bunched in a fierce scowl. "The altos are late every time. Don't wait for your entrance. If you wait until it's time to come in, you'll be late every time. A phrase doesn't start with the first note, it starts with the breath. You must breathe on the last note the basses sing." Lecture over, he composed himself. "Try it again. Begin at letter D." He tapped again, a merry, encouraging sound, and piano and singers started.

This time it was different. The music soared like a paraglider catching lift from desert thermals. It glided and swooped, and all riding with it, took wing. Finally, in the kind of hush that sounds like a miracle, it touched down.

After a long silence in which no one moved or spoke, the conductor gently laid his stick on the podium, so carefully it touched with only the tiniest click. "My friends, you humble me and touch me. That was it. You went beyond the voice, beyond the score. You *made* music. The chance to do that, just the chance, is why we're here."

"How did you fake your IQ?" Emmie's question came out of the dark. He'd been close to drifting off.

"Do you get chatty after sex?"

There was a short pause while she adjusted her pillow.

"You know, I think I do," she said in a tone of discovery. "Answer the question."

"It's easy to fake it down. It's hard to be smarter than you are, but easy to be dumber. And you know, most people find it easier to believe you're dumber than you look."

"That's not what I meant. The Stanford-Binet scores aren't supposed to vary more than one standard deviation—that's just fifteen points, right? So here you are with scores all over the map. Didn't someone smell a rat?"

"Well, now, that was a problem. A Navy psychologist actually wrote a paper on the effects of intellectual stimulation in late adolescence on the IQ score of an enlisted man."

"Meaning he thought joining the Navy made you smarter?"

"Pretty much."

Emmie snorted. "You country-slicker, you. He bought the backwoods hick act."

"What can I say? When I could see for myself that the world was round, it changed the way I looked at everything."

They had dinner with the Calhouns on Thursday night. A woman identifying herself as Mrs. Calhoun's secretary had called on Monday to issue the promised invitations.

Calhoun himself answered the door in corduroy slacks, striped dress shirt, and maroon cardigan sweater. He smelled of tobacco and bourbon.

"Glad you could come. As I told Charlotte, we are in your debt. A dinner is the least we can do, and I hope if there's anything else, you will tell us."

With only a few lights on, the entry hall seemed even larger than it had on Saturday. Two huge Christmas trees, one at each end, provided the only lights in the huge reception parlor. The effect was dramatic and professionally designed, and to Emmie's eyes, a little sad.

"You're here!" Vicky came pelting down the staircase, her hair drawn up in a ponytail that bobbed and bounced with each step. She wore green jeans and a sweater embroidered with snowmen.

"Vicky, as you can see," Calhoun commented tongue in cheek, "has deigned to join us."

Calhoun ushered them into the smaller parlor on the other side of the house. Smaller was a relative term, and this room was just as formal as the other. Twin camel-back sofas upholstered in yellow silk flanked a marble fireplace where Charlotte stood conversing with guests who had arrived before them.

All three turned to face them. "How wonderful you could come." Charlotte extended her hand to Emmie and Caleb. "Emmie, I'm sure I don't need to introduce you to these guests. Chief Dulaude, this is Dr. Blount Satterfield and Dr. Sally Armitage."

Emmie tried to keep an alert expression while Blount, Sally, and Charlotte discussed the politics within the state university system. Charlotte had graduated magna cum laude and now sat on the board of regents of the university in an appointed, non-voting capacity, but she made it clear she took her position seriously and worked hard at it.

Everyone, including Emmie, had assumed she would wish to participate in their discussion, since she had the most in common with them. As she listened she made an important discovery. She didn't lack the ability to handle herself with them. She just didn't care. She tried to think of a way she could join Vicky and Caleb in a corner. After Vicky had been shushed a couple times, and her mother had apologized twice for allowing her to join the adults, Caleb had drawn Vicky away. Now she listened enrapt as he told her a story that involved a lot of hand motions.

Emmie might even have liked to talk to Uncle Teague, and since he had known her mother as a girl, ask him questions about her and her grandmother. Since the advent of email, Vicky kept in daily or nearly daily contact with her parents, but of the people here in Wilmington, Calhoun probably knew the most about her family's past. Edward Fairchild had drawn him out of the room halfway through the meal, saying there was a call he had to take. He hadn't returned, although Emmie had seen Fairchild pass by in the hall several times.

"Charlotte, " she said, "I was wondering if might use your powder room?"

"Emmie, what are you doing with a man like that?" Edward Fairchild's voice was pitched low. Fairchild had accosted her in the hall as she returned from the powder room. She had seen him twice that evening although he hadn't joined them at dinner. Charlotte had explained that Fairchild had an office on the ground floor and that he "kept his own hours." Apparently, that meant that he had the run of the house. She had the feeling he had been lying in wait for her, determined to talk to her out of the others' hearing. "Emmie, do you know what he *is?*"

Emmie paused to think over the question carefully, knowing there might be subtle power plays at work here. At the university she was used to the lecturer's trick of rhetorical questions, set up to reveal personal brilliance or prove the listener stupid. In this case, she suspected the latter. "A SEAL?"

"Don't you know about SEALs?" he demanded. "They're trained killers—assassins."

"Are you under the impression that anyone in the armed forces *isn't* trained to kill?"

"That's not my point."

"Oh."

Fairchild blinked at the deliberately dropped conversational ball, but quickly recovered. "My point is that you can't trust him."

"Trust him to what?"

Fairchild waved that away. "Emmie, I'm trying to warn you. Your grandmother was a dear friend. I'm trying to give you the same advice she would have: stay away from him. If you know what's good for you, stay away from him."

"I can't tell whether you are warning me or threatening me."

"My dear—" Fairchild shook his head sadly. "I'm *warning* you, of course. But being seen with a SEAL won't improve your standing in the academic community."

Emmie studied the senator's advisor. He was no more than an inch or two taller than she, and wearing heels, Emmie could look straight into his pale blue, but still sharp eyes. He kept claiming a need to look after her based on deep friendship with her grandmother. She couldn't remember her grandmother speaking as fondly about Fairchild. Emmie wished she had paid more attention to who was who in her grandmother's activities. All she knew was he'd never tried to counsel her before.

"You're smart, Emmie. Your research credentials are noteworthy, and you have the right connections. You can choose where you want to go in the university system. All I'm saying is don't shoot yourself in the foot by allying yourself with someone who will be a liability."

Emmie's jaw tightened. She might have no gift for politics, but she knew she'd just been told if she went along, she could write her own ticket. If she didn't, her career was likely to stall. Charlotte and Teague had the clout to accomplish all Fairchild promised with no more than a word dropped here or there. Most universities had far fewer tenured positions than they used to. Just like big business, they had figured out that hiring short-term contract employees who didn't have to be given benefits, who weren't earning seniority, and who didn't even have to be fired—they simply weren't renewed the next quarter—saved a lot of money. Tenure-track positions, such as Emmie's, were halfway between no job security at all and the holy grail of tenure. The competition for them was fierce.

Once in line for a tenured position, the competition turned fiercer. No matter what anyone said about rigorous scholarship, the name of the game was money. Who could bring the most money into the department by obtaining grants for research. And who had powerful connections with the legislature and policymakers.

This was heavy, and cutting Caleb out must be vitally important to someone.

There was the implication that Fairchild was carrying out someone's directions, but he might be acting on his own. He obviously had a lot of autonomy in the Calhoun household and the Calhoun organization. She couldn't believe Calhoun and Charlotte would invite her and Caleb to dinner and then sic Fairchild on her to do a hatchet job—but it was the sort of backstabbing she had seen before.

It was a situation she hated and had avoided as much as possible. She had no idea what to say next. She was almost relieved when Blount, stylishly professorial in a chocolate leather sport coat and turtleneck, came into the hall. "Emmie," he squeezed her shoulder in a one-armed hug, while extending his right hand to Fairchild. "Good evening, sir. I'm Blount Satterfield. Emmie and I are colleagues."

Cripes, this evening had gotten strange all of a sudden. Blount was touching her in public and acting like they were the best of friends and maybe more. She laughed out loud when she got it. Emmie removed his hand from her arm. "Blount, if you're hoping to make points with Mr. Fairchild by claiming close association with me, your timing couldn't possibly be worse. He thinks I have poor taste in the company I keep."

❖❖❖

Emmie turned on her side so she could run her hand across Caleb's bare chest. "You know what I liked best about tonight?"

Caleb captured her hand and twined his fingers with hers. He smiled out of the corner of his eyes. "Chatty, are we?"

"You know how I get."

"Okay, what did you like best about tonight?"

"Watching you with Vicky. You're so good with her."

"I like kids. As much as I can I volunteer with SEAL Pups. The children of SEALs don't spend a lot of time with their fathers. Other SEALs try to be a male presence in their lives."

"And you know what else? I thought I could see a family resemblance between you. It's funny, neither of you looks like Teague."

"Do you do that to turn me on?" Emmie asked, not looking up from the ecology text she was halfway through.

Caleb *did* look up from his book. Except for reading, the only thing he had been *doing* was lying beside Emmie in bed, oh, and he had his hand on her shoulder.

Most people had an agenda when they asked a question. They were trying to plan their next move or they needed you to agree to something. Not Emmie. Emmie asked because she wanted to know. As near as he could tell, she liked to know everything, but particularly how this bit connected to that bit. Probably what led her into a study of ecology.

The fact that she didn't have an agenda—she simply

liked to acquire information—shouldn't blind him to the fact that she looked for connections all the time, and she might have asked the question because she saw a possible connection. Remembering this salient detail was the only way it was possible to keep up with her.

He drew a circle on her satiny skin with his finger. "I do it because I like to. He closed his book and set it in the small bookrack on the nightstand. These days there was a matching bookrack on Emmie's side of the bed too. "*Does* it turn you on?"

"Yes."

He stroked the top of her arm over the feminine swell of the deltoid. "Here?"

"Yes."

"I'll keep that in mind." He slid down the bed to get a better angle on her mouth. Just before his lips closed on hers he thought he detected a cream-pot glimmer. No agenda, hell!

She'd been running an experiment. He'd been had!

There is nothing more contagious than chuckles when you're in contact with the diaphragm of the person chuckling.

Chapter 31

"EMMIE, THIS IS CHARLOTTE CALHOUN." CHARLOTTE had a voice like the center of a Three Musketeers bar. It was sweet, soft, soothing, just substantial enough to say you could always depend upon her, but need never fear she would be difficult. Like a Three Musketeers it was always exactly the same. Emmie had been dragged to Charlotte's wedding by her grandmother. Charlotte and Teague had attended her grandmother's funeral, where Teague had delivered the eulogy. Nevertheless, until this morning, Charlotte had never called Emmie. "How are you this morning?"

"I'm fine, thank you. How are you?"

"Fine, thank you. I hope you'll forgive me for calling so early. I called because I was hoping you'd know how to contact Chief Dulaude."

Emmie chuckled inwardly and filed the exquisitely tactful phrasing of Charlotte's request for future study. Now that she had accepted that she shaded the truth from time to time, she had decided she should become more skilled at it. Nothing about her choice of words suggested Charlotte had called her because she figured Caleb had spent the night at Emmie's house. In her bed.

"He's not here right now, Charlotte, but I am expecting him." Emmie was rather proud of her answer. She wasn't in Charlotte's class, but she was making progress. Both statements were true. He had kissed her thirty minutes ago before his morning run and promised to return. Neither sentence admitted he *had* spent the night. In her bed. "Can I give him a message?" Emmie reached for a pencil to jot down a telephone number.

Charlotte hesitated. Emmie could hear a man talking in the background. "I need… I need to talk to him. Will he be there soon?"

Emmie took back everything she had thought about Charlotte's perfectly controlled voice. Charlotte was just barely hanging on.

"Probably not too long, maybe half an hour. Is something wrong, Charlotte? Can I help?"

"I'm at the doctor's office with Vicky. He wants her to go to the hospital to run some tests, but she's… she's hysterical. She knows 'tests' mean more blood draws." Again, Emmie thought she heard a man's voice. Though Emmie couldn't make out what he said, Charlotte apparently answered whoever it was. "She's *not* a spoiled child! She tries to be brave, but she's so scared of needles. She's had four blood draws in the last two weeks, and it's horrible for her. Every time is worse than the last."

Not sure if Charlotte had been speaking to her, Emmie made a sympathetic sound. "I'm so sorry. Does the doctor suspect something serious? Silly question. Of course, he does. What can I do?"

"Vicky says she will stop fighting and go to the hospital if Chief Dulaude will come with her. I don't know why she's fixated on him." Emmie thought she heard a male voice in the background say, "… can't believe you indulge her like this." Charlotte talked over it. "Do you think Chief Dulaude would do that?"

"She's trying to control you," the male voice in the background put in.

"I'm sure he'll do what he can," Emmie reassured her. After getting Charlotte's number and the address of the doctor's office, she assured her she'd get right back to her.

Caleb felt ridiculously good when he saw the phone number his cell phone displayed. He'd called Emmie's number enough times to memorize it. This was the first time she'd called him though. He slowed down so that he wouldn't be panting when he called her back. Man, it felt so good. He laughed at himself. He was as eager as a kid. Wanting to be cool, to play it right. His heart thumped with anticipation at talking to her, although he'd left her less than forty-five minutes ago. Maybe she wanted him to pick up milk or bagels. That would be good. In fact, even if she didn't ask, he might.

"What's up?" he asked, when she answered on the first ring, knowing he had a huge smile on his face.

"I just had the strangest phone call from Charlotte Calhoun. Vicky needs to go to the hospital for some tests, and apparently, she's flinging a fit, unless you'll go with her."

"Why me?"

"Charlotte says she doesn't know why. I think it's because she respects you, plus she's got a bit of hero-worship going on. Do you want to know what's really strange? Caleb, Vicky's afraid of needles, just like you. Do you think something like that could be genetic?"

"According to some studies, it may be. About eighty

percent of people with trypanophobia have a relative with it." At the time he had come across an article on the phobia, he hadn't known any of his relatives—assuming he had some—so the information had been totally academic. He hadn't considered how it would feel to recognize *kin*ship. Suddenly, the implications of phrases like *member of the family, blood kin, like a brother to me,* took on personal meaning.

He wasn't starry-eyed about how well kinship always worked. A lot of his friends thought their relatives were pains in the ass. But people like that, people who were *kin* to each other, understood at a deep cellular level what it was like to live with certain traits. They understood, from the inside, what it was like to be you.

"That's the medical name for it, trypanophobia?" He heard the scholarly curiosity in her voice and knew she was writing it down, probably to research it the first chance she got.

"Or belonephobia. Or needle phobia."

"So. Do you think this means Uncle Teague really is your father, and she's your half-sister?" He hadn't corrected the impression, okay, the lie, he'd handed Emmie that he thought Calhoun *might* be his father. The DNA test he'd had run on the glass Calhoun had used at the wedding reception made paternity ninety-nine percent certain. Strange. There could be a link with Vicky when he had nothing at all in common with Calhoun. "Caleb?" Emmie asked when he didn't reply.

"I'm getting used to the idea."

"I don't understand. What is there to get used to? Do you think she's your sister?"

Caleb wrenched his mind from the thousands of

competing thoughts about what it meant to be related to a little girl and accepted that he was in charge of getting the kid to the hospital. "Can you pick me up? I'll call Charlotte and tell her we're on the way, as soon as I shower."

"No! I'm not going to do it. You say 'just one,' but it *isn't* just one. It *never* is." Caleb could hear Vicky's raised voice as soon as the elevator stopped on the pediatric floor. He shoved past the man and woman in front of him and turned down a corridor, guided by her voice. "You lied! You said we'd wait. *No.* Get away from me. No more sticks! *No* more sticks. *No* more sticks." Vicky's protests dissolved into sobbing screams. Caleb slapped the room's door open without slowing.

In one glance he took in the cowering child squeezed between the bed and the nightstand, her tear-stained cheeks and terrified eyes, the elderly man, Fairchild, pulling the little girl's arm, and the shocked young woman, her blue lab coat and carryall of vials and test tubes proclaiming her a lab technician.

"Stop," he commanded. All three took his command to mean them. Vicky's wails ceased, the technician took a step back, and Fairchild released Vicky's arm. He stood and straightened the cuffs of his gray suit.

Vicky scrambled to her feet and launched herself at Caleb with a frantic cry. Not content to fling her arms around him, she tugged at his coat and belt as if she were to trying to climb him. He lifted her into his arms, and she immediately clung to him, arms around his neck, legs wrapped around his waist. Deep tremors shook the little body.

Little kids were his soft spot. He hated to see them scared, hurt, or neglected, and he had seen too many in Afghanistan. Many of the mountain villages were preyed upon by the Taliban- aligned forces, and terrible reprisals threatened for any resistance to their tyranny.

"You are interfering," Fairchild snapped. His pale blue eyes glittered with dislike.

"Yes I am." Caleb kept his voice light, as if the notion had just occurred to him. For now, Fairchild was powerless, and they both knew it. A pissing contest would only upset Vicky further.

Caleb carried Vicky to the bed. She tightened her arms into a stranglehold around his neck. "Easy, Little Bit. I'm not going to let go of you. I'm just going to sit on the bed, so you'll be more comfortable."

"Where's Emmie? I want you, and I want Emmie." Vicky sobbed. The breathless quality of her crying, and the way her little heart pounded against his chest scared him.

"Emmie's coming." He arranged her on his lap and cupped his hand around her head when she hid her face against his chest. "She'll be here in a minute."

The lab tech edged toward the door, a placating smile on her face. "If it's all right, I'll come back in a while."

Fairchild ignored her. "You're not doing her any favors you know." He sneered at Caleb. "Sooner or later she will have to do as she's told, and you're just making it harder." At face value his words might be reasonable, but Fairchild's tone dripped contempt.

His presence challenged Fairchild's authority. Caleb wondered if that was enough to make the older man dislike him. Not that he gave a shit what Fairchild thought. He had no intention of discussing Vicky with him. To Caleb's way of thinking, Charlotte Calhoun was the only person with the authority to direct Vicky's care. "Where is her mother?"

"Here," said Charlotte from the door. Despite her smooth, imperturbable face, her deep brown eyes burned hot. The tech ducked behind her and escaped. "What happened?"

"The technician came in a few minutes after you left." Fairchild adjusted the amount of white cuff showing at his wrists, again. "I saw no reason for her to waste her time. After all, we're here to have these tests done. The sooner they're complete the sooner she, and we, can leave. You, Charlotte, have spoiled Vicky. You have refused to set firm limits, and now *she* is paying the price. She has no respect for authority. I have told you again and again, and now you see the results. She refuses to cooperate even when it is for her own good."

Charlotte let her leather bag slip from her shoulder. "Wait a minute. The technician came in to do a blood draw, and you *let* her? When you knew how hard I had worked to persuade Vicky to trust me? I had promised her nothing, *nothing,* would happen until Chief Dulaude got here."

"You shouldn't have to bribe her with rewards for being obedient."

Charlotte tilted her head to one side, her eyes narrowing. "I was not out of the room for ten minutes—and the woman in admitting said I needn't have come at all. She planned to bring the papers here. I'm putting a lot of things together, Edward. You said the Senator couldn't be reached for several hours. You said it would cause speculation if Chief Dulaude walked into the hospital with us, and you talked us into arriving separately. You suggested I get the papers out of the way while we waited. You didn't just disagree, you deliberately undermined me."

"Charlotte, you're upset about nothing—a child's tantrum!"

Charlotte's face turned hard and her voice very, very soft. "Get out. Do not come near me or my child again."

"As usual you're reacting emotionally. You're being unreasonable."

Apparently, Fairchild couldn't grasp, "Get out." Caleb thought he would have to add his persuasive abilities. Fairchild's weapon was words, his favorite ploy driving like a tank over anything he didn't agree with. Any SEAL worth his salt knew you didn't engage an enemy where he was strong. The more he could make his point to Fairchild without saying a word, the more effective he could be.

"I'm going to put you down on the bed," Caleb told Vicky softly. "You're all right now." Vicky's arms tightened briefly, then let go. "Good girl."

His size alone was probably enough to intimidate Fairchild, but Caleb didn't underestimate small men. Neither Caleb's height nor his spare build were necessarily assets in SEAL work. Many SEALs were average and shorter, and he'd had his ass kicked more than once. If there was going to be a confrontation, he wanted Vicky behind him.

Caleb stood. He smiled. Not a nice smile. He took a step toward the much older, much smaller man.

Fairchild fell back a step. Good. Caleb smiled again and jerked his head toward the door. The man's pale blue eyes went to Charlotte. He caught the cuffs of his coat in his palms and jerked the sleeves tight. It made him look like a stick puppet.

He stalked to the door Charlotte had left open, but turned back to fire a parting shot. He didn't see Emmie, who hesitated in the doorway, taking in the tense atmosphere in the room. "Charlotte," Fairchild warned, "do not think this man is your friend. He's trash. A low, manipulating opportunist."

"That's funny," Emmie exclaimed from behind him as if she'd made a delightful discovery. "That's what my grandmother said about *you*."

"What?" Fairchild whirled around.

"Um-hmm." Emmie gave him her most wide-eyed look. "'Opportunist.' That was her very word! Hey, Charlotte—" Emmie peeped around Fairchild and waved. "Mr. Fairchild, you know when you said the other day that you and my grandmother were friends? I didn't remember that, so it got me thinking about what I *do* remember. You know my grandmother liked to speculate about how people arrive at their places in life. She was talking about you one day. I wish I could recall more, but what I do remember her saying was, 'I reckon Mr. Fairchild was useful to Mr. Calhoun—she always called people Mr. and Mrs.—of course, *Mr.* Calhoun was Uncle Teague's father—but (this is what she said) 'personally, I don't see why Teague keeps the little toad around.'"

Caleb bit down on the inside of his cheek. Emmie was channeling Aunt Lilly Hale. Just when he thought her tone couldn't get any blander, it did. *And* her eyes got wider. "Don't you think that was interesting, Mr. Fairchild? I do. I'd be happy to tell you more about it sometime. Of course, like I said, I don't remember much more she said about you." Fairchild was edging away. "But I remember things she said about other people—oh, but you were leaving, weren't you? Don't let me keep you."

Fairchild threw a glare at Caleb and Charlotte, and a look of disgust at Emmie, and stalked off.

"I don't know when I've laughed so hard!" Charlotte wiped her streaming eyes. "Look at that!" She examined the dark smudges on the balled up tissue in her hand. "Emmie, you've made me ruin my makeup. I haven't done anything to destroy my eyeliner in public since before Vicky was born!"

Emmie chuckled to think a woman could live for ten or more years with perfect makeup. She was still challenged to remember to put on lipstick, and she knew she would never take it seriously. Somehow, there wasn't a gap between her and women like Charlotte anymore. They were part of a continuum.

"Fill me in," Emmie said, from her perch on the arm of the room's easy chair in which Caleb sat. Anyone coming into the room would assume she was on his side. Well, she was. Sometime in the last few days, all feeling of existing at the edge of life, of being insignificant even to herself, had disappeared. She enjoyed feeling like a participant, and even more, she appreciated knowing she and Caleb could relate as a team. "I'm sorry I couldn't get here earlier. I had to go over to campus long enough to hand out exams. A graduate student will collect them, but I'll need to go back soon. Talk fast. What did I just walk in on?"

Charlotte stroked Vicky's hair. "Sweetie, tell us what happened before I got here."

Vicky's lip quivered. "She was already in here."

"You mean the lab technician?" Vicky nodded. "When we came in downstairs," Charlotte explained to the adults, "Edward suggested I stop by the admissions desk, and he would bring Vicky to the room. But the technician was *already* in the room. Vicky, are you sure?"

"Uh-huh. And I said I didn't want to. I wanted to wait for you and Caleb. But they wouldn't let me, and he said you wouldn't come for a long time. And he said he would hold me down, but I got away and ran around the bed. Then he caught me by the arm—" Vicky hid her face against her mother.

"When I came in, Fairchild had her trapped between the bed and the nightstand." Caleb's voice was darker than Emmie had ever heard it.

"Caleb picked me up and didn't let them get me."

Charlotte closed her eyes. "How long was it until I got here?"

"About a minute," Caleb replied.

"I never dreamed he would do such a thing. He won't come near you again," Charlotte reassured her daughter.

"Mommy told him to get out," Vicky explained as she took up the tale, "but he was arguing, so Caleb *stood up*." Her eyes got big, and her golden freckles danced. "It was scary. And fun. I thought Caleb was going to fight him." Vicky looked quite satisfied. Now that she was safe and enjoying the attention of three adults, she was recovering fast. "And then *you* came in and Aunt-Lilly-Hale'd him to pieces. I didn't know you could do that," she said with admiration. "I didn't know anybody could except Aunt Lilly Hale. Can you teach me?"

Emmie hadn't realized it was possible to feel guilty and pleased with oneself at the same time. After all, every word was an out-and-out lie—and for the pleasure of watching Fairchild try to figure out if he had been insulted, and if so, by whom, she'd do it all again. "I didn't know I could either," she admitted, "until I did."

"Did your grandmother really say that—that he was a toad?'

As a teacher entrusted with the task of guiding young minds, Emmie was always conscious of her need to set a good example. Admitting to Vicky she had lied and then telling *her* not to, wouldn't fly. "Grandmother would have said it, if she'd thought of it."

"Does that mean she did, or she didn't?"

Her mother gave her an admonitory look. "That means, it's something it would be better if you don't ever repeat, young lady."

Vicky looked mulish. "Well, he is a toad."

"Vicky, when I heard him call Caleb 'opportunist trash,' it made me mad. But if I'd known what he tried to do to you, I promise you, *Grandmother* would have called him much worse!"

Caleb stood. Deep inside he still shook with rage at what he had witnessed earlier. He would do what he could to protect Vicky from Edward. First though, there was the need to protect her from the enemy inside her. "Charlotte, Vicky and I need to talk. It isn't cold today. Is it okay with you if I take her outside the hospital?"

Vicky kicked at a pine cone. "Are we out here so you can tell me needles can't hurt me, and I have to grow up, and not be a baby, and not upset my mother by making a fuss?"

Beyond one of the hospital's parking lots Caleb and Vicky had located a landscaped area of lawn, pines, and magnolias where they had grass to walk on. It was as emotionally neutral as they were going to find.

He wanted to hug her. Vicky was no fool, and she was no coward. "No."

"All right. What then?"

"Your name's Victoria, isn't it? 'Victoria' means 'she who wins.'" At least, he hoped it did. Bound to mean something close, and it was too good not to use. "When I came into the room, you were on the floor, and you were losing."

Vicky looked at him with deep disappointment. "That's not fair. I'm just a little kid. I was kicking."

"Yeah, we need to work on that. You need to learn how to kick so that you do some damage." Vicky looked at him, shocked. Caleb shrugged. "No point in kicking if you're not trying to hurt someone."

"Will you teach me?"

"If you want me to."

"And then anybody who comes at me with a needle I can fight and get away."

"You'll never win—not by running away."

"I thought you said—"

"You weren't losing to the people, Vicky. You were losing to the fear."

"But it's there. I can't help it."

"I know."

"No, you don't."

"Yes, I do. I hate needles too. People tell you it won't hurt, or it won't hurt but a little bit. And if you'll be brave it will be over in a minute. You know *that.* You're not afraid of the pain. It's the needle-feeling, right?

Her eyes filled, and her lips quivered. "Yes."

"You know exactly which feeling I'm talking about."

"Yes."

"Okay, don't think about it anymore." There were people who could faint from just remembering what a needle stick felt like. For some, needles caused a sudden drop in blood pressure called a vasovagal response. "I just wanted to make sure we're on the same page. You can't control it, and you can't make it go away. Trying to stop the feeling, not to have the feeling, will not work. Trying to endure it won't work either."

"Then how can I win?"

"There's a way to win, but it's not by fighting the needle or running away from it."

"What else is there?

"You can have the problem and be bigger than it."

"But I hate it."

"Um-hmm." If he said anything right now, she would look for ways not to do what he said. He set them in motion again.

He had understood Vicky's temperament at a glance. It was clear her parents had little control of her and no realistic ideas of what she was capable of. She wasn't the kind of kid who would ever be held by rules someone else made. Put her in charge, and she'd be steady as a rock. He understood her because he had been the same kind of kid. Anytime he didn't agree with the adults' rules, he'd done as he pleased. And usually gotten away with it. At the age of ten, he would have been capable of going out a three-story window.

Keeping a problem instead of fighting it *was* counterintuitive. He'd seen from the first that Vicky was strong-willed. Doing things because she was told to didn't sit well. She wasn't rebellious or contemptuous of authority (as he admitted he sometimes *was*). For Vicky, it just felt better to do anything she did because she had decided to. The needle phobia was probably distressing because it overwhelmed her and blocked her ability to decide for herself. He was offering her a way to be in charge.

He'd done all the persuading he could by telling her she was losing. Now she had to make up her mind if she wanted to move on.

He kept the pace slow. He'd felt how quickly her arms had tired even under the stimulus of extreme fear and anger. Something was wrong. He prayed it was easily dealt with. He could do nothing to shield her. He could only offer her a way to deal with it from strength.

"Do you really hate needles too?" As he'd guessed she would, she had been thinking through everything he had said and coming to her own conclusions.

He nodded.

"You weren't just saying that?"

He shook his head.

"What does 'be bigger' mean?"

"Every problem has an edge." The ground under a magnolia was littered with large brown leathery leaves and seedpods the size of Vicky's hand. To illustrate what he meant, he picked up a magnolia pod, some of its bright red seeds still attached. He brushed sandy dirt from it and handed it to Vicky. "Hold this up to your face, right in front of your eyes." He pushed it even closer to her face. "Now can you see anything but it?"

"No."

"But you know it has edges, right? Even though you can't see them?"

"Yes."

"I want you to remember that you can know it even when you can't see it."

Childlike, Vicky was already playing with the pod, turning it in her hands. "You know, it's kind of interesting when you look at it up close like this."

Caleb smiled. "Some problems are like that. When you look at them real close, they turn out to be kind of interesting. Suppose you want to know what the edges look like?"

Vicky held the pod at arm's-length.

"Right. And once you look at the edges, not at the pod, what do you see?"

"Nothing."

"Nothing?"

"Well, air, but you can't see air."

"How about your hands? Can you see them?"

"Oh!" Vicky laughed, delighted to suddenly see things

a new way. The sound warmed in Caleb all the way to the bone. It was what he loved most about kids. They could shift on a dime. “My hands, yeah. And trees and bushes and grass. If I hold it up like this, I see the sky.”

“You have a choice about how you look at it. Both ways are interesting. If you want to choose the best way to pick it up and move it around, what’s the best way to look at it?”

Vicky extended the pod to arm’s-length again.

“What do you think?” Once again, it was up to her to make the choice to go further. He was telling her she could do something many adults had never learned. It was impossible to solve a problem at the level of the problem. And yet people refused to grow beyond it—sometimes it seemed like they were afraid they would lose *themselves* if they did.

“I’m bigger than this.” She held up the seed pod. “So looking at the edges is easy. How do I get bigger than the needle feeling?”

“You already *are* bigger than it. You just need to look for the edges. See what’s on the outside of it.”

“But I can’t. I can’t see any edges at all.”

“Remember what I told you to remember?”

“I can know the edges are there even when I can’t see them.”

“Right, and if you know they’re there, you can find them. Fortunately, when it comes to things you are afraid of, things you hate, all you have to do is think yourself bigger, until it is on the inside of you, and you are on the outside of it. When you do, on the outside of things you fear and hate, you’ll find people and books and TV programs—all there with some of the answers you need to win." Caleb checked his watch. "Your mother is going to be looking for us. Ready to go back inside?"

"Can I carry this?" She held up the pod.

Chapter 32

Charlotte stood to greet them as soon as Emmie and Do-Lord were ushered into the doctor's office.

"Thank you for coming." Charlotte held out a hand that trembled slightly. "As you know, my mother isn't well herself, or she would be here." Charlotte didn't mention Fairchild. He hadn't been at the hospital again. She hadn't said, and Emmie hadn't asked, what had happened to him. Charlotte also didn't mention Calhoun. Emmie also didn't ask. There were details she simply didn't want to know.

"Vicky trusts you, and so do I." Charlotte smiled apologetically. "I must ask you not to reveal anything that's said here to anyone—even the family—until the senator's aides can prepare an announcement." Emmie, seeing how Charlotte and Teague lived at close range, understood what compartmentalized lives they led. Information, even among their intimates, was shared strictly on a need-to-know basis.

Charlotte bit her lip, one of the few signs of agitation Emmie had ever seen her make. "The specialist in blood disorders, the hematologist, said he wanted to go over some tests with me, and I didn't want to hear it alone."

A man in a lab coat entered through an interior door. "Good afternoon. I'm Dr. Koppleman. I'm glad you could come in Mrs. Calhoun. Will the senator be coming?"

"He's been delayed and asked us to start without him,"

Charlotte replied smoothly. Emmie wondered if any part of that speech was the truth. "These are members of my family, Dr. Emelina Caddington and Chief Petty Officer Caleb Dulaude."

Caleb might be considered a relation, though Charlotte didn't know it, but Emmie wasn't one at all. Emmie guessed it was easier to say they were family than explain who they really were.

Dr. Koppleman shook hands all around and asked them to be seated. He shuffled papers for a minute. "Mrs. Calhoun, as I told you, we're still waiting for some of the tests to come back, but they won't change what we know. Vicky has a rare form of anemia. A disease called Fanconi anemia."

"I've never heard of it," Charlotte said faintly.

"It's rare. There are fewer than one thousand cases."

"Is it serious?"

Dr. Koppleman nodded gravely. The compassion in his brown eyes told the rest of the story. "It's a bone marrow disease," he explained. "Her bone marrow isn't making red blood cells as it should."

"Are you sure?"

"I consulted with two nationally known specialists. They concur."

"Can it be cured?"

"Fanconi anemia, or FA, is a genetically transmitted disease. Since genes can't be changed, at least not at the present stage of stem cell research, we don't speak of cure. FA is usually diagnosed between six and eight years of age, and there's a wide range of how severely the child is affected—how many organs are involved. Fortunately, Vicky seems to be largely unaffected by the disease. She's nearly average in height and weight, normal in appearance, and she's highly intelligent."

"Normal in appearance?"

"Yes. We'll need more tests to determine organ function, but just at a glance, she looks normal. Some children are not."

Charlotte's eyes filled with tears, which she managed not to let fall. "There's no cure?"

"The bone marrow failure can be cured with a transplant. You will want to educate yourself about FA, but my recommendation would be to take her to one of the centers that specialize in Fanconi. It's not a simple diagnosis, and you'll want to know everything that can be done is being done."

"Does *genetic* mean my husband or I passed it on to her?"

"Fanconi is an autosomal recessive disease. For the disease to manifest, both parents must have the gene. If both have the gene, their offspring have a one in four chance of developing the disease. Two will be carriers like the parents. They have one gene for FA, but because they also have a normal gene, they don't have the disease. And there's a one in four chance of not having the gene at all."

"You say she can be treated with a bone marrow transplant?"

"If the transplant is successful, the anemia can be completely eliminated."

"Can I give her my bone marrow?"

"Because the parents have the gene, they can't be marrow donors."

"Who can be a donor?"

The doctor looked at his papers. "I see here that Vicky doesn't have any brothers or sisters. That's a shame. The best donor is a sibling who doesn't have the gene."

"Are you going to say something to Charlotte?"

Caleb didn't have to ask what Emmie was asking. The fact that Vicky might have a close relative who might not carry the gene had rumbled like a cart on the way to the guillotine since they had left the doctor's office.

They had driven Charlotte home, then stayed with her while she made calls to her mother and Calhoun. She had been given pamphlets on Fanconi anemia, but she wanted them there in case they could better explain what the doctor had said about Vicky.

Vicky's grandmother had been understandably upset. Charlotte had shed tears for the first time that Caleb had seen. He was beginning to know where Vicky came by some of her grit. After Charlotte hung up from talking to her mother, she called Calhoun. She seemed unsurprised that Calhoun couldn't talk to her right then, and instead, described all that had transpired to an aide.

"Not yet," he finally answered Emmie's question.

"Are you ever going to?"

"I don't know how Calhoun would feel if he knew about me, but Charlotte has enough to deal with. She doesn't need a long lost bastard stepson to show up right now. I'm already a registered marrow donor, and the first thing they'll do is check the registry. You heard what the doctor said. Only thirty-five percent find matches among family. Why upset her if I don't have to? I might be a gene carrier, but even if I'm not, since I'm a half-sibling, the chances are even less that I match."

"I guess you're right. After all, you don't know for sure that he is your father, and you are Vicky's brother. But I wish you had a way to get closure—for your sake."

Caleb had never been so aware that he was lying by indirection.

He couldn't tell Emmie that even if he knew he was a perfect match, he couldn't donate his bone marrow. He looked at himself through her eyes, and he didn't like what he saw at all: a man who would let his agenda threaten a child. But *he* hadn't. That's what he had to keep reminding himself. By his own choice, he would never, ever have put Vicky in danger.

When he'd gone looking for Calhoun's vulnerabilities, he'd been thinking he'd find a scandal, some malfeasance. Maybe that the man looking to become a North Carolina "favorite son," was getting some on the side, and if the universe was really benevolent, from a man.

He had already stayed his hand because fellow SEALs would be threatened if he killed Calhoun. How many more perfect opportunities would the universe offer him? This, after all, was the most exquisite justice he could ever ask for. The perfect eye for an eye. He could do exactly what Calhoun had done—nothing—and Calhoun would get exactly the same results.

No, he never, never would have chosen Vicky to be the instrument of his revenge, but the perfect symmetry of the situation was awe-inspiring in its destructive beauty.

He could make it even more perfect by telling them now that he might be a match. He would be a gift-horse they couldn't afford not to look in the mouth. And when they did? He would win either way.

And yes. He *could* contemplate a course of action he would have found despicable at any other time. It was part of being the man he was. He'd done things and been part of things. There were terrible things that happened in war. Innocents lost their lives, were burned and maimed, in gruesome accidents and miscalculations.

There were other horrible things—*not* accidents—that happened because the innocents simply weren't as important as the objectives. You didn't justify it. You accepted it. He accepted it. This was part of being the man he was.

Chapter 33

CALEB BROUGHT IN A LOAD OF WOOD TO REPLENISH the family room fireplace at Aunt Lilly Hale's. Pickett and Jax and Tyler had been able to come for Christmas, filling Pickett's mother's house to capacity. So Emmie and Caleb were spending the night with Aunt Lilly Hale. The family would come over tonight to have supper and open presents. In the morning, Emmie and Caleb would go to Pickett's family's house for more present opening and to have Christmas dinner.

The next day, the day after Christmas, Caleb's leave would be up. He had been so right that they didn't have time to waste. Emmie was clinging to him a little, and she knew it. Every sight of him was precious. They had already talked about how they would adjust their schedules to have time together, but it wouldn't be easy. It was too soon to talk about forever, yet Emmie knew she had found exactly what she had always dreamed of in Caleb.

A future together shone with bright promise.

Caleb hunkered down in front of the fire, arranging the split logs with the same attention to excellence that he paid every job. His open-weave sweater revealed the play of muscles in his back, and the light of the fire burnished his golden skin.

He'd been a little quiet for the last hour, but so had she. There was still much to say. And the knowledge that their time was almost up made the smallest observation about the weather or what they wanted to snack on, unbearably poignant. It was easier to remain silent.

When the log had caught, Caleb added another. One-handed, he checked the number on his cell phone without removing it from his belt. He frowned and went back to his fire tending.

"Do you have to return that?" Emmie asked.

"No."

It was the second or third time in the last couple of hours that there had been a call he hadn't taken. Suddenly, it all clicked into place. The phone. His solemn silence.

"Caleb? That's the donor registry calling, isn't it? Oh, my Lord, and I mean that in the fullest and most reverent sense. That means Teague Calhoun *is* your father. And you *are* a donor match for Vicky!"

She knew she was right—she never been more sure of anything—but a cold hand touched her heart. He was so… still.

"Caleb. What's going on?"

He dusted his hands and replaced the fire screen. "You remember when I told you about the portrait of my grandfather?"

"Oh, yes, the portrait in the library."

"I didn't need this," he said as he tapped the phone at his waist, "to confirm that Calhoun really is my father."

"What? I thought you said—"

"I *know* he's my father. I palmed a glass he had used at the wedding reception. I sent it to a DNA lab for a paternity test. He passed. Or failed, depending on how you look at it."

"What do you mean, failed?"

"There's something I didn't tell you." His hazel eyes sought hers. "When I saw the portrait of Calhoun's father and I realized my mother's stories might be true, I didn't research him out of curiosity."

Her stomach dropped. "You went looking for him."

Caleb unhooked the brass-handled hearth broom and dust pan from the fire tool set. He stood there holding them in his hands. "My mother caught the flu. A couple of weeks passed. Then a month, and she didn't bounce back. One day her lips were blue. They said she had myocarditis, caused by a virus. Many people recover, and for a long time we thought she would."

Slowly, starting on the left, he swept bits of bark and ash from the green glazed tiles of the hearth. "We went back and forth to the hospital. At a hospital, they don't refuse to treat you if it's an emergency. But their only objective is to get you well enough to walk back out the door. They'd run more tests and give her a different medication. She'd be better for a while. An emergency room doc finally sat me down and told me she wasn't going to get well. She needed a heart transplant. And if I wanted her to live long enough to see a transplant, her case needed to be managed. She needed regular appointments with a cardiologist, not crisis-to-crisis care in an emergency room. We didn't have insurance. Do you have any idea how expensive heart medications are? It was taking everything to keep her prescriptions filled." He carefully swept a gray piece of bark into the dustpan. "It was the first time I ever thought I needed him."

"Needed your father," Emmie clarified.

"When I walked into that library, I had an hour to kill before I could complete my deliveries. When I finished them, I'd have enough money to keep the company that supplied the oxygen off our backs for a few weeks."

"How old were you?"

He took his eyes from his sweeping long enough to throw her a surprised glance. "Sixteen."

Emmie's face burned to think she had once told him he didn't know what it felt like to be helpless. "Okay. What's the rest of the story?"

"I saw the portrait of Calhoun's father, and I realized my mother's stories might have basis in fact. It might have really happened like she said. My father might have been a good man who had loved her. A man who would help her if he knew.

"It *is* true that I did some research. I found the address of his law firm in North Carolina. I bought some good paper, the kind that comes from an office supply store, not a tablet from the grocery store—'white wove' it said on the box." His lips twisted at his naiveté. "I wanted to make the right impression, you see.

"I wrote a letter. I got no answer, so I found another address and wrote another letter. And another. Almost a year passed, while my mother got sicker. I called his law office. I could do a better job locating someone now, but back then it was the only phone number I knew how to find.

"'Mr. Calhoun cannot be reached. Can someone else help you?'" Caleb singsonged. "I became a little obsessed with finding a way to reach him. By then, I didn't hope he would do anything. I had figured out that he probably wasn't going to come through. I just wanted to find him. You know?"

Emmie nodded her understanding. "You must have felt so powerless to do anything that made a difference, but that was *one* goal where success was measurable."

"I saw an article announcing that he was running for the senate and had opened a campaign office. I called that number. I told the man who answered I thought Calhoun knew my mother. He asked questions—my mother's name, where I was calling from—like he was interested. He said he'd be sure to give Calhoun the message, and I'd hear something soon."

"Oh, God. Did you start to have hope again?"

Caleb opened the fire screen and threw the tiny pile of debris he'd collected into the fire. He shook his head. "I had never heard of *denial,* but I think I had been in denial and was coming out of it. I was facing reality. There wasn't any hope. She wasn't going to get better, no matter what I did—no matter what anyone did."

Emmie hated the grimness in his tone, the harsh judgment of himself for not accepting reality sooner. "You know," she put in, "it might not have been denial. It might have been ignorance. You were smart and extremely competent for your age, but you hadn't had much life experience. Even if you knew the words, I'm sure you needed time to understand emotionally what it meant for your mother to be dying."

Caleb gave her one of those sympathetic looks people give those who have just revealed themselves deficient in the most basic understanding.

Emmie refused to be intimidated. "Don't give me that look. You couldn't possibly have known how bitter being helpless in that situation would feel. If you had known, you would have crumpled under the load."

The stubborn man shook his head again, refusing her comfort, refusing to acknowledge that maybe a little comfort would have been good for him. She threw up her hands. "Okay, you *didn't* get your hopes up, you *weren't* angry about what you had gone through, and there was *no reason* that a seventeen-year-old trying to shoulder a load like that, *by himself,* would become bitter!"

She stopped to take a deep breath. She was angry for him, but it wouldn't help for sympathy to turn into being angry *at* him. "Sorry I went off on you. I guess you never heard from him."

"Well, actually, I did. Four or five weeks later, there was a letter in the mail from a law firm—not his. Heavy cream-colored envelope." He huffed a sound that could have been a grunt of pain or a mirthless chuckle. "That envelope taught me the difference between white wove and vellum. And there must have been fifteen names on it." He quirked a sardonic eyebrow. "Do you want to know what the letter said? I can still quote every word."

Now the anger was there in his voice, cold and grinding forward with relentless, measured tread, like a doomsday machine freezing and killing all in its path. *No,* she didn't want to hear what the letter said! It was a bullet she would have happily taken for him, but she could not stand to know the pain he had felt when it hit *him.*

His question was rhetorical. He continued, still cold and relentless.

"Dear Mr. Dulaude,

"Be advised this firm represents Teague Calhoun. Mr. Calhoun has forwarded your letters to us.

"Mr. Calhoun categorically denies any improper relationship with your mother or even any knowledge of her existence.

"While Mr. Calhoun is sympathetic to your predicament, his sympathy does not extend to allowing himself to be blackmailed and defamed. This is your one notice to cease and desist such false and defamatory statements. Failure to comply will result in immediate action against you on both civil and criminal levels."

A threat added to an insult. Emmie could feel the lash of the injustice Caleb had endured as if it had landed on her own flesh. She slapped her hand over her mouth to stifle an outcry. Tears spilled down her cheeks.

For someone like Caleb who so generously shouldered others' burdens, to have admitted his need and then been attacked—it would inflict a wound that would bleed from his very soul. It was a betrayal of every principle on which civilization and all social cohesions stand. It was the law of the jungle shined up in stainless steel.

"I'm so sorry, Caleb," Emmie spoke through her tears. She wasn't the perpetrator, but *someone* needed to say they were sorry. Someone needed to acknowledge that it shouldn't have happened. "The only person you knew with the money or power to help you, and he used his power against you."

They were silent a long time. There wasn't anything else to say. The fire hissed in the fireplace. Ashes sifted into the grate.

After a while Emmie wiped her cheeks with the flat of her hand. Gently, in the low hushed tone people use outside hospital rooms, she urged him to return to his story. "Did your mother live long?"

His lips slanted in an oddly young, sad smile. "At that time, the doctor had changed her medicine, and she seemed better for a while..."

His voice trailed away, while he looked out the window as if he could see through it into the past. While they had talked, dusk had fallen. A pale blue veil of ground fog floated over the dark stubble in the peanut field. The pine forest at the field's edge looked almost black against the sky.

At last he turned back to Emmie, a gentle smile tipping the corners of his mouth.

"She was so pretty." He shook his head in fond amazement. "She told me my father was a handsome prince, and I believed her longer than I should have, because she looked just like a fairy-tale princess from my books. She was tiny and had long golden-red hair.

"When she died, it was like some sort of malignant enchantment fell away, and she looked about fifteen, so beautiful and so completely pure. She was propped on pillows in the back bedroom, and the last red rays of the sun glowed in her hair and made her skin translucent as a rose petal. You could see what she was supposed to be, had been meant to be. She had a believing heart and a gift for dreaming. Instead of treasuring her, he had taken one sip of her sweetness and thrown her down in the dirt.

"I swore she would have justice, Emmie.

"I promised if I ever saw him face to face, I would kill him."

Chapter 34

SLOWLY, CAREFULLY, HE TOLD HER THE REST. AS THE day grew darker, Emmie learned the story of a man in the midst of a public war, who sees a hated face left over from his private war.

She listened to it all.

All he had done.

The reasons for all he had done.

Right up to the phone calls from the donor registry.

Which he hadn't answered.

And did not intend to answer.

Her face burned hot. And then froze into a perfect wooden likeness of herself. Thoughts, like cool, slow drops of dispassion, spread ripples across her mind.

That's what this has been about. Revenge.

Everything from the day of Pickett's wedding on. It was only a way to get past the layers around Calhoun.

From the beginning. Oh, wait. That wasn't the beginning *in Aunt Lilly Hale's office. That was the third act.*

The plan was clever. Very clever. I was a walk on. Anyone could have played the character who shows up in the third act and announces, "Come, sir. I will lead you into the citadel."

And then the thought that squeezed the last trace of illusion from her heart: *Oh, Caleb, were you really willing to marry me?*

She knew the answer. Caleb was a man who would do whatever it took to reach his objectives. He wasn't mean or callous. He had never treated her unkindly. He would fulfill any promise he made. And he would let nothing stop him.

It felt like the very bones of her spine were crumbling. None of it had been real. She wanted to crawl into some deep, dark place like a wounded animal seeking its den, someplace she could bleed to death in peace or lie still enough, for long enough, to heal.

This was the experience she had always feared: to find out she didn't matter. Her life hadn't been about her, because she hadn't chosen to be significant to herself. She had kept herself small, unimportant, had crept around the edges and lived a life that *she herself* was missing from, so that she wouldn't feel this.

Well, now she felt the pain, and it hurt as badly as she had feared, but it wasn't dull. It *was* real. She had been living in a fantasy that someone would come along and she would make a meaningful difference to *him,* simply because she existed.

One lesson her newfound self-esteem had taught her over the past several weeks: she knew when it was about her and when it wasn't. This wasn't. She couldn't accuse him of betrayal. She winced at the irony. He hadn't betrayed her. What he was doing didn't have anything to do with her.

The forces at work here had started before she was born. She'd stumbled in a tragedy already in progress, but it was *not her story.* This story began long before Caleb met her.

Now that she looked at the truth—what the last few weeks had really been about—the story of her great love affair turned to nothing. It was like ashes on a fireplace grate still holding the shape of a log. If she touched them, they would fall in soft gray whispers, leaving only the memory of warmth.

She touched them.

And having let all the pieces of her fantasy collapse, she learned something.

Even if she could no longer pretend they had a relationship, all the reasons she loved Caleb were still there. His integrity. His imagination. His courage. His largeness of spirit. No matter how narrow his choices, he had never allowed life to make *him* small. He was a hero.

Oh, yes, she loved him still, though he was keeping himself in the past, and his keeping himself in the past had doomed their love from the beginning. She grieved for the tragic story he was living.

She could see so clearly that he would not have the flaws of a tragic hero were it not for his great strengths. Great loyalty. A capacity for generosity that made him able to make greater sacrifices than other people could contemplate. A self-discipline that held him to his course undeterred, no matter what the temptations.

What always made a tragedy so sad was the sense that it was inevitable, and yet it was unnecessary. She could not have the love she wanted from him, but she couldn't, *wouldn't,* let him go through this alone. She could offer her friendship.

❖❖❖

Why didn't she say something? Purple wool clogs kicked off, she sat on the maroon leather sofa with her feet tucked under her. All day he had known this moment would come. As he waited for her judgment, the back of his neck was so tight he thought it might snap.

Finally he could take the silent waiting no more. "Aren't you disgusted that I wanted to kill him?"

She pondered the question. She looked at the ceiling. She clasped her hands loosely in her lap. Emmie-like, when she had organized her thoughts, she said, "Soldiers kill. They take on terrible psychic wounds in order to keep the rest of us unwounded."

With the lecturer's skill, she looked at her hands for a moment to insert a thoughtful pause. "Teach a person to kill and you've taken away some measure of the person's peace. They've crossed a line, and they know it. Call war peacekeeping all you want. It might even *be* peacekeeping, for all I know." She shrugged. "Certainly, soldiers lose their peace so that people like me can *keep* mine. Some people are born to soldiering." She gave him another Emmie-look that signaled a dry joke. "I can't call it SEALing—for now, we're stuck with 'soldier.'"

She went back into lecture-mode. "They come into the world knowing that they're the ones. They know they are the protectors, the defenders, and the fighters. They know when the shit hits the fan, the wolf attacks the fold, and the terrorists have taken over the plane—it's their job to deal with it. They are in charge, and since they are serious about their duty, they train for the day it will come. Soldiers have skill at killing. At the risk of stating the obvious, that's what their gun is for. The most natural thing in the world is to see a problem in terms of the skills you have to bring to it."

Having delivered her meditation on the subject of

killing, like any good teacher, she left him to draw his own conclusions. She rose from the sofa, and crossed the heirloom carpet to study a small painting. After looking at it for a minute, she turned her wide blue eyes straight on him. She said pensively, "Anyway, I don't think you wanted to kill him."

His laughter cracked through the room like a rifle shot. "Oh, you're wrong." His hands clenched. With the black joy of hatred throbbing through him, he could feel a smile that had its origins in bared teeth.

He *knew* what he looked like.

And *she* plopped her hands on her hips and tilted her head at him. "If you wanted to kill him, you'd have done it by now. You've turned down chance after chance. It's not that you don't know how," she added reasonably. "I'll bet you know ways I couldn't dream of—ways that would insure you were never caught."

She sauntered up to him (yes, sauntered!) and tapped his chest with one shapely forefinger. "I'll bet you could do it, and do it in a way that would make your fellow SEALs look like frigging heroes."

A corner of his mouth kicked up.

"What?"

"You said *frigging*."

It was her turn to smile. "So, I did. I've acquired all sorts of verbal abilities I never thought I had."

She walked over to the table and switched on a lamp. She turned to him, her arms crossed loosely under her breasts. "You told me one time that you supported yourself and your mother with crime."

Caleb nodded. "They say crime doesn't pay, but it paid better than anything else in my neighborhood."

"I suspect there are areas of crime that pay very well indeed."

"Some."

"I expect you knew what they were, and you knew the people you'd have to hook up with. You could have made the money you needed yourself, couldn't you?"

"Maybe."

"But you'd have had to get into the criminal world a lot deeper. You'd have been in at a level you never would have escaped. Drugs, human-trafficking—probably other crimes I don't know about, but illegal businesses where a lot of money and a lot of human suffering is involved. We both know how smart you are. If you had chosen that path, you could have succeeded. But let me repeat. *The course of your life would have been set.* You would never have gotten free. That world would have owned you."

"And your point is?"

"I don't think you needed Senator Calhoun to save your mother," she spoke gently, as if to a slow student who must be carefully led. "You needed him to save you."

"No, I never needed—"

She brushed his objection aside. "You're in the right, Caleb. He *was* the grown-up, and he should have been responsible. But that's hindsight talking. To find the truth we must look at the situation from the perspective you were dealing with then. If he had stepped in, you wouldn't have to feel guilty because you drew a line."

His heart beat stumbled, then found a new rhythm. At last she was pleading with him as he had expected her to do, but it sounded like she was pleading *for* him.

"There were things you wouldn't do. If you had chosen the route of getting a lot of money in ways you knew how, whether she lived or died, you would never have been free. You felt guilty because you drew a line." Tears filled her beautiful wide eyes, eyes the color of honesty. "And *she* died. And her death set you free, finally, at last."

"How can you be so sure of this?"

Emmie made no attempt to stop her tears. She laughed through them, sadly. "After she died, you went to Six Flags Over Georgia and rode roller coasters for a week. And then you went to Charlotte Motor Speedway. And then you went to the beach."

He could tell something about that trip really touched her. She thought it was significant. He wanted to understand it—if for no other reason, so she would stop crying—but he didn't.

"*So?*"

"Oh, Caleb," she explained softly, "that's what a kid who has been let out of school for summer does."

Chapter 35

SHE'D TALKED ENOUGH, SHE THOUGHT, BUT SHE STILL wasn't getting through. Teacher that she was, she asked a question. "You told me you *liked* the Navy. I kept wondering, what's wrong with this picture? You? A natural-born rule breaker. Antiauthoritarian. Independent thinker extraordinaire. Tell me, what did you like about it?"

He shrugged. "Three meals a day. Somebody else bought the groceries and cooked them. All I had to do was show up. After my duty was over for the day, I had time to read all I wanted. They sent me to schools. They sent me to college."

"And you had your friends, Tim and Weed, to teach you how to go on, how not get into too much trouble, and how to massage the system so it yielded what you wanted.

"You came to the Navy with an extraordinary, mature degree of discipline and the ability to accept responsibility. You'd already had the freedom teenagers say they long for and often must rebel to get. What the Navy gave you was the freedom most teenagers have and don't appreciate. And when you'd had enough—you'd rested your soul and your extraordinary capacity demanded expression again—you moved to the SEALs.

"The Navy gave you the space and shelter in which to grow up. And you did.

"Caleb, I don't blame your mother for confining you with her overwhelming need. I know you loved her. And yet, your life improved when she was gone. You need to face that. Whatever guilt you feel about being freed—accept it.

"Make reparation where you can, and ask God, or whatever deity or Power you understand, to forgive you for failing her. And I think you've felt guilty about that. You're so generous, you probably wished over and over that you could buy her presents or take her places once those things were options for you. But if she'd been around, they wouldn't have been options.

"You thought looking after your mother was your responsibility. Looked at in that light, you failed her, and she died. Teague Calhoun is guilty of plenty, but don't blame him for what *you're* guilty of.

"Now, you're trying to assuage your guilt by making Teague feel as you do. Except you've got the guilt in the wrong place. You were *not* guilty of your mother's death. But if you allow your sister to die without trying to help her, you *will* be guilty, and you *will* turn against yourself.

"You were powerless then. You're not now. Let go of your guilt. You don't deserve to suffer the way you will. And your mother would never have asked this of you."

Emmie let her hands drop into her lap. "Well, I've preached like the child of missionaries that I am, and I've lectured like the professor I am." She stood and shook the wrinkles from her slacks. "You've listened to me patiently, and I think I've said all I have to say."

Caleb halted her, one hand upraised. "One more thing. Why?"

She looked at him blankly. "Why what?"

He covered his chagrin at needing to 'fess up to his hidden agenda with a little shrug. "I expected you to talk me into donating my marrow. I thought you would talk about duty, kindness, or mastering the situation by being generous."

"Oh, Caleb." She laughed a helpless, painful laugh. "You don't need a 'talking to' about those things! You could give lessons!"

Now, he knew he had to be straight. "I was hoping you could talk me out of letting Vicky be my revenge. You haven't mentioned her. Instead you have talked only about the situation from my side. Only my side. Why?"

"You're in a very heavy, hard place. I'm your friend." Her eyes filled with tears again, and she smiled upside down. "I didn't want you to face it alone. I will be your friend, and I'll care for you no matter what. I want you to do what's right for you. I would love to see Vicky get better. I will pray that she does through whatever agency God selects. But this isn't about her."

The moment felt fragile. And yet all the confusion he had known fell away. He loved Emmie and knew he loved her as never before. The whole time he'd used her, he tried *not* to use her, although it was not a distinction he was sure she could appreciate.

He took her carefully by her elbows to draw her to him, but he wouldn't confine her in his arms. He kissed the tear tracks across her cheeks, drying her silken skin with his lips. The space underneath his heart contracted so hard he couldn't breathe for a minute. She'd protest and get all prickly anytime he got high-handed with her, but she'd always turned her face up for his kiss with such simple trust. Just as she was doing now.

Their bodies knew how right things were between them. Always had. He could feel it now.

"Emmie," he whispered against her lips. "Emmie, I love you. The best thing about all this is that it brought me you. Now that you know all of it, I realize you're disappointed in me. Is there a chance for us?"

She twisted her shoulders hardly at all. But he was holding her lightly, so it didn't take much to break the connection. She looked away for a second, a *far off* gaze, as if she could see a distant reality. She stepped back—if she wanted to put space between them she would have to do it, because he wasn't going to move away from her.

"Oh, Caleb." She took a deep breath, the way someone does when breathing through pain.

She smiled that upside-down smile again. A smile he couldn't remember seeing her use before today. He hoped he hadn't been the one to put it there.

"Oh, Caleb." Slow and final, she shook her head. She sighed, and said, in a voice he'd never heard before, "There never was an *us*."

She took another step back and ducked her head like she was embarrassed. Then turned and walked away.

Chapter 36

THE KIDS WERE IN THE FAMILY ROOM WITH THE TV and the host of electronic gifts from Santa.

The adults, having cleaned up the supper dishes, the litter of paper from presents, and sticky fingerprints from every surface in the house, were sprawled in various states of exhaustion around the living room.

Tonight an eight-foot Christmas tree shed colored lights in the room, while only a month ago, the same space had been piled with wedding presents, a fact that had been remarked on again and again, as if they all needed to search for the roots of the mystery of change.

Grace got up to extinguish a guttering candle. "Emmie, I know you're sorry that Do-Lord's leave was cut short." That had also been remarked on a number of times.

Emmie smiled, but didn't comment. She hadn't told anyone that the decision to leave a day early had been Caleb's. Aching numbness would probably be replaced by pain tomorrow when the full truth that he was gone—and would be gone the next day, and the next—descended on her. For now, she was grateful for whatever anodyne was giving her a period of grace.

"Everybody come in here!" Grace's oldest son called from the family room. "They said Vicky's got a donor."

"North Carolina senator, Teague Calhoun, announced from his home in Wilmington, where he and his wife are spending the Christmas recess, that a bone marrow donor has been found for his daughter, Vicky, who is suffering from a rare form of anemia."

The picture switched to Calhoun and Charlotte on the porch of the mansion, the huge Christmas wreath behind them.

"Do you know who the donor is Senator?" a heavyset reporter called out.

"The donor wishes to remain anonymous, nor will they be told that Vicky is the recipient—though I imagine they might guess." He flashed his famous folksy smile. There was a murmur of chuckles. "Charlotte and I wish to express our gratitude to him or her. Not only for Vicky, but for all lives that are extended and made better by the extraordinary generosity of people willing to give of themselves in this way."

There was a bit more with the anchor recapping the procedure and an interview with a doctor who made it clear that Vicky wasn't out of the woods—there was no telling if she would survive the procedure—but at least she had a chance.

In the family room, children were cheering and clapping—even the littlest who probably didn't know what was happening—while adults were embracing one another and wiping away tears. Parents stole looks at their children and whispered prayers of gratitude that for tonight their children were safe and well.

Emmie sat on the big teal hassock where she had landed when her legs had given out beneath her.

There was only one possible donor.

He had done it. Somehow, he had found the generosity or the forgiveness or the healing to free himself of the past and had chosen to have a sister—one he could hold in his heart, even if the relationship was never acknowledged. The first truly altruistic prayers of her life had been answered; her tragic hero was tragic no longer.

"Emmie, darling!" Grace—Sarah Bea—*someone*—exclaimed. "What is it? What's the matter?"

The adults, their faces full of shock, concern, or embarrassment, according to their temperament, were staring at her. Emmie regarded them in confusion.

"You're sobbing."

Emmie touched her face. It was true. Her cheeks were slick with hot tears; her fingers came away wet.

Faces swam into and out of her line of vision. She could hear voices over the babble of the TV.

"Is it Vicky?"

"Are you worried about her?"

"She's sad Do-Lord left."

"She and Do-Lord spent a lot of time with them in the hospital."

"Tell us what's the matter."

"Someone, get Pickett!" Mary Cole snapped.

In a minute, Pickett was there, wrapping her in the scent of wholehearted comfort, murmuring and stroking. She took Emmie in her arms and led her from the room.

She shepherded her upstairs to "Emmie's room," lay down with her on the candlewick bedspread, and held her close, even after the tears ceased.

Jax stuck his head in the door and pantomimed "Need help?" and "I'll take Tyler." Pickett smiled her gratitude over Emmie's shoulder and continued to hold her.

Chapter 37

"WHAT DO YOU WANT?" HE GROWLED FROM THE hospital bed.

Well, she hadn't really expected him to greet her with open arms. He was a proud man. The last time they met he had let himself be vulnerable to her. He had told her he loved her and she had walked away. He wouldn't easily let his guard down again.

After she had collapsed, overcome with mingled grief and joy, she had leaned on Pickett for twenty-four hours. And cried. And poured her heart out to Pickett and cried some more. She'd pictured Caleb in a hospital facing needles. Big needles through which they would extract the marrow from his hipbone. He'd be under anesthesia, of course, but still. He was facing needles and not even for his own good. For someone else's.

"I want to hold your hand."

"Why?" he growled again.

He was trying to put on his hard face. It didn't fool her. *She* could see his stoic, brave, generous face, and the hard face just made her ache for him. Maybe someday he would be able to hear her say, *because you need me*.

"Because you're my friend," she said. "Can you please hold my hand?"

He was generous. If someone asked him for what he had to give, he would give it. He offered his hand.

She put her hand in his and almost cried at the warm, rough weight of his fingers as they curled around hers.

She took a deep breath for courage. With a lot of help from Pickett and others, she had come this far.

Because it didn't matter where the extraction was done, Caleb had elected to go on to his new assignment at the SEAL training base at Coronado, California. However, Caleb wouldn't return her phone calls, so she'd called Lon Swales, the kindly senior chief. He'd found out the date of the marrow extraction in time for her to catch a flight across the country. Now it was up to her.

"Caleb, I told you there was no 'us.' I was wrong. There is an 'us.' *This*" —she gripped his hand more tightly—"*this* is us, and to *be* us, all we need to do is sit together and hold one another's hand."

"You're saying we do have a relationship? I thought you said it wasn't real." Wary hope kindled in his hazel eyes.

"I don't know if I can explain. I had a fantasy 'us.' The fantasy is what wasn't real—never existed."

He stroked the back of her hand with his thumb. "What was your fantasy?"

"That there would be this person who wants me for myself alone and couldn't care less what I bring to the table and will never leave me or send me away."

Caleb sat up straight, making it clear he was not in the hospital because he was sick. He was wearing a T-shirt and shorts. Every powerful, vital line of his body was revealed.

"But I do want you for yourself alone." He pushed his hair back, even though it wasn't in his eyes. He used to do that, she remembered. And just like now, he looked so young. "That's what kept confusing me! One minute you're this kitten. A kitten with a genius IQ," he clarified, "pretending to be a nerdy professor, and I fall in love. The next, you're this totally hot babe, who is also a vulnerable and courageous woman—and I fall in love again. Then, you're this transcendent being with a voice like an angel, and I fall in love a third time. And no matter which one you were—or how hard I tried to remember it was all about making Calhoun pay—all I wanted was to be with you."

"Well." Emmie looked down at her hands. "That humbles me."

"It shouldn't." He lifted her chin with a gentle finger. "I blew it with you. I couldn't see the truth about how I felt until I could get Calhoun out of my eye."

"And until I let go of the fantasy, I couldn't see that I'd *rather* have you. Pickett straightened me out. She said, 'Many forces bring a couple together initially. It's up to them to choose what will keep them together.'"

"Where do we go from here?"

"I've been thinking about that. Neither one of us has had very good models for long-term relationships, so we're not good at it. But I am good at friendship. And so are you."

"Wait a minute." He flung up a hand, palm out. "No. You didn't come here to give me the 'can't we be friends?' speech, did you?"

"Well, no. I'm just thinking we should go with our strengths and see if we can work the rest out."

"Does this mean we can make love?"

"As often as possible."

"Same rules? Marriage is on the table? Faithful and loyal?"

"A couple of hounds, that's us."

"Goodwill, tolerance for human shortcomings, and forgiveness?"

"Those weren't part of our original deal."

He used his strength to pull her down on the bed with him. "I've been taking love lessons. I might be further along than you think."

And that's how they finally found…

The Beginning

Epilogue

"CALEB, I'M SO GLAD YOU'RE HERE!" LILLY HALE HELD out her arms in clear expectation of a hug.

Caleb had another one of those "Where the hell am I?" moments. There were many descriptive names for the phenomenon: *déjà vu, déjà vécu, jamais vu.* In itself the feeling wasn't evidence of psychic activity, and yet in his own experience it signaled that a turning point in his life was approaching. He didn't need psychic powers to know a turning point was at hand. He was on long term loan to an agency working on a project to determine if SEALs could be taught to access and enhance their psychic abilities, by helping them to recognize it in context. He was excited about it as he hadn't been excited about operating—not for a long time.

Emmie had accepted a post at the University of California in San Diego, and he had come back East to help her pack. They had timed the trip to coincide with Aunt Lilly Hale's family reunion—the summer one, that over one hundred people came to.

He knew about hugging old ladies now—it wasn't a strange experience anymore. As she pulled away her gray curls brushed the underside of his chin, and his throat tightened around a strange lump. *That* wasn't unfamiliar at all. It always happened when Aunt Lilly Hale hugged him. Maybe his unconscious was signaling him to pay attention because this time, for the first time in his life, the family he had come to visit was his own.

"I expect you're a very useful young man," Lilly Hale twinkled, so obviously sizing him up, it was impossible to take offense.

"Yes ma'am, I am," he laughed. It had become a private joke between them. "Need some tables set up?"

"Not today, but I've been waiting and waiting for you and Emmie to get here. I need the piano moved."

"Mama," her daughter, a plump fiftyish woman with a severe gray haircut, overheard the conversation, "We've already told you, nothing short of a crane is going to move that piano. We lost the poplar that shaded that wing in that storm in the spring," she explained to Caleb, "and now the sun comes in. Mama's worried that the sun isn't good for the piano. Which it isn't, but that Victorian monstrosity weighs about a million pounds. Even if it could be shoved to a different place it would leave gouges in the hardwood floor. We're just going to have to order shutters for that window."

"I don't want shutters in there," Lilly Hale objected. "If we rearrange the furniture we can put the piano on the side where the sun never comes in."

"But mama, that mahogany love seat alone—"

"Elizabeth." Lilly Hale silenced her daughter with the one word. "I value your opinion, but I do *not* wish to learn why I can't. I want to know how I *can.*"

Calling the piano a monstrosity was a trifle harsh, Caleb decided when he studied the problem, but the instrument, true to its Victorian aesthetic (although completely rebuilt on the inside forty years ago) looked like a piano on steroids. By themselves, the fat scroll legs ending in massive claw feet had to weigh two hundred pounds, and the total weight probably topped one thousand. Enough men could lift it, but Lilly Hale probably knew that. Why did she need *him?*

Beside him, Lilly Hale folded fleshy arms under matronly breasts. "Did I tell you," she asked, blue eyes twinkling up at him, "my great-niece has brought her children who don't seem to relate to anything that doesn't run off batteries?"

It took rousting most of them out of the pool, and rescinding the "no bathing suits in the house" rule, but shortly Caleb had twenty-two kids, ranging in age from ten to twenty, rimming the piano shoulder-to-shoulder. He showed them how to spread their hands palm up against the undercarriage.

"We're going to pick it up?" A kid missing twelve-year molars asked, blue eyes round with awe.

"Pick it up and carry it," Caleb affirmed. "Remember, we only need to raise it three inches. Hands in place? Everybody ready? I'm going to count to three—"

"Wait, wait! I want to do it!" A small figure barreled into the room. Orphan Annie curls of newly re-grown hair sprang around the golden freckled face. Peachy color bloomed in her cheeks, which were filling out again.

"Hey Victoria," the kids called. "Come on. We're lifting a piano!"

"First give me a hug," Caleb forced his voice around a lump the size of an aircraft carrier.

Skinny arms circled his waist in a reassuringly vigorous squeeze, and he inhaled little girl smell. He cupped the curly head. "Victoria, huh?"

She pulled away enough to grin up at him. "That's what I make everyone call me now."

"We're read-d-d-d-y," one of the kids yelled impatiently.

Caleb promised himself he'd find her later for a good long hug, and let go of her reluctantly. "Move closer together, you guys. Make room for Victoria."

"Come in."

Teague Calhoun, his Gulf-blue polo shirt the perfect shade to bring out his eyes and white hair, lounged in Miss Lilly Hale's desk chair, his expensively manicured fingers relaxed on the polished walnut desktop. He had sent for Caleb to meet him in Miss Lilly Hale's office. Caleb, non-commissioned officer that he was, knew a power play when he saw one. Every instinct he had put him on guard. Calhoun's choice of venue and posture were intended to make the statement that Calhoun's position was secure, while Caleb's wasn't.

Caleb didn't like being summoned, and he didn't like the subtle disrespect Calhoun showed to Miss Lilly Hale by appropriating her desk. When Calhoun didn't suggest Caleb sit down, Caleb took advantage of the omission by leaning nonchalantly against the wall beside the long window, thus putting his own face in shadow. "Yes, sir?" he inquired politely.

"I wanted to talk to you"—Calhoun squinted, trying to see Caleb's face—"where we could come to some understandings in private." Belatedly, the senator realized his mistake and waved at the room's other chair. "Why don't you have a seat?"

Caleb shook his head, grinning inwardly. *One point to me.* "I'm fine. What exactly do 'we' need to understand?"

Calhoun stood up—ah, that was better, his body language now acknowledged they were equals. *Two points to me.* Calhoun squeezed around the desk until he could see Caleb's face. "Charlotte and I consulted a geneticist. He studied the DNA of Vicky's bone marrow donor."

"Victoria's."

Calhoun's jaw tightened. He clearly wasn't used to anyone correcting him, but wise enough to pick his battles, he nodded shortly. "Victoria's. Don't you want to know what the geneticist said?"

Caleb felt his face harden. "Why would I?"

"Because he told me, that there is a ninety-nine percent probability that the donor is my son. The donor was you, wasn't it?"

A tap sounded on the door. Almost immediately it opened, and Emmie's head appeared. "Caleb? Sorry to bother you. I need someone to hold my hand. Can you come?"

Caleb laughed aloud at the wide-eyed innocent look and rather vague tone. She was being protective of him again. It did something to his heart every single time. Protective females were often likened to she-bears, but Emmie didn't do things the way anyone else did—including bears. She had apparently learned he was closeted with Calhoun and was determined not to let him face the moment alone.

He outstretched his arm in invitation. "Why don't you join us? I can hold your hand here. Mr. Calhoun tells me Victoria's donor is his son, isn't that interesting?"

"Interesting," Emmie agreed, letting him tuck her against his side.

"He also wants to know if *I'm* Victoria's donor." What a politician the man was! With DNA evidence in his hands, he refused to commit himself. He had neither claimed he was Caleb's father, nor that Caleb was his son. Only that the "donor" was his son. He didn't want to know who his son was. He was only trying to get Caleb to tell him how much damage control was needed.

Emmie, of course, recognized the implications instantly. She squeezed his waist to tell him she understood what this confrontation with Calhoun meant to him and that she would wait for his lead. Knowing she had his back, suddenly, he was no longer tense—in fact, the situation was a little funny. He thought he would enjoy watching Calhoun sweat for a while.

He'd already prepared an explanation in case anyone ever noticed the resemblance between him and Victoria. He put on his country-boy persona and turned to Calhoun. "Well now, Senator, they didn't tell me who my marrow went to, and I didn't ask. Still and all, you and me, we come from the same isolated area. I wouldn't be a-tall surprised to learn we were kinfolk." He widened his smile as if he'd just made a discovery. "I expect just about everybody in Rose Hill has the same DNA."

The senator flicked a glance at Emmie, then back at Caleb. "Do you know who your father was?"

Caleb chuckled in reluctant admiration. He had to hand it to the senator. He was starting to sweat, but he still wasn't admitting anything. Caleb tightened the screws. "Yes, sir. Sure do."

This was the moment he'd thought about many times. He had Calhoun exactly where he wanted him. He could destroy Calhoun in the media, especially if he told not just who he was, but exactly how his mother died. It was an option he'd refused in the past because coming out would put other SEALs in danger. No longer. At Emmie's urging he'd been seeing a counselor. He had accepted that his days of operating were over. He was of more use in other areas now. He was free to make Calhoun pay and pay. At the very least, he could make Calhoun lose sleep for a long time, wondering when, or if, Caleb would drop his bombshell. Funny how none of that mattered anymore.

"Was it me?"

Little as Calhoun wanted him to be his son, Caleb wanted even less to have Calhoun for a father. There was only one answer because there was only one thing he wanted from Calhoun now. Do-Lord looked Calhoun straight in the eye. And lied. "No, sir."

Calhoun had the grace not to look relieved. Instead, he took on the expression of benevolent concern that made him beloved by the voters. "Being a donor for someone, whether or not you were Vic—Victoria's, was a brave and generous act. I like to see good deeds rewarded. I have some pull in a few places." The senator smiled at his little self-deprecation. "Is there anything I can do for you?"

"There is." Caleb squeezed Emmie's waist. She hadn't moved a muscle, but she was vibrating with such intense joy, he expected her to start humming any second. When he'd cut Calhoun loose, *he* was the one who was freed, and she had felt it. "I want Victoria to be my little sister. The way I see it—if I *was* her donor—*my* marrow is making her blood's red cells. Even if we weren't blood kin before, we sure are now."

Calhoun looked surprised for a moment, but canny manipulator that he was, he calculated the cost-benefit ratio to himself. Caleb's explanation of their kinship would work, if anyone questioned Caleb's sudden inclusion in the senator's life. He gave a genial chuckle and reached out to shake Caleb's hand. "Son," he boomed, "we'd be pleased to consider you an honorary member of the family."

Caleb closed the office door behind the departing Calhoun (noting with a certain satisfaction that in the end, *he* was the one who held the territory). He leaned against the door and opened his arms for Emmie.

"Just a second." She extracted an old-fashioned key from a pocket in her skirt, inserted it in the huge old keyhole, and turned it. There was no click.

"You know"—Caleb crossed his arms over his chest and looked down to watch the proceedings—"the morning of Jax and Pickett's wedding, I thought you were pulling me in here for a quickie. Is it too much to hope that's what you have in mind now?"

Emmie jiggled the key, feeling for where it struck the lock's tumblers. She snorted and rolled her eyes. "You can take the man out of the jockeys, but you can't take the jock out of the man."

Caleb laughed. "Taking the man out of the jockeys works for me. Specially if we can get the girl out of the… Hanes Her Way?"

"Victoria's Secret."

"A thong? Oh hell, don't tell me. You've got on a thong under there!"

"Well, I do, and if you behave"—she aimed a sultry smile over her shoulder—"maybe I'll show it too you—later!" The bolt at last slid into place with a solid clunk. She straightened and gripped his upper arms, digging into the warm, solid flesh with her fingertips, since her hands didn't go even halfway around his biceps.

She steered him—he *let* her steer him and they both knew it—until his legs bumped the big desk. "Sit. Somebody is going to come looking for us in a minute though, and we need to talk."

"The four scariest words in the English language." He opened his legs and pulled her between them. "How 'bout we make out instead?"

"Caleb, be serious a minute. You just got as complete a rejection as possible. I'll never feel sorry for myself again because my parents' work took them away from me. How do you feel?"

"Okay."

Emmie frowned at him.

"Good."

Good Lord, this *was the man's idea of sharing his feelings.*

"Sort of light. You know, it's strange. I had decided if he didn't know I was his son, I wasn't going to tell him."

"Except we both think he did know. Fairchild did anyway. Fairchild knew your grandfather when he was a young man—he guessed who you were as soon as he saw you. After that, he tried to keep you as far away from the Calhouns as he could—including offering me inducements to dump you."

"Where is Fairchild, these days? Charlotte called me every few days with an update on Victoria's condition, but she never said anything about him."

"Charlotte relates only on a need-to-know basis, but Wilmington gossip says she kicked him out of her house. And don't change the subject. We're talking about how you feel. Will you be okay if Teague never acknowledges you're his son?"

His expression changed. His mobile lips moved in a sweet smile she'd never seen before. His eyes widened and softened in a look of awe. "You're protecting me again, aren't you?"

Emmie bit her lip and nodded. "I love you."

Caleb pulled her into his arms with a sound between a groan and a laugh. "Okay, little she-bear." He rocked her in his arms. "Okay. There was a moment when I realized I was free to destroy him or torture him for the rest of his life. It was like the Lords of Karma said, 'You dreamed of this a long time. Are you sure you want to let it go?'"

"Yes, you were locked in a struggle for power when I came in. What made the difference?"

"You did."

"Me?"

"Yeah. You said we needed to stop so I could hold your hand. And I remembered I had you, always at my back, ready to guard my six. Nothing that Calhoun did or didn't do mattered. I had already gained more than I had lost. Now let me ask you a question. Are you still willing to be engaged to me, knowing I'll never inherit the Calhoun millions?"

"Do you love me?"

"You know I do."

"Then I don't need the promise of millions. I only want the promise of life with you."

Acknowledgments

I'm always amazed and humbled when I start counting all the people who contributed to a book.

Former SEAL, J.C. Roat, author of *Class 29,* is always there for me, discussing ideas, lending a shoulder to cry on. He located another former SEAL, Rick Bremseth, Captain, USN (ret.) when I needed someone who could talk with me about Remote Viewing (clairvoyance) applications within Special Operations. Both tease me about writing "mush." Both are always ready to help with whatever background I need.

Tim Ward thought I was putting him on when I walked into the Southern Firearms Gun Shop and asked what kind of rifle a sniper uses and how it works. A former Army sniper himself, he showed me an M-14 rifle and gave me insight into how Caleb and his team would react to any dereliction of duty.

The house where Senator Calhoun and his family live is modeled on the Bridger's Mansion, today the elegant Graystone Inn, a B&B in the historic section of Wilmington. The innkeeper, Richard Moore, took an afternoon to show me its grandeur and its secrets. We discussed the feasibility of escaping via a bathroom window.

Speaking of the AWOL scene, it wouldn't have been written without the assistance of V.K. Powell. Drawing on her experience as a former police captain, she helped me design a boyhood for Do-Lord and lent me insight into the phenomenon of hypervigilance.

I'm fortunate to have two critique partners: Jennifer Lohman and Yvonne Harris. Charlotte Lehecler is a romance reader, not a writer. Her insights were invaluable.

Special thanks go to a bunch of rowdy ladies: Dr. Elizabeth Vaughan, Gail Durgin, Julie Milunic, and Elva Pugh, who convinced me the plot of *SEALed With a Promise* worked, dragged me out for cinema therapy when I felt overwhelmed, and made me wear celebrity sunglasses.

Every writer is dependent upon other writers for source material. I would particularly like to acknowledge *Inside Delta Force* by Eric Haney, *Commandos: The Inside Story of America's Secret Soldiers* by Douglas Waller, and *Down Range* by Dick Couch for their discussion of the role of SEALs in Afghanistan. *Cold Zero* by Christopher Whitcomb will tell you everything you ever wanted to know about snipers. Finally, I must acknowledge Richard Marcinko, founder of SEAL Team Six, the first counter-terrorist SEAL team, whose autobiography *Rogue Warrior* gave me the idea for Do-Lord.

My agent Stephanie Evans and my editor Deb Werksman know writers, and they know writing. I am indebted to both for their insights and encouragement at every step of bringing *SEALed With A Promise* to completion.

About the Author

Mary Margret Daughtridge, a Southerner born and bred, has been a grade school teacher, speech therapist, family educator, biofeedback therapist, and Transpersonal Hypnotherapist.

Since 2002 she has been a member of Heart of Carolina Romance Writers, Romance Writers of America, and Romancing the Military Soul, an online writing group. She is a sought-after judge in writing contests.

She loves hearing from readers and can be found at marymargretdaughtridge.com.

SEALed with a Kiss

BY MARY MARGRET DAUGHTRIDGE

THERE'S ONLY ONE THING HE CAN'T HANDLE, AND ONE WOMAN WHO CAN HELP HIM...

Jax Graham is a rough, tough Navy SEAL, but when it comes to taking care of his four-year-old son after his ex-wife dies, he's completely clueless. Family therapist Pickett Sessoms can help, but only if he'll let her.

When Jax and his little boy get trapped by a hurricane, Picket takes them in against her better judgment. When the situation turns deadly, Pickett discovers what it means to be a SEAL, and Jax discovers that even a hero needs help sometimes.

"A heart-touching story that will keep you smiling and cheering for the characters clear through to the happy ending." —Romantic Times

"A well-written romance... simultaneously tender and sensuous." —Booklist

978-1-4022-1118-8 • $6.99 U.S. / $8.99 CAN